THE BRIDGE

THE
BRIDGE

JANINE ELLEN YOUNG

SIMON & SCHUSTER
A VIACOM COMPANY

London . New York . Sydney . Tokyo . Singapore . Toronto

First published in Great Britain by Earthlight, 2000
An imprint of Simon & Schuster UK Ltd
A Viacom Company

1 3 5 7 9 10 8 6 4 2

Simon & Schuster UK Ltd
Africa House
64-78 Kingsway
London WC2B 6AH

Simon & Schuster Australia
Sydney

A CIP catalogue record for this book
is available from the British Library

ISBN 0-743-40415-7

Printed and bound in Great Britain by Omnia Books Ltd, Glasgow

To Doselle,
who taught me to aim high,
to reach for the moon and build bridges between the stars.
Thank you for being there to share the stardust
and to dance with me at the center of it all.

Acknowledgments

This book would not have been possible without the imaginative help of some brilliant and very generous folk.

First, a special thanks to my aunt, Sheila Merritt, who took me to the bookstores and introduced me to the novels that inspired me to write what I write. Without her initial and continuing inspiration, this novel would never have happened.

Thanks also to my uncle, Professor Louis Narens, whose musings on alien communication were essential to this particular book.

Next, I'd like to thank a handful of unofficial advisors, including: W. A. Bill Thomasson, John Wilson, Dr. Eric Roche, and, most especially, Dr. Steven A. Carder, M.D., for the e-mails, articles, and critiques on engineering, biology, and physics that helped me to brainstorm ideas.

Of course, not to be forgotten are those noble souls who frequent Compuserve's sci-fi lit forum, in particular the Science Fact section. These kind strangers, who have also become such good friends, let me grill them mercilessly; they battered about ideas with me and promptly shot down theories that just wouldn't work. So, I'd like to offer my grateful thanks to: WizOp Marilyn L. Alm, Jim Baerg, John Barnes, SysOp Cassy Beach, David Gerrold, Roy Gillett, David Gillon, Jim Irwin, Dennis W. Keim, Lance

Kennedy, Paul Knibbs, Dr. Fionnbar Lenihan of Dublin, Ireland, Barnett Steven Lerner, Tom Ligon, Steve Lopata, Thomas K. Martin, Phil Masters, WizOp Wilma Meier, Kenneth Porter, Steve Renwick, Joe Rosenman, David Sattar, Steven Van Dyke, Torge von Zengen of Hamburg, Germany, and Jon Woolf.

Thanks also to my editor Jaime Levine, whose insight and faith gave this novel a chance to shine, and to a handful of unofficial editors: Sande Simpson, for letting me know when the emperor had no clothes; Melissa Lee Shaw, for her editorial support; and the lovely Rachel Brown, for her assistance with all things Indian.

Equal thanks are due to the friends who put up with my questions regarding Manhattan, including Bruce Tartaglia, Jennifer Smith, Leslie Converse, S. R. Sirot, Dana Kurtin, Emma Bull, and Will Shetterly. No outsider can hope to ever truly know this remarkable city, but the natives who walked me through its majestic streets, sent me photographs, shared their memories, and allowed me to see it through their eyes brought this native Angeleno as close as possible to calling those faraway streets home.

And finally, I would like to refer readers to *The Great Bridge,* by David McCullough. It is perhaps for the best that no fictional work about engineers could ever match up to the true story of the Roebling family, but I have done my best to honor their memory and their most remarkable achievements.

Engineers are all too often unsung heroes; if we are ever, in truth, to travel between stars, it will be thanks to their aspirations and imagination . . . for they are the bridge builders.

Make no little plans; they have no magic to stir men's blood . . . make big plans; aim high in hope and work, remembering that a noble, logical diagram once recorded will never die, but long after we are gone will be a living thing, asserting itself with ever-growing insistency.

—Daniel Burnham, 1907

We have no precedent just like this bridge.
—Washington Roebling

THE
BRIDGE

Prologue

1926

FOR THE MOMENT, HIS MIND REMAINED SHARP, EVEN AS his body continued to waste away, sinking deeper into sleep and death. Eighty-nine years old, and Washington Roebling no longer had his teeth, had lost his hearing along with much of his sight, had been robbed of any physical strength.

But the clarity of his mind remained a pleasant surprise. Like that night-blooming cereus stalk that his second wife, Cornelia, had brought to his bed one crisp May evening at around ten P.M.

It had blossomed for that one night, filling the room with a delicate, exotic odor. And then, come morning, the white calyx had suddenly vanished from its leafy stalk as unexpectedly as it had appeared.

It was summer now, and the humid New Jersey heat seemed to weigh him down in his bed. Billy Sunday, his anxious Airedale, nosed at his hand, licking it questioningly. Washington stroked the animal's sleek head with a trembling hand. The poor dog had been trying daily to push him out of bed so they could take the trolley to the mill complex, as they had for the past five years.

He was sorry to disappoint the animal, but he was well aware that he was not improving, and, frankly, he just wanted to be left in peace. It was long past time he left this world, as it had left him. He didn't understand its motor cars or the dapper, boyish-faced lads driving them. And he understood the young women, with their bobbed hair and flattened figures, even less. He hated their bee-stung lips, which seemed to have been cropped, crimped, and trussed, like their hair and figure.

Nothing like his Emily had been. The photographs had never done her justice, never revealed her stately grace, poise, or keen intelligence. When he'd built this Tudor mansion for her, with its grand stained-glass rendition of the bridge, he'd tried to infuse it with her elegance and self-possession.

Twenty-three years since Emily died of stomach cancer. His Emmie, the only soul in the world he'd never tired of. Em would have appreciated that leafy night-blossoming cactus, its single flower larger than a rose, the fine, milky petals curving outward. She would have understood why it reminded him of that bright May day when the bridge had finally opened. Their greatest accomplishment, that bridge, eclipsed only by the grand success of their marriage.

Of course, most people believed his father built the bridge. Worse, they believed that Washington, not John Roebling, died back in '69.

Once, against his better judgment, Washington had posed for a statue of his father because, as the sculptor argued, there were no good photographs of John A. Roebling. That image now stood in Cadwalader Park, cheating Washington out of not only the credit he deserved, but also his identity.

The bridge was like that too; earmarked with his father's style, impregnated with his father's genius down to the steel wires that had been his father's invention. It spoke with his father's Prussian accent and had the old man's steel will: ingenious, tireless, resourceful and unbreakable. And impressive. His father had always captured the attention, deservedly so. There was never a moment when the air didn't spark around John Roebling, modern Prometheus and a student of Hegel; never a time when his aura didn't hum with the energetic promise of a train coming down the tracks.

But John A. Roebling had never even seen his crowning achievement, his last and final dream. In 1869, while surveying the location for a bridge which, he insisted, would be the most stupendous engineering structure of the age, a supply ferry had crushed his toes against a docking slip. The old man went on shouting directions until he finally collapsed in pain.

When informed by the surgeon that his toes would have to be amputated, Roebling agreed, refusing anesthetic and insisting on binding the foot himself.

Washington had fully expected the old man to pull through, as he always did, but this time, the worst happened. Not long after firing the physicians his son had brought in, John Roebling's expression had gone rigid and he began to die by inches of tetanus. And yet, all the while, he continued to write notes and sketch drawings of his great bridge.

During those final days, amid terrible seizures, tears streamed down his rictus face, the first Washington had ever seen on his father's cheeks. It was an image that would haunt him for the rest of his days, as would the phantom stone and steel of the old man's bridge, which would, over the next fourteen years, threaten to bury the son along with the father.

John A. Roebling died during the early morning hours of July 22, 1869. A good day to die, Washington thought; he might arrange to go that day himself. It was coming up. Might as well make the merging of the two of them, father and son, complete; wrap them about one another like strands of steel wire.

After his father's death, Washington was left with piles of plans and surveys and the task of holding up his father's last, great dream. And that, Washington had to admit, was fitting; while his father had been all fire and ideas, Washington had always been chained to the earth, studying fossils and minerals. He was no Prometheus, but he could be Atlas. It was he, after all, who had gone to Europe to learn about caissons. And it was he, not his father, who was the expert on that single, most important subject. Sunk down to bedrock, the caissons were the bases on which the bridge towers stood, the whole structure relying on their success or failure.

Washington had created caissons half the size of a New York City block, the largest ever constructed. Inverted wooden boxes lined with tin and boiler plate, filled with compressed air and fearful, sweaty men swinging sledgehammers at obstinate river boulders, they were Washington's first and greatest achievements, and, simultaneously, his worst nightmare.

He never imagined that he would spend the better part of three years in that pressurized atmosphere, splattered with mud, sweating in the steamy heat, directing the men. Nor that his time under the river, living in a great air bubble, working by the white light of calcium lamps, would be his only time on site with the bridge.

He remembered that worst night, the night of the fire in the Brooklyn caisson. After exhaustive hours directing workers and firefighters, Washington had collapsed and for hours he couldn't feel or move his limbs. They saved the caisson, dug out the burned portions, repaired it, filled it with concrete, and began to build up the tower as planned. Washington went back to work. The second caisson was set in place on the New York side and sunk down underwater. But the men who worked in that caisson digging out river mud and clay began to suffer.

And then they began to die.

Caisson disease it was called then. Now it was known as the bends.

When the masonry tower on the Brooklyn side had reached a hundred feet above the river and the second caisson was set in place on a substratum of ancient fossils, Washington collapsed for a second time.

It was as if the weight of his father's bridge had finally crushed him, leaving him an invalid, barely able to walk or see, weak, nervous, and in terrible pain. For years afterward he would be confined to his bed, tired all the time, imprisoned in his Brooklyn Heights home.

Only his mind would continue working.

Emily saved him, of course; she was his tower of strength. Over the nine years that followed, she observed for him, spoke for him, argued for him. She learned engineering for him. Without her, he would have never survived the pressures and humiliations of those next long years, fighting the deceitful, self-serving trustees of the New York and Brooklyn Bridge Company, facing the biting editorials, the embarrassing delays of steel and floor beams. And, worse than anything he'd suffered in the caissons, enduring the Haigh wire fiasco.

All that time under political caissons. And then, like the cereus stalk, a day in May arrived when the cactus finally bloomed. On that day, over forty-three years ago, he watched through his field glasses as Emily's open carriage traveled across the bridge, its first passenger. The workmen stopped to take off their hats and cheer as she passed. She carried a rooster in her lap, to symbolize victory.

And she waved to him along the way.

He did not go to the opening ceremonies themselves, being too weak and having suffered too much at the hands of the trustees. But Emily went, acting, one last time, as his surrogate. And from his window he saw the hordes of people, in their festive frock coats and lace and silks, as if on holiday, heard their cheers and felt their excitement. He watched the boats, sailing down the East River, bright flags fluttering from their yardarms.

The rippling water had never looked so blue.

And when the gold of the sun vanished into the bay, a necklace of electric lights lit up, one after another, from the Brooklyn side of the bridge to New York. Watching them, Washington thought of how the world had changed in his years of servitude to this engineering feat. The electric light had been invented, and the telephone. As bells rung, people cheered, and bands played, he reflected to Emmie, who stood by his side at the window, that the bridge was a journey into the future. He had built it by candlelight and with steam engines. But it would now and in years to come wear the electricity of a modern age; the horseless carriages of the future would drive across it.

The festivities climaxed with rockets and noise. And then a sudden quiet. During that lull, as if it had been waiting for just such a moment, the moon suddenly appeared and sent its pale beams down across the silvery cables.

And that was when it finally hit Washington that he'd built the longest, highest suspension bridge in the world, he and the workers and assistant engineers and his wife, and their wives . . . and one old man who had dreamed it all.

Forty-three years ago. Almost everyone who had worked on that bridge was long gone now. He was the last leaf on that night-blooming cereus. Some, like his father, believed that the dead could return, speak to the living, or even come back for another lifetime. Washington's particular lifetime had been so long, so exhaustive, he could not imagine wanting to come back. But as he considered his life and his accomplishments, another bridge seemed to open up to him, a bridge with cables made of stars and a walkway of pure, white light. And, as Washington Roebling stepped onto that magical bridge, Billy Sunday at his heel, the engineer saw Emily and his father waiting for him. He met them at the center, and they strolled across, talking of leafy cactuses, electricity, the philosophy of Hegel, and of that which, in many ways, would remain forever theirs alone: The Brooklyn Bridge.

And it was then that they all agreed, that if they could come back for another lifetime, like a calyx in the dark of night or a full moon rising quietly after an explosion of fireworks, they would . . . *if* they could again build something as grand and fantastic as that bridge.

A dream that aimed so high would be worth another turn on that strange wheel. Well worth it.

PART I: Let It Be Me

Chapter 1

Year of the Pandemic

ONLY PORTIONS OF THE CRAFT EXISTED IN THREE-dimensional space at one time, the whole of it impossible to see with the naked eye. At best, it would have appeared an inconsistent thing, like a shimmering, celestial sail shifting in and out of view, or a cross-hatching of colors, like a net cast out to sweep up the stars.

But no human eye saw the craft as it spearheaded in tandem with its million siblings toward a titanic pair of rings, the nearest of a dozen frost and silver tori, each with a small sphere of superdense matter centered within. Acting as shepherd moons to the Saturnesque rings that thickly belted a nameless gas giant, the tori turned with the patience of great clocks. By comparison, the craft floating through them might have been a bit of ocean spray or a puff of mist.

And yet those fantastic tori acknowledged, with a gentle dimming of diffuse blue light and subsonic deference, the school of flickering, billowing curves that passed through them. And bid them all farewell and Godspeed.

A symphony of commands rewove the threads of space-time, allowing the crafts to fall over a tachyonic event horizon onto a fantastic bridge. Slipping off this bridge at the last, the travelers found themselves transported, in an instant, over three thousand light-years away.

Far from their solar system and with no intent of ever returning, the crafts ventured into this interstellar wilderness, then separated, casting off at odd vectors, each to find its own adventure.

Theirs was a lover's quest and nothing short of death would stop them.

The vast majority would continue to travel, finding no rest, no hint of what they sought; others would inevitably collide with celestial objects large enough to stop or obliterate them: stars, comets, meteors.

One of those million craft, however, would find its Holy Grail.

Pitted and scarred, soiled and burned so that it no longer resembled the curve of a silver wing or a netting of sunset, the craft came within reach of its Mecca. To the radio satellites that saw it, it appeared to be an oddly-shaped rock, small, ugly, and ungainly.

For the last hundred years the craft had followed the unmistakable bandwidths of radio waves and radiation, altering its course as necessary. Artificial debris at the edge of a solar system had caught its attention, giving it the impetus to quicken its pace. Had it been living, it might have sighed a great sigh of relief at finally seeing that beautiful, blue-green planet, and all the clutter that orbited it.

Approaching cautiously, the craft examined the planet, using light, radar, and subatomic particles to touch on the highest mountains, peer through the thickest forests, and plumb the deepest trenches under the darkest oceans. It analyzed gravity and temperatures. Most especially it searched for information on the sophisticated tool users of the planet, those that had created the artificial satellites and what seemed to be an orbiting space station. Using infrared spectroscopy and microwave radiation, it learned all it could.

It even searched and found, most rare and precious of all, a few crystals of organic waste product, vented, it might have guessed, from ship or space station. These held faint traces of DNA.

For the craft, such traces were more than enough. It would have swelled with joy had it been able. Accordingly, it altered its microscopic passengers, readying them for what was to come.

When there was no more left to be done, the craft finally dropped out of orbit and into the atmosphere. As it neared the planet it ignited, burning brighter and brighter until it was consumed in a fiery butterfly's kiss. And so it sweetly greeted the planet it had worked so long and so very hard to reach.

Released into the atmosphere over the Bay of Bombay near Calcutta, the craft's passengers, countless billions of them, each so tiny that three hundred million could rest comfortably on the tip of a needle, dispersed themselves upon the air currents, northwest into India, northeast into China. They rode the winds, drifting down over many months to the surface, binding themselves to dust and pollen, the better to swiftly travel around the globe.

Some landed on the green ocean waters, taking their message beneath the waves. Some few settled on snowy mountain peaks and polar ice, remaining crystallized and buried.

The lucky majority, as was intended, found their way into the alveoli of living creatures, the small, honeycombed cells of the lungs where oxygen was exchanged for carbon dioxide. If they were especially fortunate, they found themselves in human beings, their intended hosts. This spurred the messengers into multiplying and sent some of them up through the nasal passages into the brain, where at long last they could consummate this strange and wonderful romance.

Varouna preferred the taste of mass-produced poison, which was why she smoked only American cigarettes.

She loved drinking Coca-Cola, too.

Sitting on the window ledge while fighting back the dull

ache in her head, Varouna eyed the bruised color of the late-evening sky and took another drag on the Camel Filter. Her brother, Bhaskar, was always complaining, always whining about this or that, lecturing her about the terrible effect smoking would have on her lungs, arguing with her about the expense.

His arguments, of course, weren't about health. They were about culture. To Bhaskar, America was almost as vulgar and culturally impoverished a place as India.

"If you must give yourself emphysema," he groused as he buzzed around the apartment packing an old Halliburton suitcase, "do it on someone else's salary!"

Varouna adjusted the skirts of her violet sari and kept her own counsel. Bhaskar didn't understand and likely never would. It wasn't breathing the smoke into her lungs that she enjoyed, it was the bright cherry tip of the cigarette that she kept alive with that breath, it was watching that tiny fire-blossom float languidly on the night like lotus petals on dark water. She liked cigarettes the way she liked the prayer candles that floated down the Ganges mirroring the Milky Way overhead.

Tonight, her vision blurred, making those distant lights waver, as if they were deep down under the water, floating to the surface. As a child, she'd had the same illusion about the stars: that they were coming ever closer, that one day they would blossom across the night and ring the world like a marigold garland.

"I think I caught your cough," Bhaskar threw out, shattering the vision. Dressed in black pants and a pressed white occidental shirt, he looked very much the doctor he was.

"You said it was caused by smoking."

He coughed a little. "Yes, well, I saw a lot of patients this week with the same cough."

"And you waited till now to tell me?"

"Why are you complaining? It's eased up, hasn't it?"

"And turned into a headache!"

"Then you shouldn't smoke, it will only make your head hurt worse."

That was Bhaskar's favorite and most self-righteous trick, to substitute her accusations with one of his own.

"They've a new procedure in Britain that can put an end to nicotine addiction in a few days," he added.

Bhaskar wanted to move to Europe, badly. Cambridge wanted him, and so did schools in Paris, which was where he was going this evening. One day soon, he promised, he would move them to London or Marseilles and they would never look back.

Varouna secretly hoped that day would never come. She felt it essential that they stay in the land of their birth, as if cutting that umbilical would send them drifting into the void.

"Have you seen my striped tie?" He was now searching under and around the bookcases she tried to keep clean. But the dust always came back, and there always seemed to be flour and ash upon the floor.

"Ah!" He held up the silk tie triumphantly, and folded it neatly into the suitcase. "You forgot to pass this on to the *dhobi,* didn't you? Well, never mind."

One day, her brother would marry. A British girl, most likely, with yellow hair and rose cheeks, who'd never forget to have his ties washed and pressed. And then he'd finally settle in Europe where, as he liked to say, people *really* lived in the twenty-first century. Hang his shingle in the land of clean running water and reliable telephone service, a land of cold churches and even colder whey-faced denizens. Which, perhaps, explained why Bhaskar wanted to live there. He was a cold fish, a nervous soul searching for importance and structure. India, with its erotic sculptures and honey-skinned princes would forever disturb and confuse him. But in Varouna's eyes, India was life; here was the heartbeat of humanity, most especially here in Varanasi, which Hindus called Kasi, the city of light.

A light her brother refused to see.

Her brother was a handsome man with that sense of entitlement that many Indian men had. Their father, a third-rate cotton merchant, had spared no expense to send him to the most competitive schools: to Varanasi Hindu University and even to a Paris medical school; and their mother, while she lived, had always made sure the best food went to Bhaskar's plate.

To give him his due, Bhaskar had shared that food with Varouna, even when their father had ordered her from the table and out of sight. More, her brother had shared everything he learned with her . . . although likely, she reminded herself, more out of expedience than altruism. He'd wanted someone in the household who could test his mettle as he sweated his way through exams, someone he could practice his French on, and who understood his passion and interests.

Hungry for the attention, Varouna had been happy enough to oblige. And she'd had her own interests to fulfill. Bhaskar's textbooks fascinated her, particularly those on microbiology and genetics. She found hidden stories within the cold descriptions of viruses, bacteria, and prions; like a theatrical dance, sometimes stylized and formal, filled with the crispness of a Bharata Natyam performance, sometimes shaped with the elaborate curves and bends of an Odissi ballet. It moved her, the myriad systems and methods by which life expressed itself to itself. Among the paisley whorls of genetic information, of proteins and Fullerian sphere, Varouna saw, if not the gods, then certainly the complexities of step and gesture, the subtleties of expression by which such entities might make themselves known to the world.

"I'll be back in about three weeks," Bhaskar coughed, breaking through her concentration yet again, and snapped shut the suitcase. "Leave the computer on and the door closed!" He pointed into the spare room with his medical texts, an American-made air conditioner, and his beloved computer-cum-fax machine. It was the only dust-free room in their apartment, the only cool room given the heat this time of year. Bhaskar had installed a generator he'd brought back from Germany to make sure that the air conditioner and the computer it kept cool and dry were never interrupted by the frequent power failures.

"I've impressed on everyone that they cannot send faxes while I am gone." Bhaskar allowed his machine to be used by a lawyer, a writer, and two other doctors. Though he did not make them pay for the privilege, he was miserly about the number of faxes they could send. "And I mean it. I don't care how important it is."

Bhaskar had taken her in after their father's death, rather than marrying her off. There'd been plenty of talk among the relatives over that decision, a shaking of heads by disapproving aunties. But Bhaskar had been determined; money for a bride dowry would be better put to use moving them to Europe.

Likely he had done the right thing. Bhaskar always knew what was best for them. So, no *bindi* dotting her forehead, not yet; not until they reached London or Marseilles and her brother urged her to marry a European doctor.

To whom he would not have to pay a dowry.

That, she thought, was bitter and unkind. She ought to be grateful to Bhaskar. Ought to touch his feet and thank him for taking care of her, for wanting to take her with him instead of marrying her off to an uncaring husband and a domineering mother-in-law, or leaving her in the hands of overburdened relatives.

But she only felt a kind of tired disgust.

She took another drag on the cigarette. The headache pounded behind her eyes; she was going to have to lie down.

"Varouna?"

Odd how the pain made her see the movement of the city. She took it so for granted; but, from their high window, she could almost see it as a tourist might this evening: the narrow twisting lanes and the wider, teeming streets with their clattering rickshaws, buses, scooters, and tongas. The gruff complaints of camels, the sour smells of cow dung, exhaust, and spices. The torn banners, trampled garlands, and fading floral designs painted on the dusty walls, remnants of the recent Hindu New Year.

It was April and the dry summer heat had arrived, baking the city's nearly two thousand temples. Only now, with the sun down, was the furnace that was Varanasi beginning to cool. She caught sight of students in uniform rushing home, priests and nuns and pilgrims in robes of saffron, orange, or white, some naked, their skin painted blue or red, making their way to evening prayer. She watched women with fire-wood or clay urns balanced on their heads, dragging children by the hand, and observed the perpetual flow of souls carrying tapers and lamps down to the Ganges.

India, she thought past the headache (or because of the headache?), was made up of human rivers, human wanderers. *Samsara,* the eternal wheel of rebirth, meant "to wander." To flow in the river of life and death. But those who circled through Kasi, the luminous city, transformed their human river into a river like the Ganges, a means of ascending to heaven. That had confused her when she was a child, that a river could be a way of crossing over rivers.

Now it made perfect sense.

"Varouna?" her brother said impatiently.

"You'd better hurry. You'll miss your plane," she said; the stars that were beginning to appear were so bright they seemed to jump out from the sky, as if they were trying to warm themselves by the earthly fires below.

"I'll fax you from Paris," Bhaskar said; it was cheaper than calling and easier given the time difference, but Varouna suspected that her brother simply preferred writing to talking. She'd suggested e-mail, but he'd rejected that. He didn't want her touching his beloved computer.

She smiled a little as she heard the door shut behind him.

Alone in the apartment, the noise from the streets seemed amplified, cutting into her head: the arguments and shouts, the ringing of bicycle bells, the chants of pilgrims and vendors. She put the cigarette in her mouth and took a last, delicious puff, releasing the smoke into the cooling air, watching the red light at the end float in the darkness.

It burned through the night like a prayer.

Chapter 2

April

When those years are re-created in dramas, the focus is either on the tragedy (the suicides, nervous breakdowns, kidnapping of little children by grieving, delusional parents) or the wild years that came immediately after. We see the chromatic clothing worn by the Shoal Movement, the indulgent parties on the great, whalelike floaters, and a baby boom of parents pushing strollers of cloned toddlers.

This is, however, an incomplete image of those amazing times. What needs to be remembered is that, at the onset of these years, single-stage-to-orbit spacecraft was uncommon, chartered spaceflights expensive and rare, and mono-matrix sheets to build such spacecraft and their stations had not yet been invented. These years would see all that and more come into being.

For all the apparent manic-depressive chaos of this era, the bridge builders were filled with a sharp and poignant focus, a will to succeed, and a dream that, despite all arguments to the contrary, was as much theirs as not.

—The Dancing Wheel:
Science and the Biological Lexicon

"*THEY LOVED HER IN FRANCE.*"

Judas Tarkenton, Jude to his friends, rolled that line over in his head as the elevator doors slid open to the vaulted penthouse alive with the murmur and glitter of New York society. Just a snippet of a phone conversation, the last he'd had with Warren. Warren McAllister, who was married to her, the only girl who had ever mattered.

Valerie.

They loved her in France.

Fighting an urge to punch the elevator back down, he crossed out and down a short staircase, past laughing women in beaded evening gowns and loud men in severe tuxedos.

And kicked himself for wearing his second best suit instead of renting something better.

Self-consciously he combed at his hair with his fingertips. He knew he stood out in this exclusive crowd in more ways than one. His mother had been coffee-colored, with beautiful hazel eyes, his father almost albino, with thin, pale hair. Their union had produced a son with tawny skin, angular features, curling dark hair, and deep-set hazel eyes flecked with gray. Several women had assured Jude that he was quite sexy, but whenever he saw himself in the mirror, he felt frumpy and unkempt, as if genetics had tossed him together like old clothing out of a closet.

At parties, guests tended to stare at him, as if he looked as motley and out of place as he felt.

Well, fuck 'em. There were only two people in the whole of Manhattan whose opinion mattered, and Warren's only mattered half the time.

Valerie.

He could feel her in the decor of the penthouse; her touch, delicate as the cherry blossom design on the gray silk wallpaper. And the way she settled, with her ankles crossed and a little to the side, he could see that in the rose damask armchairs now occupied by thin white women in black silk and diamonds. Her gentle fragrance hung on the white camellias fountaining out of lacquer vases and her confidence and energy issued down in the soft lighting.

She was everywhere. Damn her.

He was reminded then, painfully and acutely, of the first time he'd been to the penthouse. Perched atop a grand rose and white stone building on Central Park West, it required that the doorman key down a private elevator.

Another McAllister purchase, he'd thought at the time, a tree house for the very rich. But he hadn't even stepped out of the elevator before Warren informed him, "Dad tried to get me to purchase a place on the East Side, of course, but I told him that wouldn't be right for Valerie."

And that's when Jude knew that the penthouse had not been bought on a whim. No, not at all. It'd been hard, after that, but he'd managed to follow his friend dutifully from gourmet kitchen to closet wine cellar, from library on up to the gym with its Jacuzzi and tiny steam room. He had made all the right noises.

"You really think she'll like it?" Warren had nervously asked.

And Jude had honestly answered, "How not?" Every princess deserved a palace.

A few days later, Valerie had met Jude for coffee, an exquisite diamond and sapphire engagement band on her tapered finger. Oddly, the one thing he always remembered from that lunch was how beautifully manicured her nails were.

She'd told him the story in crushing detail. After a romantic dinner at One If By Land, Warren had taken her to see his castle in the clouds. They had toured it, just the two of them, arm in arm, ending out on the terrace. There'd been champagne waiting, and roses.

Down on one knee, with ring in hand and the lights of Manhattan glistening brightly behind, Warren had proposed.

"I cried like a fucking baby," Valerie had confided to

Jude. And in his mind's eye, he'd seen that moment: her narrow white fingers touching together before the cupid's bow of her lips, her lashes, brushed with mascara, fluttering over the deep blue of her eyes as the tears began to well up.

The image had been that vivid, that haunting.

She might as well have ripped him apart with hooks. Why couldn't *he* have been the one to bring tears to her eyes?

The night before the wedding, there'd been a private supper at the penthouse, just the three of them, groom, bride and the bride's "man of honor." Afterward, they'd gathered around the freestanding fireplace to sip brandy.

"Had to steal away my only real choice for best man," Warren had jokingly complained.

"It was a political move," Valerie had flashed back, and lifted her nearly drained snifter in toast to the boys. "It forced you to ask your dad. Now he'll have to approve the marriage."

Warren had laughed out loud and toasted her back. And Jude, observing how the firelight cascaded over Valerie's vibrant red hair, had laughed along.

He'd gotten good and drunk that night, so fucked-up and deathly ill that the next morning he'd nearly missed the whole damn thing.

With a queasy stomach and a cracked head, he'd arrived at the penthouse, now festooned with marigolds, snapdragons, bicolor roses, and irises. Cushioned chairs had been neatly set out on the terrace, and the guests, quietly arrayed in spring pastels and broad-brimmed hats, were being greeted by Warren's father and the nervous groom, who kept going up on tiptoe, waiting, it seemed, for Valerie to appear.

Was he afraid she would change her mind?

She didn't. When everyone was seated, Jude got the signal. To Pachelbel's famous canon, he walked down the aisle ahead of Valerie, the gold ring she would place on Warren's finger heavy in his pocket. Just before slipping it away, he'd shamelessly read the inscription: *Grow old along with me, the best is yet to be.*

He hadn't known whether to cry or puke.

At the altar, he'd tried to keep his eyes on his shoes; but there was one moment when Valerie shifted. He'd glanced up at her then, and felt a moment of profound disorientation. Beautiful as summertime in a vintage Dior gown of ivory satin, a crown of little blue irises holding back her soft red hair, she had, for just a second, made him feel that *he* was the groom.

But then the pastor had spoken Warren's name, and the illusion dissolved. Judas, having walked through fire, was sure he'd be numb. He found, to his chagrin, that he could still feel more pain.

A great deal of it.

This time it was Warren who blinked back tears of joy.

The rest of the wedding passed as a grainy blur: dancing awkwardly with Valerie, mumbling some toast or another, the guests laughing at his halfhearted jokes, and the obligatory applause afterward. Exiting the building with the newlyweds, fighting off the photographers who were clustered out in the street begging for a sweet shot of the happy couple. Escorting his two best friends to a private jet, kissing Valerie, who'd changed into a comfortable but equally flattering sage green dress.

He'd only shaken Warren's hand. That was the best he could manage at the time.

He had not been back to the penthouse since.

"Just a masochist at heart," he murmured to himself, pushing on through the crowd.

He ignored the snobby stares, idle chatter peppering his ears.

". . . Daddy McAllister got him the appointment of course," divulged one guest, "but they say he was actually pretty good at it."

". . . only twenty-seven years old. You want to be president before you're fifty, you gotta start early."

"I hear they love her in France," some woman remarked,

plucking a shrimp off an hors d'oeuvres tray and dousing it in red sauce before popping it between her thickly painted lips.

". . . told him, 'If you want the fuckers to take you seriously, you're gonna have to run for governor.' " That from the edge of the bar, where a bevy of guests ordered colorful cocktails from a ragged trio of overworked bartenders.

"Got that young Jack Kennedy thing going. But no brothers, so he'd better not get shot." Followed by nervous giggles.

Fuckers.

Jude made his way out onto the patio, where the native New Yorkers stood defiantly at the balcony rail enjoying the nippy winds of early spring and the music of distant traffic. At a few small tables, draped with milk white tablecloths and protected by the orange-red glow of heat lamps, a handful of out-of-town guests huddled, like hobos around campfires. Behind them, at the buffet table, a team of chefs worked diligently, filling the Manhattan night with the smoky scent of roasted garlic and seared tri-tip. Their assistants piled chilled crab claws, oysters, sashimi, and lobster onto a table layered like a wedding cake with circular blocks of ice.

All of which made Jude really, really wish he hadn't worn his brown suit.

"Jude!"

On a parquet floor a few couples gamely danced to old Duke Ellington tunes played by a three-piece ensemble. The men sent their sparkling ladies twirling out, and then, with a tug, spinning back in.

"Jude!"

Why had he danced so awkwardly with Valerie at her wedding? He suddenly found himself wondering. He liked to dance.

"JUDE!"

Valerie cut a swath through the crowd, a confident smile lighting up her lovely, androgynous face. A dimple appeared at the left corner of her mouth, only on the left, turning the androgyny angelic, and Jude felt his heart pounding in rhythm with the click of her heels, felt the entire room pull into focus behind her, as if she were spinning within like a solitary ballerina.

That was Valerie.

Her long arms flew around him and he found himself holding her, scenting the powdery fragrance at her shoulder. Cool hair cascaded across his cheek. In that perfect, solitary moment, everything else became imaginary, flat as a comic strip.

That was *Valerie.*

A kiss against his cheek.

Had he remembered to shave?

He pulled back at last, taking in the whole of her. Her dress was hyacinth, low cut to show off an accent of gray pearls around her swan neck. Her titian hair was parted elegantly to the side, a white camellia blossom behind one ear. The film-star look made her appear thinner than usual, pale as alabaster, and full of charm, like a gawky schoolgirl just come into her own.

Jude had trouble swallowing. A lump had formed in his throat just that quick. "Val," he stammered, "you look . . . fantastic."

"And you . . ." she said, plucking a bit of lint off his coat, "you look just the same. Come on"—the hand that grabbed his was surprisingly light, and just as surprisingly strong— "Warren's been waiting for you all evening!"

Holding court at the very edge of the terrace, farthest from buffet and band, was Warren McAllister, his smile bright and disarming, eyes green as shamrocks. With his bow tie loose about the neck, his jacket unbuttoned, his straw hair ruffled, Warren had the mischievous look of a boy who'd just come back from a day on the river with Huck and Tom.

Catching sight of Jude, Warren politely and hastily extricated himself from a cluster of admiring guests. His summer smile broke into a laugh as he captured Jude in a hard embrace.

"You son of a bitch!" He pounded on Jude's back. "Where the fuck have you been?"

"Europa Corp. keeps me pretty busy." Despite everything, Jude felt himself relaxing. It *was* good to see Warren again, he couldn't deny it.

"No, you asshole, I meant what took you so long to get *here*?"

"Oh. Traffic on the turnpike," he said, and they all laughed like excited children.

"I'll be just a moment," Valerie said then, touching on her husband's arm. "One of the bartenders is flagging me. You'd better sneak Jude off to the breakfast nook, unless you want to be interrupted every two minutes." A quick indulgent smile thrown Jude's way, "I speak from experience."

"Come on, then," Warren said, picking up a drink and signaling discreetly to an aide. The man, conspicuous in his black suit, nodded and followed them.

A hand at Jude's back, Warren directed them toward a darkened area of the terrace. With a surreptitious glance, he pulled out an electronic fob, beeped open the door to the breakfast nook, and hustled them in. The aide fell into position by the door.

"Joss will keep away the inquiring minds," Warren said, securing the door. The voices and jazz music became muffled, the clink of glasses and the rush of cars and rustling trees from Central Park quieted. The inside of the cozy breakfast nook was made to look like a Japanese garden, with small potted cherry trees and a stone fountain. The walls were glass on three sides; even its little domed ceiling was carefully constructed of triangular panels. Jude could well imagine what it would be like to have breakfast here with Valerie on a spring morning.

A beautiful teakwood table with a quartet of matching chairs stood in the center. A lamp hung down from above, but

Warren didn't bother to switch it on, he just pulled back a chair and collapsed into it.

"Remember—" He coughed a dry, rough cough. "Remember when we could go till five in the morning, then walk to the Night Owl Diner for corned beef hash and waffles?"

"Yeah." Judas sat himself down opposite Warren. "And potatoes with ketchup and eggs with hot sauce. We were pigs."

"Yeah. We'd always go there after getting wasted at that club—what was it called? The one on the East Side, with the steel door from a Prohibition speakeasy?"

"Aces."

"Yeah, Aces! Now there was a place to party."

"Aces was a piece of shit dive."

"It was a cool piece of shit dive."

"Yeah, it was."

Warren leaned back, pale face illuminated by the second-hand glow of the city. "So, Jude. Why have you been hiding from us, huh? We've been back for four months."

Jude felt as if he'd just been poleaxed. "Warren, I *work* for a living, in fuckin' *French Guiana*. You think I've got time to visit New York City? I can hardly make it to Jersey!" He tried to lighten his tone. "And why didn't you ever hop on your private jet and come see me, Mr. Junior Ambassador? Two years and you never found the time?"

"You're still a bitch, Jude, know that?" Warren coughed again. "Because I was too busy arguing immigration. That's all anyone talks about in the EEC, immigration and refugees. They don't want their huddled masses, we don't want them . . ."

"So you were the only idiot who gave a shit about the poor, tired bastards yearning to be free?" Jude grinned; he couldn't help it. "Well, aren't you the hotshot reformer."

Warren got that indignant, puzzled look on his face, the one that feared he was being mocked. And then his green eyes flickered and he released a breath. "Asshole. And it's 'breathe free' not 'be free.' " A sip of his drink. "Yeah, I was the only one arguing that we should lift 'our lamp beside the golden door.' It was a lost cause. Can't say I'm sorry to be out of it. It's good to be home."

For a moment they sat in companionable silence, listening to the sound of water trickling down over the stone fountain.

"How was Valerie? She like being a junior ambassador's wife?" Jude ventured then.

"She was fucking brilliant at it. I'm going to try and talk Dad into pushing her into politics. *I'll* be the supportive spouse."

"That would be a waste."

"Don't you start." Warren took another sip of his drink, as if embarrassed, and he probably was. And that was when Jude experienced a flash from their college days, breakfast at the Night Owl Diner at an hour so early it was still dark outside. He remembered Warren shaking hot sauce over his corned beef hash and eggs over easy, the clank and clatter of the diner, the smell of fried onions, the steam on the wide, square windows. Warren had picked up a knife and fork, and then stopped, blinking up at Jude hazily. And, right out of the blue, he'd said, *"God, how I envy you!"*

Jude remembered how he'd felt at that moment, a strange mixture of shock and threat, as if Warren had just pointed a gun at him and demanded his wallet.

"Why didn't you stay in grad school, Jude?" his friend asked now, bringing him back. "All the time we were at Princeton, that's all you talked about, the weird grad courses you were going to take with all those weird professors. What happened?"

Jude glanced away. "Europa Corp. wanted my ass, and they're where I ultimately wanted to be, so why waste more years?" he said, pointedly leaving out how he'd given into depression and cheap beer after Warren and Valerie's departure, burning almost all his bridges, and the grades that had maintained his scholarship, in the process.

Warren frowned, unsatisfied. "That's what you *really* wanted? What about T.Z.I.?"

"Mars? Hell, no. I'm not into long-term terriforming. Give me a mining operation on the moon. Okay, so right now it's just a handful of robots in a garage, but I designed that garage, and it's the *moon,* ya know?"

"No, I don't."

"You wouldn't. So . . . how's the old man?" Jude asked, a touchy subject.

"Making more money than God. Buying me votes with it."

"He doesn't have to buy you a godddamn thing," Jude said indignantly. But Warren wasn't hearing.

"He adores Valerie . . . now," Warren mused. "Know what he said? He said marrying a 'woman of the people' was a smart move. Can you believe that?" He chuckled, but there was a bitter edge to it.

"He tries," Jude offered, "and you know how little empathy I have for the rich."

"Yeah. I know." A shrug. "He's fulfilling an old dream. That has to count for something."

"God, how I envy you!" Warren had said, right out of the blue.

And Jude, who was fighting to get ketchup out of the bottle and onto his potatoes, had looked up, startled. Unlike Warren, who was still in a liquored haze, Jude was on his second wind and wide awake. But he wondered if he'd misheard. "What the fuck are you talking about?"

"You have your own dreams."

"So do you!"

"No," Jude's friend had said, and cut into his eggs. "I have an inherited dream. The only reason I'm here is to fulfill three generations of McAllister ambition. I am the dream. I don't get to have one."

"Matter of fact, Dad was just asking about you," Warren said now, and coughed again. This time, Jude noticed.

"How long have you had that thing?"

Warren straightened up and took another gulp of his drink. " 'Bout a week. Wish it'd go away. It's giving me bad dreams."

Judas grew very still; suddenly things became very clear. "It's not the Epidemic. Is it?" The Epidemic had been making its way across Asia; some alarmists said it was already too late to stop it from infecting the rest of the world. Reports were appearing regularly on the nightly news, quarantine measures were being put into effect and health officials were sending out fearful warnings.

Warren glanced away. "I don't know."

Jude stiffened with alarm. "Warren, *is it*?"

"I talk to a million people a day," he replied lightly. "And, you know, it doesn't matter how many shots the doctors give you, there's always some sort of crud—"

"Jesus fucking Christ, Warren! Have you seen a doctor?"

"In Manhattan?" His tone wasn't angry, just tired, very tired. "You've got to be fucking kidding. I'd walk in and before the thermometer was out of my ass, every news organization from here to Washington would know I was sick. That would be the end of my political career."

"Warren, this is serious! It's contagious as hell—"

"Only for a couple of days, and I've had it longer than that, in case you're worried."

"I was thinking about Val—"

Warren winced. "She hasn't got it."

"You should see a doctor—and so should she! What if it's something else entirely?"

"Judas," he said, which stopped Jude, since Warren rarely called him by his full name, mistakenly thinking he might be embarrassed by it. Jude found it rather amusing actually. His namesake was not the biblical traitor but a soap opera villain so popular that the show had transformed him into a good guy. Thanks to this character's brief popularity there'd been five Judases at Jude's elementary school and he'd met upward of fifteen others since then.

They all went by "Jude" anyway.

"Judas," Warren repeated, stifling a cough, "any chance you could take time off?"

"What has that to do with—"

"If you can't get a paid vacation, I'd be happy to—"

"Christ, Warren. You don't have to pay me, man. You know that."

"You want hockey tickets?" Warren grinned, and Jude was forced to smile back.

"Damn it, McAllister, what the fuck are you going on about?"

The green eyes came up, and Jude noticed for the first time that there were circles under them. "Valerie's pregnant."

He winced. One more arrow like that and he'd be dead. Jesus! Pregnant? . . . with Warren's child. Jesus.

"When's the blessed event?"

"December. What a Christmas present, huh? We wouldn't have known except that she went to see her OB-GYN for some tests. You're the only one we've told."

"I'm honored."

For a moment they were silent; the noise and the music from the party made its way through the glass.

"Why don't we go to Aces and get wasted?" Jude offered. He suddenly wanted very much to be alone with his friend. He wanted to clown around, drink and laugh and share secrets, like they had in college.

"I should get back out there," Warren demurred.

"They don't give a shit about you, Warren! Come on. We'll take Val. We'll stay out till dawn and have breakfast at the Night Owl."

"Don't tempt me," he muttered, and slid down in the chair to stare up at the transparent ceiling. "I've arranged to see this specialist in Paris . . . Dr. Fortier. He's the Epidemic expert. Can you take a leave of absence? I want you with me."

Jude sat back. Warren's voice had that same earnest note that had made them friends in the first place. Third year of college and Jude had been waiting in line at the arena for hockey tickets. A winning streak had made Devils games popular, and outside of scalpers, the only way to get tickets was to drag one's ass, in person, to the ticket booth in hopes of a cancellation.

Jude, wearing a jacket and gloves against the cold, had somehow managed to be first in a long line of blue-collar guys and struggling students, their breath forming white puffs in the icy air. Behind him, a brawny group of laborers were wolfing down flatbread sandwiches that reeked of onions and talking loudly in a language that sounded something like Russian. Jude had been trying to ignore them, reading a book on the history of New York engineering projects and waiting for the ticket window to open, when a clear, earnest voice said: "I'll give you eight hundred dollars if you'll let me go first!"

Jude glanced up from his book. The voice belonged to a fellow Princeton student, a few inches shorter than Jude, handsome, expensively groomed, and shivering in the cold because, it was all too pathetically evident, he'd left his coat in the car. His shock at the length of the line and his Princeton jacket with its exclusive monogram finished off the story.

"Thought you could just run up to the ticket window? Not have to wait?" Jude couldn't keep the jeer from his voice. "Why don't you just call a scalper, rich boy. For that kinda money, you could buy ten or twenty tickets."

"I can't." The young man looked utterly miserable. "My girlfriend's waiting in the car." He stopped rubbing his hands together long enough to point back over his shoulder toward the parking lot. "She sent me. I, ah, have to get the tickets my-self, you see?"

Jude did. And whoever this girl was, he wanted to give her a big, grateful kiss.

"She's a big Devils fan," the fellow added, a wistful look of pride coming into the bright eyes, and for the first time Jude felt a touch of sympathy for him. This student might be a spoiled aristo, but he really loved and admired this girl.

The laborers behind them laughed loudly. The blond man glanced over and his shoulders slumped. Jude could almost see him thinking and rejecting the idea of dealing with *them* for a place in line.

The green eyes came back to Jude with something very like a plea. "I'm Warren," he ventured, holding out a hand.

"Jude." He nodded briefly, pointedly refusing to shake.

The hand dropped. "Devils aficionado?"

Jude closed the book and crossed his arms. "Long time Rangers boy, actually. And you should quit while you're ahead."

The young man shifted from foot to foot, trying to warm himself. "I don't want your sympathy. I just want you to take my money." He grinned, and Jude had to admit it was a winning smile. "What's that you're reading?"

Jude raised the book so that Warren could see the cover. "There's a graduate engineering class touring the skyscrapers this week."

"Really? Wow. You, uh, an engineering student?"

"Nope."

"Graduate student?"

"Nah," Jude mocked, and popped open his book again. Warren shifted nearer, his teeth chattering in the cold. There was a photo on the page Jude had turned to, black-and-white, showing several construction workers walking narrow beams, fifty stories above the city.

"Christ!" Warren said. "I'd shit myself! How'd they manage to do that?"

"They made it their world."

"Scary."

"Inspiring. It shows you what people can do. They just forgot about gravity. All they saw was what they were creating."

He caught Warren staring at him then, still shivering in the cold but with a different look in his eye. As if he were seeing Jude, *really* seeing him, for the first time.

Yeah, he thought then, *look at me, rich boy. I got into Princeton by using my brain, not Daddy's pocketbook.*

"Would you want to do that?" Warren asked then in a wondering tone.

The question took Jude by surprise. "Me? Fuck yeah. And I'd want to come up with the idea in the first place. And draw up the design. And probably rivet together the steel beams. *'Make no little plans.'* Daniel Burnham, 1907."

"Yes," Warren said, with an unsettlingly intense expression, as if he'd just found a diamond in the dirt.

"Not that it does me any good," Jude heard himself say, heard the strained frustration in his voice. "That's what architects and engineers used to do: they helped put up the steel beams, dig out the mud, lay down the brickwork. Now all they do is sketch the blueprints. And they used to come up with these grand, onetime creations. Like the Empire State Building. Nothing like that's ever going to be done again. To bring something together so perfectly that it just seems to grow right out of the ground . . ."

There was a stir from the ticket window; it was preparing to open.

"So." The blond man glanced back at the laborers. They were pulling out wallets from their thick, worn jeans. "Whaddaya say? Could I . . . pay you for cuts? Eight hundred, I'm serious. Give you the money right here and now." And he rubbed hopelessly at his arms.

"Don't be ridiculous." Jude grated and slapped shut his book. "You can buy cuts for the price of a ticket."

Warren had searched Jude's face then, disbelief on his

open features. "Done!" he'd said, with fierce energy. "You wait right here!"

They would joke ever afterward about how cheap it was to buy Jude, anything for a hockey ticket. But Jude sometimes wished he'd just taken the damn money.

The girl who'd driven Warren to such extremes was, of course, Valerie. But what really surprised Jude was that, when he went to the game that night, his found his seat right next to Warren and his girlfriend.

"I wanted to finish our conversation," Warren told him later. But Jude suspected that what Warren had really wanted was to show Valerie off to him, and vice versa.

The three of them talked all through the game, and Jude found that, no matter how hard he tried, he just couldn't hate Warren, no matter how rich the bastard was.

Afterward they'd somehow ended up at the local pancake house for coffee and cheesecake, which turned into breakfast when they saw that they'd talked the night away.

And so began a long and complicated friendship.

"Will you?" Warren said now, and to Jude's consternation, his confident friend looked broken, lost. "I want someone I can trust, someone Valerie can trust if . . . if . . ."

"Jesus, Warren!" Jude felt cross. "It's not like—I mean, most of the people dying from this are in third world countries for fuck's sake!"

Warren laughed, and coughed. "Yeah. I feel like a real shit, rich as I am, to be so afraid."

"Yeah, well, you should." Jude pushed up out of his chair, uncomfortable.

"Think about it," Warren asked him, then finished off the drink and got to his feet. He seemed a little wobbly, but he slapped Jude on the back with warmhearted strength.

The aide followed them when they exited, and they met Valerie back on the terrace.

"My turn," she said, taking Jude by the arm.

"Everything okay out here, honey?" Warren asked, exchanging a quick kiss with her.

"A tray of broken glasses. Nothing serious. Oh, and Senator Raymond's been asking for you. And Senator Shayne and Judge Hernandez. Come on Jude, there seems to be room at the railing for us."

"Play nice, Val," Warren said, coughing, and headed back to the penthouse.

The railing was of dusky, rose stone. A line of guests had made themselves comfortable leaning on it, drinks in hand, looking out at the skyscrapers that glowed from within like magic lanterns. The three-piece orchestra was playing a soft, slow-dance version of "Let It Be Me."

Damn them.

"Warren talk to you?" Valerie wasted no time.

"He did."

"And . . . ?"

"Fly with you to Paris? You know I will."

"No. I mean, after, will you stay with us? All expenses paid, of course," she added, arms crossed and looking a little uncomfortable. "Shit. Never thought I'd be living this kinda life. Crazy, huh?"

"You deserve it," Jude said thickly.

"Yeah, sure. So what about it?"

"This is ridiculous, Val. Why doesn't he just fly this doctor here?"

"Because the bastard's swamped and can't come. And you know Warren; he won't insist." Her smile vanished. "I love him so much, Jude. This is really tearing me up. Would you stay for me?"

I'd do anything for you, damn it, he thought, *and you know it!* Only he wondered if she really did know it.

"Maybe," he insisted, though he knew he was caught. A long silence between them, making him aware of the soft chatter of the partygoers and the rhythm of the dance music.

"Warren told me you were, uh, in the family way. Congratulations."

Val smiled then, a gentle, inward smile that brought out her one dimple. And he knew then what he hadn't wanted to know, that she was truly happy. Not just on the surface, not just for the moment, but deeply and contentedly, for a lifetime.

The only problem was that it was not, and never would be, his lifetime.

And that's when the one memory he didn't want to recall came back to him, all in a flash, like a camera bulb. It was a moment that extended forward and back in time, a moment when, for once and for only, he'd come together with Valerie.

It'd been in September in Brooklyn, an Indian summer with warm breezes that brushed past their cheeks like kisses. A rare occasion, just the two of them, Warren away with his father meeting political movers and shakers. Valerie had worn a deep blue sundress that intensified the sapphire of her eyes. He'd bought her ice cream rippled with caramel that she'd insisted they share, bite for bite. And he'd walked her down the promenade by the water, which looked cool under the yellow, harvest sunlight. With a Kleenex from her purse he'd brushed clean a spot on a bench with a splendid view of the Brooklyn Bridge, and there they'd sat, enjoying the peace of the day.

He remembered with crystal clarity the sounds of children's laughter, the patter of joggers, the bark of dogs, a young man with a guitar, diligently practicing a classical riff. He remembered the odd mix of seasons, autumn rust coloring the last bit of summer green, the flower seller with bouquets as bright and fresh as spring, Valerie's white chocolate fragrance.

And, in the distance, behind it all, Manhattan, like some tomorrow city, its skyline all promises and dreams. He could almost hear the rush of cabs from it, the voices, the footsteps, past to future making their way to some pure, new beginning.

It might have been the equinox that day, as it seemed to

him that the normal course of the world was suspended, lost between what was and what would be.

And even then he knew that this was a day to store away, to lock in his heart like childhood or summertime for moments when he felt cold and aged. Over the last four years he had taken this particular memory out time and again, holding it like some warm and fragile creature in his hands, loving it all over again and wishing, in vain, for it to grow the way it ought to have grown, but had not.

The turning point, at least in Judas's mind, had come when he'd looked up at the bridge cables and announced aloud that he would have wanted that job: to suspend the halves of the walkway together into a magical whole.

"So that's what you were in a past life," Valerie had said, and laughed. "That's what I love about you, Jude. Warren's, well . . . Warren's a dream for others. He paints people glorious pictures, and they love him for it. But you . . . you draw your own pictures, dream your own dreams."

"Yeah. I'm a selfish, misanthropic bastard," he'd surmised, half in fun.

"No, no you're not," she'd retorted, much to his surprise. "If people can't understand the pictures you draw, that's their problem." Her eyes drank him in as she said it, seemed unable for a moment to reach their fill. And in that heartbeat, he almost believed that she loved him as much if not more than Warren. "But if you ever get a chance to make those images real, Jude, they'll understand. I promise you."

And then she smiled at him, and rising to her feet, she took his hand.

They made love that day. Only that one day, there in her old Brooklyn Heights apartment, with the windows open, the hot wind blowing in the curtains. He'd always imagined that their lovemaking would be fierce, desperate as he was for her. But it wasn't. That single time with her was the sweetest he'd ever known.

He loved her still; together or apart, he always would.

"All right, Valerie," he said, reaching out to comb back a tendril of her coppery hair. "I'll come with you to Paris, and after, I'll stay right here."

He did not know at that moment just how far that promise would take him. And even if he had, it would have made no difference. He was bound to Valerie McAllister body and soul, for the length of this and every other lifetime.

Chapter 3

VAROUNA, LYING ON HER SIDE, POPPED ANOTHER square of nicotine gum into her mouth and gathered the blankets tighter around her. The headache had been getting steadily worse, so bad that she'd thrown up her breakfast this morning. She'd had the maid close the shutters tight to keep out the sunlight, which cut right through her eyes and into her head. Despite the sweltering heat outside, a perpetual chill infected her skin.

She would have killed for a cigarette, but her hands shook too much to try to light one. The gum satisfied her craving and kept her mouth from getting dry.

She suspected, with a fear that was dull and depressed, that she was only going to get worse. At least the cough was gone.

Bhaskar had actually called from his conference, making some sardonic remark about the telephones working and how, in Paris, the lines never went down. He told her that it was *spring* in Europe, all green and cool, with the cherry trees in bloom. "Not murderously hot," he said with disgust, as if Varanasi were not the holiest of cities but hell itself.

He hadn't bothered to ask how she was, but he must have been pretty worried to have actually phoned. He asked, instead, if there had been any special mail or messages for him.

"No," she had told him, not bothering to try to explain that she'd been too weak and sick to get the mail.

"I'll call you again in a few days," he'd said, and she'd heard him coughing before he hung up.

The neighbor women had been by to help, poking their heads in to check on her, bringing by home remedies; they were honestly concerned, and friendly enough. They were also dreadfully stupid, gossips who couldn't or wouldn't control their children. They hated their husbands, who were always at work or out carousing, and frequently told her how very lucky she was to have such a smart, such a very good brother who earned good money and was willing to take care of her. More than one of them had an eye on her brother, but she doubted he'd have an affair with any of them. They weren't European enough.

The headache seemed to be subsiding, at last! But now she was feeling hot. No, icy cold. And sick to her stomach. A fever, she thought. And there was no one here to take care of her. Bhaskar had at least done that; in their childhood, when none of the aunties could be bothered with Varouna no matter how ill she was, her brother had placed cold cloths on her forehead and taken her pulse. And explained, all the while, how her body worked and why it was doing what it was doing.

She had often wondered if her brother had nursed her out of love or because he was practicing, even then, to be a doctor.

Pulling herself up, she poured a cup of chilled water from a carafe the maid had brought to her bedside. The effort brought her close to fainting. So, she was sick, she thought, draining the cup and collapsing back onto her side. Her body shivered.

Very sick.

The virus could not know that it was failing. In point of fact, it was not, technically, failing at all. After multiplying in the lungs so that it could efficiently spread itself to other hosts, it had ridden back up to the nasal membranes and into the brain. There, the electrical activity had jolted it into its final activity: infusing brain tissue with encoded proteins and acids. Eagerly it etched itself deeply into as many pockets and wrinkles as it could.

It found the human brain wonderfully receptive; it was shockingly easy to encode this mind with vivid new images and feelings, to engage the imagination and stimulate desires.

There were, however, problems that the virus failed to recognize: it could not pass on its entire message because only certain areas of the human brain were designed to absorb information, and those areas differed from person to person. Furthermore, the virus had been designed to download its message into a storage brain while leaving other brains, like ones dealing with motor skills, unaffected. But this planet-bound species didn't have separate brains for such things. And so the virus, unwittingly, put other functions at risk.

The virus meant no harm, quite the opposite, since to do any damage to its host was to sabotage its mission. And that was unthinkable. The host was sacrosanct, to be venerated and worshiped. But the virus did do damage, terrible damage, especially when it summoned the body's defenses.

Horrified by the attack and seeking to rid itself of a foreign intruder, the antibodies gathered and the temperature went up. The body was selfishly determined in this. The invader was trying to alter the brain. It could not be allowed to do that. Whatever it took, it would be destroyed.

And so the body tried to purge itself of the invasion, even to the point of death.

Her mind seemed to have been cut adrift. That bothered Varouna because she prided herself on her sharp mind. Sharper than Bhaskar's, smarter too.

Once, when she was sixteen, she'd enthusiastically tried to explain to her aunts and cousins why ghee didn't require refrigeration and about the gluten proteins in flour, chemistry lessons she'd learned from her brother and his books.

"What will matter to your husband is if you can cook the food," they'd impatiently responded, "not analyze it."

And that was the real sticking point. She ought to have been given the same rarefied education as her brother, the same chance to develop her mind.

But no one, certainly not Bhaskar, had ever cared to know that. To do so would have been to give her an identity, a purpose in life.

So it scared her that she couldn't seem to hold on to that mind, or will her thoughts to go where she wanted. Odd remembrances kept walking in and out, unbidden: the memory of her favorite powder blue sari, the one she'd worn as a girl at festival times, and the marigold and hibiscus flowers her favorite aunt had liked to pin into her hair. The day she'd found a litter of gray kittens by her brother's bicycle, the huge black umbrella her father had always carried during monsoon season, and the baskets of wedge-shaped, yellow candy, bees buzzing around them, that were set out before the sweet shops every summer.

But what really bothered her was that the memories tended to shift, to lose parts and put in new ones, ones that made no sense. The flowers flew from her hair to attach themselves to floating stones, petals waving like wings. The monsoon rains became a deluge of coppery dust falling around her father's umbrella. The summer candy floated up out of the baskets to dance across the sky.

As she moved down the street, avoiding the crowded buses, the perpetual tangled knot of motorcycles, bicycles, scooters, and skeletal cows, she felt that she was floating. And then she saw that she *was* floating, and that all the vehicles were really asteroids.

There were thousands and thousands of them, multiplying until weightless rocks surrounded her in all directions, heavy chunks the color of raw sugar. Some were veined with amber and bronze like nutmeg fruit, or covered with vibrant blue fronds that gushed out, long and soft as peacock feathers. Others offered up silken pastel leaves or sprouted spikes vibrantly red like chili peppers. One cluster of moonlets had long jade stalks topped with round, lacy blossoms.

The rain of copper dust poured past and she saw the gray kittens leaping from stone to stone, pale cotton threads trailing out behind them.

No sounds, as there was nothing for sound to travel through. No smells. No atmosphere. She could sense that as she floated, there beside the bicycle, its wheels silently spinning. And yet there was life here, as in the waters of the Ganges.

Quite suddenly, the bicycle wheels broke off and flew past the strange, colorful flora, past the rain of copper dust, up to the black, starry sky. They lost their spokes and one shrank to fit inside the other. Then the slices of candy began to wedge themselves into the tires, forming a pattern of rays.

But the transformation did not end there. The coloring of the wheels changed from black and honey to silver and white, and they slowly enlarged, until finally Varouna faced two enormous ice and silver rings, the larger one turning like a great waterwheel around the smaller. And, at the center of that smaller one, a dense white ball spun, tossing out colors like crystal.

What is it? she wondered. And in answer to her question, she finally saw the creators of those two great circles peering out from between the traffic of asteroids: enormous, prickly shapes, with a drapery of delicate teardrop leaves.

Travelers, she thought. Or would-be travelers.

As they neared her, they brought the stars with them, until they were able to hang the Milky Way around her neck like a welcoming marigold wreath.

That is when she understood what they were, and what they had brought her.

She understood everything.

Chapter 4

May

THE CITY FATHERS OF TORONTO HAD PROMISED THAT they'd hire more personnel to handle the paperwork, thus freeing up the police to do their job. And the city fathers had kept their word. But as the Epidemic made its way through the ranks, extending the rolls of workers on sick leave, constables and detectives like Gordon Demme found themselves back at the computers, typing away.

As his clumsy fingers pecked at the keys, he reflected that he should have worked harder and done better in his typing and computer classes. Silly him, he'd imagined that joining the department meant that he'd be chasing down perps.

He sipped at his coffee, which had gone cold and oily, and copied his handwritten notes into the files. He already suffered from a small bout of carpal tunnel syndrome ("It's your posture," the chiropractor had told him, "if you fix that, you'll fix everything"), eye strain ("If you'd just take some time for a simple laser operation," his ophthalmologist had told him, "we could probably do away with your nearsightedness. At least stop wearing those chunky old glasses and get some proper contacts. Those frames went out with Woody Allen"), and a headache.

A streak of hypochondria had him fretting about the headache. He had fears that the twinge he felt on his left side was the onset of a heart attack, or that a headache was the signal for an aneurysm.

They never were, but, of course, one day it would happen. Sooner or later, he'd feel something funny, and this time it wouldn't be harmless. Age, bad coffee, job stress, life, would eventually catch up to him.

And what would he have to show for it? Paperwork.

The phone connected to the monitor rang and he clicked on the icon to answer it. In the corner, a little picture of his wife appeared. Mae was Asian-American, with dark, shiny hair and sharp, long eyes. She was also eight months pregnant and suffering from a cough.

"Would you stop at the store before you come home?" the image asked.

"Did you call the doctor?" His hypochondria worried for her as well as himself.

"Don't be ridiculous." She sighed with exasperation. He often felt her impatience was with him, especially when they talked like this, over the computer. He knew what she was seeing: a sad, average-looking fellow with a droopy face, unshaven chin, drab dun hair and mustache, and weak, gray eyes behind square black glasses. He still had no idea why she'd ever married him, outside of the fact that he had been, and still was, crazy about her.

"The doctors' offices are closed and the hospitals are a fucking mess." Irritation was in her voice, a restlessness that had been building with the pregnancy. The two of them ought to have been happy and anxious, or excited and nervous, first child jitters and all that. Instead, they were bleak as ghosts. "Can you stop at the store? I need more cough syrup."

"Anything else?"

"Yeah, eucalyptus tea and stew meat and a few other things. Don't worry, I faxed the store a list. They should have it ready for you."

He noted that she hadn't bothered asking the store to deliver, that cost extra and they were budgeting, cutting corners for the baby. "All right, then. See you later, and get some rest."

"That's all I ever do." She sighed, and her picture disappeared; the word DISCONNECTED flashed at the top for a little, then stopped. What had happened to their marriage? Was it just the slush on the streets which seemed to keep spring from arriving? The pregnancy? It wasn't the job; the department had long since worked out everything from stress leave to couples' counseling to vacations and shorter hours. And, unlike most spouses, Mae had never worried about his getting shot or hurt, although that was always a possibility. She shrugged off all thoughts of the future, leaving such anxieties to him.

Really, *she* should have been the cop.

"Demme! Detective-Sergeant wants you." A young constable coughed.

"Coming!" he said, pushing up from his desk and rolling down his sleeves. He knew already what the detective-sergeant was going to tell him, that more constables and secretaries, another desk sergeant, a prisoner or two in the lockup, another judge at the courthouse was at home sick. Or in the hospital or in a coma. Or paralyzed. Or dead.

And he would hear it, and pray to God that his wife was only sick with a simple, normal cough that cough syrup and eucalyptus tea could cure. And he would type up more reports and do double duty and come in on his days off and pretend that this crisis would eventually end.

Gordon shrugged on his jacket and brushed the lint from his tie. No one else wore a suit and tie these days, but he was hopelessly old-fashioned, with his black horn-rims and droopy mustache.

Maybe if he shaved the mustache off, it would change his marriage.

*　　*　　*

In their first years of marriage, Mae's buoyant, "Que sera, sera" philosophy had helped Gordon from sinking down to rock bottom.

Mae's recent brooding had left him desperate.

He unlocked the door one-handed, his left arm clamped around a bag of groceries. He almost wished she'd handed him a list of groceries to get, like his mother used to hand to his father, rather than faxing the list directly to the store. Just picking the groceries up never seemed enough. Lately he'd wondered what exactly she needed him for.

And what would happen when their son finally arrived? That question scared him most of all, because Mae seemed to resent the baby now, to despise every hour it was in her body.

The house was dark, which meant that Mae was probably asleep. He flipped on a light in the dining room, then made his way to the shadowed kitchen and began unpacking the bags. The open refrigerator shed harsh, chill light across the dirty tiles. Mae hadn't been well enough to do any housekeeping and Gordon hadn't been home.

And the maid services were no longer in business because everyone was sick. Hell, there'd only been one cashier at the store and two bag boys, all three of them hiding the fact that they were coughing.

"Gordon?" Coughing from the bedroom. He hated the sound; everyone he knew, everyone he met, seemed to be coughing. It was as if the whole world were populated with sick and dying invalids.

"Yes, dear?"

"Could you make me some tea?"

"Right away. How are you?"

"I've got a fucking headache and I feel sick to my stomach. But the cough's better."

During the first three months of her pregnancy, Mae had smiled, even when she'd gotten morning sickness. They'd talked about their kid's future and held hands during the ultrasound. They'd even agreed on a name: Scott. Mae liked it because it was short and simple.

Now, she seemed indifferent to it.

God, don't let her die. Don't let her and Scotty die. He began to bustle around the kitchen. He hoped the boy took after her because he had this awful fear that Mae would hate the kid if it resembled him.

The kettle was on, a cup and saucer set out. Gordon removed his jacket and tie, draping them over a chair in the kitchen. The table was old and round, the chairs a worn teal. They'd been saving up for a new house when Mae found out she was pregnant and subsequently quit her job to have the baby. It didn't matter to him, if having the baby made her happy. But he wondered now, fretted over the possibility that she regretted choosing a child over a new home.

He crossed down the hall and into the bedroom. The small lamp on the dresser had been left on the low setting. It illuminated Mae's small, cluttered makeup table, the twin nightstands, the square mirror atop the stained pine dresser, and the bleached wood crib in the corner, waiting for Scotty's arrival. Gordon removed the gun that he wore at all times now, holstered under his arm, and took care to unload it and put it in a safe place in the dresser. Then he turned to his wife.

Despite being eight months pregnant, Mae barely seemed to be a lump under the knitted white blanket. Her face was lost in the feather pillows that surrounded her, including the full-body pillow he'd bought to support her. As he stepped up to her he saw that she was wearing her favorite nightshirt, the soft, ribbed, periwinkle blue one. Her hair streaked down behind her, oily from not being washed.

As he leaned down to kiss her, he noticed, not for the first time, that she smelled ill. She was also hot. Burning hot.

"Mae." He touched her shoulder; she stirred a little, mumbling, but her eyes did not open. The teakettle in the kitchen started to whistle.

"Mae?" A little harder this time. This was ridiculous; he'd only talked to her a minute ago. *"Mae!"*

"Why?" she barely responded, and then, "Golden Gate."

"Golden Gate?" Mae came from San Francisco. They'd flown there not six months back to spend the holidays with her parents and sisters. Last Mae heard from them, they were sick too.

"Bridge," she said, eyes glazed. Her voice held a note of awe and there was a smile on her face the likes of which he'd not seen since the doctor had first told her she was with child.

"You can step across the stars," she told him.

"I'm taking you to the doctor!" Gordon said, shaken, but even as he said it he knew, who better, that there was no getting her there. The ambulances, what few of them had drivers, were barely running, and would take hours to get here. He could drive her himself, but they'd end up waiting the night away in the overcrowded emergency room.

And when they saw a doctor, Gordon knew what he'd be told: *"It has to run its course. Maybe she'll live through it."*

He dropped to one knee then and pulled her head to his chest. "It's all right, Mae. I'm here. I'll keep you cool, and I'll get you through this. Don't worry. We'll survive this."

Mae, dilated eyes sliding open and then closed, kept a weak hand on her belly and said nothing.

Chapter 5

THE NEWS WAS ON, STILL SOUNDING IN THE BACK-ground. Valerie ignored it; there was, after all, only one subject ever discussed on the news these days: the Pandemic. That's what they were calling it now. And at the moment, nothing could interest her less.

"They say you can have some time alone with him. They say they don't have to . . . to take him right away. Val?"

That was Judas. Poor Judas. She could have loved him as passionately as she'd loved Warren if she'd allowed herself; hell, she could have loved them both, and they probably would have bowed to her will, adoring her as much as they did. But they hadn't that kind of sophistication or maturity, the three of them. Judas would have worried over what he lacked that Warren gave her, and Warren would have feared, rightfully so, that she would eventually tire of the arrangement and leave them both.

Better to choose and hurt one of them. Better to hope that the friendship would survive her than to destroy it with childish whims. And so, at one crucial point, Valerie had searched her heart long and deep. She'd held a certain pride that neither Warren's money nor Judas's lack of it had swayed her decision, though she was sure Judas thought otherwise. Her decision had been based on only one question and a gut response: *Which one can't I live without?*

Warren.

She remembered how clearly that name had come into her, how sure she suddenly was that Warren was the one. She could be a part of Warren's dream, even if he doubted that the dream was his own. What's more, his aims gave her a chance to shine, to stand in that warm, bright center with him.

But no matter how close she got to Jude, she knew that they would never stand together; as much as he loved her and she loved him, she was not the one who could partner him in that strange and frightening vortex.

That made her terribly sad, as if, for the first time in a life of awards and achievements, she'd discovered that all she was and all she'd accomplished meant nothing. There was one thing she could never be. And she was the less for that.

"I could stay, if you'd like." Judas was trying hard to sound compassionate. He sounded wooden instead; Jude was not good at expressing his feelings, especially in such circumstances. Especially when he was hurting so much himself. Poor Jude. Who would comfort him?

"How's Warren's father?" she asked then, and was surprised at how calm and quiet her voice was.

"Not . . . not good. They had to sedate him."

How sad. The one thing Warren had never wanted to do was disappoint his father, and now he had. No. That was uncharitable. The old man's grief, and love, was genuine, perhaps more so than ever.

"Let me sit with you," Jude tried again. She could hear the desperation in his voice; he wanted so very much to help her through this.

But, "No," she said; and, after a moment, she heard the door shut.

Poor Jude; he probably feared she was hysterical, that she might not know that Warren was really dead. He would have a harder time with that, with her mental collapse, than with Warren's death. He was being absurd, of course. She knew that the thing in the bed wasn't Warren. It looked like Warren, his soft blond hair and handsome features. But it wasn't Warren, just a waxwork of him.

She did feel her heart waiting, however, for Warren to come back to this shell in the bed. His spirit, she felt, was soaring around the room, out the window and over New York. She was glad that, having checked Warren over and given him some shots, their much vaunted Paris doctor had urged her husband to go home. They both loved Manhattan, and Valerie felt sure that his spirit wouldn't have been happy anywhere else.

Was he playing around the giant billboards in Times Square? Swirling round the spires and the ringing bells of St. Patrick's Cathedral? Or enjoying a moment at Rockefeller Center, trying to buy an exotic blossom for her from a flower seller, or maybe a scoop of caramel ice cream? They'd always had remarkably similar tastes, a weakness for caramel, for relish on the hot dogs, for waffles, and for grilled cheese and tomato sandwiches. Jude's tastes were completely different from theirs, mustard on the hot dog, a preference for French toast over waffles, and an indifference to grilled cheese.

Funny how well she knew them both.

Perhaps Warren was on his way back. He'd come through the window, enter the body in the hospital bed, open his beautiful green eyes and smile at her. Perhaps that was him now, fluttering the curtains—

She'd had long curtains in her old Brooklyn Heights apartment. How she'd loved that place. An afternoon with a warm breeze billowing through. She and Judas making love, because she knew that if she didn't, she'd wonder about it for the rest of her life.

She'd never told Warren about it. That was the one thing she'd never imagined about marriage, that she would still keep secrets. Naively, she'd imagined that true love meant complete honesty. But it didn't. What it really meant was that the other person's joy warmed you like the sun.

"Val?"

Funny. She'd often worried about what Warren would do if she died. She'd honestly never considered that he might predecease her. There was even, in her dresser drawer, a letter to him, just in case.

Warren,

    You're going to cry when you read this—and you're probably going to think of it as some weird message from the dead to the living. But remember that I wrote it when I was very much alive, and so it is not a message from the dead, but a legacy from one who lived and loved you.

    There is someone else out there for you! That is what I want you to know, why I wrote this letter; another someone who will love you as much, if not more, than I. You won't believe that just yet. But when enough time has passed, I want you to seek out and find that someone. Because I love you, and I want someone to be there for you, to care for you and keep you warm at night. I don't want you to spend your life pining for me, that's foolish. What I want instead is for you to be happy again.

    More than anything in the world, I want you to be happy.

Stupid, sanctimonious piece of shit! He'd better not have written a similar note to her. She'd come to his grave and scream at him; she'd tear it up and litter the grass with it!

"Valerie, it's been an hour."

Unlikely that he had written a note, though. Warren had always been the demonstrative kind, wanting to show rather than tell his love. In her scrapbook, she had the one and only love letter he'd written her, a clumsy thing where he'd composed a silly if heartfelt poem, rhyming, rather pathetically, the line "Hair red of flame" with "A spirit no one can tame."

After they were married she'd told him, jokingly, that it

was a good thing his speechwriting was nothing like his poetry, else his life as a politician would be over.

He'd gaily retorted that that was what speechwriters were
for.

"Val?"

"Go away, Jude."

The television was still on in the background, the news
yammering on, something about the death toll in third world
countries. The more civilized parts of the world had medicines, sanitary conditions, food, and so they were managing to
keep the death rate down. But in the poorest parts of the world
the bodies were piling up at a rate quadruple that of the
wealthier—and that was with the population differences fac-
tored in.

Not that that had made any difference in Warren's case.
Here they were in a hospital room with brocaded couches and
leather armchairs, with twenty-four-hour nursing, with the
best doctors and food trolleyed in on a silver cart by a tuxedoed waiter.

All for nothing. Warren had still heaved his guts out for
two days, unable to keep even water down, had run a deadly
fever for almost a week. His brain had swelled, and he'd gone
into a coma.

Agonizing week. Would he be left unable to walk? Unable to breathe without mechanical assistance? Would he even
come out of the coma?

So, now she knew. She wished, she wished, she still had
that thread of hope, no matter how it had wrapped around her,
slicing her heart to pieces. She wished, she wished, that Warren's spirit were still in the room with her, even if it wouldn't
open the eyes and smile at her.

"Val?"

"What is it, Judas?"

"They . . . they need to remove the body."

This was tiresome. "Can they give me a little more time
alone?"

"You've been alone with . . . with him for three hours."

Really? How time flies when you're having fun, she thought, and almost laughed, but didn't. If she started, she'd never stop.

"Just a little more time, Jude. I've got the money to buy that."

"Yes," he said, and she felt him leave this time.

Warren had better have left a note for her. Please God, let him have left a last letter. She needed to hear his warm, engaging voice again, if only in her mind, hang on his words again, even if they were only symbols on a page. And she wanted something, anything, that was not a memory, that was new, so that, for one minute, she could forget that he was never coming back, that she'd never speak with him again.

How, she wondered, did people in the third world countries cope? A life of misery, of sickness and constant work, hunger and fear. And death always right at your side, like a toy a child might take with it to bed. Time on this earth must seem so short and terrible to such people.

Life shouldn't be like that.

She and Warren had had youth and health, and more money than any two people ought to have. They'd lived in obscene comfort, had the best educations, grandest dreams, brightest futures. How dare she even think of this, her life, as a tragedy? What sick and starving third world woman, the skeletal bodies of her family piled round her, no luxurious hospital room, no tuxedoed waiter to bring her whatever she might care to eat, wouldn't mock Valerie's grief right now? She probably ought to be thankful and consider herself lucky.

Fuck that.

The only comfort anyone had was in another's arms. Tear that away, and only pain could be put in its place.

"Valerie." Judas was back. Poor, poor Judas. "They really—they *really*—"

"All right, Jude." She stood up. She'd waited long enough. Warren was not coming back. Time to embrace the pain, to hold to it. And hope that someday . . . someday, it would go away.

"At least she still has the child," she heard some fool relative say as Jude escorted her out of the room.

She laughed then, and, as she feared, couldn't stop. The idiot. Didn't they know the child had been for Warren? Besides, she wouldn't be keeping the baby for long. There was a 98 percent chance of a miscarriage for pregnant women sick with the Pandemic. The percentage got better if the woman was farther along in her pregnancy, but those in their first months were likely to lose the child.

"Are you all right, Valerie?" Judas asked awkwardly, arm tight around her. She was still laughing, though softer now.

"I'm fine," she said, and coughed.

Chapter 6

THEY DIDN'T WANT TO LET HIM TAKE ANY MORE TIME off. They even threatened to fire him if he didn't come in. He almost laughed at them; it was all so very pathetic. Over three-quarters of the city sick or dead or, like him, hovering over loved ones hoping that they'd recover from the illness—including most of the police force—and they wanted him to punch in for work!

What crimes could he possibly stop when the most terrible and inevitable crime of all was happening right before his very eyes?

He hadn't ever thought of himself as a superhero; joining the force had been a way of escaping his alcoholic father and a sister who went off with bad boyfriends and had screaming fights with their mother. But he'd vowed to be different and to make a difference. He'd given his heart and his life to the force. And now he saw that none of it mattered. What mattered was a woman whose hot, dry hand held his, her dark hair a tangled mess spread out across the dirty sheets, her eyes glazed.

A woman who was going into labor and didn't even know it.

Gordon had tried calling the paramedics, but even with his police radio and codes, it had gotten him nothing. There were no paramedics well enough to drive, not one in the whole city of Toronto. And even if he could get Mae to the hospital, it wouldn't do any good. According to the news, the sick were so numerous they were now being laid out on hallway floors of the hospitals, in the lobbies and emergency rooms. Most were still in their street clothing. Some were lying in vomit and diarrhea.

Mae's belly moved and rippled with contractions, but Mae just stared at the ceiling. She was completely unaware of the birth, of its pain and need to push. Gordon wiped down her hot skin with wet towels. No matter how much he poured over her, it all seemed to evaporate when it touched her.

The fever had risen very quickly this morning, a digital thermometer touched into her ear pegging her temperature at 104 degrees; it had held steady, refusing to break or back down. Not long after, her water had broken. He had no idea how long she'd actually been in labor prior to that. And there was no telling if, as was common with the sickness, the body was trying to miscarry.

He was a police officer; he knew what to do. He cut her out of the nightshirt, even though it was her favorite, shoved the pillows under and around her, and propped up her legs. Then he readied blankets for the baby; it would be premature, so he set up a heat lamp over the crib to act as an incubator. He put out string and scissors for the umbilical cord and brought in water he'd boiled earlier. Then he took off his tie and jacket and rolled up his sleeves.

He was trembling from fatigue; seventy-two hours and he'd barely slept; his knees were wobbly, his sight blurred. "Mae," he said, moving to her upraised legs, "Mae, you've got to push. Please."

With each minute of labor her skin got hotter, her eyes more distant; she might not be feeling the pain, but it was dehydrating her and sapping her of any strength she had to fight the fever.

He'd tried to get liquid into her but she'd just vomit it

back up. He was close to panic now; all he could think was to try to get the baby out of her before the birth killed her.

"Gate, golden golden, gold—" he thought she whispered. Her lips hadn't stopped moving, not in two days, but no sounds came out; even her breath was faint and shallow and silent.

"Mae—"

The crown of the baby suddenly appeared, just like that, and Gordon breathed a sigh of relief.

"He's here, Mae. He's here—can you push?"

He wasn't sure if she finally heard him, or if her body just did what it had to do, but the baby broke past the cervix and little Scotty slid into his quivering hands, warm and damp with Mae's blood. Gordon got his little finger into the mouth to clear it, and Scotty gave a mewling cry.

"He's all right, Mae. I think he's going to be all right!" His hands trembled as he tied off and cut the cord and washed the blood from his son. Scotty screamed and shook as the warm water was sponged over him. His arms and legs were thin and tiny, the ribs visible. He was all soft, veined head and red, wrinkled skin.

He's so small, Gordon thought, afraid.

But he couldn't take Scotty to the hospital; there were other infections that could kill a vulnerable newborn there, outside of the virus. He would have to create something better than the heat lamp. For right now, he had to get Scotty some formula. He couldn't expect Mae to feed him, couldn't even trust the milk in her breasts.

Mae.

He turned back to her, his son, a thing of flesh and bone still crying in his hands. The afterbirth had come and was pooled under her bloody thighs. Her skin, so dry it was almost scaly, was fiery to the touch. But when his eyes found hers he saw life still in them.

"Golden . . . bridge," she breathed, and Gordon believed that she saw and recognized him, saw their boy cradled in his arms. He didn't want to leave then, but Scotty needed food. The crib they'd bought was waiting in the bedroom corner; a nest of towels and the heat lamp were ready. He would have to trust that they'd keep Scotty alive for the ten minutes he'd be gone.

He rushed out, sped to the store though it was only a few blocks north, breaking seven different laws along the way. It hardly mattered; the streets were deserted. The store, which he had visited only a few nights ago, was now closed. That hadn't stopped looters, or perhaps just desperate folk from breaking the windows and raiding the place. The alarm was screaming, but no police responded. As Gordon feared, there was no preventing what could be prevented anymore. If someone set fire to the city, it would burn down unchecked.

He would get Mae and Scotty out before that happened.

If they were alive when he got back.

"Please," he said under his breath, broken glass cracking under his feet. "Please—" He passed scattered groceries, kicked away canned soup and cereal boxes, cat litter and scouring powder. There were no medicines or antibacterial products, clearly the first things to be ripped off the shelves by panicked shoppers.

Gordon finally found formula and bottles. Whatever looters had come, they hadn't wanted baby items. Filling his arms with diapers and formula, stuffing bottles into his pockets, he dashed back out to his car.

"Be alive, please, be alive," he wished on the way home. They were all there was in his life now, he realized. It had narrowed down that little, or that much.

His wife and his son.

He wanted to dash right from the car to the house, but he knew he'd need the car and so took an extra precious minute to park it in the garage and lock it. When he finally broke back into the bedroom, Scotty was still whimpering.

"Oh, thank God, thank God—" He skidded back into the kitchen and almost spilled everything trying to fill the bottle, his hands were shaking that badly. He warmed the formula in the microwave.

Scotty was barely making a sound when he finally got the rubber nipple to the little toothless mouth. The newborn refused it, fussing weakly.

"Come on." Gordon tried again, twice; Scotty was having none of it. His father began to sweat. At last, on the fifth try, sucking response took over, and the infant pulled at the nipple, lightly at first, then stronger.

In his time, Gordon had saved lives, but the satisfaction he felt feeding his son for the first time was unlike anything he'd ever experienced before. It was a warm glow that held his heart, like the embrace of a lover. He felt the tears rolling down his face and did not bother to wipe them away.

"Hi, Scotty," he said, and gently scooped up the babe into his arms.

And that was when he finally saw and realized that Mae was dead. The head was turned, the eyes flat, the flesh finally cool to the touch. The bloodstained legs were still up, and Gordon's one thought was that he wished he'd bothered to wash her clean before he'd left.

He stared at her body for a long time. Meanwhile, in his arms, Scotty finished with his bottle, yawned and drifted off to sleep, snug in his swaddling of blankets, with the comforting warmth of his father's heartbeat next to his tiny ear.

Chapter 7

June

IN THE HOLY CITY OF VARANASI, WHICH SOME CALLED Banaras and others Kasi, at least one cremation fire was always burning on the *ghats,* the broad, stone steps that lead down to the Ganges. Now that one cremation pit encompassed the whole city.

> *"Om Bhur Bhuvasva,*
> *Tat Savitur Varenium—"*

The pilgrims still sang in the morning and waded into the Ganges, but the water they gathered into their hands no longer glowed with the light of the sun; instead, the drops shimmered with the fires that burned on the balconies and pavilions.

> *"Bhargo Devasya Dhimahi,*
> *Dhiyo Yo Nah Prachodayat. . . ."*

The hymn went on, but there was no heart in the words that acknowledged the light of Lord God and asked that it illuminate the minds of men. The sun was lost behind the inky smoke that blackened the skies, and when it could be seen at all, it was a fat, red ball, a dying nova, not a Lord of Light.

And so the fires illuminated the night and oppressed the

day. They turned the waters of the Ganges pewter with ashes and forced those who remained in the city to wear veils over their faces.

There had been times in the past two months when the flap of the cremation flames had sounded like sails in a storm, when they were the only sound in the city, and Varouna felt as though she'd been transported to a strange, other world of darkness and white noise. The bell ring of bicycles, the honking of horns, the shouts of children, the laughter, conversation, and songs of life no longer existed. Instead, Varanasi hissed with the constant crackle of the fires and the buzz of flies, the only life teeming in the hot, hellish city.

For a while, there had also been the screams and sobs of grief, but they had stopped weeks ago. There was no way for the living to possibly mourn for all the dead or perform rites for them all.

Still, hundreds of brave or foolish or devout or sacrificial souls took it upon themselves to push wheelbarrows or drive oxcarts of bodies, hour after hour, to the fires, and toss the corpses on the flames, and recite the chants. The bodies on the carts were often so encrusted with flies that they looked gray and seemed to be rippling. When thrown on the fire, the flies broke apart into a million buzzing spots and spun around the inferno as if angry. The worst of it was that each day, one less brave or foolish or devout or sacrificial soul pushed a wheelbarrow or led an oxcart to the fire. At least thrice she'd seen one of these former souls tossed along with the rest onto the flames.

Varouna, curled by the window, watched with eyes reddened by the smoke. She was twenty pounds lighter and her muscles were so weak she could barely walk. She often had to crawl to the stove to boil her drinking water, a painstaking but necessary detail. Clean water was even more difficult to come by than usual. No water pumped through the faucets or appeared in the water closets and there were no water sellers on the streets anymore. The sick and dead had long since infected the wells and fountains and the Ganges with vomit, feces, and their own decaying bodies. An outbreak of cholera had caused almost as many deaths as the virus. Varouna had had to venture into other apartments in search of water, sometimes stumbling over bodies while lugging back jugs and bottles.

Food was another precious commodity. Thanks to her brother's taste for European foodstuffs and her own weakened needs, the tinned and canned goods in the pantry had lasted through her slow recovery. But she was almost out. Soon, she would have to search for food. And that, after surviving all this, might get her killed. Looters had been breaking in and stealing goods from those stricken ill; Varouna, having gotten the virus early, had rallied in time to bar the door against them.

Lately, however, out of boldness or desperation, the looters had begun to steal from the healthy as well. There'd been bodies thrown on the fires with broken skulls and slit throats. There had been screams from apartments not of grief but of terror. And there was horrible laughter, sounds that made a mockery of the dead, sounds that were, in their own way, as much an attempt to outface the fear as the hymns that, every morning, still rode on the flesh-tainted air.

The strange thing was, Varouna felt no horror at any of it. Since her illness, the days passed by her like a languid dance. She felt no boredom with Time's leisurely pace; quite to the contrary, it hypnotized her, like those odd lamps in which colors flowed like sea creatures.

India, she felt, tested the soul; she knew this, could almost hear it, in her blood and bones, as if it were a part of her cells, as if it had been formed with her at birth. India taught patience and adaptability. Here was the cradle not only of civilization, but also of humanity's struggle to be the fittest. Here is where all might have been lost or won at any time.

Even now.

India, she knew, must be one of the worst places hit by

this epidemic. There'd been too few doctors, too many people, and too little medicine to combat what came with such an illness, including the aftermath of cholera, pneumonia, infection, dehydration, starvation.

And it would only get worse when the monsoons came; they were due any time now. At first it would be pleasant. The torrents of warm rain would strike the sizzling pavement, douse the funeral fires, cool the air and cleanse the smoke from the sky. There would be plenty of fresh water. But the downpours would also flood the city, drown the sick who were too weak to climb to higher ground. Bodies would be left to float, grotesquely, down the watery streets. And soon after there would be mildew, fungus, and mosquitoes.

No. They were not done suffering yet.

For all this, India had an advantage: it knew what it was to suffer from plagues. It did not fight sickness as others did, seeing it as death and life at war with each other. When the Epidemic came, India built its fires and sent the dead off into the sky, to orbit round the universe and return. In the meantime, the living that could left the cities, knowing that this, too, would pass, that they, too, would eventually return. They'd lived through such cycles before. They would again.

And so Varanasi, for a time, became a city for the dead; no offerings of fruit or candy were given to the Ganges, no candles or paper prayer boats took their messages down its waters. Instead, whole families were laid out on rafts, doused with oil, and set aflame. Varouna watched these drift down the blackened waters with an odd sense of peace. This illness was like another season. It had arrived and was now coming into force. It would taper off.

And the survivors would continue.

There was, she had to admit, just one small problem: the knowledge that was now in her mind, information that did not belong to her. In her experience, the alchemy of time and hardship was like turning off one road on to another. But this was like being pushed off the road to walk on water. No one should be able to do that, and yet Varouna knew that a part of her brain, very likely a part of every brain of every survivor, now allowed humanity to do just that.

She had been set on a river that crossed over the old river.

It gave Varouna a purpose deep within to know this, a gratifying ambition that had her equally elated and horrified. She could not be the only one who knew the cause behind this virus, but she wondered if she was the only one who understood the inner biology and thought patterns of the ones who had created it. She wanted to find others, if they existed. She wanted to discuss what she knew with them, make sure she had gotten all the lore and not just bits of it.

And if she was the only one, well then she wanted to explain what she knew, teach it. To just hold it in her mind was to look on a handful of diamonds in the dark. Out in the sun is where they would sparkle and flash.

Western thinking might ask if such information was worth the death of so many, but Varouna knew that the deaths had nothing to do with it. The knowledge had been passed on. What came with it was what came with it. No value could be put on either because both were beyond measure.

The horror, the flies, the stench, the screams, the prayers, the death, all of it, was ephemeral. The great wheel was turning, here and now. One had only to look to see it, and to know that humanity, should it survive this, was moving into another time, as a body might become smoke, as a baby might be born.

And so she sat in the window, drawing in as much fresh air as would come her way, ignoring the charnel house stench, drinking boiled water, figuring on ways to regain her strength and survive. And when she had time, she glanced down at the fax that had come from Paris, that had arrived during the last time that there was electricity and the telephones were still working, when she'd still been lost in a fever and insensible.

Sorry to inform you, it said in French, *but your brother died quite suddenly of the virus. We tried to save him, but the drugs the doctors have been using to combat the fever either had no effect or were given too late. He passed on 3:34 A.M., Tuesday. Because of the pervasiveness of this pandemic, the government is now requiring that all bodies be cremated, no exceptions. We will keep the ashes and send them to you when possible, or you can come for them yourself. Our most sincere condolences.*

And so the wheel turned.

Chapter 8

September

ON THE TELEVISION, A FOUNDRY BILLOWED SMOKE charred black, the wind pushing it up into a polluted sky. In the foreground, leaves changing over from living summer green to early autumn gold fluttered and held.

Valerie stared at the leaves, feeling her hands turn and flutter with their movements, absorbing the sunlight.

"Worldwide, foundries and factories like this one have been made into crematoriums—" said the newscaster, a mocha-skinned teenager who'd been a cameraman not a week ago.

"The smell is terrible. And the sky is a constant shade of dirty brown. Bodies are brought here, sometimes by the truck-load. And the one thing everyone wonders is, how many more have to die before this nightmare finally comes to an end?"

And then he coughed.

Valerie smiled. So. He would learn. He would know.

She changed the channel, came upon a repeat of old news from June. Images of nurses, each standing beside a trash barrel brimming with small vials and boxes of disposable hypodermics, giving shots to the public. The National Guard, faces covered by sleek fiber-optic gas masks, stood by their side, keeping the peace.

Views of impossibly long lines of Americans, sweating in the hot, summer sunlight, waiting for those precious shots.

"The lines reach upwards of five miles in some places," the voice of the female newscaster, "people hoping for drugs stockpiled by the CDC to counter an influenza epidemic." An overhead view of women with children, teenagers, the aged in walkers and wheelchairs, winding down streets, through neighborhoods, past stoops and porches and storefronts. On and on and on. Several were bundled up, coughing. "But there are fears that there will not be enough to go around. And doctors want to remind people that, so far, these drugs have only succeeded in alleviating the symptoms, not stopping the virus.

"Your best chance," the newscaster continued, as the image changed to that of hands reaching, thousands of wide open palms and straining fingers, groping for nasal sprays, "is to make use of microbe-destroying emulsions or the new artificial antibodies being given out free at local pharmacies." Another shot of trucks emptying out piles of inhalers into crowds who crushed forward to snatch up handfuls.

"Temporary," Valerie judged softly, and changed the channel. "One unprotected breath is all it takes."

"Val?"

She glanced up, annoyed. Judas was setting out her breakfast on the night table. His curling, molasses brown hair, which she'd seen him trying to cut with a pair of scissors and a mirror, was falling into his eyes. Skin shaded gold, like a brown pear, hazel eyes flecked with winter gray. Not at all like Warren's more dramatic coloring, his sunny hair and summer green gaze.

There was feel to the color green, deep in the skin, to all colors. A feel to the shadings and spottings, to ridges of a darker hue, to the way colors overlapped, one into another from head to tail. Complex poems could be written on the skin in this way, flashed in one second and seen by a thousand dark eyes. And then responded to with a variety of rainbows.

Hard to be back in unresponsive, dull-colored human flesh, hard not to see colors as ideas and thoughts.

How very much she and Warren could have said to one another with chromatics.

"Valerie!"

She jerked, Jude's angry face nose to nose with hers. He had her by the shoulders and she felt he would have shaken her if he could. *"See me!"* he hissed in her face. *"For God's sake!"*

"It's too cold," she said, glancing away from him, and switched the channel. It didn't do any good. She either hit snow, blackness, or news. That's all that was ever on.

"I'll turn down the air-conditioning," Judas snarled, and headed out.

Valerie shrugged. Warren had installed generators so that they'd have climate control year round, even in a blackout. At this time of year, when the brick of the buildings absorbed and radiated the late-summer heat, the interior of the penthouse automatically maintained a cool 72 degrees Fahrenheit.

But Valerie knew she would feel cold even if she were to walk out into the sweltering heat. She'd grown used to having a skin that kept out the atmosphere, a skin layered like apple peels, Granny Smith green and shiny Rome red and pale yellow delicious. And there were silvery leaves that reached out and gathered in more light and heat than a human could bear, converting all into movement and nourishment.

As if reading her mind, Judas came back with a plate of sliced apples sprinkled with brown sugar. There were even raisins on top. She caught him looking at her, waiting, perhaps hoping she'd ask him where he got the apples. She knew she should care; difficult to get fresh fruit or vegetables since the Pandemic hit critical mass in July. Few farmers had been well enough to harvest their crops, even with the help of modern machinery, and few truckers had been well enough to transport the produce even if it had been harvested. Daily announcements on the television begged those who could pilot a plane or drive a truck to help the government transport food and goods to devastated cities. And volunteers were wanted to work on the farms.

On the other hand, most New Yorkers had already left the city for the summer when the wave of sickness broke. This had eased the run on grocery stores, the hoarding, theft, and mass exoduses tangling up the highways.

Those still alive and well in Manhattan were finding new ways to subsist. A spate of small vegetable gardens dotted Central Park and made for potted greenery on terraces and fire escapes. Boats of amateur fishermen with rods in hand went out daily to toss their hooks into the Hudson, and, of course, there were rumors of pets being eaten, rats and even roaches. On every ledge there was a cage to trap pigeons.

But finding fresh fruit . . .

"Apple farmers," Judas said, clearly tired of waiting for her to ask. "They were passing out bagfuls from the back of a truck in Times Square. Please, eat, Val."

What he really meant was that he wanted her to enjoy it. She didn't know if that were possible; she could feel the gills opening, the fine dust that passed through and stuck and was absorbed; this had flavor. Her tongue did not, no more than it seemed to have words.

She could still feel Jude's disappointment, however. Sensations to the skin might be different, taste and sight altered, but love and tenderness were still there; if anything, they were more intense than ever.

She sighed and rested back, one hand on her swollen belly. Going on six months. The pregnancy was the strangest feeling of all; inside her was one kicking stranger instead of a parcel of eggs to be expelled into the claws of a waiting male and set under his leaves to hatch.

The baby, swimming and somersaulting within, kept her bedridden. That was strange too, to be so weighed down. As soon as her fever had broken, Jude had called obsessively, all over the world—or as much of it as still had working phone service—in search of a doctor. He'd found one in College Station, Texas, and convinced the man that the baby was still alive and in the womb. The doctor, a young OB-GYN, had coughed throughout the entire conference call.

"You're still likely to miscarry," he'd warned Valerie, *Cough! Cough! Cough!* "Don't leave your bed except to go to the bathroom!" *Cough!*

And Valerie, still fragile from three weeks of illness, had said to Judas, "Why would I ever want to leave my bed?"

She changed the channel.

"We know that it goes through the nasal passages right into the brain, while simultaneously breeding in the lungs." CNN had interviews running continuously, most of them three months old. The one on now was an early interview with Dr. Fortier, the same Paris doctor they had flown across the ocean to see. The same one who had failed to save Warren.

"It vanishes from the lungs at about the same time that the effects on the brain become serious enough to notice." The doctor, a ginger-haired, bearded fellow with large teeth, spoke English carefully. "By then it's too late. We think that it is similar to . . . what is the American term?" He glanced back at some unseen assistant, then smiled a little furtively. "Yes. Chicken pox. Very contagious. Very hard, I am sorry to say, to treat or cure."

And then the doctor coughed.

Valerie smiled and changed the channel.

"Bad buildings"—old footage of a newsman pointing to a particularly ugly New York tenement—"are those with out-dated and very poor air circulation. Someone coughs and the virus is spread through the vents and infects the whole building. The Pandemic has made these death traps."

"Do you need anything else? Anything at all?" Judas was hovering again, hands shoved in his pockets with an attitude between need and dread. She was beginning to hate him. Which was unfair. Jude was wearing himself to the bone caring for her. Every day he went out into a city still sweating under an Indian summer and risked his life and sanity to find food and treasures for her.

She should be here for him; it wasn't like she had anyone else. Her father had not survived the illness, nor her mother or brother, or any of her in-laws. She was glad, in a way, that Warren was gone; he'd been painfully close to his family and their deaths would have destroyed him.

Jude, mercifully, hadn't had to go through any of that. His mother had died some years back in a traffic accident, along with his sister; his father had been lost, not long after, of a heart attack.

All he had to worry about was tending to her, poor, orphaned Jude. But she just couldn't put down the roots for him, not now. Perhaps never again.

For Warren, she thought, she could have done it; she could have come back to Earth for him. To hear his optimistic laughter, his energetic voice. She would have come back so that they could get hot dogs with relish, or so that he could buy her a rose, or so that she might fetch him a fresh cup of coffee as they sat together in the breakfast nook, planning his next big move into politics.

But Warren was gone, and so there was no reason to stay on Earth.

"You know, Val," Jude said at last, and that's when she heard him cough, loudly, dryly, "you're not the only one who *fucking misses people!*"

He coughed again, and this time she saw him. Really saw him.

Oh, God.

There was a terrible expression on his face, fear and loss and despair. His thoughts were there, clear as clear. And then he ran out of the bedroom, nearly slamming the door behind him.

"If it arrives slowly, you're probably in luck." Another doctor, this one a coughing Asian woman with a Japanese dialect. "If it comes on fast, right from cough to fever, that's bad. But if this leads to a lingering headache then flu symptoms before the fever, the prognosis is good."

How long had Judas had the cough? She was ashamed to say she hadn't noticed. It lasted on average two to three weeks.

She would have to nurse him, no question. Even if she lost the baby doing it. She caught sight of the apples and thought of how thin and tired Jude was, how badly nourished and stressed he must be.

No doubt the fool was thinking of giving all the apples to her. Damn him!

Surely. Surely he had the strength to survive! If she could only convince him that it was nothing to fear . . . but it was difficult to explain the experience to those who hadn't traveled through that dark tunnel and been lit by a different sun.

She picked up an apple slice and nibbled on it. There was no taste, but that didn't matter. She had to be ready, had to be well and strong, for Jude.

Because he had to survive this. She stroked her swollen stomach. It was more important than he could possibly know, or she, without colors, could possibly say.

She ate her apple and changed the channel.

Chapter 9

October

THREE OF THE TORI ROTATED CLEARLY INTO VIEW. The asteriated silver and frost pattern of the enormous nesting rings recalled the art deco cornice work of the Chrysler Building.

Clockwork halos silhouetted against a river of stars.

At the center, equally distant from the edges of the inner ring, hung a solid sphere of matter like a pendulum waiting to swing; infinitely dense, sometimes insubstantial, it was the heart of these great machines.

They were so large that they created enormous black shadows, making for times of artificial hibernation for those of his race, phototropic by nature, who wandered too close.

Large as the Empire State Building.

"Nearly four hundred and seventeen meters tall; and they constructed that monster in a record time of fifteen months!" he had once informed Warren, proud and wondering, as if the success of those historical workers were his own.

Who was Warren? What history? Confusion took him. Where was he? Who was he? He felt as if his mind were in a revolving door, outside in Manhattan one second, inside in . . .

He rotated his dorsal trefoils, as a river of coppery dust, trailing past slow and steady as the electric signs that wrapped around Times Tower, cut off his view of the tori. Dipping down, he skimmed over the telescope farm he and his shoal tended. The optics, dark, inky lenses, clung to the irregular surfaces of the asteroids where they were grown. They were turning now, and colors forked across them, violet and jade, indicating their new direction. From the sides of the asteroids the delicate optic roots, pale lemon and mauve, reached out for astronomers to use.

As one of those astronomers, he had frequently brushed his side eyes by the stiff roots to view the misty nebulae and distant star systems of the universe. And like all his race, had lost his heart to the sight.

He wanted to fall into those nebulae, right through the tori into the universe beyond. But to venture through, to try to reach those faraway suns, was to shut down, to drift in hibernation mode till the body exhausted all reserves of solar energy.

A craft filled with artificial light could be created. Replenishable food could be taken along. New generations could be brought forth to continue when older ones died.

But that was a poor way of finding sentience in the vastness of the universe.

He craned back his long neck to take in the rest of his shoal. Large and long as subway trains, with flower petal skin stretched over their sinuous skeletons, they twisted their silvery leaves to capture light and heat. Ridges banded them up from the whipcord tails to the spindly claws and equine heads.

The fore-eyes were as liquidly dark as the optics they grew, but intelligent. Pure, brilliant thought.

The minds behind those eyes . . .

Jokes and games were evident in the color patterns, which matched and altered, rippling out through the shoal like sound waves, a continuous murmur, an ever-ongoing conversation.

Yet it was deathly quiet, so profoundly quiet that his heartbeat was all that reverberated in his ears.

"Judas. Judas! Here!"

Leaning over the side of something, almost falling. Vomiting and vomiting into a china bowl with flowers around the rim. Looked too pretty for vomit. Sour taste, rank smell. GOD! He felt so heavy, like he was stuck to the earth or trying to keep his head above the water. Easier to sink, to float, to reach forth leaves for light from the sun, for heat from the planet. Easier to go back in through the revolving door to—

A second shoal passing by. They looked, he thought for a wondering moment, like strands of holiday lights, deep emerald, for this moment, along their length, their leaves glowing. They all moved as one, like pedestrians crossing a busy street. This flock cultivated and refined the minerals that had built the tori.

Asteroids, with crags sharp and tall as cathedral spires or pits wide and deep as tunnels, veered around them. Some shimmered white with sheet lichen or swayed with electric blue fronds, or dripped off a slow, viscous liquid like the corn syrup his mother used to put into her pecan pies. A yellow taxi flutter of solar moths held to one, a forest of tarnished copper leaves with rusty red blossoms clustered around another. Life crawled over the leaves and in and out of the blossoms, butterscotch shooters tossing out silken webs to gather up mineral powder and lemon-drop skuttlebugs to refine copper sulfate.

"How the fuck," he heard his own voice whisper *hoarsely, wonderingly, "did they bioengineer an entire nanotechnological ecosystem?"*

"Hush, hush, don't try to work it out. Just let it come; you'll get through it."

"Might die," he observed objectively.

"No! No, Jude! You can't die! Think of the baby. The baby is going to need you!"

But what about you? he wondered, *even though he didn't know who she was or why she might need him.*

"Can you skate backwards?" he heard himself say.

What the fuck did that mean?

Hockey players shooting across the slick, black darkness of hibernation, that's what it meant. Hibernation was when the shoal's orbit took them away from the sun, to the far side of the gas giant they perpetually circled.

It was a short time, twelve to fifteen hours at most. But when that total darkness hit and the temperature fell hundreds of degrees, the bodies shut down utterly. The leaves curled in, hoarding all the heat and light soaked up on the other side, and the minds went to sleep, all save the one (not the brain in tail or head, the central one), which worked like a hockey game, sending ideas shooting across the dark. Working out DNA as if it were a chess game, formulating ways to seed nearby moons, create life, materials, biological nanotecs which would build organic radio telescopes.

His race, he realized, saw nothing as beyond them, and they dreamt dreams on only the largest scale. All and every one of them, reaching for the infinite.

When members of the race came back around into the light, and awakened together, as shoals did, they had the answers. This was how the great scientists had long ago worked out that the seemingly endless seas of dust and stone formed one great circle about a gas giant.

Frozen and then torn apart by some massive force, the icy, ecologically rich surface of what had once been a planet in this very system, perhaps several planets, had been captured and added to the ring. And between the light of the sun and the heat of the planet, life had, incredibly, been given a second chance to evolve.

Or so they theorized.

And if this was true, then there certainly could be life on other planets. Easier, in fact, for life to evolve on a planet, some said. And if such life could evolve . . . surely, they all agreed, *surely* some of it *must* be sentient.

Did such life change colors and flash silver trefoils to communicate? Did they dream nonlinear answers to problems while hibernating? Did they give the best of their desires and traits and memories to their young? Did they stare out at the stars and wonder what might be living around those distant suns?

He had in his mind every picture of these creatures ever imagined by his kind. Sometimes, he could almost feel the touch on his tail of the planet dwellers.

I will find you, he would promise then, with a wash of hot colors down his length. *I will!*

"I will," Judas said to the white face above him, *a face so strange-looking, so round and soft, not ridged with the sharp, beautiful bones of his kind. There was a wispy titian netting about it, pretty, but nothing like true foliage. He tried to read the color, but it made no sense to him. Maybe the white of the face.*

A wet cloth on his forehead, dripping down the sides of his neck. Tickled.

"God. You're burning up!"

Was it the wet cloth? Or tears?

"Always comes back to Newtonian physics," he muttered. "Particle physics, evolution, basic science, if it works it works."

"Hush, hush."

He wasn't moving. That was bad. To be still was to be dead. But the white-faced creature above him smiled very sadly, very painfully, and said, "It will be over soon, I promise."

"No," he croaked, "No, not yet. I haven't gotten to the answer, what they did, why they did it—"

Why?

The first had been soaring between his mates at the time, his female drifting to one side, his co-mate to the other. They had been foraging at the very edge of the rings, where the nourishing copper dust was abundant. It was his turn to carry the family's eggs, and so the other two guarded and protected him. He and his co-mate had already fertilized those eggs, altering the color of the tiny ova from dull gray to ruby red. And then the three of them had set the eggs beneath his foliage, so that they hung like ornaments from a Christmas tree.

He had been thinking of how the hatchlings would sparkle like amethysts when they arrived, and unfurl tiny tendrils to gather light and heat for the first time. How their secondary eyes would glow along their sides, and they would drift and bump, and change their colors with erratic laughter.

He and his mates would corral the infants within the triangle of their combined foliage and they would teach them how to change direction and flow with the inner rivers. They would show them how to help each other by picking out stones from along their length.

The poetry of his thoughts came out in a variety of hues, his mates matching and contrasting to form a visual song.

Driving across country with Val and Warren in an old gold Cadillac so large they were all able to fit in the front seat. Crossing the desert at night. Warren had never done such a thing, spoiled rich boy that he was. He laughed and leaned against the dashboard, excited as a little kid. And Val cranked open the window to the warm night air, which stroked and fluttered her soft red hair. And as the radio played "Let It Be Me," they drove, over a horizon of sand, the stars so bright and close they seemed within reach.

Together, they dreamed of the future, hardly noticing that they had left the dust rivers behind, and up ahead, lightning flashed, leaping between asteroids with a brilliance that blinded. Past the lightning was darkness, the very edge of their home, the eternal hibernation of space . . . and the stars.

The first dreamer saw how very sharp the stars could look, like ice crystals. He found them arresting. Fascinating.

And then, just as he was about to turn away, one of the stars flared bright and strong.

He hardly knew he had left his mates until he found himself soaring toward that brilliant glow in the dark beyond.

Bolts of lightning arched overhead, tossing shadows across spheres of layered stone and ice.

With his tail-eyes he caught sight of the flowing chromatics of dismay from his mate and co-mate. who were growing small and distant. But he had to see. He went as close as he could to the edge, where the spaces between were large, where there was little dust and less ice. And then he telescoped his predatory forward eyes on that single, brilliant star. It looked . . .

It looked . . .

It looked like the sun!

Was it a sun?

The others were coming after him, fearful. And for a moment, he felt trapped.

Was it a sun?

And if it was . . . did it shine on others like him?

Amazing thought, that.

What might they be like, those others? What might they say to him, or he to them?

There was, he realized, with an agonizing ache, no way for him to learn the truth. He couldn't leave, his foliage would shrivel, the eggs would die and then so would he.

And that meant that he would never know. And that was suddenly terrible, unendurable.

Was it a sun? Were there other suns?

How could he find out?

He couldn't.

But perhaps, he thought, grabbing at the hope, perhaps, . . . just perhaps, his descendents could!

Focusing on the sunlike star, he spread his desire, his intense need to know, to the gleaming garnet eggs clustered on the underside of his leaves.

"Go," he told them, "find a way to soar to that other sun and meet those who absorb its light!"

"I will," Jude whispered. Were those tears running down his face? "Already said it . . . I will, I will . . ."

"It's all right, Jude. Fever's broken. You're going to make it. Here, try to drink something," Valerie's voice urged him.

Liquid down the throat. Odd sensation after the copper dust, which was really a mixture of copper-sulfate and seeds fine and tiny as those found in a vanilla bean; the dust had a creamy texture like ice cream or rice pudding. And he wanted, wanted badly, to feel it flowing through his gills.

But he wasn't . . . one of them. He wasn't a thing that swam in a living ring. He owned no leaves, no gills, no line of eyes. And his designer's mind could barely conceive, let alone understand, how to grow and create a stargate. . . .

The vast ice and silver tori hung like moons in the sky. He knew what they were now: *bridges*, or rather, half bridges.

They had harnessed the powerful electromagnetic charges of their system to power the tori, to leach from the center of those rings even the smallest particle-field interactions, thus creating a tremendous quantum vacuum. In the midst of this absence, there appeared a tunnel of gray space that could take a traveler from the ring and deposit him several light-years away.

The aliens had wanted to go through, but it was only half a bridge. It would only leave them in the ocean, not on some distant shore.

So what had they done?

A billion lifeless craft, iridescent, netted and shifting and curved like sails, passed by him. They were heading into the huge tori, so tiny by comparison that they might have been a puff of pollen or bit of spray off the sea.

These, Jude suddenly realized, could search, for as long and as far as it took, for another sun, another species. But there was more. As he watched the craft float toward the inner circle, he understood, as one of the builders might, that each was a biofactory able to produce special infections.

That, after all, was how the aliens passed on information, to their offspring and to each other. Through viruses.

By way of Pandemics.

Oh God. My God, he thought. *They killed us!*

And then he was traveling with the craft, falling into the gate, looking back, recording onto the viruses an image of fantastic creatures as large and long as supertrains. Creatures with spines like stones poking out from a brook, colorful skin thin as flower petals, and foliage that drifted out from their sinuous forms like silver pennants in the wind. Here and there along the lacy length of those creatures jeweled eyes glowed bright with hope and passion.

They didn't want to hurt anyone, they just wanted to make contact. Just make contact.

The creatures altered color, their thin, tough hides shading from topaz to pink sapphire to ruby and finally deepening into garnet. The leaves moved and shifted, steel and chrome, waving and flagging.

And Judas read that message, he read it clear and clean as if the words had been sung to him.

Here's where our half of the bridge is, they said. And here is how we built it. Will you meet us? To know ourselves, we would know you, Planetdweller.

Will you?

The glowing tori took on the shape of the Brooklyn Bridge as Jude went through, curved round, spires inward, cables like drapery about the edges. And so he seemed to cross the universe, back to his human side.

He opened his eyes, home again. For the first time, fully awake and aware. It was dark, but he could make out Valerie on the bed beside him.

In bed with Valerie? In *Warren's* bed? He felt a second of alarm, and then he focused on her, on the stringy, titian hair, on the figure which, thanks to seven months of pregnancy, was no longer lithe or androgynous. She was decidedly feminine, for all that he'd had to urge her to eat and keep up her weight. She was dressed in one of Warren's oversized T-shirts and a pair of sweat pants stretched taunt over her heavy belly. She smelled of sweat and old clothing.

He remembered her illness, his almost hysterical relief when she survived. Her strange distance over the past months. Now, at last, he understood it.

For a moment, he just looked at her; then he touched her belly and felt the child tumble beneath the taunt, warm skin. *Floating,* he thought. *Floating and drifting.*

He felt guilty that he wasn't carrying the fetus, that he wasn't doing that job.

Complete disorientation.

Not his offspring, he remembered. And, *I've been sick. Val must have exhausted herself taking care of me. Stupid! She could have lost the baby!*

He pushed out of the bed, his feet wobbly beneath him. Hard having weight, even though he knew he was lighter than he had been. He must have dropped ten pounds; there was a weak, bony-ness to his naked body, a feeling like he'd been starved. He wanted food but didn't know how he was going to eat it. Suck it in like rice pudding perhaps?

Forward; feeling the carpet beneath his feet, such an odd sensation. The sound of his footsteps, the ugly smells of the apartment, rotting food and unwashed toilets, all so very strange.

Stumbling, he made it out into the living room and headed for the terrace. When he pushed open the door an evening wind hit him, icy on his bare skin. He smelled autumn on it, October. He could almost feel the golden hues of the leaves.

And that's when he came back to Earth, back into his planet dweller body that understood seasons, that lived with an atmosphere, with gravity, with weather cold enough to make his teeth chatter.

He went forward, the balcony icy beneath his feet, the phantoms of Warren's last party surrounding him. He could almost see the fluttering tablecloths, the dancers that spun out and were pulled back in again. Overhead, the stars shone bright and sharp. Warren had bought a penthouse because he loved to look out at the city, but the lights of New York had been lost to power failures, and so the city was almost invisible, and the stars closer than ever.

He knew exactly how to get to those stars, he realized suddenly and completely. Goddamn it! He could take the human race farther than they'd ever been before.

Jude lifted his arms to those stars, holding forth the white of his palms like leaves flashing silver.

"I will!" he promised, feeling the hope, the passion, and his voice rang out over the city and into the sky.

"I Will!"

Chapter 10

December

THERE HAD BEEN NO COLUMBUS DAY CELEBRATIONS, no Halloween candy to hand out, no Thanksgiving Day parade. And there would be no Christmas. On the shortest day of the year, there were no skaters at the ice rink at Rockefeller Center. No great tree towered over the lower plaza, aglow with Christmas magic, sending its light across the city.

There was a wreath, a large one. A circle of black twigs with a wide black bow.

Judas, making his way south to Central Park, took a long, parting look at the wreath. Someone had placed it on a stand of chicken wire right behind and above the golden statue of Prometheus, a kind of critique on the gift that had been given to humankind this year. It was chillingly apt. The city was in mourning, not just for the dead, but for the death of all the joy it ought to have, the busy, bustling spirit that New York usually had at this time of year.

Gone with the people. There was snow—in fact they'd had one of the harshest winters in five years—and there was a mist that hung over that snow. But there were no people. No bundled shoppers racing in and out of the stores, no Santas ringing bells on street corners, no children in colorful scarves and caps pressing mittened hands to the frosted windows of FAO Schwarz department store.

Also no crime, for a wonder. Because the criminals had all died, or because there was no point to it? Whatever a criminal wanted a criminal could take. But then most of the human population, what was left of it, now held in their minds alien ideas that made greed and selfishness petty even to those who admired such foibles.

But Jude had another reason for his interest in the wreath. Its shape, a circle with a thorny circumference . . . *That was close,* he thought, and brought out his book and pen to add a few more notes to the sketch he'd been working on all morning. Dozens of diagrams already lined the living room walls, and he'd filled four books with meticulous drawings. But this was the first time he felt his efforts coming together. *He could make this work.*

He *would* make it work.

The problem, he thought, walking slowly down Fifth Avenue, was that the aliens had created their huge tori specifically to harness power from the electrostatic bursts created by the highly conductive metallic hydrogen so plentiful in their gas giant. But humanity didn't have the capability or resources to build a gateway near Jupiter or Saturn. They would have to find a different way of manufacturing that kind of energy.

Judas shut the book and slipped it back in the deep pocket of his overcoat. He was determined to be the first to find the right answer, whatever that might be.

He checked his watch. Almost noon. He'd better get back.

"Here we come a-wassailing," he sung to himself, crossing the snow-covered pavement of Central Park South. "Among the leaves so green—"

The park on the other side was a wonder to behold, Manhattan's backyard completely empty, its bridges and sculptures coated in ice so that they glistened and sparkled. And it was quiet, so eerily quiet. No cars rushing or honking in the background, none of the distant sounds of construction, no children screaming, no people trampling down the pristine snow into muddy slush.

It was unnerving.

"Here we come a-wassailing, so fair to be seen." He watched the words float out as smoke upon the air as he traveled the path pass Wollman Rink. Not a single skater made patterns upon the ice, which was, in any case, mostly covered with snow.

The Pandemic was, according to what few news reports still appeared on the television, tapering off, and with food and volunteers reappearing, emergency measures were finally being put in place. Sidewalk markets and hospitals were reopening. But it hardly mattered. The aftermath was just beginning.

Judas crossed through the park, his booted feet sinking down to make a troughlike trail behind him. The trees were crowned with fans of bare branches. And in that dead stillness, as in a winter cemetery, Judas's inner eye imposed over the park images of it at the height of spring. He saw a rain of fluttering pastel petals and the bright green of new leaves on the branches, saw riders on the bridle paths neatly dressed in jodhpurs and jackets, dappled horses cantering beneath them. He saw a rich cross section of people in bright polo shirts and shorts traveling up and down the pathways on bikes and skates—and he flowed with them, watching the wheels spin.

He felt the people, felt the world, felt it living again.

And then he came back. He always came back, to a world still and frosted.

"Love and joy come to you." He tried to break through that quiet. "And to you your wassail too . . ."

Electricity was back and the street lamps stayed on almost all the time during these short, dim days; they floated in the misty air, hazy circles of light through the fog. He followed them back into the trees, to a snow sculpture he'd been working on near Tavern on the Green. A raised circle. Originally, it had been the familiar double rings of the aliens. But he'd gotten rid of the center ring almost immediately. Recently, he'd added rays around the outside, making the single ring look like the crown on the Statue of Liberty. That was close, but not quite there.

He knelt and set to work scooping snow, packing it. The air was frosty, and he could feel the damp chill working its way through the plastic ski pants he wore. He ignored it all, concentrating on lengthening the points around the edges, shaping the frost until the snow ring began to look like twigs.

In their college days, he, Warren, and Val had routinely headed upstate to play in the snow. They had created a lot of sculptures in their time; Jude remembered one in particular that Valerie had done of a youth bending over a girl lithe as a ballerina. The pose had had the lovers about to kiss, arms around each other, seeming to draw love from that circular connection.

That sculpture had given him one of his few insights into Valerie's mind; in it he saw her need to dance with another, to form a bond where feelings were exchanged with a kiss.

Once, only, she'd allowed him to connect with her in that way, linking with him so powerfully that he'd felt the tie for years.

The Pandemic had come close to severing it.

Getting ill himself, finally learning what Valerie had experienced, should have made things easier between them, should have created a new connection.

But Valerie had become more distant than ever of late. She'd gone back to her room, and they hadn't shared a bed since. Sometimes, she would sit for long hours in the breakfast nook wrapped in blankets, flipping through a photo album of her wedding and honeymoon or just staring out at the snow-frosted city. Other times she hid away in her bedroom, for days on end. She ate more, looked healthier, but she wasn't there, on Earth with him.

He hadn't, in fact, seen her since yesterday afternoon when he'd left her lunch by the bedroom door. The tray of dry crackers and jam had still been outside the door this morning, untouched.

Any day now she could go into labor, and Judas knew he ought to be there with her. But he could hardly bear to stay in the penthouse. Whenever he saw Valerie he was reminded of the Pied Piper story, the part where a lame child tries to follow the piper and his friends into a beautiful land. In the end, unable to keep up, the crippled child is forced to watch as rocks close off heaven, leaving him forever on the other side.

Valerie was like that; in her mind, Warren had traveled to Nirvana, leaving her behind, crippled and lame. Jude understood; when he looked at her, into her eyes, he felt he'd lost paradise as well. Not the paradise of the aliens' ring system, but his own, the one he hardly recognized he had had, here on Earth.

His snow sculpture now had faint branches radiating outward. Snow and ice and freezing temperatures, he mused, *that* was the answer! Judas was an armchair physicist at best, but he knew all about Bose Condensate. Microscopic atoms rendered visible, like water vapor turned to snowflakes, via the application of tremendous cold. Temperature controls and lasers set in the branches of this wreath could chill space down just below -459 degrees Farenheit, causing clouds of atoms to achieve the same quantum state. These superatoms would maintain their essential behavior. Several clouds of varying charges could be set within the ring and made to chase one other about like dogs on a track, producing a tremendous amount of free electricity, enough to begin the process—to create a quantum vacuum.

He rounded out a snowball and set it in the center of his masterpiece. Couldn't forget that, he thought. Like the alien bridge they needed that pearl in the center to keep the tunnel open and stable. He wished he had some idea of how he was going to make that part work.

Rising, he stepped back to admire his work. If he was allowed to make it, he decided then, with black humor, he would plate it in gold and hang it in orbit like a welcoming wreath on a door. Maybe he should etch an inscription on the inside? "Give me your tired, your poor . . ."?

Or should it be: "Come, grow old along with me"?

With an exchange of rings, he thought then, came an exchange of vows. Vows that were sometimes difficult to keep: in sickness and in health, for better or for worse . . .

It was getting dark. He checked his watch and was stunned to find that it was nearly five o'clock.

"And God bless you and send you a Happy New Year," he whispered to himself, gathering up his courage and trudging back toward the penthouse. "God bless you and send you a Happier New Year."

Scotty, dusty brown hair and almond eyed, made loud laughing sounds from his high chair and waved a plastic spoon. He was zipped up in a toddler's flannel sleeper which was far too big for him; Scotty was tiny for his age.

"Doing all right, son?" Gordon lifted his boy into his arms and took them both to gaze out the farmhouse window. Snow was swirling down outside, covering the fallow fields and creating ice patterns on the windowpanes. Icicles hung from the eaves over the generous, Victorian verandah.

Like bars, Gordon thought, feeling desolate and alone.

After being on the move for nearly two months, Gordon had found a refuge for Scotty and himself in upstate New York. He had taken charge of a troop that guarded a small farming community and their harvest through the end of summer and fall, loading up the trucks, helping to organize workers. The total population in both North and South America was being estimated at something like two hundred and fifty million. Which meant that work, once again, was a very valuable commodity.

But there still wasn't much farming to be done in the winter. And so Gordon spent his time staring out at the snow and listening to the fire spit and crackle in the stone hearth.

The Pandemic, everyone was saying, was over, at least in North America. That, Gordon knew, was a lie. It would never be over, not if what the survivors said was true: that the virus had been otherworldly. That it was a message that stained the brain like indelible ink with alien knowledge and memories and images.

There were all sorts of Web sites popping up on the resurrected Internet, all sorts of stuff on the news. He'd seen drawing after computer-simulated drawing of the ring creatures, ridged along their sinuous length like seahorses and sprouting tendrils of leaves like grotesque rose stems. They changed color and moved the leaves to communicate, or so said those who had survived the Pandemic.

Gordon didn't know what to believe. Hard to dismiss it all as mass hypnosis or hysteria, especially with some people saying they had technical knowledge in their heads that was light-years ahead of what humanity was working on now.

Didn't matter. Scotty, going on seven months, and Gordon, himself, had never fallen ill; that's what mattered.

It was still strange, though, to walk out the door to snow covered farmland instead of pavement and traffic. Gordon had always thought that he'd live out his life in Toronto, practically because that was where he'd been born and raised, more importantly because Mae loved it. But then, he had never anticipated anything like the Pandemic, which had made all cities dangerous places to be . . . and he had never anticipated Mae dying.

She'd been in his dreams over the last seven months. He'd feel her beside him in bed, hear her say, "My turn," when Scotty cried in the early hours and imagined that she was getting up. Even after he left Toronto, he was sure he saw her, there in the dark of motel rooms and strange, abandoned houses, slipping the cream satin robe he'd given her over her smooth tawny skin.

He'd even smelled her perfume.

Then, of course, Scotty's cries would get more desperate, and Gordon would muzzily come out of sleep to realize, with a painful shock, that Mae was gone, and he would hurt all over again. He'd bundle Scotty up then, and slip them back in the car, hoping to outrun the hurt.

There'd been kindnesses along the way: a man at a filling station who'd given them his last can of gas, a worn, middle-aged woman on a farm who'd supplied him with several jars of babyfood.

"They were for my granddaughter," she'd said on handing them over, and looked away, eyes glimmering. "I had such plans. . . ."

God, thought Gordon, *didn't we all.*

And then there were the close calls, like the coughing lunatic who'd come after them with a bat.

"Get out!" he'd screamed, "You don't be bringing your plague here, *you Godless fuckers!*"

But for now they were settled, safe in a cozy, old fashioned farmhouse.

At least, Gordon thought, shifting Scotty restlessly in his arms, till spring.

Judas, stomping snow from his boots, heard the baby crying as soon as he exited the elevator.

Valerie!

He panicked and ran to the bedroom. *God, God!* She hadn't said anything about being in labor! He would have never left . . .

The bedroom door was open, the still untouched lunch tray carefully set to the side. Skidding to a halt in the doorway he saw her. There were a dozen pillar candles burning on the dresser; they gave the room a soft glow and matched patterns with the snow that had started falling on the other side of the windows. She must have had them hidden away somewhere because Judas had long since used up all the candles he remembered finding in closets and drawers. The room was not quite cold, but it felt as stark and terrible as a morgue.

She'd taken down the hanging lamp above the bed and

knotted one of Warren's belts to the hook in the ceiling. He had a horrible suspicion that she might have prepared all this days ago. He hadn't visited her room in over a week and wouldn't have known.

A tumbled stack of books on the bed showed how she'd reached the noose and dropped herself down.

She was dangling there wearing Warren's old college jacket, the monogrammed one he'd worn that infamous day Jude had first met him. Her body was limp and breathless, blood from the birth drying on her bare legs, staining the whole of the bed, which had been stripped down to the sheets.

His knees hit the carpet and he stared up at her as he might a goddess who'd turned her face from him. Her face was, in fact, turned away. He had no desire to see it. He just looked at her silky red hair, haloed gold in the candlelight, and found himself wishing, expecting, that she would turn around and say it was all a joke.

He couldn't, afterward, say how long he stared at the body. Finally, the screaming cut through to him. Its pitch changed from begging to demanding, a shriek that insisted he take notice.

The baby was on the floor by the bed: naked, white, stained with a bit of red, shaking in the cold room. The cord had been tied off with shoestring.

Judas wasn't able to stand. Trembling, he crawled over to the infant. It was a she, and she had a beautiful down of red hair covering the back of her head. She was screaming at the top of her lungs, absolutely alive and healthy, resting on a wool blanket with two bottles of breast milk next to her. Last week, after searching through half a dozen deserted stores, he'd finally found the bottles and pump for Valerie. He'd been proud of that discovery. Now it sickened him.

There was a handwritten letter folded between the bottles. But he wasn't looking at them or the note; he was looking at the squalling newborn.

My God.

At last, he wrapped the blanket around the baby and picked up one of the bottles. It was still warm, which stabbed him right to the heart. Had he only gotten there seconds earlier . . .

He should have never taken that long, lonely walk! What had he been thinking?

The nipple touched the infant's lips and she latched onto it. She began to suck greedily.

"Poor little girl," Judas whispered, though he knew the words were for Valerie, or maybe for himself. "Poor little girl," he said, and began to cry. He felt the tears falling, the pain rising up his back and into his throat. "You didn't have to go! I would have taken care of you, you stupid bitch! Oh, God, Warren, I'm sorry!"

He could barely hold the bottle as he sobbed; the shadow of Valerie's body fell against the wall, across them, and he could almost feel her heat and soul leaving her. That made him cry all the harder.

The baby, quiet now, looked up at him with surprisingly alert eyes and sucked, not caring that he was staring at her, or that his tears fell on her.

At last, she finished feeding, and Jude ran out of tears. He ventured to lift her then, to lean her over his shoulder and stroke her gently on the back.

"I'll take care of you," he promised, though he had no idea how he was going to feed her when the breast milk was gone.

And Valerie. What of her?

His eyes fell upon the note. He could see that it was written on large legal paper, two sheets, in Valerie's small, fine hand. The writing covered both sides.

Not yet, he thought. *Not yet, I can't.*

He would get Valerie down first. Put her out on the balcony, in the snow, until she could be properly cremated, like all the other victims of the Pandemic.

Yes. That would do.

"Poor girl," he echoed, tenderly adjusting the baby's small, ridged tail as he wrapped her up more snugly.

And then, with the blanketed newborn still in his arms, and Valerie's shadow still on the wall, he picked up the note.

Sometime later, by candlelight, on the longest night of the year, with snow falling and blanketing the city of New York, he read it.

Judas,

Warren didn't leave me a note. Not that he should have, he didn't know he was going to die. But it still hurt me not to have one. I know I'm going to die, deliberately and within the next three months; so I'm leaving you one. Maybe you'll tear this up or burn it or flush it down the toilet, but I kinda suspect that you'll hold on to these last words. That, like me, you'll want a note.

Here it is. I hope I do it justice. And I hope it makes you feel better. That's ridiculous too. I'm dead and nothing's ever going to make you feel good about that.

As I'm writing this, you're sick with the Pandemic, lost in a hundred and four fever; so this note is also a note of hope—because I fully expect for you to live through this to see what I wrote.

Bad joke, huh? But you have to understand, killing myself is my hope. Having you live is my hope. Having my baby live, with you as its father, is my hope.

The money, the McAllisters' billions—it's yours. Do what you want with it. No point leaving it to the only surviving McAllister, the baby—someone would have to watch over it anyway, and invest it and all. And I know you'll do right by my child. I've left a last will and testament of sorts in the drawer; use it if and when the banks ever open again. And there's a note for my lawyer if she survived.

It's what Warren would want, too, though I don't suppose you're going to like it. Too bad.

Main thing you probably want to know is why I

did it. Actually, you already know why, but I'd better say it in writing or you'll waste your time wondering what you could have done to prevent me.

I did it to join Warren. Simple as that.

Blame the Pandemic. Not just for killing Warren, but for making me see it clearer than clear. I might have gone on, half here for the rest of my life, if I hadn't gotten sick. All those times when I wasn't paying attention to what you were saying, when I was ogling my coffee or looking like a rubberneck at an accident, I was actually ringwalking. With Warren.

Funny thing, I always saw him as himself, floating there. I know you understand, because you've been there too. Though I think, listening and watching you, that you're experiencing something I didn't. You always do that, Jude. You fly farther and higher than the rest of us.

When I'm in the ring, letting the memory carry me away, I see diamond stars and the sweet night of space and the sun, farther away than ours, but whiter, brighter. The stars are above and below, even around the sun, more than I've ever seen before on Earth. Copper red dust floats by in misty clouds, like a million new pennies ground to powder and tossed to the wind. It sparkles as deep and gold as that champagne we used to drink, and in it there are glints of teal and rose and violet, like misty rainbows. And I'm weightless, floating on my back it feels like. I reach out my leaves, and it feels so good, like a stretch first thing in the morning. The light from the sun is a mother's hand and the heat from the planet is a warm, fatherly hug.

Something is holding my tail; I curve my head back and I see Warren. It would be stupid if it didn't feel so real. There he is, with that cockeyed smile on his face and a shy look in his eye, blond hair floating, and I know he doesn't belong there.

But there he is.

And we talk in colors. We say things to each other we never could in words.

It's wonderful.

I've traveled the ring with him, and we still haven't seen it all. I think I must have absorbed into my mind some kind of alien travel log. Every time I drift off, I see something new. Did you know that there are these large hollow caves like geodes? You can drift inside and be surrounded by shimmering facets. And there are tunnel forests which are stone on the outside, and tropical-looking forests growing within; they maintain their own heat and light and moisture!

In the innermost rings there are these strange little glowing creatures that move like amoebas. And did you know, in one part of the outermost ring, there is a fog of flaked ice? It looks like snow, only it glows like limelight.

I could go on and on. The thing is, I've come to believe that I can join Warren in the ring, permanently.

You're probably wondering about the baby. I suppose there's an argument that even a bad mother is better than no mother, but I don't want to do that to the kid. If I lived, I'd never be there, and that isn't right.

I know you'll love my child, because you love me. You love me as much if not more than Warren. You always have. Probably the worst thing I ever did to you was to ask you to stand by me at my wedding. Maybe that was my selfish way of trying to marry you both.

I'll tell you, Warren knew how much you loved me, too. Maybe, when he began to realize how sick he was, he hoped I'd find a new love and life with you. Maybe that's the real reason he wanted you to come stay with us.

In all honesty, I thought about it too. But I've al-

ways known that would be unfair to you. You're just going to have to trust that I know what I'm talking about here. I'm not saying that we couldn't have been happy, but I am saying that, with me, you'd never be all you might be. And that would be terrible.

I want you to know that that brief afternoon we had together was one of the best of my life. It's one of the few memories that's kept me Earthbound all these months. That and the baby. Who would have thought it would live? I can feel it kicking like a mule and I know it's going to pull through. Ironic, huh. So many mothers who'd kill to have what I have, a live baby, and I'm ready to leave it behind.

You might be wondering why I waited, since I was never very religious or anything. But you see, Jude, I do love you. And the baby is all I have to leave you. And I just can't kill what might be the only baby to survive the Pandemic—in the womb no less!

Warren and I had such a very short time together. But he lit up my world. I think about all the conversations, all the dreams we never had a chance to share, and I want to be with him again. This is the only way I can think to do that.

Hate me, hate Warren, hate the Pandemic if you can. I can't. The aliens never meant it this way, it just happened, like a meteor hitting the planet. You can curse the dark or invent a light bulb. I think I know which one you'll do.

Fly as high and far as you can, Judas. And teach my child to do the same. Tell my little one as much about me as you think he or she ought to know—let the kid see this letter, too, when you think they're ready.

You have my love, and you have always and will always have Warren's, forever and always—

—Valerie

Chapter 11

DECEMBER IN VARANASI WAS A PLEASANT TIME OF year, especially during the day when the weather was cool and dry. The air was clean again, the epidemic of flies gone, the stink of burning flesh all but vanished in fact if not in memory; and the stone sculptures and complex pavilions which had lasted over two thousand years were still standing. Pilgrims and priests scrubbed the ashes and stains from the scratched white stone and cleansed the temples with incense and holy water. Flowers appeared on altars and steps once again, before statues and in garlands that everyone wore around their necks.

Farmers, those who had survived, brought in oxcarts of rice and vegetables. One such farmer had brought in handrolled cigarettes as well. Varouna still missed her American cigarettes, but these were more than serviceable. Leaning back from the computer she gazed out the window at the peaceful haze that cloaked the river, and felt the morning silence surround her. It was always silent in the morning now; eerie that silence, especially the missing laughter and playful screams of children.

Initial estimates put the world death toll at four billion. And that was just from the virus; that was not factoring in the cholera, starvation, disasters, and murders.

Yet life returned to the world, and people finally came back to the cities.

There was, however, a difference. The survivors raised their right arms, and with a twist of the wrist, turned out their hands toward each other, no matter where they were from.

It was akin to a namaskar, an echo of the last gesture made by the aliens, that final wave as they watched their ships vanish through the portal, through doorways that danced round a planetary ring like a garland around a young girl's neck.

"*Kasi-Samsara,*" they said. *Kasi-Samsara.* It hinted at what they had experienced and seen including wheels of light that allowed the soul to cross over yet, at the same time, were also wheels of life and death, Samsara.

Kasi-Samsara also implicated that other Kasi, out there among the stars, where the inhabitants wandered round and round, trapped in a luminous circle of life and death and re-birth. The word, which was making its way across Asia and into Europe, had been shortened and corrupted to "Kasara." A Russian astronomer, claiming to have found the aliens' star, was even calling his new discovery *Kasara,* and on Web sites, the aliens were being referred to as the Kasarans.

Closing her eyes, Varouna imagined those aliens, nearly four thousand light-years away, conceiving and creating the superdense matter that floated at the hearts of their star gates and made the magic possible. She ought to have felt over-whelmed by beings who, with single-minded purpose, ac-complished the impossible, but something, she realized, had been done to her mind. It all seemed so right, so familiar. Like looking in a mirror and recognizing her own face.

Kasara. Luminous and transcendent *and* Earthly. A para-dox embodied in the aliens.

And in humans.

She could almost see humanity reflecting the aliens, set-ting pieces in place until their own portal was built.

It had to happen, she thought.

Out her window she saw candles on small rafts floating down the Ganges; not many, but a few, and flowers, too, and messages written on the sides of paper boats. She wondered how many of them were trying to speak with the aliens.

Certainly the candles and flowers and paper boats the aliens had sent had reached *them*.

With a touch to the computer, she sent her own message, an e-mail to Paris. She was going there in a week, to the city where her brother had died, a cold, European city. And given what she was going there to do, she might never return to Varanasi.

A year ago that would have terrified her, like cutting a lifeline. Now it felt a little like being born.

Or set adrift on the Ganges.

At least she would have access to American cigarettes in Paris. She lit up another of the small hand-rolled ones and released the smoke to mix with the morning haze which drifted with the candles and prayers down the river.

PART II:
I Only Want to Be with You

Chapter 12

April: Four years after the Pandemic

The shoal clustered together as the sun vanished from sight behind them. Mist froze and liquid slicking the rocks hardened until the red-hazed world glistened softly in the dark. There were no sounds, but the vibrations of the universe quieted. Distant lightning flashed and flickered amid the floating boulders and asteroids. It illuminated the coppery dust that drifted like smoke around the lumbering shapes.

As starry darkness tucked in around them, the members of the shoal curled their leaves in, tucked their claws, shut their eyes, and coiled their bodies until they resembled craggy oyster shells on the seabed. The colored skins, which had been shading down from their usual brilliance, darkened to that of a black pearl, and the creatures went to sleep.

Their minds drifted then, traveling out to the edge where six of their twelve portholes hung on the starry sky, dim, silvery shapes. Should anything come through during the short time they were locked away in sleep, it would exit out on the sun-side gates where lucky shoals, not hibernating, would greet them. But these closed portholes, keeping pace with the great wheel that ringed their system, allowed the sleeping ones to envision tiny planets in distant corners of the galaxy, planets with strange vegetation, incredible topography and huge bodies of water.

Life-forms too strange for them to even imagine lived in such places.

The members of the shoal orbited such planets in their dreams, yearning to reach down and speak with the inhabitants.

And they wondered, had their message made it to such a planet? Had the inhabitants understood it? Could they build their half of the bridge?

Would they come?

And not a few of the shoal, their sleeping minds twitching within their hibernating forms, wondered . . . was it a good message? Or had it done something terrible to these unsuspecting strangers?

Far too late to wonder that, they knew. But they dreamed the question all the same, and through their night, they formulated answers for when they faced the sun and came awake once again.

THERE WAS A CLIMBER ON THE BROOKLYN BRIDGE.

When he got the call, just before dawn on that Sunday morning, Gordon's initial response was to bitch and swear.

"There's a climber," he heard as soon as he touched on the speakerphone. Loretta's pragmatic voice.

"Yeah? So? Why the fuck are you calling me?" Gordon squinted nearsightedly at the curtained window across from his bed. It looked to still be dark. Through the curtain he thought he could make out a few lights on in the neighboring brownstones, the only hint that it might be morning.

"Brooklyn Bridge."

"What else is new?" Gordon growled impatiently and reached for his glasses. In San Francisco, or so he'd heard, the climbers showed up on the Golden Gate in July. Other places, especially on the Eastern seaboard, got climbers in autumn, presumably to see the leaves change.

In New York, the climbers rose out of the ground in spring, just like the flowers. And they usually headed right for the Brooklyn Bridge.

"And why can't you handle this?" Gordon added. His mouth tasted foul and his stomach was growling something fierce, but he forced himself to be patient. There had to be more to this problem if Loretta was calling him. And given that the woman hadn't come out and said what that problem was, it must be pretty bad. He scratched at the stubble on his chin.

"It's Kyle."

Gordon threw back the covers, his feet hitting the cold hardwood floor. "Kyle?" he repeated, searching for his slippers.

"I don't think he's going to jump. But he's climbed up on the Brooklyn side. I thought I'd better let you know before sending Burke up after him."

"Jesus Christ." Gordon went for his robe and crossed to the door. "Wait just a minute! Just a goddamn minute!"

He was out the door and moving through the rooms of the brownstone. The second floor that he and Scotty called home had been beautifully restored by its previous owner. That didn't stop the polished wood floors from creaking, or the drafts from getting in through the windows. It was icy cold in the long, narrow rooms.

Gordon went first to the guest room. He knocked gently on the door a few times, then ventured to turn the cold knob and peer in. He could tell it was empty even before he switched on the light. Blinking against the yellow glare, he noted that the daybed, covered with a few brown wool blankets and a trio of pillows, was neatly made, perhaps had not been slept in. On several hooks hung a small wardrobe of blue, gray, brown, and brick red shirts, several pairs of dark trousers, and some ties. He wasn't sure which shirt might be missing, but the dress jacket, which always hung on the room's single chair, was gone.

On the army trunk by the bed, which acted as a worktable for an old radio Kyle was restoring, Gordon caught sight of a book on beginning physics and one on electronics. He'd hoped to find a note, but there was nothing.

All too aware that he didn't want to be convinced, Gordon made a fruitless search of the study at the far end of the hall, with its abandoned baby grand piano. Scotty was learning to play, but Gordon didn't feel right about touching it or even getting it tuned. He had, strangely, no compunction about using anything else in the apartment. But he couldn't help feeling that the piano still belonged to whoever had furnished, decorated, and lived in the brownstone before the Pandemic.

The study, with its Moroccan carpet and sound system, was quiet and empty. Gordon went back down the hall and checked the two bathrooms, with their white diamond tiles and oval mirrors. Nothing. The front living room that opened into the burnt orange kitchen was also empty. But the smell of cooked oatmeal and brown sugar hung in the air.

Damn.

He headed back and, with a mixture of hope and dread, cracked open the door to his son's room. He heard soft breathing and, in the dim light, caught sight of a small shape burrowed under the warmth of several quilted covers, a tousled head on a big blue flannel pillow.

Drawing in a breath of relief and disgust, he hurried back to his own room, with its wood-framed bed and spare walls.

"Still there, Loretta?"

"Still here."

"I'll be down fast as I can. Don't do a thing, you understand, *not a thing* till I get there, not unless it looks like he's going to jump."

"Gotcha."

Gordon hung up on Loretta and speed dialed Ruth, who lived downstairs.

"Hello?" her muzzy voice answered.

"Ruth, it's Gordon." Gordon pawed through drawers for a pair of wool pants and a sweater. "Emergency. Can you come up?"

"It's Sunday."

"I know it's Sunday, goddamn it!" He was having trouble getting into his trousers. They didn't seem to want to cooperate. "Can you just skip church this morning?"

"Gordon—" She didn't sound happy.

"It's Kyle," he said briefly, throwing on a sweater and dragging on some thick socks.

"Oh. I'll be right up." A pause. "Scotty's going to be disappointed."

"I know, I know." He found his rubber-soled shoes, the ones he kept for just this situation, and tugged them on. On Sunday, Gordon always made Scotty pancakes for breakfast. It was their special tradition. "Tell him I'll be back soon as I can . . . no, on second thought, don't make any promises. This could take quite a while. Just let him know that Kyle needed me. He'll understand." That, Gordon thought, was probably a lie, but at the moment it could hardly be helped. "I have to go now," he added.

"You go," Ruth said, "and whatever it is, good luck."

"Thanks."

Gordon took only time enough to grab his blue jacket, the one with the big white PATROL letters on the back, and his keys, then he was down the curving, wrought iron stairs and out the heavy front door. He was thankful that the local patrols had been issued electric cars, and ghoulishly thankful that the Pandemic had cut the number of drivers, and therefore the number of cars on the road, in half. It had brought a serene and eerie quiet to most cities, including Manhattan.

He rubbed at his frozen hands, wishing he'd thought to wear gloves, switched on the device that made sure the stop lights turned green at his approach, and cut down Fourth Street.

What was Kyle thinking?

Not that he might ever really know. Kyle was a Pan, as those who survived the Pandemic were now being called. And Gordon was a Tenor, one of the ten percent who had escaped the virus, who had never had that particular experience, or suffered from the ongoing results of it.

All the same, he had thought he understood the young man. He had even maintained the arrogant hope that he had saved Kyle from himself.

They'd met during Gordon's first year on the Manhattan Patrol, when he'd been put in charge of a scavenger hunt through several old police stations. Most of the stations, like Egyptian tombs, had already been raided, their walls graffitied, their furniture trashed, the computers and equipment stolen. The rats had their nests in the files. But the Patrol still made periodic searches for spoils, hoping, as gravediggers might, for a secret cache. It gave them the feeling that they were a team on an archeological dig. Gordon's crew even made jokes about wearing pith helmets and mining hats.

They might have been exploring a junkyard to furnish a new clubhouse, that's how giddy they'd all felt.

"I'll take lockup," Gordon had said after they'd pushed open the doors to abandoned desks, the dusty light pouring through greasy, broken windows.

"Want me to come with you?" Burke had asked.

"What for?" Gordon wasn't worried. Dark and window-less, lockup was not a place wandering Pans made their home. As for bodies, there likely wouldn't be any of those either. During the year of the Pandemic, prisoners had been moved from the lockup to regular hospitals or prison hospitals. That had been standard practice throughout North America so far as Gordon knew.

And so he'd blithely taken a flashlight that flickered and tended to go out and headed down the back stairs. He went down the narrow hall, checking into each of the small, utilitarian cages. Being the absolute last thing he'd expected, he'd mistaken the body in the last cell for a pile of blankets. Then the light steadied and he'd caught his breath.

He was numb to the sight of corpses, or so he thought. Bodies had become bits of trash, rotten meat to be burned or buried in mass graves. But he was disturbed, and it took him a moment to understand why: the place reeked with waste products and rotten food, and roaches crunched underfoot, but there was none of that sour, distinctive stink of decaying flesh.

And so he took a closer look.

The lockup was open, filled with canned food and Styrofoam containers of dehydrated soup. All empty. There didn't seem to be anything left, nor, Gordon suspected, had there been for some time. There was a five-gallon plastic water bottle in the corner in a cobbled-together holder, a quarter full of dirty water. A hose had been engineered to reach the bed.

The body, curled on the cot, was male, wearing only a pair of torn, soiled jeans. The ribs were showing and the angular wings of the back. Pale skin, dull, dirty black hair. It didn't smell good, but it didn't smell dead either.

Gordon's hand wandered to the gun he kept on him at all times. And then he noticed goosebumps on the white flesh. Saw a twitch and then a shiver.

"I won't hurt you," he ventured, and that's when he heard a choking intake of air and knew that the man had been holding his breath. "Are you all right?"

The man kept his face to the wall. "You can't take me out."

"You weren't *left* here, were you?" Gordon asked, outraged.

"They let me out when everyone got sick. I didn't even get to trial. But I came back after . . . after."

"I see."

"I can't go," the man insisted. "I hafta stay in the dark."

"Oh? Who says?"

"I'm a criminal. Criminals have to stay in the dark."

"You must have gone out for the food and water," Gordon tried.

"At night. But I'm not going to anymore. I had trouble giving up the food," the man confessed as if to a sin. "But I did it. Only I can't seem to fight the thirst. I'm trying. I'm really trying."

"This is crazy, son," Gordon said. He wasn't sure of the man's age, but the poor bastard sounded young. He went close to the cot. It was dangerous. But he thought of Scotty grown, Scotty left alone, and he knew he'd want someone to try to get through to his boy, if ever such a thing, God forbid, were to happen to Scotty.

He directed the flashlight aside. "Turn around. Face me."

He didn't think the man would obey, then he wasn't sure the fellow had the strength, but finally the poor bastard shifted and rolled. Dark, frightened eyes stared up at Gordon, a mass of tangled black hair, Mediterranean complexion gone sickly in the dark.

He *was* young. Seventeen. Eighteen maybe.

"What's your name?"

The young man licked his lips. "Kyle."

"Well, Kyle, I'm Captain Gordon of the Manhattan Patrol. We're the new police force in town. More like a group of scout leaders, truth to tell. Why don't you come with me? You don't really want to stay here, do you? Wouldn't you like a bath? Maybe some clean clothes?"

"I'm a criminal. Criminals stay in the dark."

Gordon didn't understand that. Sometime afterward, he'd asked Burke about it.

"The Kasarans don't have criminals," the big man had

explained. *"But those that aren't quite right head to the edge of the ring and, well, leave."*

"They just drift off into space?" Gordon asked, horrified.

"Kasarans don't just talk to each other, Gordie, they absorb messages pretty much the way we did their virus. So any that aren't right can do real damage to others. Yeah, they leave."

"But, isn't that a death sentence?"

Burke had shrugged. *"Self-imposed. Tell me we don't do the same."*

At that moment in the cell, however, Gordon just asked Kyle, "What crime did you commit?"

"Stole some stuff. I didn't need it. I was just bored. And I didn't want to get a job. Mom was giving me shit. I probably deserved it. She's dead now. So's my brothers."

"I'm sorry. But as a cop, I have to tell you that your sentence is done, your time is up."

"Can't be."

"Yes it can. I say so."

Kyle frowned at that, as if he hadn't considered such a thing. "But, what'll I *do*?"

"You'll come with me," Gordon said firmly, and this time he took the young man by the arm. Skin and dirt flaked off, but Gordon didn't flinch. He pulled and Kyle came unresisting, unsteady, almost falling on his feet. "Come on. Show me you've rehabilitated yourself and I'll make you a deputy."

It was, Gordon reflected, perhaps the strangest promise he'd ever had to keep. Not that Kyle had remained so very wigged out. Food, rest and sunlight gave him back his reason. And when he was feeling well enough, he'd come to Gordon, hands in pockets, shoulders hunched, eyes on his shoes and said, "You don't have to keep that promise you made to me, man. I know you were just trying to get me out of that hole."

But by then Gordon had made Kyle part of his family. And Scotty adored him. So Gordon kept his promise and made Kyle his personal deputy.

"You're sure?" Kyle asked then. "I mean, I probably would've joined a gang. 'Cept bangers are homophobic and I don't like to hide what I am." Which was Kyle's way of getting everything out on the table.

"I'm sure," Gordon said, and that was that.

The lad wasn't half bad at the job, come to that. And he knew how to repair the electric cars, cobble furniture back together, and get computers back on line.

Now, however, the lunatic from the lockup was back, and as his car flew across the Manhattan Bridge to Brooklyn, Gordon wracked his brains trying to think of what might have driven Kyle to revert.

He got to the Brooklyn side of the bridge, parked his car, and headed at a run for the walkway, his breath coming out in frosty pants.

The day was dawning, alive with spring air, the first songs of birds, a promise of green leaves. He saw the towers of the bridge and the Manhattan skyline that lay beyond. Something, he thought, about the Brooklyn Bridge. Not that it was just stunningly beautiful, or a national monument. It seemed to rise out of the river like a tree or a mountain. Natural. Earthbound. Solid.

Perhaps that's why climbers always chose it. It symbolized the Earth to them. At night it hung surrounded by the glitter of stars above, the sparkle of the city behind, the reflection of its own bright lights in the East River: a dark, stone planet afloat in space.

Even the cathedral arches seemed to be rocketing toward the sky.

The climbers, he guessed, were just trying to rise high enough that they might soar off into the universe beyond.

Was that what Kyle wanted as well?

He felt and heard the vibrations of the train making its way along the rails below as he came up on the wooden slats of the walkway; he tasted damp morning wind off the East River. The lamps illuminating the walkway were just going off. Dawn on the bridge, Gordon thought ironically, a perfect time to be here. But for the train and the mournful horn of an ocean liner, it was surprisingly quiet.

A small crowd, most holding bikes and pointing, was gathered at the end of the walkway. Climbers were curiosities; most were harmless, more of a danger to themselves than others. But there was always that one with a point to make, an old grief to lay to rest. Recently, Loretta had talked down a man with a homemade bomb wearing a sandwich board that read, "NEVER FORGIVE! NEVER FORGET!"

Whether dangerous or harmless, climbers rarely wanted to come down, and no few of them, some right before Gordon's eyes, had pushed themselves off their perches, arms outstretched, trying to fly.

He only hoped Kyle was not planning to do any such thing.

Burke was waiting for him, a safety belt, two headsets and a rifle piled by his foot. A huge, good-natured, blue-collar worker from Cincinnati, Burke had curling brown-sugar hair and the smile of a little boy. The story went that the ex-car mechanic had walked from Cincinnati to Lake Erie, where, in the worst storm weather, he'd sailed a thirty-foot sloop to the Erie Canal and then to the Hudson. Thereafter, the Pan had made his way to Manhattan, where, for no good reason, he'd suddenly decided to join the Patrol.

Gordon wasn't sure if the story was true, but he was glad of Burke's presence all the same. There was an easy way to the man that most Pans lacked, as if the mechanic had made peace with what had happened to him.

"Where's Loretta?" Gordon asked.

"Gone to fetch some coffee. Take a look." Burke pushed a pair of binoculars into Gordon's hand.

Gordon brought them up and stepped back. He adjusted them until the top of the tower came into focus.

Moving in and out of view was Kyle, without a doubt. He was dressed in a suit too tight in the shoulders, mocha-colored with a wide maroon tie. Taking his cue from Gordon, the younger man always wore suits to work, which made Gordon feel strange and flattered at the same time. The detective was used to constables treating him with the affection of a comfortable old fixture; Mr. Chips with a badge. It had been decidedly odd to have a deputy who actually looked up to him, who acted like a disciple desperately seeking approval.

Gordon wondered if that was why he had missed signs of this breakdown.

"Here." Burke took the binoculars back and pressed a paper cup of black coffee into Gordon's hand. "Have some of that."

"No time," Gordon protested.

"He's not going anywhere," a female voice, and Gordon noticed Loretta, her brown skin glowing like bronze in the crisp, rose colors of sunrise. She nodded to him, a lanky woman with her hair braided tight against her head. "You need t'be warm and awake, Captain. And have a doughnut. Can't go climbing on an empty stomach." She held out an oil-spotted box filled with fresh-baked crullers from a vendor in the East Anchorage. The arched chambers under the bridge's Brooklyn-side pilings had become an open market for fresh-baked goods.

Gordon, feeling his stomach rumbling, obediently picked out a French twist and got it down in three bites, all the while waxing nostalgic for the maple-flavored doughnut holes he used to eat in Toronto. He took a tentative sip of his coffee. Black and sweet, just as he liked it.

"Going to give me a goddamn sugar rush," he muttered.

"Kyle's been up there for about forty-five minutes," Loretta said. "That's since we heard, mind you."

"How the fuck did he get past the gate?" Gordon demanded, and nodded to the thick suspension cables that swept down from the towers and supported the towering hanger wires in their famous net pattern. Sharp, narrow gates set on those cables blocked access to the towers.

"Easy." Loretta sounded disgusted. "He went to the bridge authorities and showed them his badge. They gave him a key. Speaking of which." She handed him a key. "Kyle locked the gate behind him."

"All right." Gordon brushed sugar from the ends of his dun-colored mustache and took another, final sip at his coffee, which, in contrast to the airy, sugary twist, tasted like shit. An El Niño condition had come riding on the heels of the Pandemic, and as if the virus had not been bad enough, hurricanes and floods had hit several coffee-growing countries. The national news had announced, in fact, that a third of the world death estimates previously attributed to the Pandemic could probably be blamed on natural catastrophes and the current lack of available international aid.

In terms of the here and now, Gordon thought with disgust, that meant no fresh coffee beans and so freeze dried was going to have to suffice. It would do to keep him alert and thinking.

"All right. Let's go." He handed the cup back to Loretta. Burke gave him one of the headsets and the belt. With practiced speed, Gordon got both on and adjusted.

Burke placed the remaining set on his own large head. He was also wearing a safety belt so that he could run up one of the other cables if there was trouble.

And then Burke picked up the rifle.

"You're not going to need that," Gordon said.

"I don't want to need it," the patrolman said, loading it, and Gordon knew that protest was useless. If it looked like the situation was going wrong, Burke would take the trouble out. Even if that trouble was Kyle.

God, please, Gordon prayed, *don't let it come to that.*

Taking in a breath, the detective climbed onto one of the main cables; they were wide as a sidewalk and easy enough to run upon if one held to the side wiring that served as guide rails.

And if the wind was gentle.

The early-morning weather was cool and brisk, with a promise of rain in the form of distant slate-colored clouds. Before Gordon, the tower rose like a castle turret, the window of its cathedral arch accenting the cabling of the bridge, elegant as a song.

He started up.

The wind kicked in and he felt his heartbeat spike.

Passing through the gate, Gordon paused a moment to secure the clips on the safety belt to the guide rails. They didn't make him feel much better.

The curve of the cable grew steeper as he headed up and the icy wind got stronger, tousling his hair. As a native of Toronto, he found spring in the Big Apple mild, sometimes even pleasant. But even he felt that the April weather was unusually brisk this morning. He pushed back at his glasses, feeling them slide on a sweaty nose growing chill. His stiff hands, tight on guide wires, were already aching.

"Doing all right?" Burke's voice came in his ear.

"Fine," he muttered into the stick of a mike. "By the way, do we know what Kyle's *doing* up there?"

"Oh, yeah, he's painting something. Leastways he's got a bucket of paint and a brush."

Gordon didn't know whether to be comforted by that. It gave him hope that Kyle did not plan to toss himself off the tower. But it also emphasized that Kyle had probably snapped.

He should never have become so attached to the young man. He'd let himself care, and now there was a chance the kid would die on him . . .

But he'd seen men on the force who'd been so hurt by death that they refused to commit to anyone, men with no life or light in their eyes, just bitterness and fear.

No. If he'd learned anything, he'd learned that the risks had to be taken, the losses accepted. A human being had to care about people, and if they left you or failed you, then you had to find a way to feel it was all worth it.

But he really could hate the Kasarans for doing this to Kyle. He really could.

"Damn it!" he heard in his ear, and noticed simultaneously a helicopter flying above, swooping in. A man leaning out to point a camera lens at Kyle.

"Go away!" Gordon waved furiously at the copter, the noise of its propellers filling his ears. He moved one arm angrily, and so violently he almost lost his step.

Whether the cameraman noticed Gordon or just had all the footage he needed, the helicopter lifted and sped off.

"Who were they?" Gordon demanded, gritting his teeth. "Damn it! Don't they know not to buzz a climber?"

"Not from the news services," Burke's voice came back, subdued. "I saw the Pandora logo. Must be Tarkenton's."

"Oh, fuck!" Gordon moved, fast as he could now. Damn it, damn it, damn it! That man was *not* getting Kyle!

The wind blew fiercer.

"Kyle!" he said loudly, but the wind grabbed his voice away. He could see the young man, sitting with his head down. There was, indeed, a bucket of paint beside him. His coat and slacks, Gordon could see, were speckled with white paint.

Gordon reached the ladder that would take him up atop the tower. Should he go up? There was no telling how Kyle might react. He might leap. He might have a weapon.

He chewed on his mustache a little, then unlatched himself from the rails and reached for the ladder. There was really no choice.

"I've got you in sights, Gordon," Burke's grim voice told him. So. The big man was thinking along the same lines, curse him.

A few rungs up and there he was, atop fitted blocks, the tops hewn flat and smooth by Victorian stonecutters. Glancing up, he could see the gold domino towers of the World Trade Center, the moiré shimmer of their flat surfaces as the sunlight appeared and disappeared behind plum-colored clouds.

Below, he could see boats making their way speedily down the East River, the dark waters seeming to move very fast. It was winter cold up here and his nose was frozen, but he could feel the sweat at the base of his throat and under his arms. Although he'd been up here several times, he could never rid himself of a panicked wish for a rail.

"Kyle!" Not a shout, as close to calm as he could make it. He kept in mind that Burke was below, watching through the telescope of the rifle.

His former deputy remained huddled with arms around his knees beside the paint bucket; and Gordon could now see what Kyle had been working on. In bold white strokes in the square corner of the tower, deftly and beautifully done, was a diagram illustrating a circle from which radiated twiglike extensions like hatchmarks or ancient glyphs. They formed a netting, making the ring look like a strange nest or autumnal wreath.

Gordon was not a Pan. He had never experienced their visions. But he hadn't turned a deaf ear to what they were saying either. He wasn't one of those who thought they were crazy or under mass hypnosis or possessed by the devil. Given some of the news on the Internet, he could hardly doubt that humankind had been given a glimpse of technology and science far beyond their own. And if that glimpse had driven a good percentage of the population nuts, and killed off another portion, well, that didn't negate that it had happened.

He couldn't say for sure what the diagram depicted, but he knew it wasn't art.

"You've done what you came here to do, Kyle," he said, simple and plain, "now it's time to come down."

Kyle finally looked up. His face was naturally boyish. This was enhanced by the coal black bangs that fell over a wide forehead, by a disarming smile that could charm the skin off a snake, and by a pair of sloe eyes that both men and women found tragic.

But all Gordon could see was the scared young man he'd

found two years ago hiding in the corner of a jail cell nearly starved to death and terrified of daylight.

"I'm trying to give it back," Kyle said, his words almost lost on the wind.

"Scotty's going to be disappointed if we're not there for breakfast," Gordon retorted, and Kyle flinched. Good.

"Don't you see?" the young man tried again and waved to his diagram. "I've read the physics books, but I don't understand them and I can't make out why this is in my head! I'm not smart enough to have it. So I'm giving it back."

"I do understand. I also understand that we can talk about this down on the ground over coffee and doughnuts."

"No." This time the dark eyes were very serious. "You *don't* understand. In here." He hit at his head with his fist. "It's been in here since the moment I got sick. And I've been keeping it in my gut, trying to hold it back, because I should understand it and I don't. Because it's special and different and important. But I don't know why! And if I can't explain it, even why it's important, I can't share it. And it has to be shared. You see?"

"Yes." Gordon tried to resettle himself. He was on his knees and they were cramping. His feet, despite the woolen socks, were cold in their shoes and he felt about ready to start shivering. The wind was up and the clouds were coming.

Dark rain-filled clouds.

A pause, and Gordon could almost see a longing in the young man's eyes, a painful swallow of the Adam's apple, as if Kyle had seen his heart's desire and knew, knew without a single doubt, that it was forever out of his reach.

"You can't just give up, son. You've come so far."

"No, I haven't. I thought for a while that the reason I didn't understand it was because I was a criminal. Then, thanks to you, I thought that maybe I could understand. But I can't."

Gordon licked his lips, and realized that, up till now, he hadn't really understood Kyle, why the young man worked so hard on his appearance, why he poured over books by lamp-light, struggling with words and concepts he couldn't under-stand, why he took his failures so very hard.

What a way to find out.

"It's like you're getting ready for an important date," Kyle went on, "and you hope you can make a good impres-sion. You're so afraid you're not going to. But you're in love, so you can't help it. So you put on someone else's suit, hop-ing to look special, and instead, you look ridiculous. That's when you understand it's hopeless."

"You aren't ridiculous. You're very important. Especially to me and Scotty—and to Burke and Loretta and everyone else on the Patrol. Please, Kyle, come down."

For a moment, Gordon thought Kyle would refuse again and he'd have to force the issue. But Kyle took a long, long look at Gordon, and suddenly got up on hands and knees.

He began to shuffle forward.

"That's good," Gordon said, taking in a breath, and heard Burke's forgotten voice in his ear whispering, *"Hallelujah."*

One hand forward, then the other. One knee nearer, then the other. The crawling was interminably slow.

The wind grew cutting, causing Gordon's ears and fin-gers to hurt. His shifted off his knees and flexed his feet and the numb toes, working the blood back into them.

Kyle was within touching distance, but Gordon kept back. Finally, the young man inched past him to the ladder.

Gordon let out a breath. "All right!" he said and smiled with what he hoped was encouragement. "You go on down the ladder. I'll be right behind. Okay?"

"Yes." He met Gordon's eyes, his own gaze still looking bleak and heartbroken. "Captain," Kyle always called Gordon by his rank, no matter how many times the older man tried to get him on a first name basis. "Thank you."

Gordon heard it in the tone and lunged as Kyle threw out his hands and made to fall off the tower. He nabbed Kyle around the waist, causing the young man to land, breathless, with arms and chest half over the edge.

"*No!*" Gordon yelled, grabbing for the belt. He hardly knew where the strength came from—Kyle weighed at least as much as he did—but he pulled, jerked hard, and his deputy came, scraping back.

"*Jesus!*" Burke's voice cried over the headset. "I'm coming up!"

Gordon ignored him. "No!" he said again to Kyle, as if to a disobedient dog. "You son of a bitch! You are *not* going to kill yourself!"

Kyle rolled onto his back, trying to suck in air and shaking his head.

The older man took up a fistful of collar and leaned in. "I don't give a *shit* what you think, I'm *not* going to let you hurt Scotty that way! *Do you understand?*"

"Yes," Kyle managed, "Yes, sir."

"Good." Gordon tugged hard, nearly ripping the jacket. "Now you get the fuck down that ladder!"

"Jesus!" Burke's voice squeaked, not only on the headset but from right below. The big man was trying to catch his breath, looking as if he'd run all the way up. Sweat shimmered across his broad forehead. "Are you all right?"

"Fine, fine," Gordon said, as Kyle began to descend the ladder, rung by rung.

"Here, I've got you," Burke said to the deputy, and set a meaty hand on Kyle's arm as he stepped onto the cable. But the big man's gaze was on Gordon, and he nodded. He would make sure the young man got down safely.

Gordon nodded in return and reached his feet back for the rungs. He didn't even bother to use the safety clips on the way down.

The crowd applauded as they reached the walkway, and Loretta came up to take Kyle's other arm, as if she wanted to make sure he didn't head back up again.

Gordon got off from the rail and just sat down, right on

the walkway, head to his knees. He felt a drop of icy water on his head, then another and another. The rain had started.

"Captain Demme?" someone said.

Goddamn it, what now? He glanced up, ready to shout, and found the breath knocked right out of him.

The gentleman looking down on him from under a wide, black umbrella had a golden face with a strong jaw and dark, molasses hair. The eyes were thoughtful and intense.

"Thank you for saving that Pan," said Judas Tarkenton. "We'll take him from here." Which was exactly what Gordon had feared he would say.

Chapter 13

Beneath the obvious chromatic movement with its subtle color alterations, the viewer can perceive the reccurring use of circles and the "ray-band" design of the Kasara Gate. There are also, however, skyscrapers like the Ali Building which use the sleek lines of the X59 shuttle in their design. The truncated airplane form of the shuttle can also be seen in Wilson chairs and the sculptures of Clarence Bow.

Thus, human creations like space shuttles, high-powered orbiting telescopes, and even the robotics used in lunar mining operations were actually far more influential on artists and architects of the time than the Kasara ring system or its inhabitants, the popularity of leaf tattoos and circular rock gardens notwithstanding.

There was a new modernity at this time, which is why it was such a rich and exciting artistic period. The impetus had come from an alien race, but the feeling was one of pride. We humans could do this . . . we would do this. And so we came to admire, once again, our own ingenuity; we gloried in the beauty of our own inventiveness.

—The Strange Age

THERE WERE, IN VARANASI, HOLY MEN WHO BELIEVED that the sacred city was merely a mirage, a dream of the real Varanasi which was on the banks of the true Ganges, the stars of the Milky Way. As a child, Varouna had often gazed up at the night skies in search of that mythic city. Now, seated in the back of a black Mercedes, gazing out at the Manhattan skyline in the distance, she wondered if she might have finally found that true Varanasi or just another mirage.

There was, she had to admit, a hint of the mythic in this city, its buildings reflecting the wet, moon-silver morning, a faint rainbow arched above it.

"New York is the world's city," the driver of the Mercedes announced, as if he'd just heard her thoughts, his first words since he'd picked her up at the airport. Dressed in a smoke suit with silver pin stripes and pelican gray shirt, he was a friendly-looking man with a wild mass of wispy, faded, ochre hair. His manner was oddly hesitant, as if he wanted to make a good impression but didn't know how. Yet the one-handed way he guided the wheel, weaving his way in and out of the sparse traffic, could not have been more confident.

When he glanced back at her, she saw disconcerting blue eyes with lines at the corners like crumpled silk.

"First time here, Dr. Premjad?" he added, as solicitous as when he'd helped her through customs and taken care of her baggage. It was still jarring to hear that title, it made her want to glance around in search of her brother. But she forced herself to remember that she deserved it. Or, at the least, the Pasteur Institute believed she deserved it.

"Yes," she sighed. "My first."

"Up ahead's Brooklyn Bridge," he pointed out. "We'll be going across and then right into Manhattan."

Varouna shifted on the plush leather cushions to see, and found herself suddenly and unexpectedly catching her breath. The sense of loss took her unawares. Over the past four years she'd experienced few bouts of true homesickness. Long hours of work and study had left her no time for that. But every once in a while it hit her, hard. The bridge up ahead reminded her so vividly of the ghats in Varanasi, their strength and timelessness, that, for a moment, she flashed back to that four-years-gone world. She smelled the rich pungency of sandalwood and flowers, felt the familiar brush of river-moist air through the car window she had cracked open. On her tongue she tasted, once again, the distinct, melting flavor of *paan,* betel nut leaves filled with mildly intoxicating ingredients, folded into triangles and chewed until the juices stained the lips bright red.

When Varouna first heard the term "Pan" applied to those who had survived the virus, she had mistaken it to mean *paan.* The homonym still seemed apt to her.

A splash of water struck her through the open window; a low ceiling of tarnished silver clouds held back the sun, all but for a trio of bright shafts that played along the gold harp strings of the bridge.

"Amazing, isn't it?" The driver flashed her a smile.

"Yes."

The car turned onto the bridge and she stared at the high, intricate cabling, feeling suddenly as if she'd been split in three; she was back in Varanasi, where fishermen cast out nets fine as spider's silk. And she was drifting in the ring, helping to create a craft like nets to catch the stars.

And, with a blink, she was here, passing between a corridor of cables, racing beneath a cage of bars toward a city with buildings that rose like arms lifted to the sky. The twin buildings up ahead, the World Trade Center, said it all: impossibly tall gold ladders to the sky, they were the treasure that lay beneath the rainbow, a way to climb out of the mud of the Earth and to the heavens above.

Her brother had spent his life believing in the salvation of modern cities like this one. She could finally understand why.

She had to admit, he had been right about many things. In Europe, the air *was* clearer, as after a rainstorm; it didn't smell of dust and diesel, feces and rot, it was purer, fresh. And she'd gotten used to having running water and reliable electricity. During her first days in Paris, she'd ventured in and out of public toilets just to put her hands under the faucets and watch the water run over her fingers, crystal clean.

But there was a great deal she missed as well, in these rich, Western cities where everyone wore shoes and washed with shampoos and herbal bath gels. Absent was the taste of clove and cardamom in her food, and she missed indulging herself in *kulfi,* which was so much sweeter and richer than ice cream or glacé. And she had cravings for sugarcane juice, freshly squeezed with lime and ginger.

Most of all, she missed the colors. Against the muted palette of the West, her saris glowed, brilliant strokes in a gray world, a reminder of a distant land where all was bright, rich, diverse, even the sun-warmed browns of people's skins.

She remembered a day in Varanasi, during the Janmashtami celebrations, when she had looked down from her apartment to see a thick river of women on their way to the festivities. The vibrant, moving stream of colored veils had swirled like iridescent oils upon the waters of the Ganges, one of the most stunning sights she'd ever seen.

Such human tides were powerful, as if the whole world were coming together, not just the people, but every facet of the planet.

Would she see anything like that here, she wondered, in this young city on the other side of the world?

"Numberless crowded streets" the driver suddenly said then, with a dramatic flourish of his hand toward the skyline— "high growths of iron, slender, strong, light, splendidly uprising toward clear skies . . ." Well, not so clear skies today, but that's what Walt Whitman said about Manhattan. Wild, huh? I mean, how some people can see the future like that?"

"Yes."

"The word 'skyscraper' means a ship's mast. Whitman

use to do that too—connect the city to all the ship masts in the harbor."

"How very interesting."

"Maybe he thought the city could sail him around the world?"

Droplets began to splatter the window as the sun momentarily lost its game of hide-and-seek with the rain clouds. The car headed down the ramp and away from the bridge. The tires made a hiss through the wet pavement, as though to hush her.

"Mr. Tarkenton thought you might want to rest after your flight, so he told me to take you straight to the hotel," the driver was saying now. "It's a suite. He's made lunch reservations at the Rainbow Room. Oh, what a view! You'll love it."

"That sounds very nice."

"If you don't like that, just let me know. I mean, if you'd rather not meet with him till dinner, or if you want to hold out till tomorrow . . ."

"It's fine," she insisted. And, "Can I smoke?" She was already reaching into her nylon bag. She felt a sudden, unreasonable need to see the glitter of burning paper.

"Sure. Everyone in New York smokes."

"I don't . . . not usually," she said, dragging out her disposable lighter. "Not anymore. But every once in a while . . ."

She put the end of the cigarette into the flame and kept it there till the paper turned scarlet. She drew in some smoke. After so many months off the nicotine, it burned her lungs. She coughed a little, withdrew the cigarette from her lips and eyed the end.

The driver turned right as the wide street vanished into smaller tributaries. "We're passing by city hall and the civic center here," he said, as they made their way past majestic stone buildings made lean and tall by linear Doric columns, needle-sharp turrets, and high arches. As Whitman had suggested, or perhaps predicted, every structure seemed to soar upward.

"On the other side, back there, is the Woolworth Building, which was once New York's tallest building, and also St. Paul's Chapel, the oldest church in New York."

The reaching white government buildings were now turning into smaller brick boxes.

"If you want a tour guide," the driver said, bringing her back, "just ask for me. I'm Oliver. I've lived here all my life. I use to work as a stagehand before the Pandemic. Now I work for Pandora."

Pandora Corporation. The name was a joke. One of Varouna's colleagues had explained it to her and she rather liked it. In that name she saw an admirable acceptance of the inherent angles and sharp edges of the virus's legacy. Another source had recently informed her that, originally, Pandora had been a life-giving goddess who poured forth gifts from a honey pot, not an "Eve" who released evils from a box.

That seemed apt, too.

"Up and ahead is the Empire State Building," Oliver told her.

She tossed the cigarette out the window and turned her attention forward, to Manhattan. The car moved in among the skyscrapers just as raindrops began to fall in earnest. But a final beam of raw, yellow sunlight hit the skyscraper windows, row upon row upon row of them, causing them to flicker like a million candles.

Fugue state caught Varouna again and she saw the funeral fires that had burned during the Pandemic, saw the burning ends of the countless candles that floated upon the Ganges, carrying their messages to God.

She must, she thought, rubbing at her eyes, be very tired. She didn't usually fall into such images so easily. The scientists in Paris did find it intriguing that her images came in threes rather than singular, as seemed to be common.

Varouna gazed out to find herself surrounded by a honeycomb of windows, yellow taxis buzzing past like bees. The people flowed down the sidewalks in countertime to the cars, honey-slow in the rain.

Following the Pandemic, metropolises had felt leeched of their occupants, humanity thinned, like rare air high up in the mountains; once so much, now suddenly not enough. But three years ago, the migrations had begun. Peter Pans, survivors left with an insatiable need to circle the Earth, came and went from cities such as this, thickening its anemic bloodstream. Most of them eventually settled in the cities, nesting in the tall buildings where they could live nearer the sky, forming strange new communities. But there were still plenty of migrants, easy to spot, even here in New York: packs on their backs, well-worn boots on their feet, lean, hungry bodies to match their hungry eyes.

The Peter Pan effect, Varouna mused, could be traced to brains where the virus had affected D4 dopamine receptors— or so she and her fellow researchers had theorized.

For just a moment, that gave her pause and brought a smile of wonder and confidence to her lips. That she should know such things!

"Here we are! The Pandora Hotel." Oliver pulled the Mercedes up into the curve before a white-gold building nestled snugly amid its tall, steel and glass siblings. Arched glass doors with small marble balconies were paired to either side of the building's elegant moldings and masonry, and a crown of pinnacled chimneys and fluted gray domes marked its roof.

"The Pandora Hotel?" she echoed.

"Yep." Oliver parked the car and smiled back at her. "We own this place. A good many of our scientists live here. It's like a very pricey, very brainy college dorm. You'll love it."

A doorman in a red uniform and gloves crossed over to the car, umbrella ready, as Oliver opened his own door into the rain. "I'll take care of it," Oliver said to him, coming around and unfolding his own umbrella. "Four bags in the trunk," he added, handing over the key. And then he opened Varouna's door for her and held out a white hand to her. She saw the raindrops falling in a curve around his umbrella, saw his shoes, saw the shiny, wet-sand sidewalk and the people making their way up and down it and, beyond that, the glass doorway into the hotel.

A new world.

"Dr. Premjad?" Oliver peered down into the car, his faded blue eyes solicitous.

She experienced and fought a moment of reluctance. A step outside into that wet world was, she realized, a step into the future. A step into this new Varanasi, be it false or true.

Oliver's look became concerned. "Is something wrong?"

"No," she said. Then, firmly, "No, thank you. I'm fine."

Carefully lifting the skirts of the sari she wore beneath her heavy coat, Varouna accepted his hand and rose out of the car into the wet, cold, concrete world.

Around her, the skyscrapers towered, trying to reach the sky. Crowds of people rushed on their way, neon signs flashed on and off, and cars put on their headlights, which glowed like stars through the rain.

A new Varanasi.

Chapter 14

Earth was trapped between the steps of this bizarre new dance and a need to set its feet back into comfortable old patterns. Of course, those learning the new steps looked a lot like those desperate souls during the Black Death who danced from one village to another until they collapsed of exhaustion. We wanted to escape our despair too, but not if it meant giving into a dance of madness.

—The 10% Future

GORDON DIDN'T LIKE BEING CAUGHT OVER A BARREL.

It was nearly eight-thirty in the morning, some two hours since he'd been called out to the Brooklyn Bridge and fifteen minutes since he'd walked into the Night Owl Diner. The thing was, Tarkenton, despite asking for this meeting, could easily leave him in the lurch. They both knew Gordon had no legal right to interfere with Pandora when it came to climbers, and he and Kyle weren't family anyway, even if he was listed as next of kin on Kyle's hospital form.

If he wanted Kyle back, he would have to talk to Tarkenton; but Tarkenton didn't have to talk with him at all.

So here he was, scratching at the stubble on his chin, waiting for his coffee to come, watching customers butter their bagels and shake salt on their eggs. Waiting.

He felt locked away, tucked as he was into one of the Night Owl's private booths with its malachite vinyl benches and rose Formica tabletop. The noisy, busy deli smelled of breakfast, toast and bacon and warm maple syrup, and his stomach growled angrily at him. He ignored it. Eating would just make him sleepy and he wanted to be very alert. He stared past the chrome bar with its worn stools and small crowded tables at the wide square windows.

Outside, the rain pounded down on unfortunate pedestrians, several holding papers over their heads or lifting their coats up high to protect their hair. They dashed about as if frightened, dodging cars and the splash of puddles.

No sign of Tarkenton.

God. He'd lost already. Anyone who let himself be put on the suppliant side of the table was dead. And wasn't that always where he ended up when all was said and done?

"Isn't this better than arguing out in the rain?" Judas Tarkenton appeared unexpectedly from the side and slid in to sit across from him.

Scared the shit out of him, coming around behind him like that. He noticed, belatedly (as was intended?), the bodyguard with black skin and hard eyes: Tarkenton's shadow. The man was probably a rocket scientist, Gordon thought sourly, never mind the mean-street glares he threw, as if he was sure Demme wanted to kill his boss.

The bodyguard nodded to Tarkenton, slipped off his raincoat, and settled at the bar.

Tarkenton himself stretched out his legs beneath the table. "Ever been here before, Captain?"

"No, I've never been here before." Gordon was still angry and shaken. Very few people could sneak up on him like that, and he didn't like it, not one bit.

A nostalgic smile. "It's an old haunt from my college days."

"How nice. I suppose it's also a Pandora hangout? Everyone in here works for you?"

"Not all, no." Tarkenton relaxed back, arms across the back of the vinyl cushions. Fairly tall, with a healthy build, he looked casual and boyish in jeans and a foggy blue letterman jacket with cream sleeves and cardinal accents. Embossed over the heart where a school letter might be was the New York Rangers distinctive logo: the proud, defiant head of the Statue of Liberty, apple red piping outlining the sharp points of her crown.

"There are still a few people in Manhattan who aren't on our payroll." He offered Gordon a faint smile, as if trying to be friends. What struck the detective, seeing that smile, was how very *harmless* the man seemed. He had a toasted complexion and lose curls of earthy hair which he kept throwing back from his forehead like a little kid. Hazel eyes with just a hint of silver quietly mixed the two contrasting browns.

In an old movie, Gordon thought, Tarkenton would be the guy who wore his school colors and a letter on his jacket. The good, upstanding best friend to the hero, the sort, Lord help them, who said words like "Gosh," and "Gee whiz," and, with all sincerity and respect, "Yes, ma'am." The one who fell for his best friend's sister and eventually got up the nerve to ask her to the dance.

Yet, as dead-on as that description was, it was also utterly and completely wrong. The distance in the man's expression, as if he were doing calculations in his head, shot everything else to hell. Tarkenton didn't seem dreamy, as an old-fashioned college kid might, nor distracted. No. He had the look of a time tripper, someone who lived an hour ahead of the rest of the world, sometimes days or even years in the future. Maybe even a lifetime. Gordon knew the kind all too well; for someone like him, who was always lagging behind, they were the scariest people on earth.

And just how far ahead, he wondered now, was Judas Tarkenton?

Coffee came for both of them, delivered by an over-worked waitress in an archaic pink uniform and bib apron. Only her white walking shoes were modern.

"What can I get you?" she asked.

"I'll stick with coffee for now," Gordon said when Tarkenton deferred to him. Damned if he had given up on having breakfast with Scotty. However long this impromptu meeting took, he was going back to make pancakes for his son, he didn't care if it wasn't till midnight!

"Sure?" Tarkenton asked, then, ironically, "Breakfast is on me."

"I'm sure."

Tarkenton glanced up at the waitress. "Three eggs scrambled with lox, hash browns, and rye toast," he ordered, without a glance at the menu. "And can I get a side of cream cheese and strawberry jam?"

"I'll have that right up for you," the waitress said, and that's when Gordon did a double take. He found himself doing that a lot these days. He'd take for granted the man at the newsstand who sold him his paper or the retailer at Fulton Fish Market folding his sea bass in a sheet of butcher paper, but then they'd say something and that's when he'd notice. A foreigner himself, he wasn't sure what gave it away, but it was as if Manhattan had a whole new population, and in a sense it did. Most Pans shied from the cities, heading out in search of clear night skies and a quiet that could match the soundless ring-system in their heads. Farm communities and small towns were experiencing an unprecedented renaissance, and cities were emptying. But immigrants still came to Manhattan, this city that never slept, with suitcases in hand or packs on their shoulders, or just the clothes on their back. What they were after Gordon couldn't say, but the look in their eyes was enough to give him nightmares. They reminded him all too vividly of the teenage girls he'd known who'd been found cut-

ting their arms with razors or burning themselves with cigarette butts.

They reminded him, also, of Kyle, desperate, strange.
And when these new New Yorkers spoke, he heard that desperation in their voices, the tone of a lost child softly and pathetically asking for its mother.

"You know, some people think the Pandemic was the best
thing that ever happened to us," Tarkenton suddenly said, his
eyes watching as the waitress crossed back to the kitchen.

Gordon frowned. Had Tarkenton seen it too? "Yeah. Real
sick fucks they are, too," he muttered, blowing on his coffee.

"Yeah, well, these sick fucks have this theory that our
hyper-media age fragmented us, like fine crystal. Too many
choices, too many things we were supposed to be. The Pandemic forced us to get back to the visceral level, brought us
back down to earth."

"Is that so." The captain could hear the drollness of his
voice, the edge. "And what else do 'they' say?"

"The sick fucks?" Tarkenton needled. "They say that the
Pandemic gave us a reality we'd lost. Life and death was a
game we played on video monitors. The Pandemic forced us
to face both."

"However did we manage without the Pandemic! Tell
me, do you use these excuses to get to sleep at night?"

The smile remained, but the glimmer in Tarkenton's eyes
vanished. The face suddenly looked very cold and distant.
"This isn't about excuses, it's about understanding."

"Understanding, huh? Do you know what my first as-
signment was when I joined the patrol? I had to negotiate a
hostage situation. Some idiot New Yorker with a gun had
taken over the Lexington Avenue platform. Whenever someone came through the turnstile, he added them to his collection of hostages. Want to know why? Because he missed
riding nose to nose with strangers. There weren't enough people anymore, he told me. So he'd decided to keep people from
getting on the subway until he had enough to make for a

sardine-tight ride, like before the Pandemic. At least, that's what he said before he put the gun in his mouth and shot his head off. And this was a Pan, not a Tenor. If you don't understand what drove him to do that, what's *really* underneath this alien weirdness, then you're stone blind."

"I've seen it, Captain," Tarkenton said softly. "And my share of suicides and drug overdoses. What do you think Pandora's trying to prevent? Human life isn't so cheap that we can afford more deaths."

"Yeah, well you're going to have them if you believe that bullshit about the Pandemic being a good thing. And I'll tell you this, working on that damn starbridge isn't going to lessen the trauma."

"That's a real helpful attitude, Demme."

"Fuck you, Tarkenton. You've got some nerve talking about attitude! Tell me, do you feel any grief at all for the dead?"

"That's not any of your goddamn business, is it?"

"It is when you take away a friend of mine. There are rumors, you know, that say you stole your fortune out of the hands of a little girl—"

"Demme." The voice that interrupted was very soft, hardly audible over the clatter of dishes and voices. "*Don't* go there. I really, *really* want to think well of you."

Gordon wasn't sure whether the blood left his face from fury or shame. "I'm a cop, Mr. Tarkenton. I do what I have to do to get the job done, and a good thing, too."

The waitress, fortunately, chose that moment to reappear, an oval platter in one hand, a glass carafe of coffee in the other. She slid the plate in front of Tarkenton and poured more coffee for Gordon. And then she was gone.

Tarkenton reached for the ketchup. "We all do what we have to, Captain. Did you know," he suddenly asked, "that the Kasarans parent in trios?"

Gordon frowned. What the fuck?

"The female lays the eggs," Tarkenton went on, digging

into his breakfast. "After both males have fertilized them, the eggs are set under the leaves of one of them. The trio can only handle the number of hatchlings produced by one female, you see, which is why only one male carries at any given time—"

"What the fuck are you talking about? What has this to do with anything?"

"Just listen," the Pandora man urged with a faint smile. "You see, there are no predators in the ring, but there is danger from rocks, electricity, and other debris. That's why the aliens have forward eyes"—Tarkenton touched two fingers under his own eyes—"unheard of in a nonpredator. But then they also have secondary, infrared optics down their sides, necessary given that the shadows cast by debris are completely black."

"I don't know what you're getting at, but I've seen the pictures and watched the science stories—"

"The mates stay on either side of the carrier, protecting him, until the eggs hatch."

"All of which has nothing to do with my deputy." Gordon took a last sip of his lukewarm coffee. "You're wasting my time. I think maybe I'll make a Sunday call to the mayor. He might be interested to hear what I have to say about Pandora's kidnapping practices." He began to rise.

Tarkenton reached across and grabbed his arm, keeping him in his seat. "Have you looked around the diner, Captain?"

He was angry, almost out of patience, but he took a quick, professional scan of the place. Customers huddled together under the cream-colored lamps pouring syrup on their waffles and cream into their coffee, pushing aside dirty plates. Their conversations were intense and animated, and at almost every table there were papers spread between the plates of poached eggs and ham, sometimes napkins, sometimes computer pads. Diagrams of the aliens and sketches of strange plants. Some of the papers had formulas or maps or chemical compounds on them.

One balding man was waving a slice of bacon and saying,

"No . . . no, listen! The scuttlebugs suck down copper sulfate—"

And, "I'm trying to re-create one of their mineral gardens," a pregnant woman was saying as she cut into her poached eggs, slicing them almost obsessively into tiny pieces. "But given our fucking gravity well, it's just not working . . ."

Crazy! He thought. Whole world had turned into a bunch of mad scientists! Was that what Tarkenton wanted him to see? That wasn't anything new.

He started to turn back, determined to leave, when it suddenly caught his eye, hitting so hard he forgot what he was about.

At almost every table in the diner, the people were clustered in threesomes. Some of the square tables had been doubled up so that six or nine could gather together. But there were no couples. In fact, Tarkenton and himself stood out for that very reason.

Goddamn. He clenched his jaw.

Goddamn.

Tarkenton had released him and was calmly chewing down a mouthful of hash browns. The fucker.

"There's four over there." Gordon pointed.

"How much you want to wager they're Tenors?"

Gordon licked his suddenly dry lips. "The trio's aren't grouped two males and a female."

"Brilliant observation. No wonder you're a police captain."

"Listen, Tarkenton, you can just shove this all up—"

"We humans don't have an evolutionary mandate to partner up in trios," Tarkenton said, lips pulling back into something like a smile. But it wasn't. It was charged with anger and irony. "Most Pans group themselves in threes without knowing why. And *that,* Captain, is the reason that the law gave your deputy to Pandora and not to a psychiatric hospital."

"Because people are grouping in threes?"

"You're being deliberately obtuse. The virus isn't just information or bad dreams, it's a residue, an aftertaste. It can make you want to do things you don't understand."

"Like build a starbridge?"

But Tarkenton shook his head at that. "Especially if you didn't get the whole message . . . which none of us with a working immune system did."

He pointedly didn't mention those who'd been lacking an immune system. He didn't have to. Gordon had seen the special reports; those without had survived just fine, but they'd never resurfaced from their hallucinations. With glazed expressions, they'd gone on dreaming until they died.

The experts couldn't say if the virus, left unchecked, had taken over, or if such people were so happy with what they saw that they just refused to resurface.

"The whole idea of Pandora," Tarkenton went on, finally pushing his soiled plate away, "is to compile information, to get the whole message so that we can know why your deputy did what he did. And how to help him."

"So the sick should cure the sick, is that it?"

"We're not sick. But if you convinced your deputy that he was, and that he could cure himself if he only wanted to, then it's no wonder he ended up on top of Brooklyn-fucking-Bridge."

Gordon felt a dark flush infuse his face and focused on his cold coffee. He wanted to toss it in Tarkenton's face and tell the man to fuck himself.

But, God, if the man was right, if Kyle had looked to him for help when he should have gone to Pandora instead, if he had kept Kyle away from Pandora because of his own prejudice against it . . .

"You talk about understanding . . . do you know what I see, Mr. Tarkenton, when I look at those damn double circles you Pans insist on drawing, over and over again?"

"The stargate?"

"Yes. That goddamn gate. Whenever I see it, I feel like a

survivor of Hiroshima looking at an atom bomb. Like a survivor of the Holocaust looking at a swastika. And yet you Pans insist on shoving it down our throats. It's not *your* idea, you know, it's *theirs*."

"Ours too, Captain."

"You can't *know* that. Not until you finish it and poke your head through and maybe get it bitten off."

Brows rising, Tarkenton lightened his coffee with a dash of milk. "I bet you're a hypochondriac too. Always thinking of what can go wrong."

He felt his face go flush then. "Something wrong with that?"

"No. It just isn't how I do things. When I see something on the horizon, I run for it, fast as I can, before it disappears. I'm running for this at full tilt," he added fiercely. "The idea might be alien, but the gate we design will be *ours,* as human as any human construct can be."

"Does that mean you forgive them?"

Tarkenton's hazel eyes slid away. "Fuck no. If we Pans could do that, we wouldn't be jumping off bridges."

"I'm not sure if that makes me feel better or not."

"Since you asked, I'll tell you; yeah, there are times when I think, *'They killed my best friends, caused the death of billions, why should I want to meet them? Why shouldn't I want revenge?'* But then I also think, maybe, if I meet them, maybe I can put all that shit behind me. Or not. Thing is, I'm not going to let my grief cheat the world out of what this bridge can bring it."

"All right, so now I understand you. Now it's time you understood me," Gordon pushed on. "I don't care whether you're holding Kyle for his own good or yours, I don't even care if it's the best thing that ever happened to him. I want him back, *tonight.*"

"There is a twenty-four-hour observation period written into the law, Captain Demme, you know that."

Gordon met the other man's eyes. He was not going to

back down on this. "You say you want to help Kyle? Then send him home. He needs his family."

That seemed to move Tarkenton.

"My little boy will be worried." The detective got to his feet, feeling suddenly awkward and uncomfortable. He took down his coat, shrugging it on. "I need to get back to him and explain what happened to Kyle, if I can."

"As the father of a little girl, I sympathize. Please tell your son we're taking good care of Kyle. The best. No bullshit."

"Yeah. . . . So," he added with an awkward gesture to Tarkenton's jacket, "Long time Maple Leaf fan, myself."

A smile came to the man's face, and for a moment, he was there, all there and really seeing Gordon.

"They need a new coach."

"Yeah," Gordon said, buttoning up his coat. "The one they've got's for shit. Mr. Tarkenton—"

"You might as well call me Jude, Captain."

"Mr. Tarkenton," he insisted. "Kyle comes home tonight. That's not negotiable. And if you don't want trouble with New York Patrol, make sure Pandora keeps its distance."

He waited a moment, wondering if Tarkenton would call his bluff. He could almost feel the bodyguard, still at the bar, watching him, waiting for a single suspicious move.

But the man merely opened his hands upon the table, an odd move, very like a Pan. Pans used their hands like that a lot, in place of the leaves they did not own.

Kyle used his hands like that too.

So, Gordon thought, he's just proven to me that I *don't* understand. Not at all.

"He'll be back tonight," Tarkenton said with a nod. And Gordon, disturbed and dismissed, buttoned up his jacket against the rain and hurried out.

It was long past time to go home.

Chapter 15

*And we, shoulder to shoulder, stood. Restless pilgrim souls,
impatiently waiting for that strangest train.*

*Ascendant beauty, climbing out of that other Manhattan
on the Hudson.*

*Protean, underwater reflected. Subastral avenues of wonder
giving way to concrete constellations.*

Fifth Avenue. Fred Astaire. Broadway lights fading.

Monroe and Lennon raised hands against the glare.

*And we rose. Embracing that too, too starry night, and
sang a passing lullaby to the children of Brooklyn's older
bridge.*

—Excerpt from The Cross Walk, *by E. E. Ralston*

THE OFFICES OF PANDORA CORP. IN SoHo WERE
nothing like what Kyle imagined. Heaven knew he'd dropped
off enough pathetic, suicidal bastards in the lobby of that
brick and iron building, but this was the first time he'd been
led inside, past broad, curving stairs to a small, iron-gated elevator.

There were bikes parked everywhere, along the walls, up on the staircase, near the elevator, bikes and mopeds. He found that strange. He'd never thought of shrinks as riding bikes. Of course, there were other scientists in the building, engineers and biologists, the best minds in the world.

And there were messed-up bastards like him.

Jesus! How could he have done it? Gone climbing, *in spring,* and up on *the Brooklyn Bridge,* no less, like every other crazy . . . crazy Pan.

His escort held the gate for him, and he stepped quietly into the elevator. "Your blood sugar's probably for shit," the man said, as the cab lurched up toward the fourth floor. Compact and muscular, the man had thinning, corn silk hair combed neatly over a rounded forehead, pale eyes, and a thin, almost lipless mouth. He was dressed, like most of those who worked for Pandora, in a black suit and tie, the only difference being that the shirt was vibrant cobalt, the tie shiny and metallic.

"Fuck you," Kyle muttered. He'd decided early on that there was no point in fighting the man from Pandora. But fuck all if he was going to be polite about it.

"Here we are." The elevator had come to a stop. The man pulled open the gate. "Come," he invited, "I'll get you something." And he stepped out.

Pandora man was gonna just leave him like that? Kyle frowned and for a split second considered shoving the gate closed and pushing the down button.

But then he felt the shakes coming on and leaned his head into his hands. The memories were back like a bad taste, the Brooklyn Bridge (God! Getting the key to the gate had been too easy, he was going to have to talk to the Captain about that . . .), his failed suicide attempt and Captain Demme coming up after him.

"Ah, no," he moaned aloud. "Ah, Jesus no. He's never going to forgive me."

Pissed it all away, he thought. Everything he'd worked

for, the patrol, trust, respectability, acceptance. Even getting a new family and doing right by them this time, not like with his mom and half brothers.

And he'd pissed it all away because he couldn't keep those damn alien feelings and thoughts under wraps. God. He'd done it this time. Done it to himself and there was no escaping it. He'd fucked himself over but good.

He dropped his hands and released a heavy breath. Whatever Pandora planned to do with him, he deserved it. He stepped out of the elevator.

And found himself in a loft, cream, with sleek wood floors and paneled windows topped with round industrial fans. Not what he expected. Massive marble pillars held up the high ceiling with its pattern of water pipes and electrical cords. Along one wall were several old coatracks overflowing with dripping coats, hats, and umbrellas, and, under a bench, rows of rain boots and not a few soaked tennis shoes.

Someone's computer was playing an old vocal of the pop tune "I Only Want to Be with You." It filled the loft, rising above the murmur of voices.

But Kyle hardly noticed the rest of the room or the people in it. His attention was glued to the photos, hundreds upon hundreds of photos, tacked to the walls above the old radiators. In each and every one was an artistic depiction of the tori, the aliens' double-ringed stargate. Snapshots of the double rings drawn in colored chalk on the floor of a school basketball court and graffitied over other graffiti on a tenement wall. Artistic black-and-white photos of ice blocks carved to resemble the twin circles. A banner marked with quick, stylized strokes, hanging from the steel remnants of an old ell.

This last he recognized as Pandora's all too familiar logo.

Kyle swallowed in a throat gone dead dry. He had seen similar works, of course, on park benches, in public toilets, marking manholes and fire hydrants. They were so common, everyone just took them for granted, another form of urban scrawl. But seeing them like this, one after another, Kyle realized that no matter how abstract, the paintings, drawings, and sculptures captured the essence of the tori as no computerized re-creation could. And they exposed a yearning, a screaming need in the artist to build an actual bridge.

"It's hard to say what instincts humans have," a woman suddenly said, as if reading his mind. He spun around and almost slammed back into the wall, breath lost. His heart was pounding again, hard, as it had been atop the bridge. Not fear, but a desire fiercer than any he'd ever known.

"Need to migrate or defend our territory." The woman was nibbling on a piece of toast. Thin and middle-aged, she wore a black knit dress that made her face look pasty. She had short, golden brown hair, and hazel eyes that examined him as if he were some strange sculpture.

"Investigate what we don't understand . . . that sort of thing. You look like you should sit down," she added, waving to a desk.

Kyle noticed the rest of the loft then, the desks topped with flat multimedia screens, the piles of books and papers. There was a familiar hum to it all, that squad room feel Kyle had come to rely on, the clicking of keys, the warmth of voices.

The place smelled of hot coffee and hot cereal zapped in the microwave; in addition to a restaurant-size sink and an industrial-size refrigerator, the kitchen also had, he noticed, a huge, state-of-the-art monitor. On it was a familiar sight: live feed from the moon, where robots mined for ore. The kitchen folk seemed to draw inspiration from the huge drills kicking up fine dust, digging and digging for minerals to refine and mold into something that would, eventually, hang in orbit around the Earth.

But what was on the monitor came second to a huge model resting atop a pine trestle table. People in jeans and flannel shirts strolled around it, jotting down notes on the new I-dik pads while, at the edge, two men played a game of chess, hands slapping down to stop and start a timer. The half-constructed wire-and-Popsicle-stick doughnut was, quite clearly, the heart of the operation.

"Don't want to sit?" the woman asked him.

"No," Kyle said, wrapping his arms around himself. He felt suddenly quite shaken.

"I'm Dr. Mavis Battencourt," the woman added, finishing off the crust of her toast. She wiped her hand on her skirt and held it out.

He took it, reluctantly. He didn't want it getting back to Captain Demme that he'd been rude, not after the captain had worked so hard to civilize him. "So," he said, dropping the hand fast as he could, "are you the one who's going to fix my head?"

"Fix it? Fuck no." She laughed. "I'm an engineer. Last thing I want to do is fix it."

Engineer? "Then what the fuck are you doing here? Or what am I doing here?"

"Here you go!" The Pandora man was back with a glass and a pitcher of orange juice. He'd slipped off his jacket and rolled up his sleeves. On his exposed white skin Kyle saw stunning tattoos of silvery-sage trifoils, like those on the aliens. A good many Pans had such designs tattooed on them somewhere, a sick attempt, Captain Demme had once remarked, to look like the Kasarans. There were even some who'd gone through plastic surgery to get Kasaran-style ridges down their back.

"Why don't we take that desk there?" the man invited.

"Fuck you," Kyle murmured. "This isn't a shrink's office!"

"Catches on fast, doesn't he?" Dr. Battencourt smiled and hitched a hip up on the desk.

"Sit," the man urged, filling the glass. "And drink. It will make you feel better."

Kyle sunk into a chair, his weak knees betraying him, but peevishly refused the juice.

"It will help stop the shaking," the man urged again, and set the glass temptingly before Kyle.

Swearing, Kyle drained the juice. It tasted wonderful and it did quiet the tremors in his bones.

"There? That is better, jah? I am Sven Johannson. From Hamburg." He offered his hand.

"Deputy Kyle," Kyle responded, refusing the hand. "Can I go home now?" He winced as he said it. Who was he kidding? Even if they let him go, he wasn't going back to live with the captain, or work on the Patrol, not after this morning. No one would ever trust him again. He probably wouldn't be allowed to see Scotty. The captain wouldn't want to expose his son to a crazy, suicidal Pan.

That hurt, that kind of thought. It hurt worse than the ache in his ribs.

"You already know the answer to that, Patrolman," Sven said.

"It's a fucking hand job is what it is; Tarkenton set this up so he could pump crazy Pans before they off themselves." That was the captain's talking. Where climbers ought to go was one of the few partisan bones of contention in the Manhattan Patrol, with Loretta defending the Institute and the captain insisting that crazy Pans belonged in the hospital like all other suicides. "Just because Judas handed over thirty pieces of silver to the new politicos . . ."

"That is not kind," Sven said gently, but with an underlying firmness that had not been there before.

"Fuck you."

The man set fingers on the table and leaned forward, all seriousness, and Kyle braced himself for a fight. He was that wired that he fell back into old patterns, gave into street instincts he'd thought long dead. "You know as well as I do," Sven said with surprising gentleness, "that when a Pan attempts suicide, it is not for the usual human reasons."

"Yeah, sure, whatever," Kyle snarled, and this time he turned on Dr. Battencourt, still listening with arms crossed.

"So what the fuck am I doing in engineering? Why aren't I in psych?"

"Shrinks can't help you." Another man appeared; he was tall and balding, with pecan brown skin and sharp, penetrating eyes. He was one of the chess players and perhaps the only one outside of Kyle wearing a conventional suit, a simple gray one with a narrow tie and a very white shirt. It made him look like an old jazz musician.

A pair of long brown fingers set a photo across the desk, another drawing of the aliens' tori, white paint splashed on old stone—but it didn't look right.

It took a moment for Kyle to realize it was *his*. The painting he had so crudely done atop the Brooklyn Bridge.

"My name's Walsh, Dr. Summerset Walsh," the man said. "Dr. Battencourt and I run this section. She's engineering, I'm physics. The reason you're here, instead of psych, is so that we can ask you, did you know what you were doing? I warn you," the man added, "it's a very serious question."

Kyle suddenly felt it was, and so he took a moment to look, really look, at what he'd done. He was taken aback by the rough white image, as if seeing it for the first time. It was almost as if he'd bled it out of his mind like a poison, and yet the shape captured him, rang through him like a bell.

He had tried so hard, he thought, God, how he'd tried to bring himself back from the edge so that he wouldn't end up here. Heaven knew the captain could have, should have given him to Pandora when he found him in that cell. Instead, Demme had taken a long shot, bet and gambled that Kyle could redeem himself. But somewhere along the way, he hadn't tried hard enough. And this was the result.

Fucked over the captain but good. Failed him and everyone else. And if the picture weren't proof enough of that, his feelings now were.

"All I see is a crazy drawing done by a crazy Pan," he said dully.

"It only has one ring."

"That's because the double rings don't work," he said; it hardly seemed to matter anymore.

"But your single ring does?"

"Yes," he asserted. What could they do? Call him a liar? "Don't ask me why, but it does."

"Son of a bitch," murmured Dr. Battencourt, rubbing at her chin.

Dr. Walsh ran a hand over his balding scalp. "Yeah."

And what was this? Kyle frowned, found himself rising to his feet. "You're not gonna tell me I'm *right,* are you?"

Dr. Walsh took a thoughtful gander at the doughnut-shaped model. "Tarkenton thought of it right off. The double rings rely on a gas giant for the tremendous electricity which powers them. It's too hard for us to tap into our system's gas giants in the same way, so we need to use different physics to get the same result. If you get my drift."

"I don't even understand what you're saying," Kyle said plaintively, but he found his eyes wandering to the model, and fought off an uncontrollable urge to run over to it, to start adding wiring.

"Oh, you understand us," Dr. Battencourt accused. "You're a natural engineer. Which is why you've been going quietly nuts. The virus gave that brain of yours all sorts of starbridge information, like quantum physics, and you used it to build a better mousetrap. Unfortunately, you hadn't the vocabulary to explain what you were doing or why."

He couldn't say anything for a moment. That he might not be crazy, that these people might be able to explain it all to him, was almost too much to hope for.

"What . . ." he tried, licked dried lips and touched on the photo of his diagram. "What was I trying to say?"

Dr. Battencourt glanced impatiently at Sven, who was currently reading something on his I-dik pad. "How long have we got?"

"Herr Tarkenton just said"—he tapped the pad—"he goes home tonight."

"Bullshit," Kyle said.

"Bullshit, he says," she grumbled. "Little shits think they know everything."

"It's *bullshit*! Pandora never lets anyone go. 'Sides, where the fuck would I go?"

"Captain Demme was most adamant about getting you back." Sven shrugged.

Kyle flinched. God. He hadn't thought they'd hit him like that. "Don't fuck with me. Do whatever else you want, but *don't* fuck with me!"

Sven's fair brows went up. For the first time, something like dismay flickered across his solid features.

But it was Walsh who said, with kindness, "We wouldn't do any such thing."

"The captain really wants me back?"

"Jah." Sven's chill blue eyes were almost sympathetic. "Jah. Most definitely." He waved a hand over the pad. "Your captain was most insistent."

Kyle's heart both lightened and sunk. He could go home. But he wasn't sure all of a sudden that he wanted to. And he had this terrible fear that, with the captain, it would come to a choice. One side of the river or the other, Pandora or Patrol.

God. What was he going to do?

"You can stay longer, of course," Walsh said, thoughtfully, mildly, "if you want to."

Patrol or Pandora. He caught his breath. "No . . . I don't want anything else, thanks."

"Yes you do, Kyle," Battencourt said knowingly. "You want to build the bridge. Just like the rest of us."

It was all happening far too fast, Kyle thought. He caught in a breath, glanced over at the bicycles. He couldn't be just another crazy Pan. He was a deputy on the police force.

But if he didn't stay here . . . The images had been waiting in the alleyways of his mind, ready to ambush him, to beat him down. If he denied them, ran away from them, what might they do next time? Crack his mind wide open?

"Could I . . . go home and come back?" he ventured.

"Oh, Kyle." Dr. Battencourt's cynical face broke into a smile that she happily shared with Dr. Walsh and Sven. "We were hoping you might ask that."

Chapter 16

There are still those who righteously use the change in the status of third world women to excuse the Pandemic. The very high mortality rate of women in such countries due to pregnancy or bad health, caused a deficit of females. In the short term, this resulted in young girls being forced to serve several men, and a return to bride snatching.

But, in the long term, when such brutal practices caused the death of even more women, misogynistic countries finally changed their ways. Cultures that had once hated and oppressed women became models of equality.

But those billions of murdered women were not martyrs for a cause. They didn't die so that their granddaughters might one day live a better life. And therein lies the sophistry of such assertions. Any argument that focuses on the positive events brought about by the Pandemic is a poor, Pollyanna excuse that cheapens the deaths of so many people by making those deaths a commodity, the price paid for a future not one of us ever asked for or wanted.

—The 10% Future

H E'D BEEN EXPECTING A HEAVY, OLDER WOMAN, AN Indira Gandhi type, not this young woman with skin brown as cloves, her hair hanging girlishly down her back in a long braid. She had eyes the color of toasted almonds. From the right angle, they had a knowing, Mona Lisa glint. Whenever they glanced his way, Jude found himself strangely nervous, as if he were back in college and wanting to make a good impression.

Which made him question whether taking her to the deco splendor of the Rainbow Room for lunch had been the right move, why he now hastened to help her on with her coat as they got ready to leave. She was wearing an apricot sari bordered and embroidered with gold. He couldn't help but notice the neat figure it accented.

He took them down the elevator and out into the hazy sunlight of Rockefeller Center. The rain had let up for the moment, leaving the air smelling fresh, the skyscrapers looking scrubbed.

That pleased Jude. He wanted Dr. Premjad to see his city at its best, polished and grand.

He *had* to talk her into staying.

"Like to take a walk through Central Park?" he asked as they paused to gaze down at the lower plaza with its fountains and rain-soaked flags.

"So long as it isn't a very long walk," she agreed, burying her hands in the pockets of the thick, camel-hair coat.

"We could take the car." He nodded to the street and the double-parked Mercedes. Oliver was at the wheel, ignoring the cabs that honked and swerved around him. Davy and Jackson, Jude's two young bodyguards, had reappeared and were hanging back some dozen steps. Odd to notice them again, they'd been so invisible during lunch.

"No, no." The doctor ventured a shy smile that made her look sweet and girlish. "It's good to stretch my legs, get a breath of fresh air. It keeps the jet lag from catching up."

The rain had stopped, but slate gray clouds still hung threateningly over the sky, allowing only a narrow strip of azure to pierce through and promising one last winter storm of icy rain.

But that didn't stop those who had come to shop at the newly reopened center. There were, Jude noticed, spring styles this year, at long last. Men's suits crisp, the shoulders broad, the creases sharp. Vests and hats were back, drawing attention to the head and chest, the upright form.

For the ladies, the clothing was soft, dresses that clung to female curves and ended with rippling skirts. The form-fitting dresses, along with the popularity of thick, curling hair (pinned up to match men's hats, perhaps?), wide lips, and sparkling rose eyeshadow brought Gibson girls to mind.

Healthy was also in. Bone-thin men and women were too reminiscent of sickness, food shortages, and death. Last month *Vogue* magazine had put out its first issue in nearly five years, and between its covers were robust new models.

Healthy and confident. Yes, that was the new look for both men and women. The survivors had defied death, and after four years of grief and guilt, they wanted permission to feel pride in that, even smugness. Rich fabrics proclaimed this, countering years of practical clothing.

But silk, satin, velvet, and moiré also had a shine to them. They flowed and rippled like the fins on a fish, like the trefoils of the aliens. And then there were the colors. Metallic. Copper, silver, steel, gold, bronze, and rust. *Did anyone else see it?* Jude wondered. The shape of the clothing emphasized the human form, but the colors turned the wearers into metal parts in a machine.

"What is that?" Dr. Premjad was pointing back toward the statue of Prometheus, and Jude caught himself just short of telling her the story of the Titan who had brought fire to mankind.

It didn't take him but a second to realize that she wasn't pointing at the statue.

"It's a mourning wreath," he said shortly. "To honor the dead."

He didn't bother explaining to her that it was the same one that had taken the place of the plaza's Christmas tree that December, in the Year of the Pandemic. No one had ever taken it down, and he doubted anyone ever would. And he didn't tell her that it signaled more than just a city in mourning.

Over the last four years, there had been no New Year's celebrations and no Valentine's Day with hearts in the windows. No flower shops had yet reopened, and almost no candy stores; and what cards there were were old and meaningless.

There *had* been an Ash Wednesday this year, a wintry white day in February with anemic sunlight piercing down from overhead and the citizens of Manhattan moving like the survivors they were, black smudges on many of their foreheads. Pale and distant-eyed as they were, often still gaunt or dazed, they'd looked to Jude like the victims of an execution: the living dead wandering the streets of Manhattan, unaware of the bullet holes that marked their foreheads.

There had been a brave attempt at a St. Patrick's Day parade as well. It had been a small, weak thing compared to what Manhattan was used to, the bare remnants of a marching band, some folk in kelly green, some in dapper top hats or derbies, waving Irish and American flags. The smiles had looked forced, like those of a hysteric, and the eyes glimmered. Jude, watching from the sidelines, couldn't help but think that the parade was somehow celebrating the Irish Famine, the very catastrophe which had brought so many to this shore.

Would the Pandemic someday produce a parade?

And then there'd been Easter. Jude would not have remembered the holiday but that the renewed and reborn *New York Times* ran a full-page cartoon depicting a black Easter egg shaped like the familiar double rings of the aliens. All around the egg were dead children, and below were the words: "The Easter Egg Hunt."

He understood and felt the anger even as it chilled him. That was the paradox of being a Pan. There was no loss of human feelings or sentiments, just a secondary understanding, like X-ray vision or perfect pitch.

That black elliptical cartoon tori had haunted the city throughout this late spring, a cosmic egg that had hatched death instead of life. And everyone was all too aware that no matter the church services, traditional brunches, or new Easter bonnets, nothing could take the place of the missing egg hunt. In this time of flowers and resurrections, there were no children to dye the eggs or hide them for, no one to give baskets of cellophane grass and foil-wrapped candy.

But in people's eyes, that Easter, he had not seen sorrow or despair. Like the cartoon, he'd seen anger and a determination to finally end this perpetual misery.

Not long after, the museums, which had been locked up tight, their paintings and sculptures whisked away by worried curators, cautiously reopened. And Patrons started going out to dinner, to the theaters where actors doggedly put on strange new plays, to nightclubs and the "free love" bars where slow floating dances were in vogue.

And a lot of the women turned up pregnant. A lot. That was a very new and very welcome sight.

A new infection, Jude thought, for a new breed of New Yorker, the new New Yorkers, whose aim was to use the skyscrapers to see the stars.

"Were you born here, Mr. Tarkenton?" Dr. Premjad had the softest of voices and he almost didn't hear her over the crush of taxis clustered around the newly reopened hotels of Central Park South.

"Lower East Side." He smiled wistfully. "Mom was a nurse. Dad fixed subway cars, that is, till Mom and my sister got into this car accident. Died." A shrug. It all seemed very long ago now. "Dad moved us to Jersey. But Manhattan . . . Manhattan's in my blood . . . literally."

"Literally?" she echoed. She looked genuinely intrigued, which encouraged him.

"Mom's side goes back to freed slaves who came to New York in 1781. Some great-great-grandfather of mine, if the story's true, married a Munsee, one of the original Manhattan natives."

"Really? And your father's side?"

"Well, he liked to pretend he was descended from the first Dutch settlers, but, truth to tell, his side arrived off the boats sometime after nineteen hundred and no few of them illegally."

Dr. Premjad laughed lightly; she had a nice laugh.

"I don't know why I'm telling you all this." Jude smiled ruefully. "I'm usually pretty tight-lipped about myself."

"I am too," she said softly, pausing to look out over the pond. "Do you know why I accepted your invitation to come here, Mr. Tarkenton?"

"We offered you a bigger bribe than the Pasteur Institute?"

"No. I came for New York. Manhattan is, for me, the other side of the planet—from India, you see? The hibernation side, as the Kasarans might put it."

"You came here to dream up answers?"

Dr. Premjad kept her dark eyes on the windblown ripples of water. "We all have to take our turns around the wheel. That is why I am here. But I am still uncertain as to why Pandora invited me. I have nothing to contribute to the building of your starbridge."

Jude turned, and almost took her arm to lead her on, then thought better of it. He waited instead for her to join him before leading them down past trees just beginning to bud with new leaves.

"You're responsible for the vaccine," he said, keeping his eyes ahead. His stomach was turning with all the nervousness of a teenager on a first date.

"My name was listed along with thirty-six others credited with that discovery," she protested.

"Excuse me, Dr. Premjad, but that's bullshit. It was generous or maybe just politic of you to share the glory with your colleagues, but they hadn't anything to do with it."

"So I am to blame for the upcoming baby boom?" she asked with that Mona Lisa smile.

"You may not be able to engineer a stargate, but I'm betting you know a lot more about Kasaran chemical engineering than you've let on."

She paused for a moment then, searching through a pocket to bring out a pack of clove cigarettes and a plastic lighter. "I've managed cut down my nicotine addiction," she explained, setting a cigarette between her lips. "But I still have the oral fixation." She snapped on the lighter and held her hand around it to keep it burning. She lit the smoke, slid the lighter back into her pocket, and released an aromatic puff. "Why would you need a Kasaran chemical engineer, Mr. Tarkenton?"

"Couple of reasons. First, because we may need someone to create chemical messages so we can talk to the Kasarans. Chromatics might fail us."

She gave the cigarette a tap, flaking ashes off its burning tip. "True. Kasarans exchange complex thoughts and ideas virally. And your second reason?"

He met her gaze and took in a breath. "My daughter was born with a tail."

"I am not a medical doctor, Mr. Tarkenton. What has a vestigial tail to do with—"

"This wasn't a vestigial tail. A vestigial tail grows in the first year, this tail shrunk and *disappeared*. And vestigial tails don't have any bone or cartilage. This tail was ridged like . . . like . . ."

"I see." Her gaze was distant, the cigarette forgotten, burning between her slender fingers. "Most of the experts," she said softly, and at last, "believe that the infants who survived the Pandemic were genetically immune."

"Fuck them. What do you think?"

A strange gleam came briefly to her eye, and for a moment Jude felt as if he were looking beneath a mask at a completely different woman, a woman who liked being asked such questions.

"*I* don't believe anyone was immune. But we were discussing your daughter?"

No one immune? Jesus. What did she mean by that? "I don't know if there's another like her," he confessed, trying to keep to the subject. "I don't even know if anything unusual happened. But I've been searching for someone to trust on this, and I . . . I hope you'll accept."

The doctor tossed the cigarette down into the dust and crushed it underfoot, leaving behind only wisps of spicy smoke. "I am not a medical doctor," she repeated.

"You might be if we were all Kasarans," Jude said softly, pointedly.

That seemed to strike her. Not shake or disturb her. He'd noticed that about Dr. Varouna Premjad, she had amazing equilibrium.

This time it was she who started them walking down the path, and he doubling his steps to match hers. They passed by benches, tree branches reaching out to form canopies over their heads. And Jude half wished he'd brought Piper with him, despite the hungry, curious stares she got. In her boots and raincoat, she would have danced through the puddles, happy as a lark. To see her crouching to watch a snail make its way across the road or picking tiny daisies to hand to him was to regain a little of what he hadn't known he'd lost.

"Do they follow you everywhere?" Dr. Premjad suddenly asked, glancing back to where Davy and Jackson kept pace, conspicuous in their black raincoats. Jackson, once a martial arts teacher, was a solid man with broad serious features and skin brown as a river stone; Davy, who had been in the Israeli Army, was pale, with curling black hair and sharp brown eyes.

"Everywhere," Jude said ruefully. "My bevy of aides decided I needed bodyguards, and these two were the lucky lotto winners."

"Do you need them?"

He shrugged. "There have been threats," he said, which made him remember his conversation with Demme. He'd fucked up, fallen into condescension though he knew, he *knew* Demme didn't deserve it.

He'd have to do better next time; the Pans couldn't afford to estrange the Tenors, even if they were the minority.

They reached Heckscher playground, where a dog lay in the mud, chewing on a dirty Frisbee. The animal paused to stare at them, as if it hadn't been expecting guests. It was bone-thin and missing fur at its joints, a black dog with a hint of shepherd markings on its face and a fluffy, curving tail. As if coming to a decision, it pushed up, Frisbee in mouth, and eagerly ran up to them. It stopped, however, a few feet away, as if it had learned that not all humans were welcoming. It put down the Frisbee and sat expectantly.

"It wants to play," Dr. Premjad observed, pausing.

"Mr. Tarkenton," Jackson arrived, quickly and efficiently. The bodyguard had his hand in his pocket; if he felt there was just cause, he would shoot the animal.

"I don't think we need to worry," Jude said, but Jackson stayed where he was.

"Is it dangerous?" the doctor asked.

"Maybe. A lot of dogs were just let out to fend for themselves during the Pandemic—those that weren't eaten during the food shortages. Last year the Patrol swept through the city, killing off roaming packs." Jude shook his head, still staring at the waiting dog with the Frisbee. "They had the hardest time with the poodles."

Dr. Premjad laughed, a soft bright laugh that seemed to

soar. It was good to hear. Laughter, Jude thought, was still in short supply.

"But," he added, "I think this one was abandoned more recently."

The dog was still waiting, and Jude felt a sudden determination. The poor animal was half starved, but all it wanted was to play. And isn't that what they all yearned for, to be able to play again? Defying Jackson's worried scowl, Jude crossed over and picked up the Frisbee. The animal immediately got to its feet, tail wagging. It barked once, high and excited. Jude sent the toy flying, and the dog went bouncing and racing after.

Dr. Premjad came up beside him, watching as the dog skidded over grass, growing more muddy and dirty by the moment.

"That was probably stupid of me," he said, even as the dog nabbed the toy and came running back to drop it at his feet. It stepped back, barking and wagging its tail.

"It was kind," said Dr. Premjad.

He gave the Frisbee another throw. The dog dashed after, then bolted right back again.

"Last time," he warned it. Another throw. The elated animal was after it almost before it left his hand. It came galloping back a second later, but Jude had already turned them back on the path.

The dog watched them for a moment, then trotted after, glancing up at Jude expectantly. Jude reined in temptation and kept walking.

"Central Park is better in May and June," he ventured, as they passed among still bare trees.

"There is no need to apologize for your park, Mr. Tarkenton. It more than lives up to the hype."

"We really want you on staff, Doctor."

"You are putting too much faith in me and what you believe I know."

"I haven't any other option," he admitted, feeling that

sudden desperation, a blue-gray anxiety that captured him and kept him awake at night. "I don't mean just for my daughter. I mean for us and the Kasarans. I can bridge the distance, Doctor, but I can't bridge the differences. I'm hoping you can."

"Dharma," she said. "The path we have to follow. Those steps in the dance of life which are ours this time around the wheel."

"So you don't think it's all bullshit? Building the bridge, trying to make contact?"

"From a Hindu perspective, Mr. Tarkenton, everything we do in this life is bullshit, all Samsara. And yet it all works toward freeing us from being trapped in the illusion. Is it false? Yes. Is it good? Yes. We have been given a glimpse of humanity's dharma. This I believe. It is now up to us to fulfill it. Will you keep the animal?" she suddenly added.

"I don't know." He glanced over at the dog, who was keeping pace as if it knew that it was time to go home. "I suppose. That is, if it keeps following. It might not. It might not want to leave the park."

"I think it will," she said.

They had almost reached Central Park West, where, as arranged, Oliver was double parked, waiting to take Dr. Premjad back to her hotel.

"So, Doctor," Jude asked as they reached the curb, trying to keep his tone light, "is Pandora a part of your dharma?"

She laughed a little, the softest laugh. "Karma, perhaps. Yes, Mr. Tarkenton, since you ask so earnestly and as I am on this side of the circle, I think, perhaps, yes."

"I'm very glad to hear that." He let out a breath he hadn't known he was holding and reached out to give the dog a pat on the head. "What do you think about naming him Samsara?"

Chapter 17

It is impossible for anyone to fully apprehend the revolutionizing effect of the Pandemic on those who survived it. We can look on it with amazed horror, discuss and dismiss debates that it was attempted genocide, but we miss the point then.

The Pandemic was a wake-up call to humanity. It was, for 90 percent of the population, the Zeitgeist of having lived through a terminal disease. Suddenly, everything that once was important was trivial. The Pandemic, in short, cut away the fat. It gifted the survivors with the ability to see their own value and importance in a world that had, increasingly, made the individual feel small and insignificant.

Out of all the vast universe, we could say we had been given this rare chance. We could regret and curse it, or we could allow it to transform us into something greater.

—The Ring of Fire: Shoal Meaning and Symbol

THERE WAS A BAD JOKE IN THE WORST OF TASTE THAT, finally, it was easy to get an apartment in New York City. With the state population down to three million, it was, in the grossest understatement, a buyer's market.

Not that anyone paid out much of anything for apartments these days. Most of the landlords were missing, and staying anywhere required only the monthly rent of maintaining the living space.

There were still problems, of course. Part of Gordon's job was dealing with long-lost third cousins who suddenly appeared, a deed to an expensive house or building in hand, demanding the eviction of the "pioneers" (as squatters were now known) living there.

It was up to the Patrol to investigate and see if the claim was in any way legitimate. Usually the claimant disappeared on them when they mentioned that they would check their records and that fraud was punishable by five mandatory years in prison.

Gordon's team had framed some of the more amusing deeds, including one that laid claim to the World Trade Center.

Usually the owners were either still in their homes or gone for good. That hadn't made Gordon feel any easier about "pioneering" the brownstone he now lived in.

As he headed home after his meeting with Tarkenton, Gordon reflected that Greenwich Village was not a place he would have ever imagined for himself. He had no artistic pretensions, had always thought of himself as too dull to live in an area historically frequented by artists, writers, and philosophers.

He had heard, however, that Washington Square had once been a burial ground for victims of the plague. And that had made him feel, queerly and finally, at home in the Village.

He got out of the car, hunching his shoulders against the downpour, and made a dash past the maple tree, a tight fence of iron encircling its trunk, to the front door. Water streamed down over the decorative arch and rushed out of the gutters. Fighting with a latch that often stuck, he pushed into a cold lobby and left wet footprints on the checkerboard floor.

Gordon shook his head a little as he plowed his way up the narrow curving staircase. This was not the place he would have thought to raise a family, a stone building in a stone city, all tight skyscrapers and concrete. During Mae's early pregnancy, he'd imagined a house in a suburban neighborhood or a Victorian gingerbread with a backyard where one day grandchildren would play.

He had thought that rural community the right place for Scotty; wholesome, with swings hanging over swimming holes, fruit right off the branches, and people understandably cautious but painfully grateful to him for his help and expertise. Folks wanted to go back to old patterns, to the world as it had been before all the illness, death, and uncertainty. All they asked was for a measure of order and respect. Gordon had been happy enough to give them that.

He'd held some cockeyed dream of settling there, raising Scotty in a big house, friendly neighbors to either side, taking his son trick-or-treating at Halloween, setting up a tree at Christmastime.

But winter had found him alone with Scotty in that huge house, dreaming of and mourning for Mae. Her absence lingered in the nooks and corners.

When the thaw came, he'd packed up his suits and Scotty's toys, said his good-byes, and made his way to Manhattan. Not long after, he joined the local patrol and soon found himself down in the subway trying to negotiate with the kidnapping subway rider. Almost immediately after that he'd found himself atop a building trying to talk down his first climber, a man who'd made himself leaves of silk attached to wiring which, he swore, would help him escape Earth's gravity.

They'd gotten the man down, and Gordon, writing up his report, had suddenly felt strangely safe. It was twisted, he knew, but he needed the craziness and the grief, the adrenaline, the challenge. Anything to keep him anchored on this planet instead of wishing he had died along with his wife.

For a while he had fretted over the decision, afraid that someone might delve into his past, learn that he'd deserted his job in Toronto. Which had made him wonder if he ought not go back to Toronto. But by then he was committed, and members of the Patrol formed, organically, from military men, remnants of the state militia, beat cops, volunteers, and retired detectives, were calling him "Captain."

They never asked questions anyway, and they gave him a chance to put the world back together again, to be alive in the only way he knew how.

Only today he felt he'd failed them.

Well, he was home now. Maybe, if it wasn't too late, he'd still be able to treat his son to Sunday brunch.

But, oh God, how was he going to explain where Kyle had gone?

He opened the door to the dry warmth and struggled out of his sopping jacket. From the corner of his eye he noticed that the kitchen was clean, the pot Kyle had used to make oatmeal scrubbed and drying on the sideboard. Gordon had told Ruth many times that her baby-sitting duties didn't include housekeeping, but she never listened.

Ruth was seated on the couch, Scotty on the floor, building plastic structures with Legos; the thin woman, with her large gray eyes and graying hair, was wearing her maroon church dress, her gold cross glinting. Scotty, adding another story to his structure, was in train-patterned flannel pajamas.

"Daddy!" Scotty pushed up and ran to his father.

"I'm all wet," Gordon protested, catching up the little, wiry body; his son was still small for his age, surprisingly light and warm in his arms. He had his mother's almond eyes and soft dark hair.

"I tried to feed him breakfast," Ruth told Gordon, standing, "but he insisted on waiting for you."

"Oh, Scotty. You shouldn't have done that!"

"I wasn't hungry," the boy insisted, and then, very

quickly, "Where's did you go? Ruth said Kyle needed you. Where is he? Is he okay?"

God. Gordon winced. He had never lied to Scotty, had sworn he never would. His own family had kept his father's alcoholism hidden away for years, as if it would go away if they just pretended it wasn't there. Gordon was determined that no falsehood would stand between him and his son as they had between him and his father. However painful, however hard, he wanted Scotty always able to come to him for the truth.

So here, he thought, was his first real test.

Combing back still dripping hair, Gordon sat down at the kitchen table and set Scotty on his knee. Ruth, with a nod, quietly stepped out the door. Patience was a gift with Ruth, as well as discretion. She would get her explanation later.

"You know Kyle's a Pan?" he said to his son as the door softly clicked shut behind Ruth. "And Pans learned things from the aliens, like you learn things in school?"

"Yeah, I know that," Scotty said impatiently. He was so much like Mae in that way that Gordon almost smiled. Mae had never been patient with long explanations either, always wanting to run ahead.

"Well," he went on, "when they don't understand what they learned from the aliens, Pans can get scared or worried. And they need to talk with someone who can help them understand. That's where Kyle's gone, to talk with someone who can help him understand."

"What didn't he understand?"

"He has this design he keeps drawing, a kind of circle."

"All Pans draw circles."

"This one was a little different. He needed someone to tell him why."

Scotty considered that, then, "You know everything," he said confidently, "why didn't Kyle talk to you?"

"Most of the time he can," Gordon said, trying to keep his tone level. He knew it was childish to feel that Kyle ought to have come to him, but he couldn't quite help it. "But I'm not a Pan. I didn't learn the things Kyle and the other Pans learned. So I can't help him."

Scotty thought about that, his feet swinging. "Am I going to be a Pan or a Tenor?" he asked at last.

"You're a Tenor," Gordon said; it came out impulsively, and only after he'd blurted it did he wonder if it were the truth.

"Good," Scotty said. "I don't want to have to go to anyone but you."

It was the best moment Gordon had had all morning. And it had made him all the more determined to get Kyle back, as soon as possible. But right now he had to tend to Scotty.

"You want some pancakes?" He set the boy down.

"Yeah!" Scotty agreed, making a dash for the kitchen.

Twenty minutes later, Scotty scooted himself up on a chair, a stack of three plate-sized pancakes in front of him. He looked up at Gordon with a grin, soft, dusty hair falling into Mae's long eyes. "Syrup, Daddy!"

"Right here." Gordon lifted up the white pitcher and poured a generous stream of liquid maple over the pancakes. Scotty slid down on his chair so he could watch it run and drip down the stack. Gordon reached over with fork and knife and cut the pile into triangles for his son.

Scotty, of course, could not finish it all, but he refused to take less. Gordon remembered the day, just after Scotty's third birthday, when he had set a plate of silver-dollar pancakes before his son. Scotty had looked at the tiny flapjacks, then at his father's stack, then back again, and then, finally, pushed away his plate and, pointing a finger still tiny and plump with baby fat, had said, quite clearly, "I want like that!"

Oddly, he had not insisted on adult portions of anything else, just pancakes, as if, in getting the same as Gordon every Sunday morning, he and his father were one and the same.

Just like Mae, all stubborn and knowing. Scotty liked to talk, too. As he stabbed up a triangle of pancakes, holding it so that he could watch the syrup drip around the edges, he chatted incessantly about the book he'd been looking at on rocket ships.

Gordon didn't mind. He loved the sound of his son's voice. It was alive and happy and it filled the emptiness in the world, just as Mae's voice had.

The rain stopped around noon, and the sun actually began to peek out, so Gordon agreed to take Scotty to Washington Square. They walked there, Scotty in miniature rain boots, stopping along the way to splash in puddles. Gordon patiently kept hold of the small hand no matter how Scotty moved and pulled because he was always afraid that someone might try to snatch his son. People always stared at Scotty covetously, small children being a rarity in the world. Some reached out and tried to touch him, their eyes glazed with tears.

Scotty had learned to politely tell such people that he didn't want to be touched.

Despite pools of water, there were games going on in the basketball courts, shoes soaked and squeaking on the damp pavement, hands stealing dirty orange basketballs to slam through rusty hoops. The young men looked thin to Gordon, and desperate, as if they were trying to convince themselves that everything was back to normal. He knew that look all too well, the frantic need for activity, the attempt to keep the mind too occupied or exhausted to think or remember.

No one was playing chess at the tables, but there was a young man with a toy boat that he'd set in the fountain. With a joystick he sent it orbiting round and round along the rim. Gordon let Scotty watch and slap his hands against the water while he brought out the cell phone and checked in with Loretta.

She hadn't heard anything from Kyle, not yet.

Gordon and his son walked and talked a little longer, huddling in their jackets against the wet wind, watching rainbows appear and arch over the city. And then they went home and Scotty drew pictures.

He called Loretta again, got another negative answer. Then he went to work in the kitchen chopping vegetables for

Irish stew. Scotty, scratching at paper with his crayons, talked to him all the while, asking questions about Kyle and Pans and schools and aliens, usually answering the questions before Gordon had a chance.

Dinner came and went, and Gordon got Scotty ready for bed. He read his son a story. Characteristically, Scotty interrupted, insisting that things were going too slowly, demanding that his father skip ahead to the good parts.

Eventually, the restless boy fell asleep, just as the rain returned to dance on the roof. Gordon went back into the living room and sat. It was something he'd always been able to do, just sit and let his mind drift.

He found himself thinking of how empty the apartment seemed without Kyle, and how strange that was since he hadn't really felt Kyle's presence till now.

Why was that? Likely, Gordon thought, because it was too easy to slip into memories, as if into comfortable old shoes. Too easy to dream of his life with Mae instead of facing this cold new reality. Small things, simple things, still brought her to mind, slipping around the corners; like the way Mae had brushed her long shining hair when they were first married. Slow strokes, with the whole of her arm, like the movement of a dancer.

And then there'd been that day when he'd come home to find that she'd cut it into a stylish bob.

Stupid to still regret that he'd hadn't said he liked the new haircut, that, instead, he'd been disappointed. She'd been angry, and the coldness between them over that damn hair had lasted nearly a week.

Stupid to regret that they'd never really made up. That he'd never said he was sorry. That the anger had just died and been forgotten.

Memories like that left a lump in his throat, and a hollowness inside. But that was a bad road to go down. He couldn't live his life being eaten away by what he hadn't done or what he'd lost. And he couldn't, he saw that now, let those memories cut him off from the people around him, the people depending on him, like Kyle and Scotty, Loretta and Burke, and the rest of the patrol.

He'd let Kyle down, both before, by not seeing that the boy was in trouble, and later, when he'd let Tarkenton take him.

That wouldn't happen again, he swore. He didn't care what it took, he was going to be there for his people from now on, if he had to become the police commissioner to do it.

He was so deep in thought that he didn't hear the key fumbling in the door, or see the shadow that stood in the open doorway, not until it spoke.

"Captain?" Hesitant and scared. Very scared.

Gordon was instantly on his feet. Kyle stood there, pale and hollow-eyed, his hair dripping wet, his bare hands shaking.

"My God," Gordon breathed, "they made you *walk* home?"

"No . . . no." Kyle shrugged and leaned against the door-jam. "They drove me back, it's just that the door got stuck."

Why was Kyle staying in the doorway, Gordon wondered, alarmed. He took a cautious step forward. "Are you all right?"

"Yeah. Yeah." Kyle slicked his wet hair back, so that he looked very young, like a rebellious teenager.

"They didn't hurt you or anything?"

"No. Actually I . . . they helped. I understand something of what I was doing . . . trying to do. And I . . . I know you might not want to hear this, Captain, knowing how you feel about Pandora and all, but, I think I . . . I think I need them."

It hurt and it made him mad, Gordon couldn't help it. He stopped moving toward Kyle, feeling betrayed. But then he saw how Kyle hung his head, hands in the pockets of his rain-soaked trousers, and relented.

"Will you be going back, then?" he asked carefully.

Kyle shuffled his feet a little, like a child. "I'd . . . like to."

"You're going to live there?"

"Fuck no!" Kyle looked up, finally, his dark eyes deep

with pain, his face bloodless. ". . . Sorry, Captain. I mean . . . no. They asked me to stay but I told them . . . told them I already had someplace to live. I do . . . don't I?"

It was then that Gordon understood why Kyle was still standing in the doorway. "Come in." He crossed to take the young man by the arm. "Come in and get dry and you can tell me all about it."

The young man breathed out a sigh, looking so relieved Gordon thought he might faint. "I'd like that."

Gordon smiled then. No. He would never let his friends down again. "Welcome home," he said.

Chapter 18

It was not just their bright eyes, dimples, and soft, childish bangs that made post-Pandemic models like Carol Cooper Kay, Mao Die Chuan, and Ida West so immensely popular. Though, in a world that had lost most of its children, those youthful, hopeful features were a powerful draw. And it was not just their strong, voluptuous shapes, hourglass figures, and long legs, though in a world digging its way back from grief and illness, that, too, had an irresistible attraction.

It was their "Fuck you!" expressions, an attitude neither angry nor defiant, but vivacious, as if they were sticking a finger up at Death.

This is most powerfully evident in the most memorable of all images from that time, an image which, in later years, would appear on billboards around the world, including one of the largest to ever hang in Times Square. It is of Eve Velvet, with her blue-black hair, smooth healthy skin, and heavy, solid figure throwing up a deck of cards and laughing as she let the chips fall where they may.

—The Strange Age

Dr. Mavis Battencourt called up Judas just as he was about to put Piper to bed. Her tired face filled the monitor, lips thin. But Judas had learned to watch her eyes, not the features, which hedged as if afraid to commit.

The eyes were shining.

Judas leaned one hand on his desk. "Tell me." He was amazed at how level his voice was; his heart was pounding.

"It's a goddamn shame that kid didn't get the schooling he deserved," she growled. "He had no fucking way to articulate what he knew. No wonder he ended up on top of the Brooklyn Bridge with a paintbrush. And the answer's yes. We want him. So why'd you have him taken away?"

"Goodwill," he answered, pushing up from the desk. "We're going to need a lot of it. Don't worry, he'll come back to you on his own, you know he will."

"Yeah, I know."

He pushed his hands into his pockets, found in one, amid scraps of paper and loose change, a small game token, plastic and yellow, in the shape of a pyramid. Piper loved to play board games and cards, especially with him. She didn't care if she won or even if she understood the rules, she just liked to see the random clutter of tokens and cards, scattered about like some strange work of art.

Sometimes she made up her own rules, explaining them breathlessly to anyone who would listen, jumping plastic pieces about the squares, trying to shuffle cards in her small, clumsy hands.

Her creativity inspired and depressed him. All his life he'd wanted to be a design engineer. Now he felt that dream vanishing under the demands of Pandora.

The bitch of it was, he seemed to have a talent for organization.

"Have you noticed . . ." he said, "the numbers are up."

Mavis shrugged uncomfortably. "Sven said there'd be more suicides. Trauma . . . hangs on for years."

Jude winced. "Yeah."

Like bits and pieces of a submarine wreck, he thought. The waters grew calm, the world went back to work, but disturbing elements just kept rising to the surface, symptoms of humanity's underlying psychosis.

There was a certain desperate attempt to put the psyche back in order. Like a house that had been ransacked, the owners believed it could all be put right by sweeping up the pieces and hanging the pictures back on the walls. They went back to work, reopened theaters and restaurants, sought out luxuries they'd done without. They pretended it could all be as it was before.

And in the meantime, Jude made it his business to enter those private homes and examine the cracks on the walls. He tried to fish out the important parts and puzzle them back together.

Would it be worth it?

Captain Demme didn't think so. But then Captain Demme was a Tenor.

"Do you feel any grief at all for the dead?" the captain had had the temerity to ask.

What, Jude wondered, lay beneath his own surface waters? Would the grief rise one day, so powerful and terrible that he would put an end to it by trying to fly off the Brooklyn Bridge?

"I'll call you in the morning, Mavis," he said, suddenly shaken, and signed off. The engineer's face vanished and Jude was left with a dark monitor. It was raining again, and as he listened to the patter on the windowpanes, he thought he saw shadows reflected on the gray screen. They moved and seemed to take shape; one, he could have sworn, was Warren. The other Valerie.

From time to time, he was sure he saw them, in the mirror when he was shaving, out of the corner of his eye. They were always just behind him, just out of sight, calmly standing near, waiting.

It scared him, as much as anything could scare a numbed survivor of the Pandemic. Was that why there were suicides?, he wondered, because people were beginning to feel again, to fear again, and they couldn't bear it?

He himself was afraid not of suicide but of going mad. What he was doing, what he wanted, had to be an act of sanity. It could not be a way of running from his grief or subverting the trauma. If it was anything less than true, that would be the end of it, for him at least.

But he had to wonder if, one day, he might not turn and catch the ghosts of Warren and Valerie that hovered always just behind him. The best friend he'd ever had, the only woman he'd ever loved. Like land mines deeply buried and forgotten, one day they would explode.

And where would his credibility be then?

God! He couldn't let his mind wander around in circles. Not now, not tonight. There was too much to be done.

A shriek and a loud bark from the guest bedroom.

What the—

Jude was up running. Barking and screaming—

He came to a halt at the door. Four-year-old Piper, dressed in her favorite, kelly green nightgown, was bouncing on the bed. Sam, his fur clean and surprisingly handsome, leapt up from the floor along with her, barking excitedly.

"Hiiiiigh hopes! He had *hiiiiigh* hopes!" she was half singing, half shrieking, her favorite song. Her nightgown streamed up with her and ballooned down, her silky carrot hair flicking and swinging. Jude stood uncertain for a moment, then he saw Jackson in the corner, meaty arms crossed, an indulgent expression on his face.

The bodyguard caught sight of Jude and the arms slid down. "Piper." Jackson's voice was very deep, and she stilled. Sam was less ready to stop. He bounced up a few more times, still barking, before his excitement abated. The dog also noticed Jude then and, ears and tail up, came trotting over to lick his hand expectantly.

"Daddy! D'ya see! Watch!" Piper clambered down from the bed and skipped up to him, face happily flushed. She had eyebrows so fair they were almost invisible on her round face. Her mouth was small, almost a smirk. Hard to believe that the small mouth could really smile, but when it did, a single dimple appeared, and that's when Piper reminded Jude, profoundly and uncannily, of Valerie.

"Sam!" she said, stepping in front of the dog. The animal's head was almost level with hers. "Sit!"

The dog settled obediently.

"Shake!" She held out her hand and Sam lifted his paw.

"Don't forget to tell him he's a good dog," Jackson warned in that flat, noncommittal way of his.

"Good dog! Good dog!" Piper insisted, petting Sam's soft chest. "He can stay, too," she proudly informed her father. "Want to see?"

"Not now. Get into bed," he said, touching on her shoulder with a "scoot" motion.

"Stay!" she said to the dog, who obediently settled down in the doorway. "Can Sam sleep with me? *Pleeease?*"

Jackson, crossing to the door, sighed loudly and shook his head. Clearly, Piper had already tried to weasel permission out of him.

"Davy and I are going to make our rounds," he said to Jude. "G'nite, Pipes!"

"Night, Jackson! C'he, Dad?"

"Not tonight. If he's really a good dog, we'll see." Piper had taken to Sam at first sight, screaming with delight and throwing her arms about the animal. The dog had, thankfully, wagged its tail and happily licked her face, but Jude had taken her aside after that and given her a lecture on petting strange creatures.

"You wouldn'ta brought him home if he wasn't a good dog!" she protested, climbing back into bed.

Jude came up and tugged the blankets around her. Raising a child wasn't something he'd ever anticipated doing, most especially not at such a time in his life, at such a time in history! The hardest part, he'd decided, was distinguishing between doing his best and doing what seemed expedient.

"No more. You can play with him in the morning."

She scowled with disappointment but rested back against her pillow with its yellow star design. He sat down on the edge of the bed, touching back her hair with his fingertips, and smiled.

The scowl grew thoughtful. "Is the Pandemic still around?"

For just a moment, he felt a great and terrible stillness, as if there were ghosts standing by the bed. At one point he had considered turning Valerie's old room into the nursery. Right now, he was very, *very* glad he had not; he would have felt her body hanging over them, dripping blood.

"Why do you ask?"

"There aren't any babies," she said with a shrug, as if it was obvious, and reached for her purple stuffed unicorn. "You told me the 'demic killed all the babies 'cept ones like me and Ida," she named off her favorite playmate. "If it was gone, there'd be more babies, not just little kids."

The observation was so right that it stunned him. Not in a million years would he have thought she'd see and understand that, not at her tender age.

"There's going to be a lot of babies real soon," he said, skirting the question like a proper coward. "Remember I told you about that new vaccine? Well, they tested it and it works. So now mommies and daddies can have babies without worrying that they'll get sick. The vaccine will keep them healthy."

"Can I have the vak-seen?"

"You don't need it, sweetheart."

Her eyes grew worried. "But if the 'demic's still here, it'll make us all sick *again*!"

"No," he assured her quickly. "No, never again. It only makes a person sick once, or not at all. You understand?"

A reluctant nod, as if she didn't want to agree, but hoped to make him happy.

"Get to sleep," he urged, tucking the blankets around her and reaching to turn on her night-light.

"I don't need the light," Piper said then, all unexpected. "I'm not a baby."

For some reason, this disturbed Jude. It felt all wrong, as if another voice were speaking through her. "It's not a matter of being a baby," he said. "Some adults sleep with the light on too."

She hugged her unicorn and shook her head.

"All right, then. Sleep tight. But if you get afraid, you come on out and find me, okay?" He kissed her and darkened the room, pausing in the doorway to look at her as she twisted and turned and snuggled in. Her blue eyes stared at him for a moment and then shut, the pale lashes touching down on her round cheeks.

The dog came with him as he crossed the threshold and shut the door behind him, following him out into the hall, a strange but comforting new presence.

The living room always felt a little bare to him. Most of Valerie's beautiful furnishings were gone, in storage or used to clothe Pandora Corp. offices. Part of it had to do with an attempt to cleanse himself of the persistent memories, the rest was practical. Where the plush chairs had once been there was now a table cluttered with his drawings, paper, pencils, and half a dozen models.

He could have worked everything out on computer, but somehow it seemed right, and better, to draw them up and scan them in. There was, he thought, an artistry to this that needed a human hand.

That thought made him smile. Maybe it was just the influence of Manhattan, the inspiration it had always given him: the greatest buildings and bridges, almost all designed by hand, built by hand. That inspiration had been left behind when he joined Europa Corp. Now it was back, along with the clocks at the street corners urging people to run after their ambitions, with the skyscrapers, proud and splendid as ocean liners heading out to sea.

That, he thought, staring out the window to the balcony beyond, was what he wanted of this "starbridge." It must be as monumental as the connection it was going to make, a physical record of every one of the thousand steps taken in this journey across the universe.

"Can I get you anything, Mr. Tarkenton?" That was Davy, hanging anxiously and respectfully back, afraid to intrude. Jude could see the young man's reflection in the window, along with that of the dog, who had settled at his feet, head on its forepaws.

"No, thanks, Davy. See you in the morning."

"Yes, sir. Good night, sir." The young man vanished. The respect, Jude thought, was undeserved. Everyone who chose to work for him seemed to think he was some kind of trailblazer, the one who could make their obsessive yearnings come true. He wanted to explain to them that he wasn't building this bridge for them, for humanity, he was doing it for himself, for the alien he'd been, however briefly, in his hallucinations.

The rain was coming down hard now. The lights of Manhattan turned the downpour into a strange, glittering curtain which brought to mind a sudden and unexpected memory. Sudden because the fugue states of alien information always drifted gently to mind, like daydreaming. This one felt violent and jarring. Unexpected because it was a human memory, and over the last four years Jude had had little time for them. Or, perhaps, more honestly, he'd built up a wall of obsession to keep them out.

But this one appeared right out of the rain, as if it had been standing there all along, just waiting to be noticed. A wet day, like this one, a weekend in the past; the three of them arranging to take in a noontime matinee and he and Warren arriving at Val's place earlier than expected.

Val had opened the door in sweats and a T-shirt, nowhere near ready to go.

"Can you give me thirty minutes? I have to wash up and change," she'd said, already heading toward the bedroom. "Make yourselves at home. I'll be out fast as I can."

Jude had settled with Warren in the living room to channel surf and shoot the breeze.

At some point, Jude had gone into the kitchen to fetch drinks. The bathroom door was close by; from it he heard water running, an offbeat splash. And that's when he noticed that the door was open, just a crack. Through that crack he saw Valerie rinsing her hair. She was bare to the waist, wearing only her sweatpants; he saw the white curve of her body, the line of the backbone, her long, slender arms. Her breasts were petite, with seashell pink areolas and small nipples.

The sight drained the strength right out of him.

He stared at her for a full minute, watching the water flow off her hair, darkening it to a sleek, wet auburn. Admiring the beautiful line of her neck, the way her pale, androgynous face tilted, eyes shut as if in slumber.

Only when she turned her head away from him, hands squeezed at the hair, did he manage to find himself again.

That's when he'd gone back into the living room, two chilled bottles in his numbed fingers.

"Hey, Jude, you all right, man?" Warren, who had been watching the television, frowned at him.

"Fine," he said, passing a bottle to his friend. And then he'd dropped, weak-kneed, into a chair, and crossed his legs self-consciously.

Before that moment he'd known that he liked Valerie, and envied Warren. After that he knew he was lost. Just lost. It had seemed to him that no matter how he pursued what he thought were his goals in life, they would never match up to the lust and longing he felt for Valerie. He felt, absurdly, like some tragic hero who'd tasted of paradise and then been expelled, forced to wander, forced to be eternally dissatisfied and rest-less.

That had been his infection. Now, like the new New York-ers, he suffered from a very different disease. And yet he couldn't help but feel that the old one was still there, like his humanity, waiting to be resurrected.

And if it ever was, how could he possibly slake that terrible thirst?

The dog suddenly stood up, panting and wagging its tail.

"Daddy?"

Jude turned. Piper was standing looking tousled and for-lorn, rubbing at one bright blue eye with the back of her dim-pled hand.

"Got scared?" he asked.

"Yes."

He crossed over and lifted her up into his arms. Her size and weight always took him aback. He still expected her to be tiny, weighing almost nothing, her strange little tail wiggling about. She put her arms around his neck and he felt a sudden moment of déjà vu as her powdery cheek touched his. But then the moment passed, and he felt unexpectedly content, as if the ghosts that had been hovering at his shoulder all evening had finally taken pity on him.

"I dreamed about the long night," she told him as he car-ried her back to bed.

"It's spring. The nights are getting shorter."

"No. I heard it on multimedia." Piper insisted on watch-ing the news with her father every evening. Usually she spent the hour cross-legged on the floor, moving colored pieces around on her game boards; Jude was surprised to learn that she'd been listening.

"What did you hear?" he asked sharply.

She seemed startled by his tone. "They said the 'demic was just the sunset. They said there was a long night coming. A loooong night."

He got her back to her bed and slipped her in, silently

cursing the Tenor whose editorial she'd heard. Sam, who had been following, stuck in his wet nose, trying to help, and Piper petted his sleek head.

"They were wrong," Jude told her firmly. "There's no long night, just a bright, beautiful morning. And you know what? Even if there was going to be a night, there'd be a light on the whole time."

"Really?" she asked.

He gave her a hug and a kiss. "Really."

He waited until her breathing quieted back down again and she drifted to sleep. When he finally did cross out of the room, he made sure the night light was left on.

PART III: God Only Knows

Chapter 19

July: Thirteen years after the Pandemic

Something had come through the gate. Flashes went among the shoals watching, fast ripples of color letting everyone know that something had been seen and simultaneously warning that it was still too early to hope.

The fore-leaders made their way to investigate, a task they'd prepared for their life long, one that had been passed down to them over generations.

The thing was still. What it was or had been was hard to tell. It might have been alive, once. But now it was a cold, twisted object encased in dirty ice.

Had it tried to come through? Or was it something that had just happened to find its way across their bridge?

There was no way of knowing. It was a terrible thing to see, and it shook the whole of their race to the very core. But there was nothing to do, nothing save return to their watch once more.

Nothing but to have faith that, next time, a living visitor would come through.

THIS WAS GOING TO BE THE BEST DAY OF HER LIFE, Piper thought, as the limo drove them to the Empire State Building and the floater moored atop it. Not just any floater either. This was *Mimi's Folly,* an extravagant club with the most celebrated nightly parties on Earth.

Tonight it would be soaring over Manhattan. And she and her father and Varouna would be in it as the center of an exclusive celebration.

She petted Sam, who lay curled next to her on one side of the limo's backseat while Gabe Kryszka, her father's secretary, sat on the other. Gabe was nervous, he was always nervous, patting at his balding head, pulling at his thin black mustache, tugging at his plump fingers. Gabe had worked for her father now for nearly three years and Piper still couldn't decide whether she liked him or not.

Across from her, her father was in conference on his I-dik pad. Varouna, seated next to him, was quietly enjoying the ride, as usual. She was wearing her most elegant sari, Piper's favorite, made of peacock green silk bordered with intricate gold and silver embroidery.

It made Piper feel drab, though she found her own brilliant gold and candy pink dress beautiful and delicate. She'd done up her hair in a row of little twists at the front, each one secured with a violet enamel butterfly clip. And she'd brushed her eyelids with just a hint of strawberry and grape eyeshadow. A pair of gold sandals right out of a Greek myth were strapped onto her feet.

When she'd seen the results in the mirror, she'd been more than a little amazed. How different she looked; and how different she felt, profoundly different.

Gazing out from the air-conditioned interior of the limo, the world looked different too. When she'd stepped through the humidity and heat to get into the car, she'd noticed it; the smell of the city had, somehow, been sweeter than usual, as if the flowers from Central Park were lending their perfume to the stone buildings. She'd even noticed the sound her sandals made on the pavement, like the rasp of emery boards. Sam, his muzzle going gray, had felt the difference too, his doggy grin wide, his tail flagging hard.

Even though she knew that the weather outside was blisteringly hot, the July sun still seemed to shine through the car window with the white, cool sweetness of pineapple sherbet. The colors of the traffic moving through Times Square, grasshopper green buses and lemonade cabs, were rainbow bright, and the colonnades of skyscrapers seemed to look down on her like friendly giants. Which was strange, since she'd always thought of New York as an adult city. That's what she'd always been told, that it was a very adult city. But when she looked out at it now, she felt as if she'd returned to days when she was very little, when the dinner table was a castle in the air.

"Excited, sweetheart?" That was Oliver, glancing back through the open window from the driver's seat.

"Yeah." She only wished Rose and Violet and Ida could see her. And Randall. Especially Randall.

"Can't rely on the goddamn Eastern Coalition." That was her father talking to Gabe; whatever he was reading off his I-dik, he didn't look happy.

"No sir." Gabe had a weird accent, which, her father assured her, was an authentic Brooklyn dialect from before the Pandemic. Her father seemed to like it, but Piper found it odd and sharp; and she couldn't understand why Gabe always had to talk so fast, or use so many curse words, though he seemed to watch what he said around her and Varouna; more than her father did, truth to tell. Piper didn't quite believe it when her father told her that was the way most New Yorkers used to talk. She figured he was pulling her leg.

"Just get the motion tabled."

"Yes sir."

Something to do with the lunar mining operations, then.

Piper made it a point to know everything she could about Pandora Corp. because that was the whole of her father's world.

He had started Pandora Corp. with just a handful of engineers like Dr. Battencourt, working in the living room with sketch paper and pencils. When he spoke of those days he got a wistful look in his eye, as if he wished he could go back to them. Her father now had an enormous administration to run all of Pandora's various businesses, including shuttle service to the moon and the space station, and the lunar mining operations, which were almost entirely roboticized. Half of Manhattan worked for Pandora Corp. And every place on Earth, it seemed, had a branch office.

But her father hated the politics, which was why he had to have men like Gabe Kryszka, whose job it was to keep him informed of global developments. The Stargate Committee, world senators who decided almost everything about who was going to build the stargate and how, had to be carefully monitored. They liked to tack on problematic addendums to contracts. And there were Tenors and religious Pans who kept trying to slow down or halt work on the bridge.

Piper had written up a report on the subject for her political science class. She'd been pretty proud of it; so had her dad, who'd thoroughly embarrassed her by sending copies of it to just about everyone in Pandora Corp.

Gabe was usually pretty good at keeping her father abreast of these situations, and even had some good ideas about how to resolve them. But right now her father was royally pissed at his senior secretary.

"I'm sorry, Mr. Tarkenton," Gabe said and pulled at his tie. His ability to find ugly ties and match them up with the wrong color shirt never failed to amaze Piper. The orange shirt he wore today was already sweat-stained and wrinkled from the heat. "I should have been on top of this one; got caught with my pants down—had my eyes on that goddamn mono-matrix fiasco."

"That!" her father said under his breath, a curse. "I warned them about Luton Tec.!"

"Lowest bid," Varouna softly pointed out, gazing all the while placidly out the window. Piper wondered how she managed to do that, to always keep her balance.

She wished Dad would marry Varouna. The two shared a bedroom, but they never kissed or held hands in public, and they never mentioned marriage.

It was frustrating.

"The Stargate Committee has to learn what the lowest bid is going to get them. The news services are having a field day."

Gabe cleared his throat, a bad sign. "That, um, is another thing, Mr. Tarkenton. There're going to be inquiries and investigations. The World Congress threatened to appoint a special prosecutor, so the committee had to throw them a bone."

Her father got a very, very cold look on his face, one that said he was really, really mad. He'd never been that angry with Piper, and she hoped to hell he never would be.

Despite the air-conditioning, Gabe broke out into a sweat, which made her wrinkle her nose and shift away from him.

"So we're going to be investigated for graft, is that right?" her father asked Gabe in a quiet voice, a chillingly quiet voice.

"Well . . . given how much of the 'gate Pandora is responsible for . . . yes, sir . . . probably," he whispered, and winced, as if he thought her father was about to kick him.

"No. We're *not*. Understand, Gabe? We're going to put a stop to that right here, right now. I don't care how clean our books are, if there's an investigation it will make it appear that we've done something wrong and give fodder to every extremist group that wants to shut us down. It will also give those lobbyists time to railroad though some law or other. *No*. We are *not* going to let that happen. Is that clear?"

"Crystal clear, sir. Yes, sir."

"*Today,* Gabe."

Piper stiffened. *Today?* "You're going to miss the celebration?" she blurted, and wondered if that meant she couldn't go either.

Her father's eyes shifted her way; they were still and bleak and cold as January and that scared her for a moment, but then they seemed to see her and softened back to normal. "No. No, sweetheart, I didn't mean that. I couldn't miss this damned thing even if I wanted to. I just meant that Gabe and I are going to have to corner politicos in between cocktails."

Gabe was coming with them? Piper bit her lower lip in alarm, then remembered her frosted lipstick and forced herself to stop. She was trying to think of something to say without sounding rude when the car reached Thirty-fourth Street.

There was a mob crowded around the entrance, a line of people in dazzling outfits standing on a red carpet, and tons of photographers pressed against railings to either side.

So, she thought, her mouth a little dry, her heart pounding with sudden excitement, and she patted at the butterfly clips in her hair. They changed color depending on the light, just like her dress, which could darken to raspberry or soften to powder pink. She suddenly wondered if her look was too juvenile.

Oliver was out and opening the door for them, letting in a wave of hot, moist air.

Sliding out first, Gabe stood at the curb and offered his hand to Varouna, who tucked up her beautiful skirts and exited lightly and gracefully with his help.

"Thank you, Gabe," she said, as digital cameras swung her way. Gabe nodded in a way that seemed both distracted and shy, and then held out his hand to Piper.

Oh, God, she thought, and noticed, all of a sudden, how thick the air seemed, swampy and hard to breathe. She didn't want a picture of herself and Gabe to go out on the news services. Not with all her friends watching, Violet and Ida and Rose . . . and Randall . . .

"You stay in the car, Sam," she said, and kept her eyes pointedly on her shoes as she exited so she wouldn't have to accept Gabe's help, but the secretary touched on her elbow and assisted her to the curb.

His palm was sopping wet.

Shit!

She rubbed at her elbow as her father came out. The cameras, thankfully, were now zooming in on him. She heard shouts from the crowd, questions from reporters, comments.

"Fuck you!" someone yelled. But also, "Don't let those bastards screw with our bridge, Tarkenton!" Mostly, Piper couldn't tell what they were saying. She was just amazed that anyone would stand out in this oppressive heat to catch a glimpse of celebrities like her father.

"Let's go," he said, leading them up the carpet. Varouna moved in a step behind him, and then Gabe.

"Take care of Sam, Oliver," Piper said to the chauffeur, who shut the back door and offered her a little salute. The dog was at the window, staring out at her, his nose leaving damp, misty spots on the glass. She didn't go many places without Sam. Sometimes she even took him to school, which, her father said, proved that this was a much different era from when he was a kid.

But this was an important outing and she was not going to bring along anything that might embarrass her or her father.

Now if she could just convince her father to leave Gabe behind.

There were photographers at street level, cordoned off but still able to photograph the line of people baking under the noonday glare. One got used to that kind of attention, Gordon thought, when one became a public figure, as he had in the last six years. And one thanked God there were strict stalking and privacy laws to keep the hungry journalists at bay.

They waved to him from the sidelines, shouting their questions, immune, it seemed, to the brick-oven heat of the city, the 83 percent humidity. They even used devices to magnify their voices. "Commissioner Demme! Are you thinking of running for mayor? On what ticket?" came right to his ear. And, "There've been protests against these celebrations, Commissioner, what are you doing to protect the city from terrorist threats?" And, "Are you here in an official capacity, Commissioner, or is this a political show?"

Thank heavens, he thought, offering his palm for scanning, his party was being checked in right now.

Tarkenton, rich fuck that he was, had taken his little band right to the door, where his bodyguards were waiting for him. Didn't even have to show the attendants who he was or prove that he'd been invited. Didn't have to be checked over to make sure he wasn't carrying any weapons or explosives. Right in and probably right up to the top in an elevator all their own.

Interesting, the obsequious glances that Tarkenton had gotten from those waiting in line. New York was a city that toughened its residents, but it also respected the pecking order. At the very top, especially, there was always a jostling for position, a kowtowing to those who granted and were granted special favors.

"Your party is cleared, Commissioner," said the official, who had passed a wand over Gordon, Scotty, and Loretta to make sure they weren't carrying anything dangerous. He nodded politely and gestured to the darkened interior of the old building. "First elevator on the right. We hope you enjoy the celebration."

"The hell I will," Gordon muttered to himself as he gratefully led his family into the climate-controlled interior and out of the sweltering heat. With his arm he mopped at his damp brow. Loretta, striding next to him, her heels making soft clicking sounds on the stone floors, looked cool as a day in April in a yellow sundress with a gauzy pleated skirt. She gave him a sidelong glance of her warm, sloe eyes, and a full-lipped smile.

"Don't you dare ruin this, Gordon," she said, slipping her

arm under his. "What's happening up there is worth celebrating no matter what you think!"

"They're not even finished with the damned thing," he grumbled. "You'd think we were already sending someone through."

"Nevertheless," she added, and he heard the silent *"dear"* tacked on to that, emphasized and punctuated.

They made their way through the elegant marble lobby and joined a group waiting for the elevator. Scotty bounced with excitement, a remnant of childhood which, at fourteen, was beginning to vanish. His dusty brown hair was cut short in the back, with long bangs falling almost into his bright, almond eyes at the front. There was a mischievous smile on his face that was purely Mae's. But his shoulders were straining at his white button-down shirt, hinting a growth spurt that just might finally match him to his old man.

"It's really tork up there," Scotty said now, his new favorite word for something that was truly fantastic. His voice cracked, it had been doing that. It didn't stop him from talking people's ears off. " 'Cause the crown of the building used to be a mooring mast for dirigibles, but then it was made into a telecommunications antenna. But then satellites made the antenna obsolete, and now it's a mooring mast again!" He had a brilliant grin on his face, hands in his pockets. Gordon didn't bother telling him they'd all heard this before. He'd learned long ago to let his son run on.

And, as usual, the boy had an audience. Maybe it was because Scotty looked strikingly comfortable and youthfully slim in wheat slacks, leather suspenders, and white wing tips. The boy had a discerning and demanding eye, and despite Gordon's warnings that he was going to grow out of those clothes within a month, nothing less would do. Scotty had bought the outfit himself with money he'd saved from his allowance.

Having always had trouble shopping for himself, Gordon could only marvel at his dandy of a son.

The elevator arrived and they piled in.

"The floaters have propellers that allow them to be held steady, like a helicopter—though not if the wind is bad enough. But then they just land it in a field," Scotty was saying to Loretta and the others. The small group was an impressive collection of international movers and shakers: Chan Biao the soccer star; Adebamgbe, the famed artist from Africa; and models Tuyet Sen-Sen, Guadalupe Aznar, and the "fuck it" girl herself (a fond nickname that no one uttered in her presence), Eve Velvet. Almost all of them were smiling.

"Old dirigibles," Scotty explained as the elevator sped up to the higher floors, "couldn't be manipulated like that and so you couldn't moor 'em. They've designed this new mast way better, too. They used to descend down this narrow ramp onto a little platform with this huge airship swaying right behind them, which was really stupid and really dangerous. What they have now is an elevator shaft that locks directly into the gondola. Here, let me show you," he added, bringing out his I-dik pad.

And almost all of those famous people crowded in to watch him pull up a diagram from the New York Library.

His son had that way about him, Gordon thought with a proud smile. Scotty loved to gather in information and then offer it back again, like a treat he was dying to share. And that innate generosity made complete strangers want to listen to him.

They changed elevators, rose up the last floors, and reached the top. An attendant in gold was waiting to usher them onto the last elevator, the new one located in the new mooring mast right at the center of the building.

Scotty paused for a second to stare out the windows at the Empire State Building's famed observation deck, and at the silvery blue monster that hovered overhead. It was vast as a whale, and yet it bobbed as weightlessly and gently as a cork in a still pond.

That was the only direct view they would have of the airship. Superficially like old zeppelins, though more rocket-shaped than cigar-shaped, *Mimi's Folly* was as daunting in size as ever the *Hindenburg* had been, and edged with delicate rudders that lay like fins, top and bottom and along the sides.

The gondola hanging underneath and embedded partially within was, of course, much smaller by compare, but gigantic all the same. The outside, however, was something of a disappointment, an oval hatbox with the aluminum look of an old airplane. Huge bay windows formed a necklace around its odd shape, tiny forms shifting and moving intriguingly behind them.

"Let's go." Gordon sighed, feeling more uneasy than ever. Damn the Pans and their need to stay airborne!

The special elevator in its special shaft had etched gold doors that silently glided open. The elevator man, discreetly holding the doors open till everyone was in place, pushed the button with a gloved finger. The car closed up and rose smoothly.

"Quite a show," Loretta murmured to Gordon and smiled at him. He caught the nervousness in the gesture. He'd been married to Loretta for seven years now, and he'd been the Police/Patrol Commissioner for six, a job that was as high profile as they came, given that Manhattan was where Pandora was headquartered. He'd been personally responsible for protecting some of the most important and famous people in the world.

But no matter how many posh parties or political dinners they attended, Loretta always got stage fright.

Scotty never did. The boy positively thrived on that deadly kind of chaos.

The elevator opened up to a small hatcheck room.

"Welcome! Welcome, my friends!" Fredricko Tuturro, owner and host of *Mimi's Folly,* was waiting for them. A vivacious, sepia brown man with a pencil-thin mustache and bright eyes, he grinned like a madman as he reached out to each of them. "So glad you came! Senior Adebamgbe! My Lady Sen-Sen!" He pressed the palms of the ladies and pumped the hands of the men. "Thank you for coming. A day to remember! Please be sure you take a moment to read the emergency instructions located on any table monitor. We want everyone to know about our safety features. Commissioner! So good of you to join us! And your lovely wife." A gracious bow to Loretta, who looked suddenly shy. "And this handsome young gentleman is your son?"

"An honor to meet you, Mr. Tuturro," Scotty gamely returned.

Fredricko's grin turned genuine for a moment. "Now I *know* there's hope for the future! Commissioner, I don't suppose you'd allow me to hire this gracious young fellow to help me greet my guests? No? Well, you have a good time, young man. This is the first of two days you're going to remember for the rest of your life. The next will be the day we actually go through the gate. What a celebration we'll have on that day, eh? Make this one look like a children's birthday party."

"Yes, sir." Scotty laughed along with him.

And with that they stepped over the threshold into the airy noise of the Grand Salon. It was, Gordon thought, as impressive as he'd heard. Oval, with sleek gold parquet floors and pale blue walls interspersed with wide windows that revealed the whole of Manhattan.

But it was not the view that captured the attention, rather it was the ceiling. Two stories overhead, it had rings of softly glowing champagne and silver bands that deepened as they rose to gold and amber and finally to a fiery orange at the smallest circle near the very top. The effect was that of looking at the rings of Saturn, and it made the relatively small salon seem enormous.

Beneath this powerful umbrella was a pale, polished oakwood bar at the far end of the oval and, down the curving sides, double rows of neat little cocktail tables. Occupying these were international media stars, artists, singers, sports figures, and models, as well as a handful of senators, scientists, and government representatives. He even caught sight of Nikki Richardson, the controversial talk show host and pundit, which was a surprise given how vehemently opposed she was to the stargate. Everyone was dressed to the teeth, men in slacks with knife-edge creases and tight vests that made their shoulders look wider, women in very short, beaded or pleated skirts that revealed their plump legs. The majority of them were wearing color-altering fabric, so when the men tugged at the vests, or the women knocked those short flares out, the color changed or flashed or shimmied like fairy dust.

Wisps of trailing fabric wrapped about the upper arm or watery jewels of aquamarine and amethyst, flashing at ears and throat and around hips, accented the costumes. Eyes were shadowed with the soft triplicate colors of Napoleon ice cream or enlarged with delicate markings below the lids that seemed to be fine script. And here again, the colors changed, on eyes and lips and even the blush on the cheeks.

Gordon thought it frivolous and silly, but then, he still wore a suit and tie to work.

He saw Tarkenton, dressed in a subdued gray suit, locked in conversation with a woman from the Stargate Committee. Dr. Varouna Premjad was with him. Nearby, kept back by Tarkenton's bodyguards, hovered a number of reporters with I-dik pads. Not many, and most of them were well known, the kind that usually put the best spin on their reporting instead of the most tabloid, but the last thing Gordon wanted was to be trapped on a floater with reporters.

If he had to be here, he damn well wanted to enjoy himself.

And then he caught sight of two people that he absolutely, positively did not want to see. Two people bearing down on him. One was Governor Cornell Davis IV. Davis

202 / Janine Ellen Young

had been press secretary to the assistant mayor of New York sixteen years ago. During the Pandemic, he alone had crawled from his sickbed back to the mayor's office, there to take control of the city. Even his worst critics agreed that his leadership had kept New York afloat during the turbulence and change of these past fourteen years. Beside him was Mayor Lizbit Mindel, once of the Bronx, currently of Fifth Avenue, one of the last true New Yorkers in Manhattan.

"Uh-oh!" Scotty had seen them too, and was edging back. "You'd better move fast, Dad, or else—"

But it was too late.

"Gordon!" Davis had him by the hand, and as if she were the governor's wrestling partner, Mindel had stepped around to block him from the other side. "We were hoping we'd see you here! And Loretta, how are you?"

"Just fine, Your Honor." Loretta offered a smile but her eyes looked to Gordon with a kind of panic.

"Good, good." A solid man with midnight black skin, trim salted hair, and piercing, wide-set eyes, Governor Davis had a weighty presence that no one took for granted. "We were wondering if we could talk with you for a moment, Gordie. We promise it won't be for long."

Gordon felt his heels digging in as Davis pulled on him. He threw a pleading look to his wife and son. Loretta, looking grim, nodded to Scotty that he was on his own and gamely joined her husband.

"This is hardly the time—" she tried.

"If we don't do this now there won't be another time," Mayor Mindel put in, her thin face combative.

If it came to fisticuffs, Gordon thought, he'd bet his money on Loretta.

"Look, Gordon." Davis leaned in close; he smelled of cigar smoke and fine red wine. "Don't fight us on this. We *need* to talk. Understand?"

"Come on, Gordon," Mindel added, double-teaming him for sure. "We'll all have a drink. No harm in that, is there?"

Gordon considered it, and finally sighed his surrender.

Damn it! He thought. The fuckin' ship hadn't even launched yet.

Chapter 20

Predictably, there were members of the faithful in all religions who could not reconcile the information downloaded into their minds with their beliefs. Some preferred to die rather than recognize a fallacy in their theism. Some found ways to accommodate the new information into their religion. And some, disillusioned with a God who had done nothing to save the dying, reasoned that they might as well pray to those who had demonstrated powers equal to or greater than God. Creatures able to see in the dark, with skin that could endure extreme temperatures. Creatures who did not need an atmosphere to exist. Creatures with power over life and death.

So was born the Kasaran Church, also known as "The Shoal Movement."

Tenors, while not without doubts, crises of faith, and confusion, had far fewer qualms. They could see the Kasarans as devils, as evil come to test the world. And they had proof that they themselves were divinely chosen, for hadn't they retained clear sight while the rest of the world had gone mad?

—A Farewell to Faith

It HAD BEEN EASY ENOUGH TO WALK AWAY FROM THE adults. Her father, Varouna, and Gabe were already busy talking with representatives from the Stargate Committee. She wondered if they'd even noticed that she'd left.

She was glad, at least, that her father hadn't insisted on having Davy shadow her. She didn't know why she needed a bodyguard. There was the mandatory I-dik locator at the back of her neck and her I-dik account chip embedded in her palm. If anyone tried to kidnap her, the Patrol would find her in an instant.

There were, of course, stories of robbers cutting off hands and using them to empty I-dik accounts of all their money, but those were just urban legends. Although, when she was very young, such tales had scared her so badly that she'd kept her hand in her pocket whenever she went out. Her father had finally explained to her that the I-dik chip in her palm wouldn't work if there was no blood pumping through it, so it wouldn't do a robber any good to cut off her hand.

She was just glad she could wander unwatched through the party, like an adult, which she was . . . well, almost. Adulthood was age sixteen, only three years away.

First thing she would do when she was legal, she'd decided, was go to a bar. She'd had sips of wine and liquor, of course, at dinners and parties, but it was different to be a legal adult, able to go into a public bar and order a drink. And maybe she'd get herself a tattoo.

Maybe, when she was sixteen, Randall, who would be eighteen, would look at her differently. Maybe he'd want to be her lover. And they'd come to a party like this one, she daydreamed, weaving her way past the tables, on a floater. He'd buy her a drink, and then they'd sneak away to one of those secret rooms that Violet had told her floaters always had and they'd make love, up among the clouds.

She smiled to herself then, and gazed wistfully at beautiful fashions (none of them could really hold a candle to

Varouna's sari. What was it, she wondered, about saris that made women look so very beautiful?), trying to imagine what she might wear.

The musicians, crowded back near the entrance, were playing a mixture of colored xylophones, drums, and piano, a sound like waves breaking before an ocean liner. Pans were weird about that. *Heartbeats,* her dad once explained. The only thing one can still hear in space, the pulse and throb of your own blood.

Piper thought that eerie, but the music had a sassy tick-tock to it that was appealing. She could see herself and Randall dancing to it.

Squeezing her way to a window, she got herself a place to watch the launch. She couldn't see the leashes that moored the floater, but she could hear the *whip-snap* snaking sounds as they were set free. Nothing seemed to happen for a long moment, and then the Empire State Building receded in the windows as the floater slowly and elegantly drifted skyward.

It was difficult, over the voices and music, but she was sure she could hear the faint whirl of the propellers used to steer the great airship. It was her first time on a floater and it was stranger than she'd expected, and more thrilling. Everything moved so effortlessly, without the rumble and hum and shift of wing flaps. And through the windows the city shone in the sun, a glittering landscape of magical towers, like the floating worlds she'd imagined as a child.

"Tork, huh?" A teen came up beside her. Dressed up as he was, it took a moment for her to recognize him. Scott Demme, Commissioner Demme's son. He was one of those who hung with the drama and speech clique. She didn't know him well, but being that there were so few of them, all the kids in Manhattan that were around her age went to the same school.

They were being called the "Twister" generation, after Oliver Twist, Dickens's famous orphan, and a good many of them were really screwed up. Some had been raised by adults so afraid, in those first years, to lose them that they hadn't been allowed to go outside to play. Some told stories of how they'd been kidnapped by bereft mothers, which was why all kids now had to have a second I-dik chip on them.

Currently, the one thing Twisters talked about among themselves was how their parents routinely neglected them for their younger siblings, the new "miracle babies." A good many of them hated that damned vaccine. There were women giving birth to clones of themselves, others arranging to have a baby a year. Which meant there was no room anymore for the mostly orphaned kids who'd survived the Pandemic.

No wonder that a few of the adolescents she knew still carried teddy bears or security blankets with them. Last week, during lunch, Piper, Ida, and the twins, Rose and Violet, had stolen Reba's favorite bear, Minnow, and passed it around under the table, giggling as Reba desperately tried to snatch it back. When Reba suddenly burst into tears, Ida had promptly tossed the bear upon the table in disgust. Rose and Violet seemed embarrassed by the entire affair. Ida was annoyed.

"What a fuss!" she'd complained.

Piper had felt vaguely ashamed. She still did.

We should be better with each other, she'd thought, and so, now, made sure to smile at Scotty.

"It's way," she agreed. He was, she reflected, a nice-looking boy, if a little short. Not as sexy as Randall, but he was neat and he took pains with his appearance, and she appreciated that.

"Want a drink?" he invited.

She thought about that. If she accepted, she might be stuck with him, out of politeness, and she wasn't sure she wanted to be. But of all the young people on board, and there seemed to be more than a few darting about, he was the only one who seemed to be near her own age.

She shrugged. "Sure."

They went to the bar and slipped up onto the stools.

"What can I get you two?" The bartender smiled their way, a man in a white shirt with a gold bow tie.

"Egg cream?" Scotty asked her.

She shrugged again. She didn't quite mean to, but she felt suddenly shy and unsure; she wished she could tell Scotty to order her up a "Manhattan," or a "Cross-Walk," a stunning drink that sandwiched a layer of blue curaçao liqueur between a layer of Benedictine brandy and a layer of lemon vodka. An egg cream sounded so juvenile.

"Sure," she heard herself say.

The bartender smiled at them and next thing he was setting out two fountain glasses, foamy topped and with a chill film of condensation on the outside. They had thin black straws, making them appear to be alcoholic drinks, which pleased Piper.

The two of them sipped in silence for a bit.

"First time on a floater?" Scotty asked. He seemed to like asking questions, which was fine with Piper. She preferred answering to asking.

"Yeah. You?"

"Uh-huh. You're a Yop, like me, aren't you?"

"Yop?" She thought she knew every current slang word, but she hadn't heard this one.

"Born in the Year of the Pandemic? Year zero?"

"Oh. Yeah, I was."

"So you're fourteen?"

"In December." Which put her just under the wire for being a Yop, Piper thought. That January first, not seventeen days after she was born, had been set as the offical end of the Pandemic, even though, by all accounts, it had hung on through February.

"My birthday's in May," Scotty said, and smirked. "Two years to go. I'm gonna get legally drunk for my sixteenth birthday, what about you?"

Piper flushed a little. "Go out to a bar maybe," she admitted.

"My dad wants me to go right to college, but I'm thinking about taking a year or two, apprenticing as a journalist or something."

"I . . . don't know what I want just yet."

He nodded sagely at that, as if he understood. "They've got a media room up front. Want to see?"

Shrug. "Sure."

Why did she keep doing that?

Slipping off the stools they nabbed their drinks and headed through a door that led to a small theatre. Center stage was a huge multimedia monitor, a screen just like those hanging in almost every store window in Manhattan. In Piper's childhood, those monitors had shown images of the lunar mining operations. Trios of people would pause on their way to work or dinner to watch with that wistful expression so common to Pans.

Of course, over the past four years, the images had changed from the surface of the moon to the space factories where the parts were being made, and to where they were being towed into place and soldered together.

The circle of the starbridge with its twiglike appendages had been growing and growing until now, gold-plated so that it glowed bright and beautiful, it hung almost complete but for one last section. That section would be added today.

On the screen, one of the shuttles came close, passing by the ring and matching itself up in size to one of the slender twigs. That always struck Piper, just how breathlessly enormous the bridge was.

"Putting in the temperature controls in the branches and the magnetically levitated track in the doughnut is the next step. That'll be easy," Scotty said conversationally. "The hard part's going to be creating the dense matter for the center."

Duh! she almost said, but that would have been juvenile.

Who did he think he was talking to? She'd been raised looking at plans, computerized simulations, formulas, and calculations for the bridge. Which usually meant she ignored the monitors that hung around the city like clocks. It wasn't like she was going to see anything she hadn't seen a thousand times in a thousand different ways.

Or so she'd always thought. But like everything else, what had been ordinary seemed different and unique today. She gazed up at the screen, feeling strangely in awe of this bridge her species was building.

It's going to happen, she realized, with a sudden chill, *this is going to happen.* There was no faith needed. Allow it to happen, and it would. The understanding was like an epiphany. She could almost imagine she was the first human on Earth to ever think of it.

"A completely different species," she said suddenly, then blushed, because they were not alone, there were people wandering in and out all the time, sometimes sitting down and just staring at the monitor. But no one seemed to have noticed.

"Yeah," Scotty said. "And we're going to be the first in the whole history of the human race to meet them."

"Exactly," she agreed. He *had* understood her, as clear as if the thoughts had been his own. She smiled at him then, and got a grin in return. He had a nice smile, friendly and boyish. Maybe they could have fun together.

"Hey, Scotts!" someone said then, breaking the moment, and she glanced back to see Kyle.

Kyle had beautiful blue-black hair, the face of a knight, a tan complexion, and the deepest, darkest eyes she'd ever seen. *Kyle,* she'd often thought, when he came to talk with her father, or when her father took her to visit the engineers in SoHo, *was a dream*!

And this dream man was hugging Scotty! How did he . . . Oh, yes, of course, she had heard that Kyle lived with Commissioner Demme. Lucky Scotty.

Could she maybe get Scotty to invite her over to his house sometime?

"Hey, Piper." Kyle smiled, then, to Scotty, who had, Piper realized, asked some question or other of him, "I'm here with the engineering crew and their kids. Tarkenton got us invites, said we deserved to be here for 'the christening.' We're going to the engine room, want to come?"

"Yeah!" Scotty said, and then, as if he suddenly remembered, tossed an embarrassed glance at Piper. "You don't mind, d'ya? We won't be long."

They weren't going to ask her along? She felt her heart fall. And here she'd been afraid that she was the one who was going to have to make up some awkward excuse.

Shit.

"No," she said, her egg cream turning in her stomach. "Not at all." That was the polite expression. Kyle glanced at her with a bit of a frown, but Scotty didn't seem to hear whatever Kyle had heard in her voice.

"Come on," the teen urged his friend. Kyle hesitated for just a moment, and Piper held her breath, hoping. But then another expression crossed Kyle's face and he lifted a hand, a gesture of farewell, and followed Scotty out.

Piper felt a profound disappointment, so deep and dark that it took her a moment to realize what was in that last look Kyle gave her. She'd seen it before, the look of someone remembering whose daughter she was, and thinking that perhaps they'd better not take a chance.

Kyle had wanted to ask her along, but he did not want to risk his job, his position on the engineering team, by taking her somewhere her father might not want her to go.

And so she was left, alone in this room of strangers, with the gold mourning wreath of the stargate hanging before her on the monitor. She set down the half-finished egg cream on a side table and went back out into the salon.

The band was playing "God Only Knows," a song her father informed her was quite old. She'd only heard the most recent cover of it. A number of adults were dancing to it, slow and close, almost sadly, as if they'd lost something and could only regain it in each other's arms.

A glance out the windows showed that *Mimi's Folly* was making its way around the edges of Manhattan. It had just passed over the steel latticework of the Williamsburg Bridge and was heading for the Manhattan Bridge. In the far distance waited the Brooklyn Bridge, its cables fine and silvery in the summer sunlight.

The East River flowed below, sailing ships dotting it like folded scraps of paper.

This was supposed to be the best day of her life, Piper thought, staring out at the panorama, at the bright, pale sky in which they soared. She shouldn't feel like crying, not here, at the most exclusive celebration in the world, not now, with the party only just beginning.

It wasn't like she and Scotty were good friends, it wasn't like he *had* to ask her along.

It shouldn't hurt at all.

But it did.

"Hey, darlin', why the long face?" a man asked, and she drew herself up, brushing straight the skirt of her dress. It wouldn't do to waste her time feeling depressed, especially over something so ridiculous.

"Oh, it's nothing," she said, glancing up at the gentleman, and lost her breath for a second time in ten minutes. The man was about the same age as Kyle, and twice as gorgeous; he had long brown hair and a short brown beard that framed an absolutely stunning smile. His sky bright eyes fastened on her, piercing right through.

How did someone *do* that? she wondered. Never in her life had she experienced so much attention, as if the man's whole regard were suddenly and entirely focused on her and her alone. Her speeding heart seemed to have stopped beating.

He's wonderful, she thought.

"Are you sure?"

"Sure?" she echoed.

"That it's nothing."

"Oh. Yes. Really."

His smile widened and his eyes seemed to laugh at her,

but that was all right. It was a gentle laughter. "What's your name?"

"Piper."

"Piper. I'm Laurence. Laurence Anderson." And then he was shaking her hand. His palms were broad and thick and seemed to hug her small fingers. "Maybe you've heard of me?"

"Um, yeah! God, yes. I just saw *Red Night* and I went to see *The White Papers* when it came out . . . but I've never actually read one of your books," she confessed, and thought, *He's much, much better looking than in his pictures.*

"That's all right. They still manage to get on the best-seller list." The eyes stayed on her, clear and blue and direct. She felt more self-conscious than ever under that beautiful gaze. What he must be seeing! A chubby teenager, breasts just beginning to take on a little shape, milk pale and round faced.

Her father said she looked like her birth father. She'd seen the pictures, and she did. He'd been handsome, but she'd rather have looked like her mother. Her mother had been beautiful.

Damn it, she thought to herself, don't just stand there staring, do something! So she drew in a breath and smiled. She knew she had that at least. When she smiled, really smiled, she could get people to do just about anything. She wasn't sure why.

Laurence seemed delighted with her smile, his own becoming a grin. "Have you a last name?" he asked, and Piper felt as if he'd just poured warm water all over her.

"McAllister." She was glad, not for the first time, that she had a different last name from her famous father—and that the news services almost never mentioned her. She didn't want to frighten off this man like she had Kyle.

"Well, Piper McAllister, there's a private lounge that only very special people know about. I happen to be one of those special people and I have it on good authority that the lounge is currently free and empty. Would you like to leave all this noise and fuss and see it? We could talk."

He wasn't really asking her what she *thought* he was asking, was he? And if he was . . . ? Maybe he thought she was older, of legal age. It was wildly flattering, and strange to say, but she felt as if she could accept, more, that she could do just about anything with him, tell him just about anything.

It was real, and it was now, just like the stargate. She wouldn't have to wait until she was sixteen, wouldn't have to wait for Randall or Scotty to take notice of her. Laurence was interested in her, he was looking at her, seeing her, and he wanted her.

But did she really want him?

"Thank you . . . not just yet." Best not to cut off her options. "Later?"

He smiled that warm smile back at her. "Anytime, pretty lady." And he stepped back, releasing her. "You change your mind, you tell me. I'll be waiting."

Gabe couldn't stop sweating, which was embarrassing, especially since he no longer had the heat to excuse it. But he couldn't explain to Mr. Tarkenton that he was sick to his stomach with fear, couldn't explain to Mr. Tarkenton anything.

Because Gabe was a member of the Kasaran Church and it was a given, in his faith, that anyone who was working on the bridge, especially Tarkenton, who had designed it and gotten the whole ball of wax rolling, was doing *their* work and was to be held in awe.

He hadn't quite told Mr. Tarkenton that either. One didn't just blurt out that one belonged to the Shoal Movement, 'cause even Pans thought it was kooky and extreme and tended to be distrustful of its members. And, well, Gabe could understand that; there were a lot of obsessive weirdos out there. If he'd said in his application that he was a member of the Church, Tarkenton probably would have figured him for a fan, a stalker trying to be close to the one he worshiped.

But it wasn't like that at all. Gabe knew his position was a privilege, and he knew it carried a lot of responsibility, which, before the Pandemic, wasn't a word he would have ever applied to himself. He'd been an irresponsible and immoral jerk back then.

He knew where his duty lay now, though. And he wasn't gonna shirk it, and, well, if he had to lie to do it, he would . . . and if he had to do more to keep at it, well . . .

He pulled out his handkerchief, which was already damp, and mopped his face again.

Fuck it!

"Look, Mr. Babin," he said to the more recalcitrant of the United States' two world senators; Gabe didn't know how the man got reelected, he was heavy and ugly and always frowning. "I know you didn't come here to talk shop, but these situations come up. The sooner we hash this out, the better."

"Tarkenton has a lot of nerve, asking for this kind of favor." The man took a gulp of some bluish drink. Colorful cocktails were the current rage; not that Pans were much for flavors, but they liked the look of the liqueurs. Every time Gabe saw one he was reminded of children's snow cones, the bright lime, blueberry, and cherry colors. The senator's drink had that same blinding, cornflower hue to it.

"Yes sir," he said, glancing over to where Tarkenton was standing with the other senator, a nice if intense blond woman named Wilson. He was glad to see Jackson and Davy standing behind his boss, on guard and keeping away the media.

Good.

Dr. Premjad was there as well, a quiet, solid support. Gabe was surprised to find her looking his way. He tried to smile, to assure her everything was all right. She had the most penetrating gaze he knew, not sharp, just steady, like a slow, constant pressure. Gabe was more than a little afraid of her even though she always treated him with the utmost courtesy. She was Tarkenton's lady, for one, and nothing got past her, for another.

She'd also cracked the virus. And anyone with that amount of Kasaran knowledge, or just smarts, scared him spitless.

Piper, Tarkenton's little girl, was nowhere in sight, for which he was grateful. The way she looked at him sometimes, as if he was mud, was worse than Dr. Premjad's ability to strip him bare. Not that he blamed the kid. He'd been a real dirtbag in years past and he didn't expect that he'd cleaned it all off.

No, he thought, remembered, *not at all.* And wiped at his brow.

"Look, Senator," he tried, feeling his nerves starting to fray. "You're stuck here till midnight. What's ten or fifteen minutes, huh? Mr. Tarkenton ain't no lobbyist." That was a not so subtle reference to Pandora's ability to influence votes, which it rarely did, but could, if pushed.

The man pursed his lips, not liking how close that came to extortion; Gabe didn't like it either, but he wanted to close out this deal, and using such ploys is what made him a fair success at his job. Politicos took him to be Tarkenton's minion, brainless and obedient, they didn't expect the curves he could throw at them. And his rather crude appearance let him get away with being blunt and rough when he needed to.

"Ten minutes, no more," the senator said. "You tell him that."

"Yes sir."

"And you tell him that if the World Congress appoints a special prosecutor, it'll be out of my hands."

That pissed Gabe off. "I'm sure, should it come to that, he'll be more than happy to explain to said prosecutor that he was the one who begged the Stargate Committee, on record, to use Mono-Mat International. And that nearly everyone on the board, including *you,* Senator, voted for Luton Tec. Over, I might add, his very strenuous objections. A prosecutor might wonder why you did that."

The senator, Gabe was gratified to see, turned quite pale, and looked very worried all of a sudden.

Put that in your hat and smoke it, Senator! It was, he thought, long past time they stopped supporting this yo-yo. The man was said to be savvy, a sharp bastard who could negotiate matters the way North America wanted them, but right now he just sounded like some toady trying to cover his ass. Well, let him know if he deserted them, he'd be left naked and out in the cold himself.

"Mr. Tarkenton will talk with you right after the ceremonies," Gabe added, before stepping away. He felt as if he were escaping a straight jacket. Good as he was at this sort of thing, the politics still affected him more than they ought. Not that he didn't have a thick skin, it's just that it had been scraped rather raw of late.

"Mr. Kryszka?"

Oh, God. It was *her.* She'd come up from around the side, slithering in with practiced ease. There was a hint of condescension to the mouth, superiority in the laughing eyes. This was a woman, he thought, who loved squeezing people's hearts.

"Have you thought it over?"

"Yeah," he grumbled. He realized he was keeping his eyes down, focused on the pair of high heels she was wearing, gold, like the stargate, and very much in vogue. He forced himself to look up. "And I don't like it and I *won't* do it."

"Mr. Kryszka, I'm mystified. All I'm asking is that you help me set up a short interview with Tarkenton on this very important day—surely that's neither absurd nor unusual."

"Your trying to blackmail me into it is real unusual," he snarled softly. Very softly.

The mocking eyes slid away under lids frosted with a line of indigo and copper. She was closer to him now, and he could smell her perfume, a kind of citrus and gardenia fragrance. There was this weird belief that, having lost an appreciation for smell, Pans didn't wear perfume. But a lot of them did; smells helped to clear the head, to bring Pans back to Earth and keep them anchored there. The Kasaran Church always ended their ceremonies by passing around something fragrant for the worshipers to inhale, a rose, a salt shaker filled with cloves, or a cotton wad drenched in some essential oil. It brought closure and sharpened their meditations.

"Always remember," his minister, a tiny little woman with white hair and wrinkled black skin, liked to say, *"that you are human."*

"Yes, I am blackmailing you," the woman said, those gold-frosted lips were smirking at him again. "This would be a very bad time for the media to learn that Mr. Tarkenton's secretary used to be an embezzler. The Stargate Committee is very nervous about such things right now. Especially an embezzler who used to work graft with contractors."

That was in the past! he almost protested. And at any other time, that might have sufficed. There had, for years, been a tenant among Pans that the Pandemic had erased the past, like some terrible baptismal. To ask a person what he had done before the plague was considered in bad taste.

But Gabe had no illusion that this was different, that it would make a difference, a big difference.

"One short and simple interview," she prompted. "I'll get it on my own, if I must, but it would be so much easier for the both of us if you'd cooperate."

"No," he said flatly. "Now fuck off."

She said not another word, shrugged as she turned from him, as if to say, "Ah, well, it's your funeral."

He would have to find Mr. Tarkenton, he thought, find him and tell him, now. And then resign.

His stomach twisted and turned. He'd worked his ass off at Pandora, trying for this job not long after he'd been born again into the Kasaran Church. He'd struggled up Pandora's ladder over the last ten years until he'd reached the highest position he could, one of trust, a job he could really do, where he could make the dream come true. He'd done it because the bridge had to be built.

Mr. Tarkenton understood that. He was one of the chosen. One of the ones who would make it happen.

If I've jeopardized that, Gabe thought. . . .

He came upon her as he turned, standing right behind him, angry-eyed. Her form-fitting dress showed off the new curves that would soon mold her into a woman, an ironic contrast to its sweet pink color and the youthful butterfly clips securing the playful twists of her carrot-colored hair. Like the changing colors of those clips and the dress, her face seemed, in its fury, alternately adult and poutingly childish.

"Piper," he said, clearing his throat. Oh no. "What did you hear?"

"What are you doing talking to *her*?" she demanded.

Nothing, then, Gabe thought with a breath of relief, the kid hadn't heard anything. "That isn't any of your business."

"I'm going to tell my father—"

"You're going to tell your father?" He almost laughed. "Don't be a stupid little girl! You write one school report and think you know how things work? You're thirteen, for fuck's sake! Go and play."

He saw the change in her expression and regretted the words almost instantly. Her face flushed deep red and her eyes glittered for a moment with shocked tears. Then, almost immediately, her face paled and the eyes went hard. She spun away and ran.

"Wait! I didn't mean that, Piper—" Gabe said, pushing between a laughing couple and almost upsetting their drinks. "Sorry, sorry," he said, still moving. "Excuse me! Excuse me—Piper!"

The sickness in his stomach had just gotten worse. Much worse.

Piper found Laurence at the bar, chatting and laughing, and hesitated, not sure if she should try to interrupt.

"Excuse me," she heard Laurence say to the other man, his eyes alighting on her, "I think someone wants to talk to me." And then he was in front of her, tall and warm and strong.

"Laurence," she said, "I, um, I changed my mind. I'd like to see that private lounge, now, if that's all right."

His brows went up, but he gallantly offered her his arm. "Pretty lady, it would be my pleasure."

"Thank you," she breathed, taking the arm, and let him guide her through the crowd. The material of his shirt under her hand was incredibly soft and thin so much so that she could feel the heat radiating from his skin.

He directed them into the media room; on the screen, the final piece was being towed toward the wreath. There was a countdown at the bottom of the monitor; another thirty minutes yet.

Laurence took a sudden turn into a dark area she'd taken to be a wall, surprising her with a hidden spiral of small chrome stairs.

"After you," he said with a wave of his big hand. Piper hesitated, feeling Laurence's warm, large palm resting on her shoulder. Maybe she ought to think about this.

But then she caught sight of an orange shirt, of Gabe, barely visible in the dim light from the screen, running a hand through his sweaty hair and searching for her.

She set her gold sandals onto the stairs then, heading up fast as she could, feeling the cool curve of the rail beneath her hand and, behind her, Laurence's safe, strong heat.

If no one would allow her to find adulthood down below, she'd find it up here, with someone who cared, really cared, to treat her as if she were important.

Chapter 21

The Stargate Committee was formed because no single corporation or country had the funds or resources to build the stargate. Furthermore, as the whole planet was going to be affected by this creation, it was only right that every country have a say in its development.

Composed of twelve world senators from twelve different countries, the Stargate Committee takes bids and reports from companies, engineers, and governments around the world and decides not only how the bridge will be constructed, but who will make parts for the gate. When the time comes, they will also decide when the gate will be opened, the number of robotic tests there will be, and who will be the first astronaut to venture through.

Senators volunteer or are voted onto the committee by the World Congress, and they must answer to their countries and to the congress for any decisions they make.

—*"The Stargate Committee,"* by Piper McAllister
Ms. Yu's 6th–9th Grade Political Science Class

THE ENGINE ROOM WAS INTERESTING, ESPECIALLY with a bunch of engineers, but Scotty was still getting restless.

"We use vectoring engines and we work with the weather instead of against it," the pilot was explaining. There were four chairs for the pilots and a number of monitors indicating weather currents, flight patterns, and the status of the airship. Very tork, even if four more adults and four kids made the small space even smaller.

"Do you still use helium?" Ernst asked; Ernst was Sven's clone, eight years old, blond and thin. His father had his hands on his son's shoulders, his short-sleeved polo shirt exposing the leaflike tattoos along his arms. Scotty liked to watch them ripple with the movement of the arm muscles.

"Oh, yeah. Keeps the price up." The man shook his head woefully. "Helium ain't cheap."

"Floaters should go back to hydrogen," Dr. Walsh argued. Walsh always found a way to take an opposite side; he loved to play chess and had talked Scotty into a few games, until he figured out that Scotty was getting bored and deliberately losing to end the game. They'd since switched to poker, which made Scotty much happier. "Its lift is six percent better than helium."

"Too reactive, it's not worth it." Dr. Battencourt cut that down neatly and succinctly. It was really strange to see her in a glittering rust cocktail dress instead of a lab coat. She was holding the hands of her nine-year-old twins Arliss and Bianca. A pair of test-tube brats, Arliss had a playful smile and a complexion the color of chocolate milk; his dad was Walsh. Bianca, fathered by Sven, was, by contrast, pale and shy, with straight brown hair. They were neatly dressed in matching sailor suits, hers with a pleated skirt, his with flared trousers.

Scotty winked at them when they glanced his way. They ducked their heads and laughed.

"Of course," Dr. Battencourt added, "if you really wanted good lift, a hard vacuum—"

Sven snorted. "When you can do that, you won't need an airship any longer. You might as well build an antigravity machine."

The conversation spiraled off from there, with Kyle stepping away (one step, that's how tiny the room was) to peer over everyone's shoulders and ask about the instruments.

Scotty was delighted; he listened avidly for a moment; drawing in the unique facts like light, until his face beamed and his eyes glowed.

This was so tork! he thought, hands in pockets, and leaned back against the doorjamb.

And that was when he caught sight of a flash of red hair . . . Piper? Where was she going? He leaned out the door and saw the spiral staircase they'd come up, narrow and silvery, almost invisible. Footsteps were heading up to the next level. Now where did *that* go? He moved over to the stairs in time to see Piper's gold sandals and the soles of a man's shoes vanish into some place a couple of meters overhead.

And it occurred to him only then that maybe he ought to have asked Piper if she wanted to come along to visit the engine room. He hadn't thought about that, hadn't imagined she'd want to. But she'd seemed a nice girl, if not real communicative. She had a real smile, not fake like some girls he knew, a lot of curves and silky hair, and a thoughtful expression that made her look older, fifteen or sixteen instead of thirteen. Which was probably why he hadn't thought she'd be interested in the engine room.

But maybe she would have liked to see it.

Or maybe not. She'd had that weird gaze girls sometimes got when they caught sight of Kyle. Maybe he should tell her Kyle was dating a Broadway actor named Rob?

That wouldn't be kind, but then, Scotty reasoned, she might pay more attention to him. And since the engine room was so small, they'd have had to stand real close together.

Real close.

Maybe he could catch her and ask her to join them? It seemed a good idea, and Scotty wasn't one to really think things over; he knew if he didn't say what he thought, or do what came to mind, he'd forget all about it, and so he moved on it, right then and there.

He leapt up the stairs two at a time and got to the top in an instant. There was a curtain, and he had enough where-withal to glance around it rather than just bursting in.

On the other side was a small lounge, an ocher carpet with Native American designs covering the sleek floor and a chrome mantel with bottles of expensive liquor along one wall. A pair of cream and sienna armchairs with matching side tables and a simple rawhide lamp completed the cozy picture.

A bearded man was leaning with one elbow on the mantel, a drink in hand that he must have just poured, as it went up to the top of the glass. Piper had one too, but she was holding it in both hands with a look on her face as if hoping that she didn't have to drink it. The man was murmuring something to her, smiling in a way that disturbed Scotty. Piper kept glancing up and then back down at her feet, like a little kid.

And Scotty suddenly felt that he shouldn't even be here, because the man was, well, a man, and handsome enough to be a media star; at the same time he felt angry—not jealous, just mad. Who did this guy think he was? For fuck's sake, Piper was only thirteen!

Just as he thought that the man took Piper's drink out of her hand, set both glasses up on the mantel, and ran his hands down her bare arms.

He said something to her.

And then he leaned forward and kissed her on the neck.

Scotty flushed, and backed out, fast. He rushed down the stairs, cutting past the engine room and down the second flight, pushing past a short balding man who was coming up, sweating and puffing.

"Excuse me!" he said, taking the stairs almost three at a time.

Piper might not thank him for this, he thought, but he was the son of a Patrolman, of the police commissioner of New York City, and he knew when he was seeing something that just wasn't right, that wasn't going to go right no matter what Piper might think.

He exited out into the salon and made a beeline for his dad.

At least Governor Davis was willing to listen.

"I appreciated your faith in me," Gordon said, sipping his club soda. "But I don't want to be mayor, of any city, let alone New York."

He felt Loretta's hand on his knee as he said it, her signal that she supported him. She hadn't said a word yet, and likely wouldn't. She just drank her daiquiri and gazed out the window at the firecracker colors of the sun as it cut its way through the dusty air. Down below, the floater cast its ponderous shadow over the Statue of Liberty, the ferries, and Battery Park. Gordon knew, however, that she was listening. Loretta was a very different experience than Mae; they spent long stretches together in silence, quietly eating dinner or reading in bed. Scotty filled the silence if Scotty was there, but mainly the two of them just sat near one another, touching or holding hands. Both of them were content with that.

"I understand, Gordon." The governor was making water rings on the small cocktail table with a Scotch royal. "We"— he indicated the Mayor beside him, Lizbit was taking unladylike gulps of a whiskey sour—"we understand. But you have to see it from our perspective as well. This is my last year as governor, and if I'm going to make a bid for the White House, I have to do it now. And Lizbit here is the natural choice to succeed me, she's certainly *my* choice. That leaves the mayor's office wide open. We don't want a stranger in it, someone who might work against us instead of with us. New

York's become one of the most important cities on Earth, politically speaking."

"What makes you think I even have a chance?" Gordon tried the defeatist tack. "I'm a Tenor!"

"You're a *moderate* Tenor. The Pans won't have to fear that you're an extremist, and the Tenors will be happy to have you in office. Besides, the Tenor/Pan thing has eased in the last few years. Most Pans don't even hang out in trios anymore."

"They're still the majority, and they're not going to want a moderate Tenor over one of their own."

"Of course they will; they'll want one because their children are going to be Tenors, and the Pans need to bridge that gap here and now, before it's too late."

"Cornell, I don't want the job! I'm happy just where I am, doing what I'm doing, which I do very well, thank you."

The governor leaned back at that, lacing his hands over his neatly buttoned vest. His manicured fingernails looked very pink against the dark skin of his hands. "When I joined, for a time, with the Nation of Islam," he said then, in a deep, rumbling voice, "they asked me to change my name to something more appropriately Islamic. 'Davis,' they told me, was likely the name of whoever owned my ancestors. And Cornell was Latin, not Islamic. Do you know what I said?"

"No sir." Gordon frowned, wondering where this was leading.

"I informed them that I was distantly related to Benjamin Oliver Davis, the first black general in the U.S. Army, and, therefore, I felt no shame in the name Davis, no matter how it was obtained by my distant ancestor. As for Cornell, that was my father's, grandfather's and great-grandfather's name and I was not about to dishonor them by rejecting it. But I would, I told them, change my middle name to Mohammed if they liked, which I did."

"And your point is?"

"You don't have to surrender all that you are in order to be what other people feel you can be."

Gordon sighed.

"He's also saying you can run the office your way, dummy," the mayor threw in. Lizbit had a very distinct, very brazen manner that had made her very popular with the people and very unpopular with most politicians. With short dark hair and a narrow face that tended to wear a disbelieving scowl, she was quick to launch into people as if they were disobedient children. More often than not, it worked.

"That's not the issue," Gordon tried again.

"It *is* the issue, Gordie," she said, sounding an uncomfortably lot like his mother. "We three love this city, and we *know* what it needs. We *know* how to run it well. Cornell here can take his very good management style on to the White House, and it's long past time I moved up. So why not you? Stop undermining yourself!"

"And have you consulted with Jude Tarkenton about this? Don't tell me he doesn't get a say. I know how this city works, remember?"

"There you go again, turning poor Judas into a modern day Machiavelli," the governor observed mildly. "Despite what you think, Judas Tarkenton has not bought himself any new or special laws, and the ones modified to his benefit were changed to accommodate our new and unique situation."

"Next you'll tell me he hasn't contributed any money to your campaign."

"Of course he has." Lizbit rolled her heavily mascaraed eyes. "But he's never asked for anything outrageous. He's got a goddamn stargate to build, you think he has time to run New York City?"

"No." Gordon sighed again. "His employees do that."

The governor eyed him with something like pity, and yet beneath, there was a penetrating consideration. "Maybe you *are* the wrong man, Gordon, with that kind of cynicism and pointless anger. Sad thing is, I believe you could win just about any fight you put your mind to. Do you really want to waste your efforts on Judas Tarkenton?"

A glance over at Loretta, who had left off staring out the window and was waiting for his answer along with the rest. Gordon knew how she felt, Pan that she was. To her, Judas Tarkenton was making her dream come true, was a good man who had helped Pans understand themselves, who had gotten Earth focused on what was most important to all of them.

They'd had arguments about his feeling. And, truth to tell, Gordon knew his resentment was just that, a kind of itch that he'd scratched for so long he'd miss it if it was gone. He'd had talks with Tarkenton over the years and he didn't really count the man his enemy. More like an irritation, if that.

And perhaps that was the real issue. As commissioner, he didn't have to deal with Tarkenton over anything more than police escorts and security. As mayor, he'd have to deal with the man on a regular basis.

Was he afraid of that? Why? What did he think Tarkenton would do, convert him?

Perhaps.

"Dad!" It was Scotty, squeezing his way between people, weaving around waiters who had appeared with open bottles of champagne and tall glasses. The big moment was close at hand. "Dad, could you and Loretta come, *now*, please! I think someone might need you."

"Ever heard of Tantric magic?" Laurence asked, coming away from the gentle kiss he'd given her neck, and she felt a delicious shiver run up her back.

"Not . . . not really," she said, a little breathless, and then glanced anxiously over at the stairs. She thought she'd seen the curtain move, heard footsteps. Was it Gabe?

"Sex magic. It's believed that during sex, the man and woman exchange energies. It's viewed as a circle of fire, a kind of eternal dance."

What wonderful words, Piper thought. No wonder he was

a writer. And his voice was so beautiful, his face so hypnotizing. It made her feel she could actually do this, maybe even relax about it.

"What I'm telling you, Piper," he went on, in that low, warm, confident rumble, "is perhaps the most important lesson you can learn, more important than even how to make love and enjoy it. People come together expecting to gain something, but this coming together will only work if they understand that there will also be change, destruction as well as creation." He smiled his very white, warm smile. "But you understand all that already, don't you?"

"Well, not . . . not really." Piper flushed. She wanted to show him that she was more adult than she looked, but she also figured it was best to be honest.

Which made her wonder if she shouldn't tell Laurence about her most secret secret, that her mother had come down with the Pandemic during the first trimester of pregnancy but that, instead of having a miscarriage, she'd carried Piper to term.

That she'd been born with a tail which had disappeared, that she now had two small "brains" in her lower spine.

It had frightened her when her father told her. Seven years old and she'd had nightmares about it for months. She'd even checked out her behind over and over in the mirror, trying to find the vanished tail.

"What am I?" she'd finally demanded, and started to cry.

"Every test we've run on you says you're human," her father had assured her, which explained why Varouna did so many tests on her all the time.

Now, six years later, she'd long stopped thinking or worrying about the strange circumstances of her birth; but all of a sudden, she felt like telling Laurence her secret. She felt sure he would understand and accept it all, maybe even have answers that no one else had.

"Yes?" Laurence urged, and she realized that she'd hesitated.

"I'm not real experienced, if you know what I mean. I don't even know if I should be doing anything."

There. Her father would be proud of her for that; diplomatic, polite, but clear.

And Laurence seemed to understand. He nodded and smiled. "Hey, we'll do whatever you want. A little or a lot or none at all. I just find you really attractive and I thought it'd be nice to get to know you."

She felt her heart pounding hard in her chest then, and her head felt light and a little dizzy, which was strange since she hadn't even tasted her drink.

She went a little breathless then, especially when his face came very close. She smelled hard liquor, sharp and frightening, and his very masculine fragrance, like oranges and hot chocolate. And then his lips touched hers and he was kissing her.

It wasn't like any kiss she'd had before. For one thing, his beard and mustache were there, tickling, yet soft. For another, it was the kind of kiss used in old films, deep, and his tongue was pushing into her mouth, opening it wide. That was startling, and scary, but also stimulating in a way the wet smacks she'd gotten from boys her own age had never been. She didn't quite know what to do.

His hand moved down from her shoulder, slipping down under her dress, down, soft and shivery sweet on her skin.

He touched her breast.

She jerked back, unbalanced and scared. This was going too fast—

His fingers found her nipple.

And that's when she bit him. She just bent to his arm and sunk her teeth in, hard.

Much, much later, she would play that moment over and over again, wondering why she didn't just scream for him to stop, because he probably would have. Or, if she'd been that scared, why hadn't she just kicked him?

But then, his touch hadn't actually panicked her. It had, to the contrary, made her *mad*. She'd felt . . . affronted.

And maybe that was why she'd done it.

Stop it! was the only thought she would ever be able to remember thinking at the time. That, and a wish that she had never gone with him.

"Hey!" She heard him suck in a cry as her teeth broke the flesh and she tasted something warm and salty.

"Let her go!" she heard someone else say even as the hand went from fondling her to knocking her away. Her teeth tore out of the arm, splattering blood across her mouth, and she banged her head against the mantel. There was a bad moment where she couldn't breathe, where there was a warm, metallic taste on her lips, a slippery film that clung to her teeth and trickled down her chin. Laurence was hissing and holding his bleeding arm even as a pudgy, balding man came at him, snarling.

Should bandage that arm, Piper thought, strangely detached.

The shorter man sent his fist up, and, against all expectations, it got Laurence right in the jaw. The big bearded man went stumbling back and then he just folded, fell to the carpet, his skull hitting the wall.

That might cause a concussion, Piper thought.

"My God! Piper. Are you all right?" An orange shirt, a tie that didn't match, plump, worried hands touching her very gingerly. "Are you hurt? *Jesus!* That fuck! You're bleeding!"

She caught a breath, and it came back out a sob. And then she was in Gabe's arms, crying and shaking, even as her mind floated above her, worrying that the blood might have stained her dress, wondering if Laurence might be seriously hurt, and what she was going to tell her father?

Crying and crying, because the day, which was supposed to have been so wonderful, had just turned very, very ugly.

*   *   *

He had informed Fredricko he wouldn't be giving any interviews to journalists, and he'd reiterated that to Davy, Jackson, and Gabe. No talking to the media until that moment when the last piece of the starbridge was set in place; and then he'd hold a press conference, express how happy he was, how proud, and how much more there was yet to accomplish, blah, blah, blah.

But he found himself in a private question and answer session all the same, even though champagne was already being uncorked and in twenty minutes he was expected to publicly witness the last exterior piece of the stargate set into place.

It had happened not long after he'd finished chatting with Wilson. He'd hidden himself away in what had to be a bump in the side of the gondola, a kind of booth with a solitary cocktail table and its own little window. Two people could sit comfortably, three if they were willing to crowd, but no more. His hope was to hide there for a moment, catch his breath, have a drink with Varouna. He'd even asked Jackson and Davy to stand within the doorway instead of without so no one would notice them and figure out his hiding place.

It was relatively quiet and out of sight of the salon, but Nikki Richardson had still found it, and him, inching close enough that Davy shouldered her back.

"Mr. Tarkenton," she'd said, very loudly. "I've come to smoke a peace pipe!"

Davy had taken hold of Nikki's arm. But as he pulled her away, she'd said, "I've heard that there might be a special prosecutor appointed to investigate all companies working on the stargate. Don't you want to avoid that?"

That's when Jude had exchanged a look with Varouna and raised his hand, stopping Davy.

"What is it you want, Ms. Richardson?" he'd asked coldly.

"Just a quick interview," she'd said then, ringing all kinds of suspicious alarm bells in Jude's head. Renown for her talk show, a forum for anti-Pan opinions, Nikki Richardson was a handsome woman with roan hair pinned up in a French twist and a neat, small figure. She was also a Pan, which lent credence to her claims that other Pans could be cured of their alien obsessions. She argued, in fact, that she could "save them all from themselves," if they would only listen to her.

How she'd gotten an invite to this particular celebration Jude did not know, but he had his suspicions. Nikki was very good at twisting arms. She'd been trying to twist his for years.

"You were right about Luton Tec., Mr. Tarkenton," she'd gone on, her tone oddly ingratiating, "and I'm willing to admit it, on-line, right now. Wouldn't that serve you and your company? Especially on this night of all nights? Give me a *private* interview, a short one. I'll apologize publicly for ever doubting you, and give you a forum to air your side of the story."

"And you get what, Ms. Richardson?"

"I finally get you on my show," she'd said, seriously, almost humbly. "Ten minutes, that's all I ask."

Jude had nodded to Davy then, and Jackson had fetched a third chair, which they'd set to Jude's left.

Varouna had pointedly stayed in her seat. Her body language told him she wasn't about to leave him alone with this woman. Jude was glad enough of that; he didn't trust Nikki, but he didn't dare pass up her offer either. She was right. A real-time retraction by her, here and now, would do Pandora a world of good and repair not a little of the damage done by Luton Tec.

"Ten minutes," he'd echoed, and so ended up doing what he did not and had not wanted to do.

"This is very generous of you, Mr. Tarkenton," Richardson said, bringing out her I-dik pad and setting it up so that it would tape and download the interview directly into the Multi-Media Channel. "I know you don't much like me," she added with a cryptic smile. She did not show off her teeth when she smiled, but kept her lips pressed tight, as if holding back secrets.

"Davy, get me a drink," he ordered. The younger body-guard nodded and vanished from the door. Jackson moved to center himself, arms aggressively crossed. He clearly didn't like this.

"Let's get this over with," Judas snapped as Richardson finished fiddling.

"Of course. Let me first make good on my promise. You warned the Stargate Committee, and anyone else who would listen, that Luton Tec. couldn't be trusted. You were right. They turned in inferior mono-matrix sheets and stole nearly ninety million global dollars in the process, the largest graft operation ever. So it would seem that we all owe you a pro-found apology."

"Accepted," Jude said shortly.

"Of course," she said, eyes sparking, "it could be argued that the entire stargate project is such a scam."

"Good-bye, Ms. Richardson," Jude interrupted, starting to rise.

"You promised me ten minutes!" Richardson suddenly snapped with something like panic, something like rage.

And Jude sunk back down, startled and disturbed. Varouna was frowning. "Yes I did," he said. "That's not the same as listening to your stale tirades."

The flush left her cheeks and she subsided. "Quite so. So, Mr. Tarkenton, what do you think of how the Stargate Committee handled this embarrassing situation?"

"I'm less worried about the bad publicity than I am about the mono-matrix sheeting," he confessed smoothly. "We were actually quite lucky. The bad sheeting is only in a few places, and Mono-Mat International is replacing them as fast as they can." There, he thought. Being able to say that was worth the whole interview.

"I'm sure you had something to do with that." Richard-son's tone was noticeably pert.

"Outside of recommending Mono-Mat, no, I didn't."

"Pandora designed the stargate. Its scientists are working on how to power it, and word is that Pandora Corp. will provide the test pods and train potential astronauts. That's a great deal of power and control in your hands, Mr. Tarkenton, and in the hands of your Pandemic of a company."

"You really can't help yourself, can you, Ms. Richardson?" Jude shook his head. But she didn't seem to hear him.

"You're involved in a much more insidious kind of graft, aren't you, Mr. Tarkenton?" she went on, leaning in. "Earth has already paid out four billion lives to the Kasarans—"

Good Lord. "Ms. Richardson," he cut through, "you can have an interview, or you can make your speeches. You don't get both."

"I know how you think! I know how that alien infection makes you think!" she hissed suddenly, with surprising vehemence. "It makes you want to cheat Earth of even more human lives! Just steal them, as if they had no value at all."

Richardson was breathing heavily, nostrils flaring, and Jude blinked at her, amazed. The woman routinely got angry and yelled at guests on her show, but she usually built up to that over a good fifteen minutes; they'd been talking less than five. Had he missed something?

Unless . . . he glanced over at Jackson, hand lifting to signal. This was all wrong.

Jackson took a step forward, alerted, and that's when Richardson snapped the weapon out from the side of the pad. It was sharp and thin and made of plastic, the kind of item that would not have been expected or found in a search.

She was going for him before he realized that the blade wasn't some strange addition to her pad.

Jackson moved very fast, but not fast enough. Varouna was there first, but Nikki was prepared, determined and very strong.

She lunged and connected.

*　　*　　*

Gabe put himself in front of Piper when the commissioner and his wife arrived, it was all he could think to do. It was something of a given in Pandora, standing orders from Tarkenton to each and every employee: Piper was to be protected.

"I hit him," Gabe said as the commissioner and his wife both moved to kneel by the unconscious bearded man. "He was . . . touching Piper." Gabe ran a hand over his head. Surprisingly, he wasn't sweating anymore. Striking out had relaxed him considerably.

"So my son said." The commissioner frowned up at him. Gabe had met Gordon Demme a few times, unofficially. He wasn't real comfortable around anyone associated with the law, but Demme was as comfortable as they came. Nice guy. Sane. And his wife was a solid patrolwoman.

"Is the girl all right?" the wife asked now.

"Shook up." Gabe pulled at his tie. God. What was he going to tell Mr. Tarkenton? He glanced back at Piper, whom he'd settled in one of the chairs. She had her knees up and was hugging them. "She should be moved . . ."—he glanced pointedly at the body—"somewhere else."

"In a moment." The commissioner spoke very calmly, he looked worried. "Loretta, can I speak with you?"

"Commissioner." Gabe reached out, stopped when Demme glared back at him. For just a moment, the man who had seemed so mild looked quietly dangerous. Well, he would be mad. Who wouldn't, to have had a day off turned upside down like this? "Can we keep this under wraps?" Gabe asked softly. "I mean, the whole place doesn't have to know, does it? I'm not trying to protect Mr. Tarkenton here," he added, because he knew how Demme felt about his employer, and waved back at Piper meaningfully.

"Don't worry," was all Demme would say, and, taking his wife by the arm, huddled with her in a corner.

Gabe glanced at the bearded molester, as he was beginning to think of the bastard; the man didn't look like he was going to wake up anytime soon. In fact, he was looking pretty awful. Served him right.

"Gabe?" Piper was still staring over her knees at her toes, blood smearing her face, what wasn't on his shirt.

He pulled out his handkerchief, found a bottle of water on the mantel, and dampened the cloth. He knelt by her and gently wiped away the blood from her chin. Her eyes stayed on her shoes. "Yes, sweetheart?"

"I was . . . mean to you . . . earlier today."

He felt as if someone had grabbed his heart. He stuffed the bloody handkerchief back into his pocket. "Don't think of that, sweetheart."

"Have to think of something else," she murmured. "I'm sorry about today, about being such a bitch."

"I shouldn't have said what I said to you," he muttered, hurting for her.

The commissioner was back, his wife stepping over to Piper. "Hey, honey," she said kindly. "Why don't we go to the ladies' room, get you freshened up?"

Piper looked a little apprehensive about that, but she rose and took the woman's slender hand when she offered it. They were quite a contrast, the adult woman tall and brown, the adolescent short and very pale.

Piper didn't even glance down as she stepped over the bearded man to reach the exit. Gabe watched them leave, listened to their footsteps going down the metal stairs.

"Listen, Commissioner, I'd like to be the one to explain this to—" he began, then stopped. Demme was standing with arms crossed, his dour face very grave. "What?"

A nod down at the bearded man. "He's dead."

Gabe forgot how to breath. "Dead?" He lifted a hand to pull at his tie but couldn't seem to lift it that high. "Can't be. I—I didn't hit him that hard."

"I don't know why or how," the commissioner said, "but until I do, you're under arrest. I'm going to have Tuturro turn back and then I'm going to phone the coroner."

Worse and worse. God. Gabe wiped at his face.

"Gordon!" Loretta was back, her brown face almost gray. "Tarkenton's been attacked!"

Gabe was pushing past her before a single thought came to mind. His heart was pounding hard in his chest.

Oh, God. Oh, no! Don't let him be hurt!

Chapter 22

Amusement park rides took a novel twist during the post-Pandemic years. Pans, sometimes suffering from an almost intoxicating need to feel weightless, brought back into vogue isolation chambers and stayed for weeks at amusement parks featuring dropping elevators or parachute rides. They spent so much money on commercial spaceflight that the number of shuttles tripled and the price for going out into space plummeted.

This obsession also led to the popularity of "floaters," sporting restaurants, spas, and even elegant apartments. Spearheaded by Pandora Corp. in cooperation with the legendary Zeppelin Company, these modern airships contained solar-heated air/helium gas vector engines, fly-by-light laser controls, and weather-working computer systems. These floaters, many still in operation today, were popular settings for several suspense thrillers and hot romances.

—The Starlight Connection

THOUGH SHE HADN'T SMOKED IN NEARLY ELEVEN years, Varouna was craving a cigarette, badly, and seated there in Commissioner Demme's stark office, she'd nearly convinced herself that she deserved one. But then they brought in Gabe, who looked just awful, his jacket and tie gone, cuffs on his wrists making his hands look puffed and swollen, and she forgot all about the nicotine fix.

He stopped in the doorway when he saw her, a kind of agony in his eyes. Maybe he just never expected anyone to come get him, or maybe he wished she hadn't bothered.

If he asked her why, she thought, she might just tell him that it was far quieter here than at the hospital, where the media, camped across the street, clamored for details. They were running constant updates on Judas's hospitalization, along with stories on Nikki Richardson, who was locked away and under suicide watch.

The woman had recorded a message, of course. And being that she was now the hottest news on the planet, that message, as she had no doubt intended, was being played over and over again. It extolled the world to destroy the stargate, to find a cure for Pans instead of accepting their illness. It excused her violence against Judas as an attempt to stop the madness. She demanded that Pandora be investigated, arguing that the corporation had cheated every soul on Earth with false promises. "A global swindle," Richardson called it. And, going for the all too obvious, "Selling out the planet for thirty pieces of silver!"

But the message was backfiring, at least in the quarters where it mattered. The senators who had been on *Mimi's Folly* had gone on record as saying that they would fight any investigation of Pandora or Judas Tarkenton.

"We won't be party to anything that lends credence to Nikki Richardson and all she stands for, the violence, hate, fear, and intolerance," Senator Babin had gravely intoned on camera. And his words were accompanied by tape from Richardson's own I-dik pad of her crazed appearance, her stabbing of Judas.

And so the cowardly senator found a safety net for the

position they'd pushed him to take, and Pandora, or so it appeared, dodged yet another bullet, the most serious one to date.

But not Judas.

Should have been faster, Varouna thought, chewing on a nail. She'd reached for Nikki's arm as the woman swung the knife, but missed. Jude, who was starting to rise, was stabbed in the upper back, right in the spine. Crazed and wild, Nikki had managed to plunge the blade twice more into Jude's side even as Jackson wrestled her off.

"Don't move!" Varouna had begged him. And he had stared up at her, gasping, bewildered, his blood soaking into her sari as she frantically tried to help him.

Hours later, from the hospital, she'd finally thought to call the penthouse and ask that someone send her fresh clothing; an aide had arrived in minutes and gingerly handed her a sari pressed and wrapped in plastic. She wore it now, a brown one, quiet and subdued.

She wouldn't have the peacock sari washed, she thought, just burned. It was Piper's favorite, but the poor girl wasn't going to want to see it ever again, not after what had happened today, which included the mysterious death of suspense writer Laurence Anderson.

Varouna, her gaze returning steadily to Demme, couldn't say which way the commissioner planned to jump on that one. With his old-fashioned bay mustache and sad, gray eyes, he might demand there be a public inquest, or not. Still dressed in the shirt and tie he'd worn on *Mimi's Folly,* he sat behind his desk (tidy, that desk, not in an obsessive way, but as if he just couldn't think of anything to put on top of it), seeming pained and worried about *her.*

Yes, well, she thought, leaning back in her chair, he *was* keeping her from the hospital. But then Piper and two very guilty and worried bodyguards were pacing the waiting room floors right now. Varouna figured she was where Jude would want her, and frankly, as patient as she was, she hated wasting time in places where the waiting seemed pointless. Davy would call her when they knew whether Judas was going to pull through or not, and in what condition.

"Dr. Premjad," Gabe said as the guard sat him in the other chair. He kept to the edge of it, as if he wanted to stay standing. "You shouldn't be here."

"She's here to explain to you what killed Laurence Anderson," Commissioner Demme said, as the guard left. Then he rose and came around to unlock the cuffs.

It had been Demme's idea to explain it all to Gabe.

"You kill another person," Demme had told her, *"or even think you have, and that sticks with you. He shouldn't have to live with that. Now I can tell him a lie, or you can tell him the truth, but he's going to know right now he didn't do it."*

And *"I'll tell him,"* she said, because one did not shirk one's dharma.

Gabe rubbed at his wrists, bewildered. Demme stayed on that side of the desk, leaning back against it. Behind him, the old air-conditioning coughed out an icy breeze and the windows gazed out on a wall of other windows. That was the way of New York City, windows and walls facing windows and walls.

It had taken nine years, but Varouna finally felt she understood the city and those who were native to it, like Gabe. People crowded the streets, as many as might in the aftermath of the Pandemic; and yet there was a distinct difference from the multitudes in India, not in the level of poverty and wealth, but in their essence. In India, there was a chaos of movement that was like water or air, swirling, seemingly directionless, and yet, in the end, spiritually routed. Those who lived there took their time, allowed themselves to be captured by the festivals that swept through, by the unexpected obstacles and opportunities that might cross their path, everything from a sacred cow to a beggar to the waters of a monsoon.

The movement of life, to them, was ordered by forces of

family, by karma, by the cycle of life. You danced to whatever music was playing at the moment.

In New York, there was no nature. The citizens had created their river out of steel and concrete and glass, out of a grid of numbered streets that seemed to flow on forever. And so each and every soul moved with purpose in this city; they all had a place to be and an impatience to be there. An ambition. Like the skyscrapers, always reaching, always achieving. The trains arrived and travelers flowed on or off, the clocks struck a time and workers poured in or out. It was an attractive energy that could burn the soul out; more like magma than water, hot and beautiful.

A city of earth and fire instead of water and air. Fire and earth were both a means of burial, they consumed or swallowed the dead. And like such powerful elements, New York scared newcomers; it revealed to them, as the millions of stars in the sky might, just how unimportant they were.

But the city could come together as well, it could become one soul, with one heart, all feeling the same, all putting their energy into one aim, be it a parade or a political movement . . .

Or the building of a bridge.

"Piper told me everything," she explained to Gabe. "She's very worried about you." That caused the usually brash Gabe to duck his head like a schoolboy. "But the reason I'm here is because the coroner couldn't explain what happened and I could."

The pudgy little man looked anxious about that. "Dr. Premjad, you don't have to explain anything. I mean"—he shifted in his chair—"I mean Pandora and all, it's more important to me than *anything*. I mean that. I'd die for it, if I had to, that's how important it is."

Few things could push Varouna off balance, and she liked it that way; she'd spent her life learning how to maintain her equilibrium. But Gabe had just managed to do it, and with so gentle a touch that she was taken completely by surprise. She felt her heart tilting, wobbling, and the world seemed to rush up, close enough to smell and taste, close enough to terrify.

She swallowed hard, and pushed it back with something like a smile. "Are you offering to 'take the fall,' Gabe?"

He shrugged, chagrined. "It wasn't the kid's fault. God knows she doesn't deserve any more publicity. Pandora certainly doesn't. I can take it."

"Yes, it *was* her fault," Dr. Premjad said softly. And Gabe looked up at her sharply.

"I hit him and he hit his head, isn't that what happened?"

"What I'm going to tell can't leave this room." Varouna looked to Demme, unsure of what she might see there. He knew already, she'd told him quietly and privately, anticipating that she'd have to work very hard to prove it to him. But his face had gone ashen when she explained, and then he'd pushed a button and told them to bring in Gabe.

Now he stared down at his polished shoes and nodded gravely, as if he agreed with her, as if he'd decided instead of acquiesced.

"Piper's future depends on it," she added.

"Maybe you'd better not trust me," Gabe said, running a hand over his head.

"I have to. If Judas doesn't come through . . ." she couldn't finish. Eight years together. She hadn't thought it would work, had barely unpacked her bags that first year she'd come to live with this man who hung Rangers paraphernalia on his office walls and built models of New York skyscrapers out of little plastic Legos.

Judas, she had known when she moved in, still carried a candle for Piper's mother, the woman who had been married to his best friend, the woman who had decorated the penthouse. The one who had left Judas to join her dead husband. That one, Varouna knew, still danced at the center of his heart, and would continue to do so, no matter how many years passed.

But then Judas had taken Varouna outside on a winter's

afternoon to sculpt designs in snow. He'd bought her a Rangers hat to wear at the hockey games and on occasion he had woken her up in the middle of the night for an impromptu trip to the Night Owl. There, while it was still dark outside, they'd sip coffee and talk science. And they would call up books on their I-dik pads, downloading information, writing out formulas. Sometimes Piper would arrive, driven there by Oliver, to have her breakfast with them. That was when Varouna would realize that it was light outside, that they'd been there for hours.

And at those times, Varouna felt . . . *knew* that if she wasn't in Judas's heart, at least she danced in his head, and he in hers.

And that, for both of them, was more, oh much, much more than enough.

She could, she reasoned now, live without him, but she wasn't sure she could live in the world knowing that he was no longer in it.

"Piper is going to need your support," Varouna finished. "She killed Anderson, Gabe, infected him when she bit him."

"What the fuck?" His expression was beyond stunned, it was angry. "You *can't* be joking. What are you saying? That Anderson was allergic to her saliva or something?"

"I mean that saliva from Laurence Anderson's bite contains a kind of fast-acting and fatal bacteria that entered his bloodstream and shut down his nervous system as fast as a snakebite."

"That can't be right!" Gabe insisted.

"It is," Demme cut in, his voice sounding strained. "Believe me, we looked for another explanation."

"I also examined your handkerchief," Varouna went on. She was impressed with the coolness of her tone. The chemical composition of what she'd seen under the microscope had scared her to death. Fast and lethal. "The one you used to wipe the blood from Piper's chin? Same thing."

"Oh, God." Gabe sunk back, his thoughts were clear from

the look in his eyes; if he'd had had a break in the skin, the infection in that blood might have gotten him, too.

Varouna felt strangely angry about that, as if Gabe were criticizing Piper. "She's not dangerous anymore," she heard herself snapping. "It was a protective response, it's gone now, and for all we know it may never happen again."

"It was *deliberate*?"

"Deliberate, but unconscious, I assure you."

"How . . . ?"

"Piper's mother contracted and survived the Pandemic during her first trimester."

"She woulda miscarried," Gabe argued, as if that were a law of nature.

"Valerie McAllister did not. So far, she is the only woman on record to contract the virus that early in her pregnancy and not miscarry. Piper was born with a vestigial tail."

"A . . . tail." Now he looked scared. Perhaps this was too much for him. She hoped not. She was gambling Piper's future on her trust of him.

"They're not that uncommon a mutation. Babies are born with them all the time. Usually there's a quick surgery and that's the end of it. But there were no doctors Judas could take her to that year. So she kept it. And it did what such anomalies never do, it shrunk and vanished."

"I don't . . . I don't understand. What are you telling me?"

"Kasarans have multiple brains that do different functions, you know that. One of the brains is in the tail."

"She . . . *she has a Kasaran brain*?" His tone seemed to hover between skepticism and fear.

"She has two, to be precise," Varouna said bluntly, and watched as eyes dilated; Gabe looked dizzy, Demme nervously brushed at his mustache. "When they were first detected, we feared that they might be tumors. They weren't. They're about the size of a mouse brain, very small. They haven't grown or changed since she was five, and so far they've been completely dormant."

"So far," Demme echoed.

Varouna folded her arms, her heart heavy, as if so much had been put upon the scales that it had finally snapped and fallen. She remembered a day when Piper, knowing how much she loved candles, had set dozens of them all over the apartment. But after lighting fifty, the fire alarms went off, and that's what Judas and Varouna had come home to find, Piper, the alarms, and the smell of fifty hastily snuffed candles.

Dear, dear, thoughtful Piper.

"Does she know?" Gabe asked quietly. There was an edge of anger in the voice, outrage. Varouna felt herself stiffen, then forced herself to relax. Gabe wasn't trying to offend her, he just cared.

"About her Kasaran 'brains'? Yes. We explained it as soon as we thought her old enough to understand. About the virus she created, no. Not yet."

"Will you tell her?"

"As soon as I get back to the hospital. I want to get some X rays and blood work from her, make sure she's back to normal." Which was what? she wondered, her hands shaking as she pressed them together in her lap. So tired. Such a long terrible day, heading into a longer and more terrible night.

"I want to be there," he said grimly, and when Varouna looked his way, "She'll need me."

"After we get the tests back, Gabe," Varouna said, "but, yes. She will."

Commissioner Demme kept silent, troubled.

"What's going in your report, Commissioner?" Gabe now demanded, his body tensed and hunched, aggressive, protective. "What will you tell the media?"

Demme sighed and rubbed underneath his old fashioned glasses at his eyes. "I'll think of something."

* * *

They wouldn't let her into intensive care. All they'd allow was for her to sit in the private waiting room, watching her father on a monitor. He looked grainy on the small screen, and not real, a clear plastic hose taped to his mouth and an IV going into his arm. There were patches and wires, and machines monitoring everything. She could watch the lines and squiggles and spikes below the picture if she wanted, see if his heartbeat was still strong, his pulse and pressure regular.

She saw those lines both as patterns and as information, everything she experienced was like that. Her mind was so clear and flat, as if her emotions had gotten up and walked away.

Was this how the Pans had felt during the Pandemic? How her mother might have felt when her biological father died, or how her dad felt when her mom died? She felt suddenly very close to all of them.

"Piper?" That was Varouna, somberly swaddled in a brown sari trimmed with silver, seated next to her in a brown leather arm chair. The room was, Piper reflected, pretty nice for a waiting room.

"What?" She was having a hard time being polite. At least she could stand having Varouna in the room, because Varouna wasn't trying, like everyone else, to show her sympathy or make her feel better. Not like Oliver, who tried to hug her, when the last thing she wanted was to be touched. And then there were Jackson and Davy, who looked at her with such hurt and shame that she felt obligated to comfort them.

She felt too selfish right now to want to do that.

And there was Mavis and Dr. Walsh, and the doctors, who tried to talk to her as if she were a little girl, explaining things slow and way too simply.

That made her mad, as mad as she could feel right now, with her blood running cool as snow and her mind drifting away, looking down on it all from far above.

She wished her friends were here, kids her own age. They might not understand what she was going through, but they'd understand her. Ida and Rose and Violet would know to bring her a root beer and play cards with her.

"Piper," Varouna tried again, and this time her hand was on Piper's chin, gently lifting so that their eyes met. "Listen. About the tests—"

"Yes," Piper said impatiently, "I heard what you said. The throat culture and the pap smear were normal. Which means my saliva and vaginal fluids are human, not . . . alien. You're still waiting on the blood work and the urinalysis."

"Did you hear what I told you about the X rays?"

She blinked. "A third brain's appearing."

"Rudimentary. Right above the other two."

"What happened on the floater caused it, didn't it?"

"Likely, yes," Varouna said with gentle directness.

"They're Kasaran, aren't they? The brains."

"We think . . . We think Kasaran-like."

"Able to create viruses and . . . other things. Chemical compounds." It wasn't a question. She said it analytically, coolly. It was as if she had been folded up and reopened, like some strange origami doll, once a child, now an adult. She felt like one, thought like one.

"So it would seem."

"Why did he die?" Piper asked then, because she'd been wanting to know. At first, she hadn't been able to comprehend it, that there'd been something evil in her saliva; it sounded so absurd, but then it had all made a weird sort of sense. Of course a freak like her would be able to do something like that. But there was one thing she still didn't understand. "I only wanted to stop him. I didn't want to kill him."

"The reason that Laurence Anderson died," Varouna said carefully, oh so carefully, "is because your body hit a level of arousal that woke up the brains in your spine. It wasn't intentional; you're thirteen. No one your age is in control of their hormones, and anything could have spiked them. Do you understand? Anything."

"Are they still awake?"

Varouna pressed her lips together. "I don't think they're ever going to go back to sleep again, Piper."

Of course not.

"When they woke up," Varouna went on, "they tried to communicate what you were feeling to Anderson. Being that they're your brains, they know how to get past the normal defenses of the human body. Which enabled the message to move very quickly through Anderson's body. And as the message had only one purpose, it could also be very direct."

God. What would her friends think if they found out? What would Scott Demme think?

"We'll have to test you regularly."

"Yes," Piper said, turning her attention back to her father, lying still as death in his hospital bed. Nurses and doctors came and went, at one point pulling curtains closed around the bed so that those in the waiting room wouldn't see whatever private things they were doing.

She watched the lines and squiggles and spikes that marked her father's pressure and heartbeat and pulse.

A whole human life, Piper thought then, love and hate, creation and murder, and it all comes down to this. All just strange chemistry.

In her case, very strange indeed.

The news showed a split screen; on one side, a space shuttle towing the final bit of tubing into place, finishing out the circle of the stargate; on the other half, images of Judas Tarkenton, plastic tubing from his mouth and trailing out of his arms, being rushed on a gurney from *Mimi's Folly* to a helicopter and on to the hospital.

The voice-over explained how Tarkenton had been cut down not ten minutes before he was to usher in worldwide celebrations in honor of this first, completed step. How the festivities on board *Mimi's Folly* had never gotten under way, and how other parties around the world had barely had time to get started before the news of Tarkenton's hospitalization cut them short.

Tarkenton was now in ICU after several hours of intense surgery, alive but barely. And the starbridge, often referred to as "the Mourning Wreath" due to its similarity to the one at Rockefeller Center, had become one in earnest.

Scotty was leaning on pillows, close to the screen. Gordon rested back on the couch, drinking seltzer water to ease his stomach and keeping his free hand on Loretta's knee. Loretta was knitting, her way of calming her nerves.

Kyle had called to say he wouldn't be coming home for the night. He and the other engineers were holding a vigil for Tarkenton at the office.

Strange to say, Gordon almost wanted to ask if he could join them. Strange to say, but he felt suddenly close to Tarkenton. He had stood in that narrow doorway, stared down at the man, vulnerable and left crumpled in a pool of blood because no one dared move him. Loretta had crowded in with an ashen-faced Dr. Premjad to help. That, too, had affected Gordon, seeing his wife wetting her hands with Tarkenton's blood, tears trailing down her face because this man was her future, and he was in such terrible trouble.

And all the while, Richardson had screamed and shrieked from where Tarkenton's bodyguards kept hold of her. One of her eyes was swelling and some of her rants concerned Pandora brutality, but no one was listening. Gordon told her flatly that she was under arrest for attempted murder, recited her rights to her, then ordered her locked away until they landed.

The fury and glee in her eyes had disturbed him badly.

And at the edge of it all, Piper stood, head in hands, sobbing uncontrollably. Gabe had been behind her, tears wetting his mustache.

And everyone else on *Mimi's Folly,* the guests and the waiters and Tuturro, had remained silent as if at a grave site.

Scotty's feet were kicking, up and down, hitting the floor. Usually Gordon could ignore it, but not tonight.

"Scotty, please," he asked. "Stop that kicking."

The boy looked back, Mae's dusty black almond eyes and Gordon's own bay hair. The feet stayed up. "Sorry."

"It's all right," he said, examining his son. Could the Pandemic have done something to Scotty as it had to Piper, in the womb?

Don't be ridiculous, Gordon! he chided himself. *This is different.* Mae was in her last trimester, almost due. And she wasn't sick for long. It was different.

Oh, God, please, let it be different.

But what if it wasn't?

"Is Piper okay, Dad?" Scotty asked then, and Gordon saw that the boy was gazing his way, worried. It was the first time since they'd left the airship that he'd said anything about what had happened.

"Except for her father, yes, she is."

"Did I do the right thing?" During the madness, Scotty had run to help fetch towels and water from the bar. He'd raced up to tell the flight crew what was going on, and then hurried back to his father to await further orders. His son, thought Gordon, liked to have a purpose.

"Of course you did the right thing."

"But that man, Laurence Anderson—"

"An accident. I don't want you fretting about it."

Scotty quieted then, but he didn't return to watching the news. Instead he lay out on the rug, chin braced on his interlaced hands.

Not the same, Gordon thought. But what if it was? What if Scotty had something alien in him, something that couldn't be removed like a tooth or a tonsil, something that could show up at any time?

For perhaps the first time, Gordon Demme considered that; was that what it was like to be a Pan? To feel a kinship to the Kasaran aliens not only because you had touched their minds, but because you saw them in your spouse and in your parents and in your children?

There were those out there like Nikki Richardson, sworn to destroy those aliens because they hated to look in the mirror and see them there.

I can't let that happen, Gordon thought, watching his son. And, *God, Tarkenton, don't you dare die. Not now, not when I've finally come to my senses and know just how much we all need you and your damn stargate!*

Because meeting the aliens, healing the wounds and putting the past in the past, was indeed the only way to keep children like Scotty and Piper safe.

"I'm going to run for mayor," he said then. And Loretta paused; Scotty's eyes widened.

"Are you sure?" his wife asked. That was all.

"Very sure."

She nodded and returned to her knitting. Gordon got up and stepped over to Scotty. He slid down into a cross-legged position, which was hard at his age, with his joints beginning to stiffen. "That all right with you, Scotts?"

"Oh, yeah, you'd be a great mayor! I'd vote for you."

He smiled. "Let's see if the rest of the city agrees with you. Gordon Demme, mayor of New York City," he added, and shook his head.

However, he wondered, had he come to this?

Part IV: "I Will"

Chapter 23

November: Twenty-four years after the Pandemic

Xenobiologists at the Pasteur Institute have confirmed that Kasaran viral communications pose a significant biohazard (see diagrams on page 19).

In addition, essays contained herein by psychotherapists and sociologists, a good many of them working for Pandora Corp., argue that our post-Pandemic civilization is fragile at best. The phenomenon known as Enforced Cooperative Union, a tendency toward collaboration instead of competition, more evident in Kasarans than Homo sapiens, has produced a number of secondary phenomenological social and cultural changes the long-term effects of which have yet to become clear. (See Randow's report on the cross-tribal unification between the Hutu and Tutsi tribes of the former Belgian Congo.)

Finally, there is a strong argument that the human race is still suffering from a collective trauma. A growing ambivalence in the Pans (see Tandu's test results on page 403), including a notable schism in the Shoal Movement (see Cho Wang's observations on page 197), support this contention.

These and other essays contained herein support the con-

tention that humanity is not yet ready to make contact with the Kasarans.

—Introduction to *The Argus Report*
Commissioned by the Stargate Committee

THE ELEVATOR DOORS SLID OPEN TO THE SOUNDS OF disingenuous conversation. Scotty stepped out, well dressed in a white-water silk waistcoat, and paused at the top of the staircase to gaze out over the crowd like a prince. And that is just how Scotty felt among the cocktail dresses and smart suits, like a visiting prince. Competent and decisive, he had his mother's almond eyes and his father's sardonic smile, a smile that worked better for him than it ever had for the old man.

The smile was the key.

Scotty liked the admiring looks that came from that sea of familiar faces, Pandora scientists and engineers, primarily, many of whom Scotty had known since childhood. As for the rest, there was a healthy sprinkling of politicians, a couple of trusted news hounds . . . and a few bodyguards.

There were always bodyguards.

"Scotts!" An old friend of his father grabbed at his hand as he descended the stairs. "Good to see you!"

"Judge." He nodded back, and waved to a pair of ladies who flirtatiously smiled his way.

Released by the judge, he wandered on among the guests, admiring what Piper had done. The penthouse appeared at its most manicured. Clearly she'd gone all out for this soiree, restoring the gray silk wallpaper and trim. The Macintosh armchairs about the fireplace were a nice touch, as were the hothouse orchids, their heady fragrance riding just beneath the expensive perfume.

"Three of my father's essays were in that report," he overheard Ernst complaining to Bianca. "One we coauthored."

Sven's clone was speaking of the *Argus Report,* of course. No one in Pandora could talk of anything else. Recently, new, more cautious senators had been elected to the World Congress, and gotten themselves appointed to the Stargate Committee. They'd commissioned the *Argus Report* to investigate, they said, the possible repercussions of using the stargate. But the suspicion was that they were looking for a way to shut down the upcoming tests.

"Mom's really mad. She says this could delay the test," Bianca, looking lovely in an off-the-shoulder tea rose gown, said sympathetically. Delicate images of butterflies and swallows floated on the optic lace of her skirts, making Scotty suddenly aware of just how beautiful the women were these days. Popular styles had brought back button-down ankle boots, short, sculpted hairstyles, and the ornate jewelry that seemed to float on the skin.

Wonderfully soft skin.

". . . leaked to the press," he heard Dr. Walsh say, and saw the old physicist turning his glass around and around in his hand. He was talking to Reba, a playwright and one of Piper's oldest and closet friends. "It's going to bury us. And I don't think these festivities are the best sort of spin control."

There were a minimum of serving folk; the custom at these late-night cocktail parties was to arrange for several fully stocked carts and to set out platters of rich nibbles in the corners, letting guests help themselves. Scotty took note of the oysters nestled on ice, the bowls of glistening red caviar and deviled quail eggs, before stopping at a cart, pulling up a bottle of rye, and stirring himself a perfect Manhattan with a splash of lemon to make it an Uptown.

"We've pulled through worse than this." That was Mavis Battencourt, dressed in an archaic but elegant pants suit of gold and bronze. She was talking to her son, Arliss, one of Pandora's many publicists. Arliss was a little younger than Scotty and something of a ladies' man.

"But Baxter wasn't mayor," Arliss pointed out with that sour-tart tone of his.

Gordon, Scotty recalled, had said just about the same thing nearly two years ago when he announced that he would be retiring from politics.

"I barely stayed afloat, Scotts," he'd confessed over their traditional pancake breakfast. "And I figure I've more than paid my dues."

"So who do you think will win?" Scotty had asked.

"Baxter." A lead-heavy answer. "No doubt about it. He's got everything that everyone wanted that I couldn't give them."

Which was altogether true. Scotty had met the man. Buffed from a daily work regime, handsome, with eyes shallow and empty as black glass, he had charisma, charm, and an aura about him that most voters didn't recognize as patronizing.

Baxter's first move as mayor had been to cut the chromatics program from schools.

"An unnecessary extravagance," he had labeled it during an on-line town meeting. "Not really the business of the educational system. First and foremost should be the study and advancement of *human* history."

Which was exactly what Gen-M, the "miracle babies," who were now of voting age, wanted. After all, didn't they have their own dreams? It was hardly a surprise that they didn't want to bear the weight of their parents' ambitions as well.

As far as Scotty was concerned, Gen-M was throwing away the future of the human race.

Kids today.

"Oh." Piper almost bumped into him. She was dressed in a jet and jade gown, brilliant emerald snapdragons flying across the optic netting of its full skirt.

"Scotty," she said, her face close to his, and suddenly he felt himself on a distant shore, gazing at those features, so near, so far. She had the face of a child finding the first star; soft, round, alabaster white, with red hair cut short and silky close, as if she'd trimmed her sails so that she could soar faster.

He felt his heart begin to melt.

God. Don't let her smile.

"You're late," she said flatly. "Dad's been waiting for you. He's in the office with Gordon."

"Piper—" he blurted as she began to turn away.

She glanced back, impatient. "Yes?"

"You look wonderful."

"That's good of you to say." She seemed a little surprised. "Thanks," she added, her dress rustling as she slipped among the guests.

At least, he thought, she'd been cordial with him.

His fault, all of it.

Should have used the smile.

Scotty had practically forgotten Piper after that terrible evening on the floater. It was as if they'd been buffeted about by strange winds, blown in wildly different directions. That made it easy to forget, to get lost in the corners of their new worlds.

He heard a thing or two over the years, of course. It was only natural given the overlap in their social circles. Rumors of private tutors, of her wanting to stick by her father as he went through nerve regeneration and nearly five years of physical therapy.

But his last two years of high school had erased any casual thoughts he might have had about Piper McAllister, the girl with whom he'd once shared an egg cream. He ran the school newspaper with all the zeal of a director on old Broadway, the yearbook like an editor at the *New York Times*. Added to which, the girls loved him. Three hundred Twisters of high school age in Manhattan, about a hundred seventy of them girls, and he dated just about every one. Those years and his first two in college were spent (or, as his father liked to put it, *mis*spent) in a warm sea of a silky, sweet hair, intoxicating smells, and moist kisses.

He was so lost in girls that when he did see Piper in the company of her father, at the opening baseball game, at a concert or one of his father's fund-raisers, he hardly gave her a second look.

But, strangely, her image stayed in his dreams for nights afterward.

At NYU he met Glynis, a biology major with hands made for Chopin and eyes of cornflower blue. She gave him the nicest little hickies, and it was her idea to make love on the observation deck of the Empire State Building in the dead of winter.

He still clenched his teeth a little at the memory.

And then Glynis had suddenly gone serious on him. She needed someone, she had informed him, to help her focus down, not a horny kid.

It was right after that that Kyle had offered to take him into space.

"Everyone should go at least once," said the man who was the closest thing he had to a brother. "It puts things in perspective. And seeing the gate up close . . ." An awed shake of the head.

The next thing Scotty knew, he was suited up and on his way to the space station.

His life had not been the same since.

The door to Tarkenton's office was cracked open. Inside he saw his father, leaning against a large drafting table, arms crossed and head down. Hair almost gray now, Gordon still wore the same old black horn-rims, still maintained his mustache which, unlike his hair, was touched with bay color. Scotty paused a moment, a fond smile touching his lips.

"Dad." He stepped in. He saw Jude then. Tarkenton's long body was nestled on a pillowed recliner, sunken into the armchair as if weighed down by the bones. An ancient astronaut brought down by gravity. But Scotty still saw the ghost of the Judas Tarkenton he'd known in his youth. A tall, golden man who had graced the covers of glossy e-mags, one of the most recognized faces in the world. An award-winning image taken from those days had Jude dressed in a turtleneck shirt, long arms akimbo, dark brown hair tumbling over his wide forehead giving him the distinct feel of an impatient conductor. The color of the image had been such that his skin shone like polished brass and his large, almost oval hazel eyes seemed to be gazing far into the future. Scotty had always thought of Judas as a gold eagle after seeing that picture, soaring over the city, setting his golden crown high up in the night sky.

"Scotty," Tarkenton said, "is the report ready to go?"

Jude was angry.

"Up and running," Scotty informed him, crossing over to the floor-to-ceiling monitor. With a wave of the hand it came on. Three dozen Pandora sites registered. "We're calling it the *Io essays: Contrary Evidence to Argus.*"

"Is it?" Scotty's father threw the question at Tarkenton, not his son.

"Your dad's trying to be my conscience again," Tarkenton said with a tight smile.

"Nothing to do with conscience. I've read the report. You hired me as a consultant—well, I'm consulting."

"And they call *me* Judas," Tarkenton said it softly, but Gordon's intake of breath indicated he'd heard. Scotty tensed. Gabe and Varouna, damn them, were in India; that left him as the only buffer between the two.

But then, unexpectedly, Gordon's tight shoulders relaxed. "Just a Philistine," he gave back, mildly, which surprised Scotty.

"Too true." There was weariness in Jude's voice, which explained why his father had checked his usual knee-jerk reaction.

Tarkenton was close to the breaking point.

"Look at those fluctuations."

On the screen, the sites were displaying numbers and fifty-eight different charts, colors, pies, and waves. There were tiny images, rapidly changing, of worldwide debates from coffeehouses with a linkup to semipublic cabinet meetings. Lists of words, red-flagged because of their charged content, filed by.

"You're still favored," Gordon pointed out, nodding at the percentages. For the moment, they held somewhere around sixty, rising to seventy and plunging to fifty every other second.

"But not solidly. *Argus* has turned over the rock. Every politico on the planet is trying to save his worthless ass."

Scotty noted the reflection of images in Tarkenton's wintery eyes and considered the distinct difference between these two men, so important in his life. Both quiet, isolated even, and controlled, but his father always seemed to be right there, in the now, while Tarkenton was always somewhere up ahead, unreachable.

Like an oracle, Scotty thought, and shivered. The man saw things that might happen, acted on them. Which is what Gordon feared, that Tarkenton would act, without any seeming reason or explanation.

" 'S that the readership?" Gordon adjusted his glasses and gazed up at the number in the corner of the screen.

"That's *Io*'s download," Scotty said, touching on the monitor. Another figure appeared above it, seven times as large. "That's *Argus*."

"Shit."

Scotty snorted at that, turning away a little as Tarkenton and his father tried to absorb the information.

Outside the window, the balcony lay empty, windswept and forlorn. Potted trees had shed some brown leaves across it and there were a few dark, cold puddles from a recent rainstorm. Beyond the stone railing, the haloed lighting of Central Park seemed to float and glow, and the city itself shone cold and strangely quiet.

A plane flew in low overhead, crossing the night, running lights blinking.

That we did this, Scotty thought. *That we can do it.* That had been his thought when Kyle took him up into space and allowed him to float weightless before one of the wide station windows and see, up close, the full magnificence, the vast, golden glory of the starbridge.

It had taken his breath away, defied description. Like a ring of fire, so enormous it seemed to hold the whole of the universe within its circle.

"The sphere." Kyle pointed proudly to the glowing stone hanging and flashing at the center of the great gold wreath. "That was my bit of weird science. I worked out how to manipulate the magnetic fields to compress the carbon to the right density. You keep changing the charge and it keeps everything stable. Like a keystone in an arch. It also acts as a way to connect us to the Kasaran gate."

"Theoretically," Scotty had murmured.

"Oh," Kyle had said with a smile, "it's more than that."

Scotty had eyed him sharply then, excited. "You've tested it?"

"Not yet." Kyle had admitted, chagrined. "But we will. Soon."

I want to be there, Scotty had thought then, his heart pounding hard. *On the front lines, making it happen.* The wish was sudden, stronger than anything he'd ever wanted in his life, stronger than the lust he'd felt for Glynis.

He knew then that he didn't want to be part of the crowd when the big moment finally came, watching it as he might watch the glittering ball drop in Times Square on New Year's Eve. No. It didn't matter that he was coming in on this from the tail end, he wanted to make it happen, he wanted to help drop that ball, open that gate.

After Kyle brought him home, he promptly switched his major from journalism to business and political science. His father frowned, disturbed, when he explained what he wanted to do, but then quietly went off and spoke with Tarkenton.

After a year as a senator's aide and a stint with a political news organization, Scotty had passed on his résumé to Pandora.

Six months later, he was working under Gabe.

"Fuck it," Tarkenton snarled, bringing Scotty back. The percentage had dropped to thirty and was holding. Jude looked hollow and gray. "Scotty, get back to the party and play host for me. Send Arliss in. We've got to plot a media blitz."

"Yes sir." He nodded and slipped out. He paused there, feeling annoyed, helpless. He was Tarkenton's deputy, damn it! Gabe had left him in charge. Which was exactly where he wanted to be. So why couldn't he do more? And what *should* he be doing that he wasn't?

He crossed down the hall toward the sounds of glasses clinking and voices murmuring, but stopped when he heard an unmistakable retching.

A glance back and down the other way. The sounds continued. Someone who drank too much?

For a moment he was tempted to ignore it, but if someone was sick, he ought to take care of it. Or at least let Piper know.

The bathroom door was open, the light on. It was not the guest bathroom but the one near the office. The walls were a cool eau-de-nil green, the furnishings spare, a white claw-footed tub, toilet, urinal, and free-standing sink. One long mahogany shelf offered up perfumes, lotions, soaps, and an antique pharmacy bottle filled with white tablet painkillers.

Piper was vomiting into the toilet, her beautiful dress bunched up around her. She had her hands pressed to the floor and was being quite violently sick.

"Piper." He pushed in, alarmed, and reached to hold her by the bare shoulders. His hands nearly flew off again. She was hot to the touch, and dry.

"You're burning up!" He snatched a folded washcloth off the shelf and wet it in the sink. "Why didn't you tell anyone you were sick?"

She coughed and seemed to catch her breath. "Wasn't," she said, spitting. "Must have been the oysters."

"Here," he offered, bending to wipe her face, pointedly ignoring the stink from below. And that's when he froze. He hadn't meant to glance into the toilet, that being the last thing he wanted to look at.

But he did.

There was vomit, but there were also a handful of long black wormlike creatures, writhing in the filthy water. Only they didn't look like any worms he'd ever seen.

"Jesus Christ," he said, dropping the washcloth and backing away. He pressed his hand over his mouth, sure that he was going to be sick in turn. And right now, he didn't, he really *didn't* want to do that.

Piper blinked down, and tears suddenly swelled and trickled down her dead white cheeks. "Oh no," she whispered. "Oh no. What now?"

Chapter 24

The Forgotten Generation, originally known as the "Twisters," comprises one of the saddest and yet most inspiring chapters in post-Pandemic history. These pre-vaccine children spent their critical years in the strangest of environments: coveted curiosities expected to take the place of all dead children while enduring their own terrible loss.

And then, with the onset of the Cadeau Vaccine and the new "miracle babies," they were "forgotten." Some, once prized and coddled, were abandoned on the street!

Suffering from hypochondria, paranoia, agoraphobia, and panic attacks in adulthood, this neglected generation, so in need of consistency, loyalty, and love, purchased Labrador puppies so fast that a black market sprung up almost overnight.

And yet this same generation also produced heroic, optimistic, self-reliant, and adventurous adults. Raised during the exciting, vivacious years of the starbridge, they became, themselves, a living bridge to the future.

—The Starlight Connection

Varanasi had not changed, Varouna reflected warmly, as she sat with Gabe out on the ghats, gazing up at the stars. And yet it had. Gone was the constant roar of mechanical traffic, the rickshaws, the scooters, the backfiring buses. The air reeked only of cook fires and the distinct riverwater fragrance of the Ganges. It was, Varouna reflected, a most impressive display of what Indians could do when united.

They'd proved that when they followed Gandhi and they proved it now. The skies had been cleared, deliberately, so that people could gaze up at the stars. There was an enclosed crematorium by the Ganges, so even that smoke would no longer pollute the skies. And, here in Kasi, the luminous city, there were no longer any city lights; it was as dark as out in a field or desert, even now, on Diwali. People settled, knees under arms, crushed together on the flat rooftops, or on balconies, or, like her, on the ghats, to stare up at the sky.

And up at the new ornament that hung there. It was small, but clear as the November moon, feeling somehow near to the Earth. Its ring shape could almost be discerned with the naked eye. Not the branches, just the circle.

A gold ring, hanging in the sky like a marigold garland. They referred to it that way in India, not like in the West, where they called it a funeral wreath.

A necklace of marigolds, a mandala, there to welcome whatever traveler might come through, or whatever traveler might need to take it with them on their journey. It was a universal and sacred pattern, a spiritual message that any would know and recognize.

"Here we are," it said, "circling through Samsara, in the wheel of the universe, in the spiral of this galaxy, together. Come," it invited, "cross over with us and let us dance, together, at the center of it all."

At no time of the year did that message seem so strong as it did now, on Diwali. Celebrating the victory of spiritual enlightenment over ignorance, Diwali was the festival of lights. Residents purchased new clothes in preparation, white-washed the walls, swept, dusted, and polished till the city felt clean and new.

And then, on that first night, Varanasi came alive with fireworks and the *divas,* little clay oil lamps that every family set out by their doorway. Citizens also placed lamps out on the ghats, outlining the vast stone edifices in light, making it seem, thought Varouna, as if the stars had been brought down to earth.

"They've got that analysis of those, um, worm thingys," Gabe said, leaning over her shoulder and handing her his I-dik pad.

Varouna accepted the thin, clear pad, scanning the diagram of the autopsied worm it offered, the analysis of its makeup and the chemical contents of Piper's stomach, all the while listening to the sounds of celebration, the jangle of bells and the heartbeat of drums from the city, the pop and sizzle and bang of fireworks.

Earlier on, there had been a parade of Kasaran puppets made out of silk and paper and carried high on sticks so they seemed to be floating. And there had been a river of women pouring down the streets to the Ganges, all carrying the little lights between their brown hands, their multicolored veils making them look like a flowing rainbow. Folk passed to and from the river, lighting lamps, setting them down, giving them away.

Varouna's own concession to the holiday was a little lamp filled with perfumed oil that burned on the step at her feet; the smoke from its flame scrolling off, a fragrance Judas had liked, or rather, one of the few he'd been able to stand. He'd had a sensitivity to smoke and smells, and whenever she left candles burning he had snuffed them out as soon as he was sure she'd left the room.

"So?"

Three months since she'd left, and she still missed him

terribly. There were depths to Judas, like dark earth under sand. It had made him a passionate lover, sincere. But for all that, she'd felt that they were like the double rings of the Kasara Stargate, working together, but always apart. She didn't mind it; they weren't meant to unite as men and women sometimes could. And, at last, it had come time for them to be in different places.

She knew he was still on this Earth, that she could call him up at any hour and see his face, hear his voice, feel his presence. That was all that mattered.

"So?" Gabe demanded, and Varouna realized it was the second time he'd asked. She shook herself. Fugue state. She fell into them more often these days, and deeper.

"Dr. Premjad?" Gabe leaned over her shoulder, worried. She could smell his sweat and the spicy cologne he wore to hide it. He was scratching away at an insect bite. The hot, sticky weather had been hard on him, even after Varouna had gotten him to wear light cotton shirts instead of his usual suit.

"Drifted away there," she said. "Sorry."

"S'kay. How's Piper? She's gonna be fine, right? Just another weird false alarm?" His tone was forced, just like on the day he'd knocked on her door and, refusing to step into the bedroom, stood there on the threshold and informed her that he'd be keeping her company in Kasi.

"We're not going to let you see this through alone," he'd told her firmly, even though he was staring down at the polish on his shoes. "I spoke to Mr. Tarkenton about it, and Piper, too. They agree. You're sick; you need someone with you, and it ain't gonna be a stranger."

"You're too important, Gabe—"

"I've taught Scotty everything I know. And I can handle things from India as well as here. So we're not going to argue about this. I'm going."

She hadn't really tried to go against him. Judas might, but no one else could. And he was right, she did need someone;

and she was, frankly, very glad he was here. Besides, it wouldn't be long now, a few months at best.

"Those brains of hers are getting quite clever," she said to him now. "It would seem they're creating life-forms just like those in the Kasaran ring system."

"Oh, Jesus," Gabe breathed, with all the superstitious awe and fear of a Shoal.

At that moment, an old woman with a mud pot, moving from group to celebrating group, stopped by them and poured out chilled, spiced buttermilk into a glazed bowl. Cheerfully, she offered it to them.

"A gift from the Great Mother," she said.

"Thank you." Varouna accepted the bowl, took a delicious sip, then drained it dry. She handed it back and the old woman went on to another group of celebrants.

"That wasn't real sanitary," Gabe complained.

"Poor Gabe." She smiled now. "You remind me a little of my brother. He didn't know how to live here either. And this was the world he'd been born to."

"Just trying to keep you healthy," he muttered, which was Gabe's way of chastising her for being out so late at night.

"Too late for that. We'd better go on home. I don't want to talk to Piper out here, where it's so noisy."

"Here," Gabe said, taking hold of her elbow. "Let me help you."

She smiled faintly and let him assist her to her feet. Gabe's plump hands were very strong, they steadied her as she swayed.

"Standing and walking isn't really a problem for me, you know," she said to him.

"You could drift into another fugue state while walking," he observed gruffly, "or standing. Then it would be a problem."

"When it gets that bad, I won't be doing much of either."

"Yeah, well," he muttered gruffly, a hand still on her elbow, holding to it as if trying to keep her with him.

The fourth day of Diwali, Varouna mused, was *bhau-beez*, a day when brothers gave gifts to their sisters and re-affirmed their special bond. Her brother had always done this perfunctorily, as if getting it over with. And since they lived together, it was, in a way, a waste of time.

She had still cooked his favorite food for him on that day, as tradition dictated.

The Pandemic had severed that connection, and given her a new brother of sorts. In many ways, Gabe felt more like a sibling than her real one ever had. She would have to find a way to cook him his favorite food, although perfecting a New York pizza here in Kasi might be difficult.

"Do you miss Manhattan?" she asked him, all of a sudden.

A shrug. "Yeah." He glanced away. "A lot." Which was an amazing thing for Gabe to admit: that he wasn't utterly content being here, far from everything he knew, taking care of her.

She started up the steps, careful to keep her sari clear of the oil lamps. At the top, she paused to glance back at the *divas* along the ghats. The little lamps seemed to wink and flirt with the gold ring in the sky, waving perhaps, raising their flames like hands or songs to its beauty.

For a moment, the lines of lights reminded her, pro-foundly, of the gold-dust rings around the Ring-Walker's planet.

And also of the lights of Manhattan.

"I miss Manhattan too," she confessed then. "A lot."

"How are you sleeping?" Varouna asked, which Piper found a fucked-up question given that she hadn't gotten to sleep at all. She'd been up the whole night, surrounded by Pandora's most trusted doctors, the ones who knew of her condition. They'd pumped her stomach, empty now of worms, taken her blood, tested her saliva.

And interrupted her whole, weird, ten-hour sleep cycle.

That was the only way she slept, and Varouna knew it; ten hours sleeping, ten waking. EEGs of her REM state were normal. EEGs of the little brains in her spine were . . . inconclusive, sleeping or waking.

"You *have* been sleeping, haven't you?" Varouna asked now.

"Oh, yeah, like a log. I've been having these weird dreams about making mold into a super conductor."

"You told your father about this?"

"He has enough to worry about, don't you think?" By which she meant the goddamn *Argus Report*.

Piper stared at herself in the mirror, her I-dik pad, with Varouna's careworn face, propped up by her elbow.

What, she wondered, was Scotty going to think? That's all she'd worried about since this nightmare had happened. What Scotty would think. He didn't know about her three little friends, how clever they were at keeping her well while making her sick.

And how the hell was she ever going to explain it to him?

"So. They were just there to cure my ulcer?" she asked now.

"Dramatic"—Varouna nodded—"but effective."

"I can't believe this."

"You must watch your dreams, Piper. Kasarans work out problems in their sleep—"

"I know my brains can respond to my unconscious, Varouna!" she snapped, and then felt bad. She couldn't help feeling that Varouna had deserted her, taken Gabe and left for India without her.

At the same time, she knew, in her mind, that Varouna was sick, and going to get sicker, and the last thing she wanted was to hurt her.

"I can't be vomiting up worms in space," she said now, by way of apology.

"I know." Varouna said with that soft equilibrium that Piper missed so much. "I know how important it is that you be the one who goes. You know we all want the same. Just try to cooperate with the doctors. They're trying to help."

"Yeah right, sure."

"Get some sleep."

"I'll try. G'night, Varouna," she added, though it was morning in New York.

"Good night, Piper. And a happy Diwali."

Piper winced at that, even as the I-dik went blank. She wanted to hop a plane, right now, and visit Varouna, visit India. Diwali was her favorite holiday, especially in Kasi, with thousands of *divas* lighting up the'ghats.

But the doctors would surely object to her going anywhere right now. She gazed at her reflection, at her botched makeup and crooked emerald earrings. She hadn't had any time to wash or change before they'd rushed her to her special rooms at the labs.

Why did Scotty of all people have to have been the one to see the worms? She'd thought a lot about him over the years, even blamed him for what happened. If he hadn't ditched her, made her feel unworthy, unnoticed, maybe she wouldn't have gone with Laurence Anderson.

Of course, those were the thoughts of a spoiled brat, but she couldn't help it. Every time she saw Scott Demme, she felt an acid resentment. Bad enough the arrogant prick had been hired as Gabe's shadow, now he was leashed to her dad! And unlike with Gabe, who understood her, she had to keep her problems, and often herself, hidden from him.

And how dare he come waltzing in tonight, as if he belonged in her house! And how dare he work with her father with such competence and ease. Where had he been when her father had been lying in agony in the hospital or suffering through physical therapy? He didn't know her father!

The only problem was . . . he *was* good at his job. Damn good. And friendly with everyone but her.

Which left her staring at her image in the mirror wondering what it was in her that brought out the worst in Gordon Demme's son.

His first conversation with her, some six months ago, had gone badly.

Scotty had been working under Gabe for several months, mediating a robotics deal between the Pan-African team and the one in Munich, flying with Gabe to World Congress meetings in Madrid, calling down to Pandora's news services to fetch up the rawest data for Tarkenton.

He'd been feeling confident, even comfortable with Tarkenton and Dr. Premjad. And Gabe had warmed to him, which Scotty gathered Gabe didn't usually do.

"Most people," the older man had confided in him, "don't want to put in an effort, know what I mean? That's why we're all so well behaved most of the time. Most people are content to be jelly, unless you motivate them."

"So," Scotty said, "if we make what we want to happen the status quo, a pain in the ass to change, it'll stick?"

"Thatta boy!" Gabe had nodded, satisfied, and Scotty had finally felt a part of Pandora, not like the new kid on the block.

And then he had run into Piper.

When he first saw her she was seated at the bar in the living room wearing a stylish apple green dress with a tight waist and full skirt. Her head was bent, and he could see the fine, titian hairs on the nape, glowing in the light so that they created a kind of halo.

For a moment, he lost all breath, though he couldn't quite say why. The curve of her neck, the line of her arm, was so very natural, so very beautiful.

"Make you an egg cream?" he heard himself say.

She looked up, surprised, but not displeased. "Well," she said, slipping an I-dik into a pocket on her wide belt. "Whaddaya know? Scott Demme."

"The one and only. Egg cream?"

"Sure. Why not?"

"Haven't seen you around," Scotty chatted, slipping around the bar and pulling up the ingredients. "Gabe told me you're in training? To be on *The Magic Bullet*? Said I couldn't tell anyone. Currently classified info."

"Yep." She smiled, showing off a single dimple on her left cheek. "Got a problem with that?"

"Not at all," he said, though it had surprised him when he first heard. The Piper he'd known on the floater had seemed too girlish, too proper to want such an adventure. "But I don't know why you're not telling the world. It's great PR: Tarkenton's daughter, training to be the first to travel through the stargate her father designed. Terrific stuff."

"When it's definite that I'm going, then we'll announce it."

He measured the Fox's chocolate syrup into a glass and added in the appropriate amount of milk. "What do the other astronauts think—of Tarkenton's daughter being on the short list?"

"They think I'm uniquely qualified for the job," she said with an odd gleam in her eye.

"Yeah? Don't know how you do it. I've never felt comfortable in space."

She shrugged. "You have to make it your world."

Scotty finished off the drink with a splash of seltzer. Then, impulsively, he popped in two straws, and took a sip from one.

"Not bad, if I do say so myself." He smiled and pushed it her way.

And that was when her attitude changed, all unexpected. She stared at the straw he'd used as if it were diseased, then, with brutal frankness, she removed it, and used the remaining straw.

He didn't know how to take that; fastidious, or was she telling him what she thought of him? He waited for her to hand the drink back to him, share it, but she didn't. She held on to it, sucking it down in a proprietary manner. Which left

Scotty wondering if he ought to mix up another. He decided against it; it would put what had just happened in the spotlight.

His mind flashed then on something he hadn't thought of for a long time, of a bearded man kissing Piper.

And he felt suddenly very offended that she'd tossed aside his straw.

"What did happen up there with Laurence Anderson?" he asked, bluntly, and, he would see later, very unwisely. "On the floater?"

She stiffened, and her china blue eyes widened as if she'd been slapped. "How'd you know about him?"

"Um, I saw you go upstairs with him. And later on the news. . . ."

"Oh," she said flatly, so flatly that he felt the unspoken truth squirming in him, making him feel ashamed.

"I saw him kiss you," he confessed. "I went and told my dad."

"Oh," she repeated. "That's why he showed up. Never actually thought about it."

He shrugged, suddenly feeling annoyed. He hadn't meant for their talk to go like this. "Guess I was just an obnoxious little tattletale."

A sour expression came to her face when he said that, his mockery seeming to leave a bad taste in her mouth. Gabe chose that moment to reappear, a blessed interruption.

"Hey, Princess," he said, smiling at her with great fondness.

"Hey, Gabe." Her guard dropped away and the smile that came to her face went right to Scotty's head, like the bubbles in a glass of champagne.

There was a single dimple, and the lower lip seemed to pout. The lipstick was pink, soft as a rose petal. It was one of the sweetest smiles he'd ever seen.

For a moment, the one thing he wanted in all the world was for her to smile at him like that.

"This guy bothering you?" Gabe joked. "If he is, you give the word and I'll toss him over the balcony."

Her eyes flickered thoughtfully, and so seriously that, for a moment, Scotty's heart dropped right into his stomach.

"Not at all," she said, taking up her drink and crossing around the bar. "He made me an egg cream."

"Nice of him," Gabe approved.

And that was their first meeting.

Their second didn't go much better. It was a few weeks later, early summer, and she was out on the balcony wearing a pair of shorts. Scotty had come in search of a soft drink, when he saw her.

Her skin was like marble. So pale that at first he thought she was wearing a T-shirt with a decal on the back. Then he realized that she was wearing a halter top and the decal was a tattoo.

He stepped out to get a closer look, or so he told himself at the time.

She glanced back, small sunglasses hiding her eyes, her expression guileless and charming. It went cold when she saw who it was. The muscles in her back and bare arms, he couldn't help noticing, were finely toned.

"Just admiring your tattoo . . . Princess," he said to tweak her and was satisfied when she frowned at him. Then, gesturing with his drink, "Stained?"

"Fuck that," she said bluntly. "The only real tattoos are ones made by an artist, pricked on the skin with needles." She turned back to gaze out at the city as if showing it off.

"It's only real if it hurts like hell? That makes sense."

"If you don't want to hear about it . . ."

"No, no, please. Tell me all about the agony."

She shrugged. "It hurt. And it took forever to get it all healed and colored. But it was worth it. I got it in Varanasi, Shiva's chosen city."

"That's . . . very interesting." The view from the balcony

was certainly one of the nicest in the city. All of Central Park, white flowered trees and green lawns, spread out before them.

A romantic view, Scotty thought. Wasted.

"Why the hell are you here?" she asked unexpectedly.

"Huh?"

She glanced back, sunglasses opaque, flashing. "You must have shot your wad to get a position as Gabe's assistant. Why waste pulling all the Demme strings for that?"

"Gabe wouldn't have taken me on if I wasn't competent," he said, stung. "What, you think *my dad* got me this job?"

She should talk, he thought.

"Hey, don't get me wrong. I think it's *tork* having a Demme on this side of the tracks, the name carries weight," she said frankly, leaning back on her elbows, "and you're more than just qualified or they wouldn't have let you leapfrog into the driver's seat."

He felt his shoulders relax at the backhanded compliment, which only made him angrier with her.

Bitch.

"I just want to know why you've sold your soul to us," she went on. "I mean, if you wanted power, why not the political arena like dear old dad?"

She was, he thought then, really pissing him off.

"History is in the making here," he said, joining her at the rail, "in case you hadn't noticed."

With a deliberation that infuriated him, she shifted away, as if she feared they might bump elbows. "History has been in the making for twenty-four-fucking-years," she observed, and shrugged, as if it was no big deal to her, which it probably wasn't. That scraped a raw nerve. How could she take it for granted? Didn't she know how lucky she was, to have been a part of this from the beginning, to see every move Tarkenton had made, learn about every discovery as it happened? To be on the short list of humans who might just go through that gate someday soon? Just to think of it made him sick with envy.

Time to change the subject, he thought, gritting his teeth. "So, what's with the tattoo?"

"It's Shiva. Principal creator/destroyer in Hindu writings. In some of his aspects, he's a hermaphrodite. See," she said, turning so that he could examine the image, which covered her from just below the shoulder blades to just above the small of the back. He dared to take a step closer, and smelled a hint of the patchouli oil she wore.

It was, he had to admit, beautifully done, brightly colored with some amazing intricacies. Shiva—him . . . itself?—was dove gray, with a blue throat and a handsome androgynous face. He or she was dressed in a tiger skin loincloth, with a trailing scarlet belt. A crescent moon shone in long black hair that flew out to either side, as if he'd just come out of a spin. One leg was lifted and crossed over the other, as in a dance step. In one of his four hands was an hourglass-shaped drum; in another, raised high so that Scotty was uncannily reminded of the Statue of Liberty, the god held a brilliantly colored flame.

"In this aspect, he's Nataraja, lord of the dance," she explained, "the creative force spinning within a ring of fire, the Ganges flowing from the crescent moon in his hair. His right free hand"—she lifted her own right hand and flipped it open—"offering hope, his left offering to show the way. He terminates with the fire and creates with the beat of his drum."

"What about the . . . is that a snake?" He'd thought it was a trailing scarf around Shiva's neck, but he saw now that it was an emerald green cobra, coming up and over the dancer's shoulder.

"The snake's the best part." She grinned back. "It's the Kundalini, the serpent in the spinal column. We all have one; it contains our own innate power."

"So we all have a poisonous cobra in our spines?" he asked ironically.

She dropped the sunglasses a little, and the look she threw him was almost sultry. "Fuck yes. But there's more to it than that. Story is that the world snake tried to spit venom on humanity. Shiva swallowed that primal poison to save mankind. He holds it, still, in his throat."

"Which is why his neck is blue."

"Yep."

"You have Shiva dancing in the center of the stargate," he pointed out. Which was, indeed, the case. The deity was, anachronistically, dancing within the gold stargate.

Piper eyed him over her shoulder, and even with the sun-glasses he could feel her scorn. How could he not understand? her expression seemed to ask. "The gate *is* a ring of fire."

"I thought your dad based it on a mourning wreath," he threw back.

"He did. But it's also a ring of fire, the big bang, the exit out of the womb. It's all one and the same. The hermaphrodite spinning at the center of a circle, male and female united, dancing at a point which is simultaneously alpha and omega."

He was fascinated in spite of himself.

"And you . . . believe all this?"

She frowned at him then, her short hair glowing in the sunlight like red gold. "Something wrong with that?"

"Well, not the religion," he said hastily, "but let's face it, you're a Yop—"

"Yeah, so? Yops can't believe in Shiva?"

"Sure. But if they're rich New York Yops then they're probably fooling themselves," Scotty said, and regretted the words almost instantly. But it was too late to back down. "I mean, what the hell do you have in common with real Hindus? Isn't this"—a wave toward her tattoo—"just some modern, lightweight take on someone else's spirituality?" This wasn't where he'd planned on going with this. And yet he felt a strange, mischievous thrill as he said it, like when he was a kid and used to throw mud at women's dresses. "Have you anything in common with real Shiva worshipers?"

She had turned to face him, her pale arms folded, her head cocked as if he were a curiosity she couldn't quite believe was real. "That's the question, isn't it," she said then, in a tone that sent goosebumps running down his arms despite the heat, "what we have in common."

And then she stepped past him, heading back into the penthouse as if dismissing a servant.

He knew he'd blown it then, big time, and he could have smashed his head right down on the railing. But even as he considered this, a contrary voice within him wanted to meet with her again and tug at her pigtails.

It was, he thought, the most perverse desire to flirt he'd ever experienced.

Chapter 25

January: Twenty-five years after the Pandemic

The first photomontage actually started in South America, but took off like wildfire in the Pacific Rim and, from there, to India, the Middle East, Africa, Europe, and North America. It worked like this: someone would construct a makeshift palette, usually a collection of corkboard or wood, and set it up in a prominent place. People would then paste, staple, or hang pictures of lost loved ones on the boards. Inevitably, when no more could be added, a new section of board would appear, usually stretching outward, but sometimes upward as well.

Currently, the most interesting and famous of these "Wailing Walls" are the "Barricade" in Paris, which goes straight up for nearly a quarter mile, the "Hanging Tears" in Argentina, which winds down the coast from Bahía Blanca nearly to Buenos Aires, and the "Ring" in the Takla Makan desert. The "Ring," formed out of nearly thirty million photographs, created with the help of over a million artists, is without a doubt the most dramatic, standing like Stonehenge in the most desolate of places. Like the stargate wreath hanging over the planet, it demonstrates to the universe the grief and loss of planet Earth.

—The New Iconography

THERE WAS A MINI-PHOTOMONTAGE ON THE SPACE station, created with real pictures instead of digital images. It layered the unwindowed sides of the door to the control station, forming a bridge, it seemed, by which those working in space could touch Earth.

Kyle's chair, located just over that door, left him very aware of the images, more so than ever at this moment.

The room was humming with activity, controllers belted into the gray seats, floor and "ceiling," which ringed the horseshoe, eyes on their screens and not on the huge gold wheel that filled the tall bay of windows like a wedding ring waiting for a bride. They chattered to each other over those screens and sailed plastic bottles of what should've been water (alcohol was strictly prohibited) back and forth, top and bottom, across the space.

The chill, conditioned air crackled with nervous excitement.

It all gave Kyle a nearly uncontrollable yearning to contact SoHo, to see on his monitor the wood floors and paneled windows of the Pandora offices, imagine the smell of coffee and toast and oatmeal from the old kitchen. Not like this perpetually filtered air, so dry the residents needed to apply a daily coat of lotion to their scaly skin. All of a sudden, he was even homesick for the sound of the ancient fans in summer and the racket of the old radiators in winter, the hum and chatter of the place, noisy as the New York stock exchange.

Not that he would have traded places with anyone right now, not for anything.

"Systems stable," Rafe said, his blond, Spanish face appearing in the lower right-hand corner of Kyle's screen. "Area cleared. Probe ready for launch. No anomalies, not even a sun flare. Did you have breakfast this morning?"

Kyle threw a look at the real Rafe, who was seated on the ceiling and catercorner from his commander in chief.

"I didn't want to throw up," Kyle said to the screen.

"Then don't let them talk you into taking a sip from that bottle," Rafe warned. "You want a relaxant?"

"*Now?*"

"It's going to be fine, I tell you." The Spaniard flashed a sunny grin, his accent giving the words an easy twist, a sense of inevitability.

"Thanks," Kyle muttered back. He didn't feel like being soothed. He was hyped, and he was intent on staying that way.

"I love you," Rafe said then, and winked.

"Yeah," Kyle said back. He was trying to be better about that, especially with Rafe, who'd been his partner and spouse for six years now. But sometimes he still couldn't help but think of himself as a kid who used to break into cars, steal purses, and rob corner stores.

A kid who didn't deserve to be in a stable, happy relationship, and who certainly shouldn't be in a position of such importance and responsibility.

Which was why he sensed so profoundly the pictures below and to either side of him, pictures that seemed to be watching and waiting for him to fuck up.

In all the off-hours, when their tests were put on hold for repairs or checks, he'd scrutinized those images, even memorized a few. Like the snapshot of a young couple at a hospital, proudly, if tiredly, showing off their new baby, or the one of a child holding tight to a carousel horse. And then there were his favorites: the black-and-white masterpiece of a boxer in the ring, gloved hand raised victorious, and the old women with their arms around each other in matching T-shirts. There were old postcards as well: an obelisk in Egypt, China's Great Wall, the meandering waters of the Amazon, the St. Louis Arch, the Tokyo supertrain, the Empire State Building.

Such places, he thought, had been victims of the plague too. The Pandemic had reduced them somehow. Made them small by comparison, especially to what lay beyond the windows of the control room.

Europeans, Australians, and Africans called it "the gate," Americans "the wreath," and those from Asia or Indonesia called it "the garland." Among engineers and here on the space station, it was known only as "the bridge."

But to Kyle it had always looked like the crown of thorns worn by Jesus in a picture his mother had had hanging on her bedroom wall.

He hadn't much liked that picture, always feeling that his mother took it too much to heart, wearing her rotten life in a dirty city with bad air the way Jesus might wear those thorns. Enduring rotten kids who cursed her out as she might nails hammered into her hands.

I wasn't cursing you, Ma, he thought. *I was cursing because you weren't gonna be any more than what you were. Fat and tired and always wearing those damn slippers.*

He glanced down at the image of the bridge on his screen. Jumped, started, when he couldn't find it, glanced up, ridiculously, to make sure it was still there, which it was, of course, large and majestic, in the windows.

Then he heard snickers and took a second look and realized why the screen image had vanished. Someone, probably Rafe, had erased it and replaced it with the old whitewash painting he'd done atop the Brooklyn Bridge.

He glared then at the men and women, in Pandora gray and white, seated round the bottom, and, in a manner queasily like looking up into a mirror, on the ceiling as well.

"Bastards." He sighed.

They laughed, some of them leaning their heads back as if to take in more air. Two of them slapped hands, and the plastic bottle went floating back across for another toast.

And then they started to applaud, and Kyle really did not know what to do. They were applauding something he'd painted over twenty years ago, a rough image done in suicidal desperation, that had gone out to engineers around the world and matched up to Jude Tarkenton's blueprint, its ideas incorporated.

He looked out again at the gold ring outside the window, refined and beautiful and complex. His design as much as anyone else's.

"Yeah." He waved to his crew then, his team, feeling that connection he had to them, one perfected, neat and clean as a drill squad, over the last few years. It was the sort of trust and unity he'd yearned for his life long, offered to him now like a reward well and truly earned. "Yeah, all right, thank you. Now can we please get this test under way?"

"On your mark," Jim's voice came from his screen. And instantly order and efficiency returned to the room. Hands reached, stats were triple-checked.

Kyle's own screen snapped back to normal. The small image of the bridge twirled slowly on its axis, revealing all angles and noting all specs.

What it told him was that the gate was in perfect working order.

Here we go, he thought.

"Mark," he said to Jim, a solitary face in the upper left-hand corner. "On your ready."

Jim nodded, his eyes seeming to watch the numbers counting back on Kyle's board. "Sol is in place and ready for launch. Warm 'er up!"

"Let's get it charged," Kyle commanded the six faces along the bottom of his screen, Rafe's included.

They grinned like maniacs and Karen saluted him. Then he saw their eyes glaze as their focus went elsewhere. The bridge was never shut down completely, but it was on standby. They'd bring it up to speed now.

The stats on his board started to change, and he felt his empty belly contracting. It was suddenly hard to swallow and he felt a little light-headed.

Maybe he should have had breakfast?

"Mark!" Jim's voice, back again. "Twenty-nine and counting."

At the center of stargate, the sphere glowed, waiting to hold open the tunnel that would be created. Fringe physics turned to mainstream in one brief generation.

"Temperature at 0.01," came the warning from Patricia. "We're getting a steady charge."

The image of the stargate on Kyle's board seemed to tremble a little, as if water in the center of a pool had been disturbed.

The minutes ticked by, and Kyle felt his breath getting shallower.

Hang on, hang on, he thought. *Got to keep a clear head.*

The stars within the ring seemed to distort, as if rising from the bottom of a river.

"Launching *Sol*," Jim half asked.

"Launch," Kyle heard himself confirm, his voice sounding so very far away. He knew that only the hundreds of times they'd practiced this allowed him to do it at all. His skin felt clammy, his pulse fluttering.

Doctors were monitoring, he thought, with some panic, and took in a few deep breaths to bring himself back to normal.

"Kyle?" Concern from Rafe. He was monitoring too.

"I'm fine."

A slot in the branches opened and *Sol* came drifting out. Ungainly, gunmetal and heavy chrome, knobbed with lenses and sensors, and tethered with a length of mono-matrix cabling, *Sol* was anything but pretty. But it was adept and perfect for the job of darting in and darting out. Which was all, Kyle had been firmly warned and ordered by the Stargate Committee, he was allowed to do during this test.

Tarkenton had been with him at that meeting, and Kyle hadn't liked the looks his boss had gotten from the know-nothings on the board.

But they'd both known how much was at stake, and they'd both meekly and earnestly agreed.

"*Sol* launched. Everything spot on," Jim added.

"*Sol* responding," Gretel confirmed.

Kyle felt himself relaxing, which was strange, because the probe wasn't yet through the gate. But it was beginning to feel so right, so natural, as if it was all meant to happen.

And then his screen started to flash red.

"Abort!" he snapped, touching on a very special icon.

The controllers, one and all, turned to gape at him; he might have yelled at them then, because they were supposed to respond to such commands instantly and without question.

But he knew they were as stunned as he.

"Power down!" Rafe was the first to come to his senses.

"Terminating *Sol*!" Jim was a second behind. *Sol,* a grain of sand next to the great golden ring built by man and machine, came to an abrupt halt.

"That command was from the Stargate Committee," Kyle said then. Some would say that he didn't owe his team an explanation, but he knew he did. "They just told me to abort. I don't know why."

But even as he said it he knew he was lying. He did know, he just couldn't bear to tell them, or to acknowledge it himself.

They'd been *so* close, and it would hurt too much.

As everyone in Pandora had feared, the new Gen-M voting block had apparently seen and loudly agreed with the *Argus Report*. Joining forces with the Tenors, they'd put pressure on their parents, the Pans, and the waffling senators on the Stargate Committee to put a stop to the test.

Arguments, discussions, and investigations would follow. Initiatives, votes, and countervotes. Which meant that it might be a while, a very long while, before anyone was allowed to power up the gate again.

* * *

They took the exterior elevator down from the Rainbow Room. Installed over the last twenty years by Pans trying to escape the enclosure of the city, the elevators rose and fell along the glassy sides of the skyscrapers, glinting like jewels in the brisk January air. Looking down, Piper could see the raised matting of the sidewalks approaching, contrasting the ink of the streets, delineating each block.

This time of year, she reflected, New York had a black and white clarity to it, like old movies on silver nitrate film. It shone around the edges, the mono-matrix bridges connecting the upper floors reminding her of tightropes at a circus.

"You ate all right," Gordon Demme suddenly said to her, awkwardly, because the dear old fellow had never quite found a way to comfortably ask her about her "illness."

"Like a pig," she agreed, with a wave of her mittened hand. "Ulcer's all gone. Whaddaya think, Pops?" she added then, "will we be able to market my worms?"

"Jesus." Demme winced.

Her father looked annoyed. "You drank too much."

"I only had two aviations." The taste of the cocktail's tart, flowery cherry flavor seemed to reappear on her tongue for a moment. "They won't kill me."

"Sure of that, are you?" he came close to snarling.

Piper shrugged. Her father was in a foul mood, and she couldn't blame him, not after what the Stargate Committee had just pulled. She caught a raised eyebrow from Davy, who stood behind her father's wheelchair, his frown indicating that he agreed with her father.

Damn it. She'd only had two! Not like on her sixteenth birthday.

"You got drunk?" Varouna had yelled.

"And survived," Piper had answered, hungover. *"Well, kinda."*

"How could you? If you are going to experiment—"

"—do it in a controlled situation," she'd finished, suddenly snappish. *"Hey, this was controlled. Broadway and*

Houston in SoHo. Bar called 'the Liquid Courage.' Can't get more controlled than that."

Varouna had looked pained then, as open and vulnerable an expression in those large dark eyes as Piper had ever seen. And Piper had felt bad then, and allowed Varouna to run a battery of tests on her.

As it turned out, alcohol had no more noticeable effect on her than on any other sixteen-year-old girl.

"Nice thing to know," she'd said dryly. *"Now I can get drunk anytime I want."*

The elevator reached ground level and Davy maneuvered her father's chair out the doors of Rockefeller Center and onto the sidewalk. Ten and a half years ago, two teams of microsurgeons had reconnected the spinal nerves sliced by Nikki Richardson's assassination attempt. With the help of cells and nutrients, her father had eventually gotten back the use of his limbs, but despite all the agony the fucking doctors had put him through, his extremities were still shaky and he couldn't travel long distances on foot.

The chair was motorized, but Davy insisted on pushing it, as if in penance.

Poor Davy had never quite forgiven himself for not getting back to his post quick enough to stop Nikki Richardson. Jackson, who now headed Pandora Security, also felt responsible.

Her father pulled his wool coat tight against the bracing January weather, frosty enough to turn ears red and cause noses to run. And Piper, feeling uncomfortably superstitious, took a moment to glance back at the gold statue of Prometheus. Behind it stood the huge Christmas tree, due to come down any day now, still beautifully trimmed and lit, presiding over the skating rink on the lower plaza. As had become the tradition, the tree was incongruously topped with the infamous black wreath of Rockefeller Center.

The same damn wreath that had shown her father how to

build the damn bridge. At moments like these, she always felt that it was hanging right over her father's head.

"You're going to defy the SGC, aren't you?" Gordon suddenly said to her father. Piper could tell he'd been waiting all afternoon to pop that question.

"What else do you suggest I do?" Jude retorted; he looked as grim and tried as Piper had ever seen him, almost as bad as during those first five years.

Those had been hell. Jude in a foul, frustrated, almost panicked state over his helplessness and the crawling slowness of his recovery. And she, her teen angst magnified a hundredfold by her unpredictable physiology. They'd made quite a pair, and tested everyone's patience with their mercurial tempers.

Well, that was all over . . . mostly.

"Ever since the last election," he said now, "the Stargate Committee's been run by those chickenshits who commissioned the *Argus Report.*"

"Oh, yeah. And there couldn't be anything remotely right in the *Argus Report,* could there?" Gordon sneered, and wiped at the sheen of sweat under his old-fashioned glasses. "Just because the starbridge is ready to go, doesn't mean that we're ready to cross over."

"So we just shut everything down? *Not* an option, Gordon."

"And defying the committee is?" Demme looked thoughtful about that, head down, hands deep in his coat pockets. "We had a good run, Judas," he said then. "Eight solid years pushing a procontact agenda. We had every schoolkid learning chromatics, for fuck's sake," he added with something of a smile. That had been one of Demme's favorite achievements. "But I'm telling you, you do this, and you'll be stepping over the line."

"Would you turn me in?"

Piper felt sorry for Gordon then, he looked so angry and miserable. It was an unfair question. "The Stargate Committee was created by a duly elected World Congress. And I don't care if you think you can do better, you don't just toss democracy out with the bathwater."

"I *do* know better," her father argued, "I'm the designer, the goddamn engineer. You don't build something like that and then cower in the corner, afraid to use it!"

"Gosh, didn't they say the same thing about the hydrogen bomb?"

"Apples and oranges, Demme," he snapped, and Piper knew her father was really angry. A mean silence fell between the two friends then.

Piper tucked her mittened hands into the pockets of her kelly green, wool plaid skirt and walked on in silence. The skirt was one of her favorites, long and full so that it swirled about her legs. She wore it with a pair of shiny black boots and a wide matching belt. A short matching jacket completed the ensemble and kept her warm.

They passed a bearded man playing a trumpet at Fifth and East Fifty-third, cheeks puffing out, gloved fingers running up and down the tabs. His music echoed up and through the canyon of skyscrapers, riding over the soft, rushing sound of electric cars, the distant clang and rattle of construction. Traffic lights changed color, and pedestrians crossed, exited and entered outside elevators, rode the glass carriages up so that they might cross and crisscross black bridges high overhead.

At times like these Piper thought she could almost see the ghosts of past New Yorks haunting the present. She would catch, out of the corner of her eye, the Manhattan of brownstone blocks and brick houses, mortared with Knickerbockers or the Manhattan of the Stock Market Crash and the cool ascension of the bull market during the late twentieth century. Was that the Waldorf-Astoria between Thirty-third and Thirty-fourth Streets or was it the Empire State Building? She would hear the ghostly rumble of jackhammers, the shouts of workmen walking the steel skeletons of skyscrapers and digging subway tunnels. She would even feel the flutter of a ticker tape parade brushing by her cheeks.

And then that flutter would turn into a desolate breeze, whistling down the empty streets of her mother's Manhattan, the bleak and desolate Manhattan of the Pandemic.

"How're you getting on with Scotty?" Gordon asked, grudgingly, which jolted Piper until she realized he was asking the question of her father, a peace offering of sorts.

"He's a wonder, of course," her father grudged back. "Chip off the old block."

Gordon grunted as if disgusted, even though his eyes sparkled, pleased. "Don't bullshit me."

They reached the corner of Fifth and Central Park South, wove their way around the cabs clustered together pushing to get to the front of the hotels, and crossed the street.

"No bullshit," Jude said when they were safely on the other side. "Ask Piper."

She felt her face go hot. "He's great."

"Yeah," Gordon said with a sudden, proud smile. "He's really come into his own, hasn't he?" He glanced at Piper as if he wanted to add something, then seemed to change his mind.

Had he hoped, she wondered, that she and Scotty would be friends? Or had he feared that Scotty might "catch" something from her?

They reached Central Park and started on down the path. The muddy ground had been frozen and thawed so that splinters of thin, brown ice crunched under her boots. There was the rushing sound of traffic, the clop of horse hooves from a carriage.

"How's Varouna?" Gordon ventured, breaking the silence once again.

"Royally fucked," Piper answered for her father, which caused Gordon to cringe. He didn't like it when she used obscenities. "She's falling into longer fugue states," she added quickly. "I was thinking of visiting her, but . . ." She held out her covered hands.

"Just as well," her father said. "I don't want you getting any more tattoos."

She tsked. "And I was so hoping to stick an image of Kali on my forehead."

Her tattoo had caused an even bigger argument than her drinking, especially when she decided she wanted it done not only in India, the tropics, but the old, old-fashioned way, by hand, with needles and inks.

"If you're not going to consider what your body might do against the pain or the ink," Varouna had almost yelled at her, *"at least have the decency to think of what your blood or sweat might do to the tattoo artist!"*

"I'll provide him with gloves," Piper had answered, equally insistent.

Unlike with the alcohol, there'd been reactions. Her skin grew bumpy and turned violet, but, in the end, she'd had her tattoo.

Tantric magic.

She hadn't told anyone what Laurence Anderson had said to her on that fateful day, about the eternal dance in a circle of fire. But every word he'd spoken was seared on her brain, an incantation that had helped summon the cobra.

In the tattoo she made those words flesh, her flesh, and set her back up against Shiva's. Her hope was to make the magic hers as well, and so, control the cobra.

Gordon turned them onto a tree-shrouded path. The naked branches, slick with ice, looked like lace. Here and there Piper caught sight of a bright red cardinal, or an electric blue jay holding tight to the high, thin twigs, feathers plumped up against the cold. And she felt a wave of sadness. Sam had loved to bark and point his nose up at winter birds.

The dog had stuck by her through every bout of her un-certain "illness." When it was mild, he had laid on her bed with her or chased after a rubber ball she'd bounced against the walls, keeping her company, not caring about the strange rashes or lesions that appeared on her skin. And when the illness had grown troubling, strange aches and pains or swellings, Sam had stayed in her room, moving to stand with the physicians when they checked her over, making sure that they didn't hurt her.

And on those scary occasions when no one was allowed inside the room, when it was thought that her breath or sweat might be infectious, Sam had remained right outside her door, head resting on his paws, ever patient.

She missed him terribly.

She had some of his cells on ice, of course, waiting to be cloned. But she'd decided that her life was too uncertain to raise a puppy. Or maybe she just wasn't ready for a dog who would not be Sam, for all that he had the same DNA.

Maybe when I'm better, she promised herself. Which was a laugh, because, technically, she couldn't get sick.

"Your brains have learned from your immune system. They'll fight anything that invades your body," Varouna had told her. *"Let's just hope you don't need a transplant. I shudder to think what would happen."*

Welcome to the club, Piper had thought, because her body took care of itself in very strange ways, most notably the way it had wept a kind of blue slime to counter her teen acne. The goo had vanished after a few agonizing days, and she never had pimples again.

She'd attributed that little miracle to the brain in her coccyx. That one was named "Mirabell."

Varouna had calmly collected the ooze, analyzed it, and eventually bottled it as a skin cream they named, simply, "P." It had netted Pandora a cool seven billion.

Surreptitiously, Piper tugged back one of the mittens and took a peek. Beneath, green mold dusted her pale skin.

"How are they?" her father asked, and she quickly folded the mitten back. She hadn't meant for him to see.

"The same."

"Sir?" Davy was touching on the earpiece he wore at all times. "It's Kyle. The Stargate Committee has announced its plans to scrap *Sol* and shut down the gate, indefinitely."

Gordon cursed under his breath. Her father just looked resigned. "Davy," he said quietly, "get us home." And as the bodyguard set a brisk pace, "Gordon, are you with us?"

The ex-mayor wavered, his breath misting out. The gray eyes behind the glasses were angry. For a moment, Piper was sure he would leave them. "You'd better know what the fuck you're doing, Tarkenton."

"I do." Then, "We have to brief your son."

"I'll arrange for our flight," Piper said, paling. They were going to brief Scotty. She knew what that meant.

"Oh, now wait a minute," Gordon said with alarm. "You're not planning on sending *her*—"

"We can argue that later," her father insisted.

As they reached the edge of the park, Piper paused to check under her mittens again. The mold was gone, just like that, only a trace of it sticking to the knitted wool.

She wished she'd had a third drink while she'd had the chance.

Chapter 26

Thanks to the Cadeau Vaccine, the so-called Miracle Generation came into being, riding on the wave of a new baby boom. This confident and energetic generation, doted on, pampered, spoiled, was a power to be reckoned with even in their youth.

Fascinated with gears and moving parts, they resurrected automats; thrilled by the tastes and smells their parents could no longer enjoy, they indulged in spicy cuisine and aromatherapy. They read printed books and took to music with full instrumentation and complex harmonies.

It ought to be remembered, however, that this ad humane passion (evidence, some argue, of the race's collective trauma) started with Gen-M's elder siblings. It was the neglected Twisters who recreated old radio shows, brought back flower arranging and wine tasting, and opened theaters featuring black-and-white movies. They were responsible for this last aggressive assertion of our identity, for clearing out the dust of the past so that the future could finally happen.

—The Strange Age

SCOTTY AND PIPER MET A FEW TIMES AFTER THEIR talk on the balcony. Most of these encounters were short, a passing in the hallway where Piper shied away from Scotty, throwing him a harsh look when skin touched skin. Sometimes a word passed between them. He sometimes saw her going into the gym, where she stayed for hours on end, the door securely locked.

Once, he'd caught a glimpse of her room.

It was during the early hours of the morning, a few weeks before Gabe and Varouna were set to leave for India. Scott had been working in the penthouse office all night long and had finally left it to visit the washroom. He was about to turn on the lights, when he heard hushed, anxious voices from around the corner.

"She's been in there for three days solid." Oliver's voice, scared.

"That's it! I'm breaking open the goddamned door!" Gabe's voice angrily responded, and Scotty peered around just in time to catch sight of Gabe, hair mussed, his eyes red from being woken up, punching in a code to force open Piper's door.

What was this? Scotty wondered, staring. Gabe had on a pair of pants and a satin robe loosely belted around his paunchy waist. Oliver, on the other hand, was fully dressed, chauffeur's cap in hand, ready to take someone for a drive.

Piper? At this hour?

And then Scotty saw a third man and his eyes widened. The fellow was sealed up in a protective white plastic suit, complete with hood and breathing mask. Weighing down his hands were two bulky cases with biohazard labels.

The door swished open, releasing the mangled reek of old pizza, coffee, and raw alcohol, and Scotty caught sight of Piper's sitting room. It had white-bread walls and was furnished with a pair of the egg-shaped chairs, fashionable back in the days when he was a kid but now neither hip nor retro.

On the walls were monitors showing real-time images of the ghats in India. They contrasting the real-time lights of Manhattan flickering through the open windows.

He might have thought the room incredibly spare but for the god-awful mess that covered nearly every inch of the grape jelly carpets. There were coffee cups half filled with milky coffee, some of them overflowing with half-smoked marijuana cigarettes. Stained disposable plates were piled up in the pockets of the chairs, half-eaten pizza, chili dogs, pretzels smothered in mustard. Stained shirts, some of them looking as if scissors had been taken to them, were lying about, along with socks, bras, underwear, skirts, and, glinting here and there among the carnage, outrageously expensive jewelry.

There were also several gin bottles.

Gabe just sighed. "Think the bedroom's as bad?" he asked of Oliver, and nodded toward the spidery spiral staircase leading up to the room above.

"Worse," Oliver agreed morosely.

Worse? Scotty thought, horrified.

"Piper, honey!" Gabe called up, never entering the room.

"Fuck off!" From overhead. "I'm trying to kill some brain cells!"

"Come on, Princess, cleaning crew's here."

"You don't touch my room! You let the fucking germs multiply! I'm creating another Pandemic in here!"

"Come on. Let Oliver take you to Long Island."

Something upstairs crashed and broke, making Scotty jump.

Gabe didn't budge. "Please? For me?"

Minutes crawled by, and then a small figure, swaddled in a dark green sweat suit and sunglasses, came gingerly down the steps. Her face, what little Scotty could see of it, looked puffy and swollen.

"There's a girl!" Gabe encouraged as she shuffled out. He never touched her, though it looked like he wanted to, badly.

"You go with Oliver. When you come back, we'll have your room all spic-an'-span!"

"Yeah, and who's gonna decontaminate *me*?" Scotty thought he heard her mutter, and took that as his cue to duck into the bathroom.

He escaped back to the guest room he'd been given and lay naked on the bed, trying to get to sleep. His mind wouldn't let him. It kept playing the scene over and over again. Scenarios came to mind, most of them unlikely, but his mind was darting and drifting by then, and they seemed to make sense. He envisioned himself stepping over the trash, climbing those stairs; her yelling, refusing to leave, so that he had to sweep her up into his arms (maybe with a little kicking and screaming?) and carry her out into the beauty and freshness of Central Park.

And the man in the protective gear? Did Piper have a deadly disease? The wheel of his fantasies turned, other choices passing by like horses on a merry-go-round.

"Don't look at me!" she would say, sick with a raging disease. But he would push his way to her bedside.

"I don't care what you look like! You'll always be beautiful to me!"

He frowned at that one. No. Maybe not. And rolled restlessly onto his side.

Eventually, he drifted off, still wondering, still thinking of her.

The next day, he cornered Arliss.

"What's the deal with Piper?" he asked.

"Caught your attention, did she?" Arliss liked to wear porkpie hats and brown jackets; he had light, maple coloring, the smile of a cherub, and, from his parents, an eye for detail that could be downright scary.

"Arliss—"

"She's Tarkenton's daughter. I don't know a thing."

"Fuck that! You've known her all your life."

"Doesn't mean I *know* her, man."

"Come on, please. I won't let it get around you told me."

Arliss had given him that scrutinizing look that said he was trying to figure out an angle. Then the eyes went distant, as if he were retrieving a file from his considerable memory, which he was.

"She never goes out to ritzy dinners unless she and her friends have a private room. From experience, I can tell you she brings her own cutlery and china to five-star restaurants and insists that they be used."

Scotty shifted uncomfortably. "Even on, um, dates?"

"Especially on, um, dates. Speaking of which . . . not to tell tales out of school, but you did ask, word is she never has sex unless both she and her partner are wearing condoms. So if that's what you have in mind . . ."

"I don't know what the fuck I have in mind," Scotty lied uncomfortably. "You, um, didn't get that from experience, did you?"

Arliss eyed him with disappointment.

"Yeah, right, okay. Go on."

"She doesn't kiss, she doesn't hug, and she doesn't shake hands unless she's wearing gloves. Without warning and at the drop of a hat, she'll go into hiding at a house she owns on Long Island."

"She owns a house?"

That got him a disgusted look. "She owns several, Scotts! Wake up and smell the wealth. But the only one she visits regularly, or rather, irregularly, is the one on Long Island. It's fenced in, and under heavy surveillance, so don't even think about a rendezvous."

"You make her sound pretty strange."

"She *is* pretty strange, buddy boy. She's filthy rich, and you know that's no good for anyone's mental health, and she's a Twister, and she's a Yop. Sanity would be a miracle."

"Anything else?"

"She's set her cap on being the first human ambassador to

the Kasarans. Which is why she's always exercising and going off-planet to train."

"Yeah, I know that."

"She has a tattoo of Shiva on her back."

"Know about that, too."

"I won't ask. D'ya know she's a sociologist?"

That surprised him. "No."

"Took on-line university courses from MIT. Graduated cum laude. Ph.D. thesis was on the culture and society of engineers who spend months living on the space station."

"Logical."

"And a fascinating read." Arliss threw him a superior smirk. "She's had two serious boyfriends. One was a painter, that was the mistake boyfriend."

"Mistake?"

"You know, the one guy or girl we should have never said yes to? The one we look back on and wonder what the fuck we were thinking?"

Leah, a Gen-M musician from Georgia whom Scotty had dated for a brief month, flashed into his mind and he shuddered. "Yeah. Okay."

"Yeah, well, Picasso tried to pull a Svengali on Piper, get her to give up her fastidious fixations. She kicked his ass in this spectacular public argument, then fled to Long Island for two months."

Fucking Picasso! Scotty thought, and was surprised at the vehemence behind his feelings. He wanted to find that painter and smash a canvas over him. How dare he toy with Piper!

"And boyfriend number two?"

"An engineer as obsessive-compulsive as she was. Just didn't work out. Amicable breakup."

"And she's been alone since then?" Scotty asked, and he couldn't say himself what that tone was in his voice. Hope?

"A few dates, nothing serious." Arliss looked him up and down then, as if trying to decide if Scott was a worthy contestant. "I'm not sure I can tell you what her taste in men is, but her weakness is candy, her favorite place on earth is Varanasi, she listens to those Gen-M torch songs of old pop tunes." Arliss made a face, showing what he thought of that. "She prefers dogs to cats and her favorite color is green."

Can't tell that from her sitting room, Scotty thought. "That's . . . an amazing amount of information."

"Information?" Arliss said innocently. "You didn't get any information from me. I don't know a thing about the boss's daughter."

"Not a thing, no. Say. She hasn't asked you for the same rundown on me, has she?"

Arliss wiggled his eyebrows and turned away. "Wouldn't tell you if she had, Scotts. But you might want to hope she hasn't. I know a whole lot more about you than I do about her."

He didn't know how to take that. Or what to do with the information he now had on Piper. Thing was, what he really wanted was to talk with her again.

There were times when Gordon couldn't help but think that Manhattan, as a concept, was maintained purely by the power of belief. That if only one such inhabitant should stop believing in it, it would all come crashing down.

And it would be *his* disbelief, he often felt sure, that would end it all. He would cause traffic to block up every tunnel in and out of the city and, atheist that he was, would induce the rats and the cockroaches to rise to the surface, pouring out from the sewers to flood the streets. He would take from the city its last breath of air, blot out the last shaft of light and leave it in darkness.

And so it would all end like some strange dream of a city that never was and never should have been.

The resurrected automat at Fifty-seventh Street, however, was among the few places that gave him hope for the city's future.

Within the spacious interior, Gen-Ms in neat suits and tightly belted dresses made visits to the cream walls and their grids of narrow chrome windows with signs that said "Pies" and "Sandwiches" and "Soups" overhead. All of it modeled on the past, the food handmade, the windows automated, not a jot of microcircuitry in residence.

There were, of course, a couple of modern twists, including one section labeled "Opiates," and a small bar stocked with intensely flavored liqueurs in long-necked beakers.

All very Gen-M.

It had been during Gordon's second term as Mayor that he'd come head to head with what Gen-M was all about. That's when the twenty-year-olds had poured into Manhattan, driving up the demand for housing in their search for a bustling, urban existence. They'd started up a plethora of small, unique businesses as well: barber shops that shaved customers with straight razors, theaters featuring live shows, and corner groceries with open candy barrels.

In addition to all this, they zealously attended city council meetings to argue with the resident Pans about the zoning laws they wanted changed. These meetings were made all the more surreal when the Gen-Ms turned out to be clones (sometimes twin or triplicate clones!) of the Pans.

Gordon recalled with a twisted smile one fierce debate where the Gen-Ms had tried to get the city to return to paper money.

"Legal tender is legal tender," they'd argued, not unconvincingly, "and if we want to use it instead of electronic deductions, we should be able to!"

Which was yet another reason, Gordon reflected, that he hadn't tried to run for governor.

It was all very strangely refreshing and empowering, especially as his sentiments were usually in agreement with the youngsters.

He made his way between the noisy, bustling tables where kids feasted on hashish-laden appetizers, meatloaf sandwiches, and apple pie. Young people glanced up, surprised to see anyone over thirty in their hangout. They were, however, a polite generation, kindly drawing back their chairs to clear a path for him.

Scotty was sitting alone at a corner table, a steaming cup of black coffee and an uneaten slice of orange-glazed cheesecake before him, the same as he'd been when Gordon had called up his I-dik forty-five minutes ago.

"That's not good for you," Gordon said, removing his overcoat and, uninvited, slipping into the empty seat beside Scotty. He gestured to the cheesecake. Scotty was lactose intolerant. An implant in his stomach created and regulated the necessary enzymes, but not if he overindulged.

Without glancing up, Scotty pushed the cheesecake and an untouched fork over to Gordon.

"You ran out," his father added.

"You and Tarkenton were finished," Scotty retorted, then the brown eyes glanced up, anxious. "Weren't you?"

"We told you everything, so far as I know."

"You've known all along." It was not a question, nor, for that matter, was it an accusation. The expression on his son's face was one of distress. Scotty was wondering if he'd deserved to be kept in the dark.

"It wasn't my secret, Scotts," Gordon said carefully. "Though I grant that you should have been told about Piper's . . . problem the minute you took over Gabe's job."

"I don't know what I see in her, Dad." His voice was wooden.

Gordon sucked in a breath. "Let me get some coffee." He fetched himself one of the automat's heavy white mugs and filled it from the huge percolator. As he sat back down, Scotty pushed cream and sugar his way.

"No opiates?" Gordon asked discreetly.

"I'm not trying to lose myself, Pop. Just . . . get a hold of it all. Do you know how terrified I've been?" his son asked quietly, as if wondering at the fact. "Ever since I saw the . . . the worms . . . God, Dad, *someone* should have told me then! I thought she was dying! And I . . ." He stopped, stared off and up at the lights. Was that a shimmer of tears in his eyes?

"Is this father to son?" Gordon asked with forced casualness, and took a bite of the cheesecake. They'd worked out that essential question in his troubled teens. Did Scotty want a father, or did he want a man named Gordon Demme?

"Very." Scotty swallowed hard. "I'm scared. I'm on the inside of Pandora, just what I've always wanted. But it's old and tired, Dad. I don't mean Tarkenton, I mean Pandora. I'm scared it's going to die on me before I have a chance to— to—"

"To be part of the dream," Gordon finished for him.

"Yes."

"And you think Piper's going to die with it."

"Come on, Dad, what do you think?" There was an edge to his tone, but checked, as if trying to be patient.

"Hm." Gordon took a gulp of coffee, another nibble of cheesecake. Frowned. "What the hell is this?" He pointed his fork at the dessert. "This orangy glaze, I mean."

"Burnt orange. It's in everything this year. The color's really popular too."

"I'm not liking this decade," Gordon grunted, and gave up on the cheesecake. "I know what you're saying, son. Sometimes, I look up at the gate and I feel that it's hanging by a thread. And that someone or something is just going to snip it and send it crashing to Earth."

"Someone should have told me," Scotty echoed. His mouth pressed as if he'd tasted something bad. "You're not going to let Tarkenton send her out there, are you?"

Now Gordon had a bad taste in his mouth. Burnt orange? "That's not my decision. Do you love her, Scotts?"

A shrug of surprisingly muscular shoulders. Scotty kept himself in shape. "I want her . . . badly. I don't know if that's love. I'm afraid that I just want to have sex with her because of what she represents. That I want to fuck the stargate, if that doesn't sound too perverse. God," he added, pressing an embarrassed hand to his face. "Did I just say that to my father?"

"Don't sweat it. I am a little mystified though. How the hell did you ever become so enamored with . . . all this?"

"You mean, with the company you used to love to hate?" Despite the confusion in them, Scotty's eyes twinkled in a way that reminded Gordon of the little boy who loved to chew on maple-soaked pancakes. It made the ex-mayor feel absurdly mushy and softhearted.

"Simple jealousy," he went on. "I know, I know, I shouldn't envy Pans like Kyle, but I do. I envy them because they've met the Kasarans, so to speak, and I haven't. That's why I've been giving my all to Pandora, because they're going to give me what I want, what I missed out on."

"I see," Gordon said softly. He felt taken aback. Scotty had always been passionate, like Mae. But he'd never quite imagined what the Pans might look like to this son of his, who had, as a child, always been so glad to be a Tenor.

"You're a Tenor," Gordon had told him. And Scotty, believing that Pans needed to go to Pandora to find out the answers to the universe, had said, *"Good. . . . I don't want to have to go to anyone but you."*

Now Scotty knew different. His father didn't have all the answers he wanted. But neither, Gordon could see, did the Pans.

What Scotty wanted was on the other side of that stargate.

"Maybe," Scotty added softly, "that's why I want her. She's that promise made flesh. God, if she dies . . . Dad. I don't know what I'll do. Please tell me she isn't going to die."

Gordon got to his feet. "Come on."

"I don't want to go home."

"We're going to the penthouse."

". . . Dad . . . I don't know if I can go back, not just yet."

"You have to. They're leaving at midnight. I'm talking

now as a survivor, Scotts. You *don't* waste what precious time you've got, you don't sacrifice the chance if you get it. Not when it might never come around again."

Scotty licked his lips, desperate, uncertain, Gordon could tell. That, unfortunately, was Gordon's legacy to his son.

But so was patient, stubborn persistence.

At last, his son nodded, and they made for the door.

The images on wall screens were so good they almost seemed like windows. It allowed Piper to feel, for a wonderfully disorienting moment, that she was with Varouna in India. She could hear the jangle and rhythm of Varanasi coming from outside Varouna's apartment, the voices chanting and laughing and shouting in a thousand different languages. If she asked the camera for an adjustment, she could even peer through the window and into the distance to view the colorful crowds upon the ghats, dipping into the Ganges. Holy men scooping up the waters, letting the drops splash over their heads; women laundering sheets of bright cotton and fishermen tossing out their gossamer nets. And carpets of marigold wreaths floating upon the waters.

Kasi, her second home. A wave of longing hit her so strong it hurt her heart. She'd felt so strangely comfortable there, as if the mass of humanity were a blanket to keep her safe and warm.

"I went over the scans you sent me," Varouna said. She had, Piper reflected, grown plump over the past five years, and allowed gray to thread her hair. Varouna had never been one for vanity, refusing even the pills she developed herself to maintain a svelte figure and dark tresses. Lately, however, it had seemed that she was letting herself go. Her gaze was all too often distant, and she was slow to answer.

Piper found herself chipping at her nail polish.

"Of my spine?" she asked now.

"And of the mold. But yes, mainly your spine."

"Give me the bad news first. Then the bad news."

"I believe your biology will accept your own brain as the fifth brain," Varouna said gently.

Piper winced. "The fourth matured with the worms, didn't it?"

"Very likely."

"I knew it, the minute that mold disappeared, I knew it had to be working. . . . God-fucking-damn it! And no, I haven't told my father."

She and Varouna had noticed the fourth brain developing not long after her first, overprotected sexual experience at twenty. She'd feared that it had completed its development, but hadn't been sure until this afternoon. The newest one was located between her stomach and her heart, right up against her lungs.

She was thinking of calling it "Ethel."

"Five is Shiva's number," she murmured, faint comfort.

"You should tell your father," Varouna tried.

"Give him second thoughts? No way." No one, she thought, no fucking one, was going to rob her of this opportunity.

"The doctors who will be monitoring, they ought to know."

"So they can do . . . what? I'm living on borrowed time, and if it's up, it's up. I know where I want to go. The only thing I'm worried about is knowing what to do once I get there."

"I see." Varouna nodded, slow, almost ponderous. Then, "I've made a special recording for you, downloaded it into your personal I-dik. I'd like you to listen to it while on the shuttle. Not before. Will you do that for me?"

"If that's what you want. Varouna?"

"Yes, Piper?"

"I wish to God you were going with me."

"I am," she said then, and the smile on her face was the one Piper remembered from her childhood. "When you get there, look for me."

Chapter 27

Act II

We're on the front stairs of the church we were inside in the last scene. Maria steps out, wiping her eyes. Karen approaches from stage right.

KAREN: *Found solace, did you?*

MARIA: *Please, Karen, not now.*

KAREN: *You don't get to dictate my time anymore, Mother.*

MARIA: *I just buried your sister, for God's sake!*

KAREN: *My sister? Your clone, mother, your fucking copy! Why did you need a clone? I never understood that. More kids, that I could understand, but a clone?*

MARIA: *Maybe I wanted a daughter I could understand.*

KAREN: *You don't understand me? Is that it? Well let me explain. I won for you, Ma! So many kids dying, and I lived. You treated me like something special for four years, then a vaccine suddenly shows up and you—*

MARIA: Your half sister is dead! Do you understand? Can you get that through your selfish heart?

KAREN: My selfish heart?

MARIA: Jesus God, Karen, can't you forget for one single second the wrongs you think—

KAREN: No. No, I can't. The wrongs are what I am, Ma. That's why they call us Twisters. We've spent our lives twisting in the wind like leaves torn from a tree.

—Falling Leaves
By Reba Drago

PIPER RECALLED HER LAST DISCUSSION WITH SCOTTY, the one right before the night of the party and the worms. It had been at an off-Broadway play written by her best friend, Reba. It was called *Falling Leaves,* and to Piper's annoyance, Scotty turned up at it.

Fifteen minutes before the play was about to start, she'd been out in the lobby, greeting friends who had come to cheer Reba on. It was one of those grand openings: a red carpet from sidewalk to threshold, the rustle of silk skirts, Chardonnay and Bordeaux proffered by waiters wearing pressed uniforms. Piper had just split off from Violet and Ida when Scotty appeared, a wineglass cradled easily, arrogantly in his palm. She came to a halt. Too late. Scotty caught sight of her, lowered his drink from his lips, and smiled with a kind of wonder that irked the hell out of her.

The gaily dressed crowd seemed to vanish as her attention focused on him, and she felt her cobra stir, rising up out of her spine to peer over her shoulder. It fixed its hypnotic gaze on him. Suppressing an urge to go up and bite, she gestured with a gloved hand.

"Scotts."

"Pipes." He grinned back, which jarred her, being Jackson's old nickname for her.

Son of bitch could certainly wear a tux, she had to give him that. It was tailored to accent the broadness of his shoulders, making her wonder just what he looked like underneath the silk. For an irrational moment she half expected him to hold out his hand and lead her into a slow waltz.

She snorted to herself at that. *Pull yourself together, Piper!*

"So." He cleared his throat a little. Scotty, she reflected, didn't like lulls in the conversation. "Have you seen the play? Any good?"

"It's a fucking masterpiece. Reba's best work," she responded pertly. Scotty looked surprised. Likely he'd been expecting her to say something critical. "It's about survival," she added pointedly. "A universal theme. Even we rich, shallow Yops can understand it."

He flinched at the sarcasm, which gave her a certain satisfaction.

"Yeah, I guess you can," he ventured. A peace offering or a cautious opening gambit? "But don't you think our generation is a little obsessed with the subject? With some justification, of course. We did manage to beat the odds."

It was a petty sort of challenge, one tossed out just for the hell of it, but it got her thinking, as all his questions, damn him, seemed to. She felt the cobra go still, heard, all of a sudden, the air flowing between the milling crowd.

"Kasarans," she said, and the second the word left her lips, Scotty stepped closer, as if she were about to spit gold. He had a warm smell she'd noticed from the first. Whatever he used, it mingled incredibly with his chemistry to produce a fragrance sweet and inviting as apple pie. It made her mouth water, made him almost irresistible.

"Yes?" he said, eyes aglow with expectation, and she found herself moistening her lips.

"Kasarans," she repeated, "pass on themselves to their

young, all of themselves. Just download the chemistry, let the new gen build on it. We humans can't do that; no passing our personalities and minds down from parent to child, though God knows we try. But we do it on a cultural level. The Pans have passed their whole fuckin' perspective on survival down to us, like . . . like falling leaves." Piper watched Scotty as she said this, saw the slight nod of his head. A bell was ringing, signaling that the play was about to begin. The two of them were almost alone in the lobby. But for some reason, she couldn't leave. She felt locked there with Scotts, as if they were holding hands, allowing a current of ideas to pass between them.

Most strange of all, she felt that what she was saying and thinking was coming from him, the way it had so many years ago on the floater, when they'd both looked at the stargate and thought the same thought.

"It's what we Twisters react to," she finished. "It's what Gen-M *is* reacting to. No escaping it, even if it's no longer of any consequence."

The spell seemed to end with that, Scotty's mesmerizing gaze finally breaking off, dropping down to his wineglass. As if seeing it for the first time, he took a hearty swig of it.

"Cultural entrapment. Nice excuse. I'll be sure to use it next time I don't want to accept responsibility for my actions."

He might just as well have pinched her and yelled "Gotcha!" Or, more like, jumped a checker piece across the board, slapped it down at the end, and demanded she "king" him. She didn't quite know whether to be furious and insulted or to admire his incredible audacity.

"More like responsibility for your words," she needled, and had the satisfaction of seeing a flash in his eyes, as if he'd just replayed his words and realized that he'd blown it, big time.

"Piper—" he began, a gloved hand reaching out.

"The play's about to start," she said, cutting him off.

Enough was enough, she thought, capturing up her skirts and hurrying up the balcony.

Third time, she thought as she reached her seat. *He just keeps twisting my tail and I keep letting him. Well, no more.*

From now on, she decided, she'd keep away from Scott Demme, and out of conversations with him.

Tarkenton could still fire him for this, Scotty thought, knocking on Piper's door. It made his palms sweat just to think of it. His whole career, down the drain, because of his lustful intentions.

His body hadn't had this much control over his mind since that ill-considered venture of his into the girls' gym in high school. His father had busted him something fierce for that. The mayor's son, he'd been informed, had to be better behaved than the rest of his classmates, not less.

But this time the old man was standing up for him. Talking with Tarkenton while Scotty entered the lion's den, that being Piper's upstairs bedroom. He remembered what Gabe said about it being a worse mess and he was unsure which he was more afraid of, Piper or what her room might look like.

But if he didn't catch her here and now, he might not ever get the chance. And that would be intolerable. He'd rather embarrass himself forever, live with a memory he could hardly endure, than leave what he had to say unsaid.

He knocked again. She opened the door, registering surprise at the sight of him. Her hair was half hidden under one of the small triangle-and-string scarves that women were wearing now.

A faint frown came to her face, and he noticed how, when she frowned, her one dimple appeared at the corner of her mouth, only tightened, as if trying to be serious.

"I need to talk to you," he said.

A blink of outrage, and for a second he was sure she'd slam the door in his face.

"It's important," he added.

He thought she would come out, but then she stepped back and, to his amazement, silently invited him in.

The room was amazingly clean and spare. There was a slate gray daybed and a large white dressing table with a wide mirror, its glass shelves lined with frosted bottles, all carefully labeled, looking like it belonged in a hospital rather than a bedroom. Incongruent with this colorless simplicity was a small shrine to Shiva in the corner, exotic, almost garish. The icon rested on scarves of rose-petal silk and was surrounded by candles of marigold orange and yellow.

The only thing cluttering the floor was a special duffel for trips to the station. It was half filled with what looked like a medicine kit and the station-standardized T-shirts.

"You're packing," he said, which sounded stupid even to his ears. "I mean," he added quickly, "you're going."

"How about that. Didn't they brief you?" she said, shutting the bedroom door. She stepped back toward the shrine to Shiva in the corner. He noticed that the candles were lit and an incense cone in a little iron holder was burning.

Music was softly playing, Gen-M torch songs as Arliss had predicted.

"Why?" he asked her then.

"Why what?" There was a small bowl filled with peeled imported tangerines on Shiva's table. An offering? he wondered, even as Piper picked up a tiny slice and popped it into her mouth.

"Why are you going?"

"What kind of a question is that?" she demanded, arms crossing. "Fuck. Someone should fire your ass if you don't know the answer to that."

He looked her over then, really looked her over, trying to figure out just who she was. This was not Piper in an elegant gown or showing off her tattoo. She wasn't wearing any makeup; her face looked milky, her exposed neck thin and delicate. She was barefoot, in stirrup pants and a jade green button-down shirt. And yet he could almost feel the tattoo of

Shiva burning on her back, dancing there in the center of its fiery stargate.

Just a girl, he sternly reminded himself. And, *green's her favorite color.*

She was chipping away at the cherry coloring on her thumbnail, a gesture that undermined her confident portrait and hinted at the anxious girl that might be within.

"I found out . . . what the deal is, with you." He shifted and found himself wishing there was somewhere to sit besides the daybed.

"Well, hallelujah."

"Why didn't you tell me?"

"Gosh. I dunno. Our conversations were so pleasant and intimate. I can't imagine why I didn't just open up to you, tell you all about how I killed Laurence Anderson."

"This is different, Piper," he snapped, and his own anger surprised him; he felt it pounding in his throat and behind his eyes. "I'm Gabe's second, I should have been told! Do you know how worried I was when you . . . when you . . ."

"Vomited up worms," she finished, softly, coolly. Then, "You're right of course. But what's done is done. You know now."

And that's when he saw the look in her eyes, the one behind the coolness, the one that matched what he was seeing in those chipped nails.

"You didn't . . . expect me to come back, did you?" he ventured, and felt a faint hope beating in his heart.

She shrugged and popped another section of tangerine into her mouth; she did not, he noted, offer him a slice.

"I thought you'd run screaming into the night. But let's face it, you needed to know. I don't know if me or my dad will make it through this. And Varouna . . . Varouna is going to be gone soon as well."

He dropped his gaze, embarrassed by the naked emotion in her eyes. And felt ashamed that he only felt comfortable with her when she was fighting. Why was that? Had he perhaps sensed her "illness" all along? Did he get her fighting mad as a way of keeping her alive and kicking? Frightening thought, that.

"So, I'm supposed to keep the fire burning, is that it?" he asked, his stomach dropping right down through the floor. He'd been thinking about her all this time, what she was, the chance she was taking; he hadn't given his own future a thought.

In charge of Pandora? Him?

"You and Gabe." She nodded.

"Thank you for your confidence."

"It's not confidence. It's inevitability."

"Fatalist."

A nasty smile came to her face. "No. A rich, pretentious Yop in need of a natural man to awaken and defrost her. Right?"

He felt his face darken. Last chance, he reminded himself. Last and only chance. "I'm sorry. I was wrong. Dead wrong. I'd like to make it up to you, but you've got a flight at midnight. Why *are* you going?" he tried again, and this time he couldn't keep out the plaintive note in his voice.

"Because," she said softly, "someone has to confront the Kasarans with what their damn virus did."

Scotty caught his breath. Of all the things she might have said, that had been the farthest from his mind. Rhetoric about self-sacrifice for humanity, the future, taking great chances for greater ends, these he'd been prepared for. But not that.

It flew in the face of everything her father and Pandora stood for, everything that had been taught by Pan propaganda mongers in the elementary schools and on television specials.

It was as close to heresy as he'd ever heard.

"You want revenge," he said with a sort of wonder.

"I lost my parents, my humanity. My adopted father lost his health and my adopted mother is going to go into a coma and die. Fuck yes, I want a confrontation."

"Does your father know this?"

"You think he's blind as well as stupid? No, sorry," she growled, and chewed on a final tangerine section. The polish on one nail of her free hand was almost gone. "That was uncalled for. Look, Scotts, I'm the only one who can do this. Dad, Varouna, Gabe, they all know that. I'm like a butterfly, born to mate then die. And I will do it. I *want* to do it. But my way."

It came to him then, all in a flash, why he wanted her. Having caused someone's death, seen the world cripple her father, and lived with her own secret illness, she now held an entirety of self, a vision of the world, between her small, soft hands.

Would she offer it to him? Or would she toss it up, laughingly, releasing it like a bird into the sky?

It was all or nothing with Piper, he understood that now; and he wanted that all, not hesitant pieces, wanted her to throw caution to the winds, utterly and entirely.

And he had only this hour to convince her to give it to him. Which left him wondering, what could he possibly give her in exchange?

Crossing the distance between them he came close enough to make her instinctively take a step back. Not out of fear of him, he knew that now; she just didn't want to risk touching him and passing on something unwholesome.

Ignoring that, ignoring, as he knew he would, what his father had told him Piper had done and could do, he took her face in his hands. Her cheeks felt soft and warm and downy between his palms.

Her eyes blinked rapidly at that, and her breath quickened, as if she couldn't believe he'd touched her, as if the touch of another human being was so wonderful it might well break her apart.

Bending just a little, he kissed her, right on the mouth. Her lips tasted of salt and tangerines and they seemed to vibrate.

Sunlight, he thought, *must taste like this.*

The connection was so smooth, so strong, as if they shared the same place in time, that he didn't even realize he'd parted from her until he saw her disbelieving face before him.

"You *idiot*!" She slapped at his hands, hissed at him. "You could've just poisoned yourself! You can't trust me!"

"I don't care. I want you." He licked his lips, a deliberate show of defiance. It annoyed her, and that gave him a thrill. "Do you want me? No protection, right now." *Come on, Pipes,* he thought. *Fight back, stay alive.*

"*No protection . . . ?*" She gaped at him.

"Well, I am on MBC, so you don't have to worry about getting pregnant—"

"Did you *listen* to what you were told?" she snapped, "Did you understand? Blood, sweat, tears, saliva! *I can kill you!*"

"That isn't what I heard. What I heard was that, while you were angry and scared, you bit a man and infected him. So don't get mad and don't bite me."

"You think this is *funny,* asshole?"

"I'm a Twister and Yop, just like you," he answered, and, slipping off his jacket, began unbuttoning his shirt, a bold move, but he wanted her concentrating on him, not what might happen. "My mother was dying of the virus when she gave birth to me, one month premature. If anyone can survive you, I can."

"I *don't* need another nightmare in my life! Not tonight, not with what I'm going to do!"

"Have you thought that you might not be able to do anything without doing this first?" He slid his shirt down off his arms, and reached down to unbutton his pants.

This is going to be really embarrassing, he thought, *if she refuses.* But he knew that if he wanted her, he could hold nothing back.

"What the fuck are you doing?"

"The thing is," he plowed on, "your human body is trying to do what Kasarans do, communicate virally, and all your problems probably stem from that. What I'm thinking here is that, well, maybe we can make it work."

"All right. That's it. I'm calling your father, or mine, or someone." She sounded, for the first time, uncertain, staring at him as if he were out of his mind. He was, and it felt good.

She didn't, he noted, make for the intercom.

" 'Make no little plans,' " he reminded her.

"Then why are you taking off your pants?"

"Oh, ha ha ha. I'm talking about us, missy. About Twisters," he said, and stepping out of the rest of his clothes, he stood naked before her. "The Pans know what they are and what they want. The Gen-Ms know, too. We don't, because the Kasarans fucking made us, Piper. We were in the womb and they changed us. They're our parents too. And maybe that's why your body can't make up its mind. Well, it's about time we found out what they did to us. You and me, here and now. What are we, Piper? And where can we lead the world?"

He paused then, for dramatic effect or just to buck up his courage because he was suddenly feeling very cold and very vulnerable. He was now, he reflected, in her hands.

"Well," he said at last, when the lull finally got to him. "What do you say?"

Chapter 28

I find the myth of Pandora an apt metaphor at this time in human history. Pandora opens the forbidden box or honey pot and releases into the world all evil and disease previously unknown. Horrified at what she has done, she shuts the lid, unwittingly trapping "hope" inside.

Luckily, Pandora is persuaded to reopen her box, releasing hope, so that mankind will not despair and die.

Forgetting for the moment that this story is, as I have been told, a corruption of a tale about Pandora as gift giver, I have this thought: It is at times of great destruction when great promises, kept trapped, may also be released, to aid in an ending, or in a beginning.

Opening a "Pandora's box," as we have, we release the potential for great evil. But we also release hope, which has just as much power, if not more, to transform the universe.

—Dr. Varouna Premjad
On the Cadeau
Vaccine

*T*HINGS CAME TO AN END, PIPER THOUGHT. THE *MAGIC Bullet*'s cramped cabin was supremely uncomfortable, and there was little to do but watch the instruments and stare out at the approaching stargate on the main monitor. She was so near she could no longer see the distant thorny edges. Only the dense white matter spinning at the center of her screen.

Helmeted, hooked up in embarrassing ways so that her body didn't need to do a damn thing, she rested, half reclined, in the special seat, and let her mind wander where it would.

So many things could happen. Forces could rip her apart, even if they didn't damage the probe. She might not arrive, might be lost in gray space. Or she might arrive and not be able to get back. She would die then, too.

That didn't scare her; as she'd explained to Scotty, this was what she'd been focused on doing since that day when arousal woke her Kasaran brains and changed her forever. But she did worry about what it would do to her father if she failed. Hard enough for him if she succeeded; he was, after all, going far beyond mere defiance of the Stargate Committee.

If she died . . .

And what, she wondered, would Scotty do if she never returned? Odd how she could almost feel him with her. She had convinced herself years ago that she wasn't meant to find love. Who, after all, unless they had some very strange fetishes, could ever be content or happy with her phobias and their requirements, with the dangers of loving her?

Still, over the years, she'd reached out, hoping that someone on that distant, other shore would see *her* and not the millstones she wore around her neck. Hoping that someone would want to reach back.

Someone finally had, last night.

"Approaching the gate, *Magic Bullet*. Are you ready?" she heard Kyle's voice ask in the hollow of the oxygen-rich probe. It was so quiet inside she could hear her breath in her ears.

Small lights lit the interior and shone red and green on the control panel. She knew how to do a dozen different routines should there be trouble, but for the most part, it would all be up to the microchips guiding *The Magic Bullet.*

Our version of the virus, she thought.

"Ready," she said back, foolish as it was. There was no turning back now, even if she wasn't ready.

Only the space within the circle filled her screen now, warping and wavering as if covered by a distorted lens. The white light of the sphere at its center throbbed, pulsing, three times the size of her ungainly little craft.

Would she crash into it and make a quick end?

"Count down . . ." said a different voice, and it took her a moment to realize it was her father, who was stuck on the station, watching, the harder job.

"Thirty, twenty-nine, twenty-eight . . ."

She thought of Varouna then, and the message her almost mother had left her. And she remembered how Varouna and Jude used to sit through till morning at the Night Owl discussing science or sociology, making a connection Piper was not a part of and never would be. Varouna ought to be with her father at this moment, she thought. He should not be alone, watching his only daughter, his only link to his past, crossing into the unknown.

His only link to Valerie McAllister, a gift, of sorts, that she'd given Judas Tarkenton; one, ironically, that he wasn't meant to keep, but to use.

Was that why her father reached for the highest, most ephemeral dream? Piper wondered, because he knew he could never hold on to the earthly ones, not her mother, not Varouna . . . not her?

She had an odd vision then, of the three of them forming a stargate between their linked arms, like sky divers holding hands.

"Ten, nine, eight, seven . . ."

"I love you, Dad," she said then. She thought he said it back, but she wasn't sure. At that moment, the dense matter flashed brilliant white. She felt the distant edges of gold lattice, the ring of fire surrounding her.

"Isom namah shivaya," she said then, "speak to me the *taraka,* Lord Shiva, the enlightened words that I might chant them and cross over . . ."

Space went gray as she fell over the threshold.

The screen went blank, the lights went out, and all she could hear was her heartbeat. It was as if she'd returned to the womb.

"I love you, Dad," Piper said, or at least, that's what Jude thought she said. The words were garbled.

"Five, four, three, two . . ." Jude had heard himself counting, but he wasn't watching the countdown on his monitor, with its close-up of the probe approaching the gate. He was, instead, gazing out the window, the one in which the starbridge seemed framed. In the hint of a reflection, he could almost see Valerie and Warren standing before that golden mourning wreath. Their ghostly images looked sick, dead, as they had at the end, their eyes hollow and distant.

"Why is she doing this?" they seemed to ask him. *"She was our legacy, our future, and we gave her into your keeping."*

And how could he explain it to them? His entire hope had been to build that greatest of edifices, that fantastic and complex bridge. The only one of its kind ever built by man.

And he had done it.

And then sent his daughter out to cross over it, while he, invalid and coward that he was, sat and watched and held his breath, hoping it would get her to the other side.

It couldn't fail. It could *not* fail.

The countdown never reached "one." The manned probe,

which had been hanging there, just out of reach of the gate, suddenly flew in, as if snatched—

—and vanished.

There, and then not there. Gone.

"*Magic Bullet* has been launched!" Kyle said thickly, and Jude saw hands tremble as they reached across the controls.

So. Piper was gone, farther away from Earth than any human soul had ever ventured.

"If you're going to go through with this," Gordon had argued with him last night, "and defy the whole planet, then at least do it with an unmanned probe! Why the fuck are you even thinking of sending Piper?"

"Because," Jude had said patiently, "we're only going to get one illegal chance to defy the World Congress. We can't waste that chance."

"Killing your daughter will do that?"

Like most of Gordon's damn questions, it was all too pertinent.

"Whatever or whoever goes over that bridge must act as our ambassador to the Kasarans. Right now, Piper is the very best potential ambassador we have."

"Can't you wait on it, then? See if the committee changes its mind?"

"Pandora's hit a threshold, Gordon," he had tried to explain. "We both know it. We need to do something radical or we will die, slowly, by inches. It will be the mission to the moon all over again, only this time, the failure will be a million times worse."

And now Piper was gone.

On their trip to the space station, he'd tried to talk with her, knowing it might be his last chance. The noise and pressure and pains of launch had finally ended, and they were in the ease and comfort of weightless suborbital flight. As regulations demanded, he and Piper had stayed belted in their seats, facing one another.

"I'm sorry," he'd said then, gruffly, leaning as far toward her as the relaxed belting would allow.

"For what?"

"For not being the father you deserved."

He'd thought it would be hard to spit that out, but it had been easy as a whistle, and just as surprising.

"Dad, what the hell is this?" Piper had been quietly angry. "You've been fine."

"No," he insisted, remembering the time that Piper had tried to join the Junior Hockey League, thinking it would please him. When she didn't make the team she'd come off the ice to face him, dejected. He had taken her, still in her hockey jersey, to tea at a beautiful hotel on Park Avenue, and there they'd spent the afternoon, sipping from pretty china cups and nibbling on petit fours until he saw her smile again.

There might have been more days like that if not for the stargate. Should have been more days like that. She'd been so like Warren as a little girl, all bright smiles and sunny disposition. When he looked at her now he still saw Warren's charming face, the fey grin, but she was cool, pragmatic Valerie in all else.

He felt no joy in that. Valerie had killed herself.

"I haven't been able to make you well, I've spent your lifetime building"—a wave out the small, round window toward that golden, artificial star—"*that,* and now I'm probably going to get you killed. I hardly qualify as father of the year."

"We're not doing this to get me killed."

Then why are we doing this? he had wondered.

And that is when he suddenly felt as he had five years ago, when he'd tried to force his trembling hands to draw. It had been one of the few times during his slow recovery that he'd fallen apart, weeping into one hand when he saw the mess he'd sketched. He realized at that moment that his youth and health and future were gone, and very little of it had ever been given to Piper, or anyone else for that matter.

"Hey!" Piper's sharp voice and the warmth of her hand had startled him back. She so rarely touched anyone, even him, skin to skin. "There's nowhere else I'd rather be, Dad," she'd said then, sounding just like Valerie at her strongest. "I swear it. So don't you dare go regretting anything!"

"Highest hopes." He'd smiled wanly, their own special little mantra. "That's all I ever had for you, Piper."

"I know. I won't let you down."

He was, he thought now, very glad he'd told her that. The ghosts of Valerie and Warren, he noticed, were gone from the window.

"Stargate Committee calling!" someone announced.

"Don't answer it," Jude commanded quietly.

"They're threatening legal action. They've got jurisdiction over the military on this station, they say."

"And we have control over communications to that military. Tell them, as soon as we're done, they can arrest us."

Nods all around, one of the engineers passing the message down to Earth. They were a damn good crew, all with him, all willing to go to jail with him. This was their dream, too, and they'd been a part of it in a far more intimate way than he'd ever been.

"Bridging cycle complete," Kyle said. Jude saw the younger man looking back at him. "She's through, if she got through."

He hadn't asked Piper, when he saw her with her duffel at the door, ready to take a helicopter to the launch, what she and Scotty had done. He'd just been glad that they'd found a way, that Piper would have a connection, back on Earth, one that, unlike him, was grounded.

He was, Jude thought with wry self-analysis, too Promethean for his own good. The sluggishness of ideas, imagination, thoughts, will, that he saw in the Stargate Committee were like chains, locking him to a rock while the damn *Argus Report* ate at his liver.

He had given the Earth fire, and he wanted to watch it light up the universe.

Only Piper now knew if he'd succeeded.

Piper.

By now you are on a shuttle to the station, about to take a most fantastic trip. Before you do, there are some things I think you should know, which is the reason for this message.

You once showed me your mother's letter to Judas. She was a very wise woman, your mother. First, because she explained, so clearly, the lure of the virus which makes us Ringwalkers. It is, perhaps, the most powerful bridge on Earth, as it allows us to cross over into another species.

It is a bridge that has been calling to me for years now. As I explained, my immune system never really killed the virus, it just slowed it down. And so, the message has, if you will, made its way into my brain like a fire in a coal mine, slowly burning through.

The truth is, it is likely that you will find me in a coma when you get back. You are aware, I am sure, that I have been falling into fugue states more and more. I predict that I will fall into catatonia very soon.

I want you to know that I would not change what has happened to me for all the world. Not to get back my brother, not to get back the billions who died, not to save my life.

I also know that you feel differently.

I could tell you that I think what happened to the world, what has happened to me, was for the best . . . but my lack of regret is purely selfish. If the Pandemic had not happened I would not have become the bioengineer I am today.

It was one of the oddest things to realize about myself, that I had that much hunger, that much raw ambition. I think I always wanted to be the best and most brilliant. Thanks to the Pandemic, that is what I became. The virus allowed me to know my own mind, to live up to my full potential. And I relish that.

So I will step into my catatonic state with no regrets, Piper, my daughter, because, when I do, I will finally know it all. And I have wanted to know it all for twenty-five years.

Think as a Hindu when I fall into that coma, and after, when I die, for I will, in a very real sense, have crossed over. I am from Kasi, I have bathed in the Ganges, and I have faith in my lord Shiva. He will whisper to me the taraka for crossing over, this I believe.

That is the first thing I have to tell you. Now I must reveal to you two secrets. As with your wise mother, I refuse to be stingy. I will be dead, and you can do with them what you will. They are yours to tell or keep.

The first is this: What the Tenors have never understood is that it was more than just our understanding of how the Kasarans thought and felt that allowed us Pans to forgive them. Whether we were able to say it or not, I think we all knew that what those aliens had done was build a bridge that spanned the Earth. We all had a common experience to draw on, a common understanding. We could finally see ourselves not as this race or that race, not as this nationality or that, but as one species from one planet.

And, frankly, the virus made us more than a little bit alien ourselves. There is no way that we, as the humans we were, could have ever united the planet or come together to build the golden garland that now hangs above us.

"You can curse the dark or you can invent a light-bulb." That is what your mother said, and that is what we Pans did. Your father built his bridge, and I built mine with the Cadeau Vaccine.

Or, if you like, we opened Pandora's box, releasing the hope and changing the entire perspective on this evil that happened to us.

Which brings me to my second secret, which is my speculation about you.

I don't know if you're going to like this, but I hope you will understand all the same. It is my considered opinion that your mother made you what you are, deliberately, as a gift for your father. She said it herself, your father was going to fly high, and she wanted a daughter who could fly with him, help him soar, as she had not been able to do.

A daughter who would provide him with hope at a time of great despair.

What I am saying, Piper, is that you might not have been an accident. Kasarans know to alter their fetuses; the virus could have taught your mother to do the same.

And no, I can't prove that I am right in this, nor that, if your mother did it, that she did it consciously.

So, exactly what are you? you might wonder.

That I can tell you.

The craft the Kasarans sent us, the one that infected the world with the Pandemic, was a biofactory.

You are our version of that biofactory.

Whether knowing this or not will help you, I cannot say, nor do I know if it will help you to do whatever it is you decide to do. I advise only this: whatever you intend, do it not for me, nor in memory of your dead parents, nor for your father, nor for Earth.

Create your own bridge. You are my daughter, and I love you with all my heart. Be strong, be bold, and hold tight to whatever happiness you can find. Shiva's blessings from the city of light, little one. If we are destined to another turn on the wheel, then I promise you, I will see you again.

Kasi-Samsara.

Varouna Premjad

There had been great speculation among the scientists at Pandora as to whether an astronaut would experience any time passing while traveling through the gray space between one end of the bridge and the other.

"Absolutely," had been Walsh's considered opinion.

"I don't think so," had been Battencourt's.

Sven had refused to take sides.

As it turned out, Piper did experience time passing. But she had a feeling that the clocks would not record it, that only she, like a woman dying, could feel this split second stretch out to infinity.

And what came to her in that split second, much to her chagrin, was Scotty, unprotected and vulnerable, giving himself to her.

"Maybe," Scotty had said after, astonishingly, removing all his clothes, "you never got a chance to finish what you started. You were aroused, and that woke everything up. But it was all wrong, all premature. Maybe all the weirdness of this alien development is just that you never got a chance to fix what Anderson fucked up."

"So this is for my own good," she had sneered back, but softly. "Make me a woman and I'm all cured and back on target? And you're the man to do it?"

"It's the only self-serving excuse I've got," he'd admitted ruefully. She couldn't help noticing how compact his body was, the muscles nicely defined, the skin tanned to a soft bronze. He was handsome, and masculine, and she found herself annoyingly interested.

I've got my father's secretary naked in my room, she thought.

And,

I've got Mayor Demme's son naked in my room!

And,

Scotty is naked in my room. And he wants me.

"This is certainly the strangest proposal I've ever had. It isn't real romantic."

"Haven't the time," he'd said wryly. "When you come back, though, I'll be as romantic as you like. Right now, you're a hero off to war, and I . . . I want to give you a final fling before you go. What's wrong with that?"

"Oh, gosh, nothing. Except, of course, that you might *die.*"

In the background, a long, slow version of the song "I Will" started playing.

Damn it.

"Should I put my clothes back on?" he'd asked.

The idiot, she had thought, still staring. The idiot was a fucking genius, because he was forcing her to *see him,* daring her to give up this chance, possibly her last chance.

He did that every time, dared her like a little kid, drew a line in the sand then goaded her over it.

"Piper," he had added then, earnestly, and taken up her hands, the ones that had been greenish with a mold just that afternoon, all save the nails, which she had painted with red polish in defiance.

"I don't want to die." His face had come close enough for her to feel his breath, to remember his warm kiss. "And it seems silly, if I'm not sure this is love, to risk my life, but I just . . . want you."

Starved as she was for physical affection, his touch had been painful. She had to hold back from leaning forward and sinking her teeth into his bare shoulder. But she bent her head and touched her lips to his broad chest.

It was the only way she had of telling him that he was all she wanted at that moment, all she'd dreamed of for so very long.

His hands came up then, gently undoing her clothes, warm hands slipping under the fabric.

He'd kissed the nape of her neck lovingly.

"I'm tasting tangerines," he'd said then.

And when they'd connected, "There's a golden ring of fire," he had said softly, a smile of pure joy breaking across his dear face, "and we're dancing at the center of it."

"Yes," she'd breathed back, and for a moment, they just were, the two of them, the only two in the whole of the universe, alpha and omega.

We are the children of the Pandemic. She didn't think it, or say it, she just experienced it. She and Scotty, born in the midst of death, at the turn of the wheel.

She fell, she soared. She saw the gleam in her eyes answered in the shine in his. Their sweat mingled, their saliva, their flesh. And when they climaxed, she saw herself through his eyes and watched the flashes of his life within her heart.

She didn't infect him.

Instead, she'd met him in the center, and found there something eternal.

"Crossing completed," a prerecorded voice informed her.

She opened her eyes then. The lights were back on, and she could see stars on the screen, clear and bright as only stars in space could be . . . unfamiliar stars.

And a large red gas giant, surrounded by a golden Saturn-esque set of rings.

From the corner of her eye, a dim sun cast misty light on her probe as it hurled forward. With tardy hands that trembled in their clumsy gloves, she went through a procedure so drilled into her that even her shock and jitters couldn't interfere.

A dozen little screens came on right below eye level, each one showing her a different angle of the cluttered alien system. On one, she saw the alien gate looming behind her, the one she'd crossed through, asterated silver and pewter. It was similar to Earth's golden wreath, but with a strangely organic edge, grown like crystals or hewn like stone.

It was raw and beautiful.

In theory, she ought to be able to turn her pod around and go right back through the ring, back to her own solar system. In theory, Pandora was holding the stargate open, waiting for her.

In theory.

She was approaching the rings, closer and faster than she'd anticipated as *The Magic Bullet* fell into orbit around the gas giant. Her breathing was coming faster. None of the re-creations she'd seen matched the stunning reality.

There were rivers of coppery dust, and asteroids that glowed with lacy, neon blue fronds, incandescent mosses, and flowers bright and warm as marigolds. Spidery candy-yellow creatures drifted, trailing strands behind them, and glowing, violet tendrils wrapped themselves about small stones.

It was completely alien, and yet, uncannily, she felt that she was gazing at Manhattan from the Brooklyn Bridge, or wandering the streets of Varanasi at night. Everything glittering, active, alight.

And then they came, slipping from in between the gleam and glow of the asteroids. She wasn't prepared for how large and long they were, like sailing ships, and moving with equal grace. Their leaves were silvery, their skin thin, almost transparent, like the stretched rubber of children's balloons. They changed color gently, as a cascade of water, lilac to rose with shades of sea green.

She hadn't been prepared for that either, the sweet beauty of it.

Not really prepared for any of it, she thought, her heart racing.

The side eyes flashed along their length, and the tails curled and moved; languid arms reached for her.

A screen on the outside of the probe would show her to them, and flash the chromatic messages the experts had arranged. But would they be satisfied with that?

Could she say more to them? Should she? And how?

Varouna was on the verge of catatonia. But when she surfaced out of the fugue states for brief breaths, she always heard the song that was Kasi outside the window: the bells and noise of festivals, and the smells that went with them, the spices and oils and burning fires.

She would remember the taste of *paan* on her tongue and drift back down again, back into the ring, content.

There was excitement in the system. An alien craft, at long, long last! Oddly constructed, it was like nothing they'd ever anticipated. Something on the outside seemed to be showing them what might be on the inside.

They debated. Should they try to crack it open? Get this thing out?

But no. It would come out if that's what it intended to do. Anything wise enough to construct one of their gates, to connect, must be within the craft purposefully.

Anxious in their excitement, anguished in their joy, they surrounded it, changing their colors, trying to communicate. And, of a wonder, it flashed back colors to them! Short messages, limited, but chromatics all the same.

An amazing moment, a historic moment, one to pass on to every generation to come.

"Do not touch me," the alien chromatics clumsily warned. "I am safe. I am from far away. I have come to meet you."

The messages were gratifying and frustrating. It was talking to them, and that was amazing! But why wasn't it allowing them to feel what it was, know all it knew?

From where she drifted, Varouna smiled. *Wait,* she thought, *just wait. She won't disappoint you.*

She came back up and out then, back to Kasi. In an ash-tray by her hand a cigarette burned, almost all ashes now. It wasn't Camel Filters, they were long gone, but it was an American cigarette, still mass-produced poison.

Varouna smiled. Her reach was weak, her fingers barely able to take hold, but she managed to tap off the ashes and draw in a lungful of smoke.

Gabe didn't approve, but Varouna knew how little time she had, and she was bent on indulging in her few vices while she still had the chance.

In that sense, she was a true survivor of the Pandemic.

As was Piper.

The probe registered the viruses, as it was meant to.

A shoal surrounded her now, and more were arriving to join them. Everywhere she looked she saw those drifting leaves, the sharp ridges, the enormous fore-eyes. Colors washed by, fantastic, strange, eager.

Innocent, she would almost say. And yet the probe told her that the area around her was thick with infections. As expected, they were trying to send her viral messages.

She felt her stomach turn with anger and frustration.

Varouna came to mind then, and her father. And Earth, with all it had lost and gone through and changed thanks to these creatures who had so thoughtlessly reached out, hoping that someone would reach back.

"I've got a message for you, you fucks, I've got . . ."

And then she flashed onto that forever moment of pure pleasure with Scotty. And that's when she experienced a stereoscopic sensation of being, simultaneously, on a brick and rod-iron terrace in New York *and* in Varanasi. For a second she heard the humming sounds of Manhattan, its summer traffic, *and* the chiming song of Kasi, its winter festivals. She felt the damp of the East River and of the mist that rose off the Ganges.

Rising sun and setting, eternal human past, eternal human future, all one and the same, circling around her.

"They made you," she could hear Scotty saying to her, as if he were there with her, her other half. *"They made us, as much as our parents did. We are the bridge. Won't you let them cross to the other side, Piper?"*

She could almost see him, not floating in the ring, but in the fire at the center of that ring, the dense, hot fire around which everything spun. He was smiling at her, reaching to her.

"Come across," he was saying, *"don't keep that poison inside yourself."*

Don't keep . . .

"I'm a biofactory," she said then, blinking and bringing the Kasarans back into focus. "Like what you sent to us."

It clicked then.

"Like what you sent to us!"

And that's when she discovered that Scotty had been right. Like Tantric yoga, something had recently, finally untangled the cobra that was in her spine. It didn't control her. She controlled it; she could tap into those four little minds and produce whatever chemicals she liked.

Including a virus that would kill off every Kasaran in the system.

Hold it in her throat, or spit it out and destroy those creatures that were now turning their silvery leaves toward her like hands in a dance? Open Pandora's box and release . . . what?

"Whatever you intend," Varouna had said, a prideful glow in her eyes, *". . . whatever you intend, do it not for me, nor in memory of your dead parents, nor for your father, nor for Earth.*

"Create your own bridge."

And her father, *"Highest Hopes . . . That's all I ever had for you, Piper."*

But it was Scotty words, her father's favorite quote, that made up her mind for her.

" *'Make no little plans,'* " he had said it last night, to woo her, to win her.

If she was going to give these aliens a message from her species, the first, it was not going to be anything small or petty.

There was a special container for her to capture a viral message from the outside, a sealed specimen she could bring back for analysis. But, unbeknownst to the Stargate Committee, the tubing leading to the container could also be used to send *out* a viral message. Varouna had spoken with the probe's designers, arranging for that; the plan, originally, was that Varouna would bioengineer such a message. But it was clear to Piper that it had also been created for her to use, if she could.

And she was quite sure now that she could.

Closing her eyes, she concentrated down, reaching for the cobra until she had it by the throat; that, at least, is how she saw it. What she knew, intellectually, was happening, is that she'd sent a command to "Ethel," who, in turn, was sending orders down to each one of the other three.

They each gathered chemicals available to them from her body, and passed them along up the spine, connecting them together along the way. She didn't feel anything, but she could see it, in her mind's eye, as if she were milking the fangs.

At last, she had her virus; it wanted only a vehicle, a way to be delivered.

With a deep breath, she engorged the small, honeycombed cells of her lungs with oxygen, causing the spongy tissue to press against her ribs and spine. She witnessed the exchange, oxygen for carbon dioxide, and a special kind of venom. Microscopic messengers that multiplied a billionfold even as they passed through the cell membrane.

Pressing her mouth to the container, Piper released her

breath into it, and, riding on that breath, a virus that contained everything she was.

A human mind, she thought, spent its life searching for ways to communicate, and usually failed. But not this time. Not this time.

"Here's my *takara*," she said, as, with the push of a button, she sent the contents out into space. "Cross over."

No Kasaran eye could see that breath as it exited out, so little, so slight. Using microscopic vision, they might have discerned a tiny bit of spray or a puff of mist, but only for that split second before it dispersed. The messengers riding on that breath would, in time, bind themselves to the coppery dust and alien pollens of the system, the better to swiftly travel around the ring. Some would drift away from the ring out into space, lost forever, while others would settle on ice crystals and remain frozen indefinitely.

The majority, however, as intended, found their way right past the gills and into the brains of the Kasarans clustered around *The Magic Bullet*. In mere minutes, Piper's knowledge spread itself through the consciousness of each and every one of them.

The life they experienced in those moments was stranger than they had ever imagined in all those generations of imagining. Weight, taste, sound, smell. Communication so imperfect that, ironically, it formed itself into poetry and pictures of surpassing beauty.

A race where viruses could kill.

Did kill. Had killed, in great and terrible numbers.

A long time passed, as the stricken Kasarans came to terms with what was now in their minds, an alien way of seeing things, alien dreams and hopes and ambitions.

Alien hate and love.

But amid all the strangeness and anger and loss, they also found hearts yearning for a connection, reaching for what they knew was out there, just beyond them. Creatures waiting, as the Kasarans had patiently waited, for a day when the bridge would be complete.

At last, the fore-leader moved close to the tiny little craft, hoping that the even more fragile creature within would see him.

"Message received," his colors said, and in his mind he added what his colors could not convey, a name that required sound to be understood: "Piper."

The connection had been made. The bridge had been crossed.

Epilogue

May: Twenty-five Years After the Pandemic

We all understood, almost from the first, that the Kasarans weren't trying to hurt humanity, just the opposite. What they didn't understand was the intensity of a viral message on a species that didn't communicate that way. And they couldn't know what humans were like, our tendency to obsess, for better or for worse, on things that capture our imagination, or the way we cling to even the most dysfunctional of relationships.

They sent us a message hoping to capture our hearts. For the most part, they did. Little did they know all the crazy, mad things we'll do for love.

—Judas Tarkenton

He HAD GORDON WITH HIM WHEN THE TIME CAME to go to the bridge. Right where they'd been all those years ago, on the Brooklyn side. Jude walked with his cane, slowly, but with purpose.

They found a place to pause, making sure they were not facing into the wind, but that the chill April breeze was whistling past them. The sun was almost down, leaving only an orange glow over the gleaming outline of Manhattan, and causing temperatures to plunge so that Jude zipped tight his blue and white letterman jacket, the one with the Statue of Liberty, crowned head and torch raised, embroidered in red on the back.

He looked up in time to catch sight of the evening star appearing, as well as the stargate in golden contrast.

It had been hard that first month after his "mutiny," as they were calling it. Members of the World Congress, citing the *Argus Report,* accused him of putting the whole human race at risk and even argued for the death penalty. All the while, Shoal Movement protesters hailed him as a hero and demanded clemency.

Jude just wished there was someplace on Earth he could go where he could hide from the press, from the calls and the questions.

In the end, faced with the political clout of Pandora's scientists and engineers, the World Congress had forgone both the death penalty and prison, instead barring him from space forever. His enemies were outraged, calling it a slap on the wrist, but, in truth, it was the worst thing they could have done to him.

"They'll forgive you," Gordon had tried to assure him then. "Fuckers can't forgive you yet, but give 'em a year or two. They'll let you go back."

"Doesn't matter," Jude had said then. "I already know what's on the other side."

Most of the space station crew had gotten off, Kyle included, as their expertise was suddenly too valuable to waste. And Piper had become not only a necessity, but Earth's darling. As Jude had warned Gordon years ago, the genie could not be put back in the bottle. Contact had been made, and Piper was the interpreter.

For some twelve weeks humanity had exchanged information, passing on to the Kasarans arguably intimate details, receiving back regrets, apologies, and the Kasarans' most earnest wish to be friends.

Finally, on the very day that Varouna had finally passed away, a Kasaran drifted through the gate Jude had designed all those years ago. The creature had hung there, on Earth's side, for mere minutes, oblivious to the wild, ecstatic crowds far, far below who flooded the streets and rooftops with telescopes and binoculars, or clustered around wall-sized monitors, flashing out their hands in greeting. In ignorance of the sensation it was making, it hovered shyly, long and large as a subway train, colors bright as neon, with a sprouting of silvery leaves that seemed to wave. The first alien to ever pay homage to humanity's sun.

Fashion designers were already selling optic netting with Kasaran images floating across, and long armbands of delicate, trailing fabrics were making a comeback.

It would seem that all had been forgiven after all.

"It's time," Gordon said, bringing Jude back to the bridge. The ex-policeman was attaching his I-dik to the rail so the two of them could see it. On its small screen Jude could make out Scotty, Piper, and Gabe standing on one of the ghats in Varanasi. The sun was just coming up there, touching the misty waters of the Ganges with a sparkle of gold. Jude could even make out, in the distance, crowds of people dressed in saffron, there to greet the sun. Their chants were very faint:

"Om Bhur Bhuvasva,
Tat Savitur Varenium—"

It was hard to hear them over the noise and celebration. In addition to the momentous events of the week, it was also the Hindu New Year.

"Dad," Piper said softly. She was swathed in a white-on-white embroidered sari, her short titian hair seeming brighter and more colorful by compare. She held a box.

"We're ready," he told her. He gave Gordon his cane and took in exchange their box. It was sandalwood, with a picture of Nataraja carved on the lid. Jude broke it open, simultaneously with his daughter. He didn't look down into it, he couldn't bear to do that, but taking his cue from his daughter, he shook out the ashes, letting the breeze capture and sail the gray cloud out over the East River.

"*Isom namah shivaya,*" Piper said, as her puff of ashes flew down to spread itself upon the soft morning mist and the waters underneath.

"She bridged worlds during her lifetime," Jude said, words he'd thought about long and hard. He hadn't wanted, at first, to say anything, but they were Varouna's due, and he was damn well going to make sure they were said, no matter the thickness in his throat. "And created one the equal to any on Earth or in the heavens. She will be remembered, and she will be missed."

"She should have lived to see this new age," he heard Gabe choke, and caught a glimpse of the man wiping at his eyes.

"She saw it," Piper responded, and Jude saw Scotty wrap a protective arm about her shoulders. "She saw it all."

They were quiet then. People getting off work walked or cycled past them along the walkway. Below, within the caged road, silent cars rolled by and the subway train rumbled on its way. And far, far below, the East River, waves gleaming like polished nickel, carried boats back to their slips. The sky darkened, and a bright full moon appeared in the heavens.

All so much the same, thought Jude. *All so different.*

A memory came to him then, a very simple remembrance that he had not thought of in twenty-five years. It was a night like this one, so very clear. The three of them, Warren, Valerie, and Jude, walking across the Brooklyn Bridge, arm in arm. There'd been the smell of the ocean on the air, the feeling of being up high above it all, as if in orbit. In the distance, the fairy lights of Manhattan were appearing, smoke and steam drifting up from its towers. And the wind blew soft and crisply cold.

Then, as now, Jude had watched as a necklace of lights came on along the bridge, one after the other, from Brooklyn to Manhattan, as if leading the way from past to future. And as they illuminated the netting of the bridge's cables, the wing shapes that gave it so much of its beauty, Jude had felt a sudden and silent camaraderie with his friends. As if the three of them had built or would build something magical. He'd caught Warren's grin then, and saw Valerie shake back the soft, fluttering banner of her hair in agreement. He'd grasped Warren's arm behind Valerie's warm, slim waist, and felt Warren's answering hold, felt Valerie's embrace tighten around the both of them, pulling them all closer than they'd ever been before. The time was theirs, a now that they owned, filled with life and joy and potential.

Jude felt that same potential now, as, once again, the lights came on along the Brooklyn Bridge, seeming to travel from stone and steel past to glass and mono-matrix present. He didn't have Valerie or Warren with him anymore, but through the gothic arches of the towers he saw the stargate hanging right within the point, like a bell in a steeple. A bridge within a bridge.

And he felt their arms around him.

The barely visible circle of the stargate did not look, this night, like a mourning wreath, he thought. It looked, instead, like the marigold necklace Varouna had once spoken of, the one that would come down out of the heavens to encircle the Earth. A ring composed of every soul who had dreamed it, built it, and made it happen.

"It's the greatest bridge ever, Tarkenton," Gordon said then, coming to stand beside him.

"It's unprecedented," he agreed.

"So." The other man, once his nemesis, now his closest friend, shrugged a little. "Would you do it again? I don't mean the last twenty-five years, but, knowing what you know now, if you had the chance to build something else just as unprecedented?"

Jude thought about that as moonbeams illuminated the stunning length of the Brooklyn Bridge and seemed to give the fiery gold stargate rainbow shimmers.

Would he want another such lifetime, so terrible, so wonderful, if, as Varouna and his daughter seemed to believe, his karma might be to build another, even greater bridge?

"Without hesitation," he answered, and stepping forward, lifted his arms for a moment, as he had years ago, to the stars, reaching to the bridge around him, to the future, to that gleaming promise in the sky and what lay beyond it.

To dream a dream that aimed so high and earn a chance to dance at the center of it all would be worth another turn on this strange wheel. Well worth it.

Janine Ellen Young studied geology before receiving her M.A. in Literature from UCLA. An English teacher at Santa Monica College, she has been lecturing and teaching classes on speculative fiction for twelve years and was a recent guest speaker at the Mt. Saint Antonio's Writer's Conference. Her first novel, *Cinderblock*, made *Locus* magazine's 1997 Year in Review Recommended First Novel list. She is happily married and lives in Santa Monica, California.

interzone is the leading British magazine which specializes in SF and new fantastic writing. Among many other writers, we have published

BRIAN ALDISS	GARRY KILWORTH
J.G. BALLARD	DAVID LANGFORD
IAIN BANKS	MICHAEL MOORCOCK
BARRINGTON BAYLEY	RACHEL POLLACK
GREGORY BENFORD	KEITH ROBERTS
MICHAEL BISHOP	GEOFF RYMAN
DAVID BRIN	BOB SHAW
RAMSEY CAMPBELL	JOHN SLADEK
RICHARD COWPER	BRIAN STABLEFORD
JOHN CROWLEY	BRUCE STERLING
THOMAS M. DISCH	LISA TUTTLE
MARY GENTLE	IAN WATSON
WILLIAM GIBSON	CHERRY WILDER
M. JOHN HARRISON	GENE WOLFE

interzone has introduced many excellent new writers, and illustrations, articles, interviews, film and book reviews, news, etc.

interzone is available from specialist bookshops, or by subscription. For six issues, send £17 (outside UK, £20). For twelve issues, send £32 (outside UK, £38). American subscribers may send $32 for six issues, or $60 for twelve issues. Single copies: £3.00 inc. p&p (outside UK, £3.50; or USA, $6.00). Outside Europe, all copies are despatched by accelerated surface mail.

To: **interzone** 217 Preston Drove, Brighton, BN1 6FL, UK

Please send me six/twelve issues of Interzone, beginning with the current issue. I enclose a cheque/p.o./international money order, made payable to Interzone (delete as applicable) OR please charge my MasterCard/Visa:

Card number

Expiry date   Signature

/

Name ....

Address ....

....

If cardholder's address is different from the above, please include it on a separate sheet